SIX
LIVES

SIX
LIVES
Lavie
Tidhar

An Apollo Book

Head of Zeus
First Floor East
5–8 Hardwick Street
London EC1R 4RG

WWW.HEADOFZEUS.COM

Contents

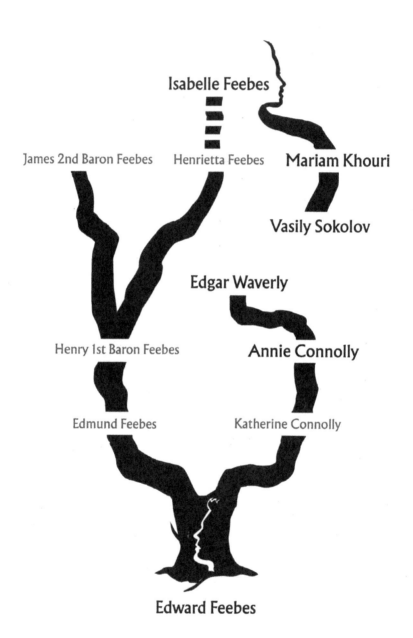

Isabelle Feebes

James 2nd Baron Feebes   Henrietta Feebes   **Mariam Khouri**

Vasily Sokolov

Edgar Waverly

Henry 1st Baron Feebes   **Annie Connolly**

Edmund Feebes   Katherine Connolly

Edward Feebes

PART ONE

THE GUANO MERCHANTS

Edward

1855

1

EDWARD COULDN'T SEE LONDON YET BUT HE COULD smell it: the unpleasant effluvia drifted downriver thick with smoke, rot and perfume, and a lone seagull cried overhead above the crow's nest as though startled by it. The bird traced a long parabola in the sky and flew back towards the estuary and the distant sea.

The ship sailed gracefully enough along the Thames. Edward did not much care for ships. He often suffered seasickness. The irony of the terms of his employment for the House of Feebes did not escape him, for they often required long sea voyages. He would be glad to be on dry land again.

The approach to London was thick with other ships. Edward stood on deck, under the billowing sails, and watched warships and trade ships, frigates and trawlers and clippers, and somewhere along the south bank a giant iron monster, one of the new steamers being built. Edward clutched a handkerchief to his face, the cloth soaked in Mrs Winslow's Soothing Syrup, which he took to ease his disposition on board ship. Breathing the faint aroma of laudanum helped his nerves, though did little to temper the London stench, which grew by degrees as the ship approached the docks.

Before you saw the city you saw the cloud that hovered above it day and night. Black soot and ash rose into the air for miles around, a fog that embraced London until it became one with it. Edward thought longingly for a moment of the clean air and sparkling sea of Cádiz, but that lay behind him, and London beckoned, for all that it stank. It was the black heart of all the world, and all the credit lines led to London. Then it appeared, gradually, the old summer palace on his left with its meridian lines and observatory, the literal centre of the world from which all maps were made. Then shortly houses and pubs and brothels and grocers, and always a milling of people, pressing against the banks, congregating like pigeons as they went about the business of living and the living of business.

'You are looking forward to returning home?' Dr Müller said. He came and stood on the deck with Edward and smiled pleasantly as he reached for his pipe. He had boarded in Cádiz along with Edward, and they had spent many a pleasant evening playing draughts and whist to while away the time.

'I am a stranger here myself,' Edward said, a little self-consciously. 'I grew up in Devon.'

'Ah, yes,' Dr Müller said. 'Your uncle?'

Edward smiled. 'It is his company,' he said.

'But he thinks highly of you,' Dr Müller said. He puffed on his pipe. 'You are a diligent clerk, no?'

Edward shrugged, discomfited. 'I hope he does look on me with favour,' he said. In truth, he wasn't sure what his future held. He had carried out his duties to the best of his abilities, but his uncle was an often aloof figure, and Edward did not know him well.

'I myself,' Dr Müller declared, 'am attending a conference of the Royal Society, which should prove most elucidating. You have heard of Charles Darwin? He is a fellow who studies barnacles.'

'Barnacles?' Edward said.

'Yes, yes,' Dr Müller said. 'Barnacles.'

He blew out smoke. The ship, meanwhile, eased its way across the water, moving slowly amidst the ungodly flotilla that crowded the docks.

'My business is in cloth and wine, mostly,' Edward said. 'I do not know much about crustaceans.'

Dr Müller's eyes twinkled when he said, 'But you do know something of birds and their excreta, eh? Eh?' He punctuated each exclamation with a stab of his pipe in the air, a habit that was somewhere between endearing and exasperating.

Edward shrugged. 'Less than you, I imagine,' he said. 'I only know them as columns in a numbers book.'

Sailors ran along deck and orders were barked hither and yon, none of which meant much to Edward. He saw they were to berth next to the *Maid of Lima*, one of the new ships leased by his uncle, and carrying, indeed, the aforementioned sacks of precious excrement. Dr Müller leaned over the side and gazed at the ship in fascination. Porters swarmed over the docks and up and down the gangplanks, faces masked against the stench of the guano as they offloaded sack upon sack from the belly of the ship. As they emerged back onto the docks they merged in turn with their fellow porters, men of all shapes and sizes, all united by a brutish strength, all swarming like ants between the numerous vessels that came to dock in London from all corners of the world.

Here were India merchants and Malay sailors, Dutch adventurers and Spanish slavers, river barges and ships of the line and fishing boats from the far north and luxury passenger ships from America, where there was no aristocracy but that of money old and new, and other ships from Peru and Brazil, bringing all that the world had to offer here to the Smoke: coffee and tea, sugar and chillies, saffron and coca, delicate china and hand-woven cloth, wood for the carpenters and wool for the milliners and silver for the jewellers and ink for the printers, and as the world brought its riches here, Britain sent back its own gift to the world: order and the law. Without it there was chaos. With it, a letter of credit issued in Natal would be honoured in Hong Kong just as it would be in London itself, in Guiana or in New South Wales. It was a world of credits and tallies that Edward knew, of tidy numbers in neat columns, of profits and loss. When he watched the ships and the moving porters this was what he saw, a great subtraction and division, figures splitting and aligning and all adding up at last, in a symphony of bookkeeping. But he could not articulate all that to Dr Müller.

'What strange creatures we are!' Dr Müller said. 'Look at them swarm, all of them different and yet all alike. God the designer had built variation into man, and given us suffering so that we might struggle for existence, for as Heraclitus said, struggle is the father of all things. I may be misquoting.' He smiled genially and tapped his pipe on the railing, sending the ash flying into the air, where it joined the billions of particles floating in the poisoned atmosphere over the Thames. Edward covered his nose and mouth with the handkerchief again and breathed in laudanum. His head swam pleasantly.

Before long they were berthed. Dr Müller had been an agreeable companion, but Edward was glad to at last be off ship. They bade each other farewell, and made tentative arrangements to dine together once more while in town. Edward made his way through the throng of people, animals and vehicles, doing his best to avoid stepping in the muck of faeces that lay on the ground. Things were no better when he emerged onto the street, where horse-drawn cabs went gaily past and small children, employed for that purpose, darted in between them to scoop up the animals' constant expelling of waste, but in vain. The smell of the city hit Edward in full then, a rank stench of open sewers and night soil and disease, and the black fog clung to his clothes even as his feet sank into wet puddles of animal discharge. He hailed a cab and ducked inside it with relief.

'To Bishopsgate,' he said.

2

THE VENERABLE LONDON HOUSE OF FEEBES & CO., OF which Edward Feebes was but a lowly, if well-esteemed, clerk, was situated close to the heart of the City, and bore a discreet façade and a modest sign upon its three-storey building. It was situated on the old Roman road; the ruins of the old Roman wall of the city stood nearby. It was a sense of continuity with the past that Henry Feebes, Edward's uncle, often expressed appreciation for. London, then and now, was a part of the global network of trade – a minor backwater in Roman times, perhaps, but the beating heart of it now.

Edward paid the cabbie. The horse shat and the cab ambled on, and Edward, one hand on his wallet, gazed around him at people flowing up and down Bishopsgate, suited bankers jumping nimbly between the filth like children at a game of hopscotch, and beggars and dollymops from the nearby tenements of Whitechapel went about their business just the same, along with the food cart vendors, the horse-drawn carriages, the omnibuses and the bobbies on the beat, who regarded the whole loud, smelly, bewildering enterprise as just another Tuesday. Edward put the handkerchief to his face, inhaled once and put it away. He opened the door and passed into the austere confines of the office.

'Edward!'

Mr Doyle, the Irishman, beamed happily when he saw Edward's arrival. Edward smiled in response. He liked Mr Doyle, with whom he first worked in the counting house when he joined the firm. They shook hands.

'How was Spain?' Mr Doyle said.

'Congenial,' Edward said. 'How is London?'

'Still standing,' Mr Doyle said, and they both laughed.

'You look well,' Mr Doyle said. 'It is good to have you back. You spent too long amongst the Godos.'

Edward winced inwardly at the slur. Like many in Britain, Mr Doyle did not much care for the Spanish, but the House of Feebes had made its early fortunes trading with Spain when there was still a blockade, and it was rare to hear such sentiments expressed openly amongst staff. It was only Mr Doyle's familiarity with Edward, based on their days together in the counting house, that loosened his tongue, and so Edward did not raise objection.

He followed Mr Doyle upstairs, to oak-lined offices where a comfortable fire burned, and was there reacquainted with his uncle. Henry Feebes shook Edward's hand with cold, bloodless fingers, but the look in his eyes was warm enough when he said, 'Welcome back, Edward. We have much work to do.'

They sat by the fire and Mr Doyle brought them both port, then departed. Edward sipped the drink and it loosened something in him. Outside the window, darkness was already falling somehow.

'You did good work for us in Cádiz,' Uncle Henry said.

He was more elderly than Edward remembered. A touch of pestilence the previous winter had left him gaunt, and when he moved, Edward noticed before they sat, he did so with a slight limp. 'You are honest, with a good head for numbers, and you do not overindulge in drink, unlike some.'

Clearly he had something – or someone – on his mind.

'Moreover,' Uncle Henry said, 'you are family. Keep working diligently and there is no telling where you'll go. After all, I will not be around forever.' He smiled thinly. 'Though I intend to remain in place for many more years to come,' he said.

Edward nodded. He sipped his port.

'I am forever grateful for the opportunity to serve,' he said.

'Good!' Uncle Henry clasped him by the shoulder. 'You are aware of our South American operations, of course?'

'Of course,' Edward said, surprised. The Feebeses had begun in the cloth trade with Spain, then made considerable sums on the West African slave trade. It was Uncle Henry himself, however, who as a young man, and prompted by who knew what premonition, chartered himself a berth on a slow boat to Peru, and there entered into negotiations and eventual arrangements with the Peruvian government. Now the Lima House handled the bulk of the guano trade with Europe, and acted as both creditor and guarantor for the government. In effect, they were all but printing money.

'Henry Feebes made his dibs, selling the turds of foreign birds,' as the popular music hall ditty went. Crudely put, perhaps, but not inaccurate. And as long as the birds continued to shit in Peru, the House of Feebes stood prosperous.

'I need you in Lima,' Uncle Henry said.

'In Lima? But—'

'The man we have there, running things,' Uncle Henry said. 'Moens. You remember him?'

Edward tried to keep his distaste from showing. Moens was a gregarious type, blustery and hale, with a fondness for brandy, cigars and the military. He had used Edward badly when he worked under him, and Edward was relieved when he heard Moens had been sent to Lima.

'I do,' he said.

His uncle frowned. 'The numbers,' he said, 'are of some concern.'

'I see.'

Nothing more needed to be said between the two of them on that score.

'I have made the arrangements,' Uncle Henry said. 'The *Wanderer*, out of Liverpool. She departs the day after tomorrow. You can travel north by train. Spend tonight in London, dine well, rest. It is a long journey to Lima.'

'Of course,' Edward said.

'Good man,' Uncle Henry said.

Edward sipped his port.

There had been much to arrange, papers to sign and packages entrusted to his keeping until Lima. He had so recently decamped off-ship and in truth was none too keen on undertaking a long sea voyage again. He had hoped for a position back in the London House.

And yet...

And yet he could not deny this was an opportunity, as

Uncle Henry had made clear. This was responsibility, and Edward was flattered that it was entrusted to him. There were clear prospects in his going, and a young, ambitious man would be a fool to turn down such a task. It was from Peru that much of their fortune came, and nothing could be allowed to harm that flow of money across the ocean. If Moens was indeed negligent in his duties, that must be uncovered, and then dealt with promptly. Yes. And he had never been to the Americas, either, he thought. It would be beneficial to gain experience there, the better to utilise when he was inevitably promoted. All in all, Edward was happy with his lot. And there were cures for seasickness.

He took a cab to Euston, and checked in to the accommodation provided to him by the firm, a modest room at Mrs Seacombe's lodging house, near the station. He had looked with envy at the new Great Northern when the cab passed it by, and rather wished he could stay there. But frugality was a byword in the House of Feebes. And Mrs Seacombe's rooms were clean and comfortable; he could not complain.

Having deposited his travelling bag, and taken a wash to the best of his abilities, Edward was eager to reacquaint himself with London. Mrs Seacombe's, like most houses, sat atop a cesspool into which the bodily discharge of guests and hostess both went daily (to say nothing of the servants). Consequently, the fumes of that combined output did rise, and were so pungent that it was clear no night soil men had come to clear the cesspit in quite a while. When Edward stepped out into the street the air was hardly fresher. It was darker now, with only gas lamps lit, and his feet sank into the layer of fresh manure drizzled with urine. There was nothing to it, though. He had soaked a fresh handkerchief with laudanum, and breathed through it as he took his stroll. He had messengered to Samuel Mardon and George Sieveking, with whom he had often dined at Newman's Chophouse on Coleman Street. They had clerked together for the firm in former days. Lively lads, he thought. The streets seemed merry at this hour, gentlemen about their business and the fancy carriages carrying the well-to-do to social engagements, the theatre and the opera. London's dirt was less visible in gaslight. Though he was not a native of the city, he had had the measure of it by this time, having shared accommodation with the lads in Blackfriars. He knew which shadows to avoid and which to embrace as he walked. Laughter, curses, smoke and the smell of beer spilled out of pub doors. He passed a man passed out in the awning of a bookshop. A painted Jezebel leered from a first-floor window. A boy sold fried eels from a cart. Edward's stomach rumbled. He wended his way through narrow alleys, avoiding excrement, horses and cut-purses as well as he could. Nearer the market the traffic of carts and horses increased, as did the cursing of the drivers and the noise of the crowds. Edward was accosted by two flower girls, one pretty in the dim light, the other less so. 'Sweet violets, penny a bunch!' the first one said. The second leered at him in invitation that had nothing to do with flowers.

He ducked into the Saracen's Head, under the grisly sign of the bloodied, hacked-off head and its dark visage, and found a place of shelter and warmth in which convivial voices were raised and glasses clinked.

'Edward!'

He found Samuel and George in the back, holding beers. He shook hands with them, smiling.

'Why, you're as dark as a Spaniard!' Samuel said. 'Is it true you are going again so soon, Edward? Your note was unexpected!'

'It is true, Sam,' Edward said. 'I was not expecting it myself. But we do have tonight.'

'And tonight we shall have!' George said, grinning. He had somehow gone and fetched a fresh round of drinks from the bar. These he put none too steadily on the table.

'To your health, Edward!' he said.

They raised their glasses, laughing. Edward let the cool beer wash away the rancid taste that the city coated his tongue with. He did not usually partake of much drink, but this one went down easy.

'How go things with you both?' he said.

'I work for Sadler, Guest & Co.,' Samuel said. 'On the German commission side. It is but a small business, yet the hours are good and the pay agreeable.'

'And I a stockbroker for the Smith Brothers,' George said, 'with a speciality in railway shares. You should come and work with us, Edward. You always had a good head for numbers, and my masters are constantly in the market for top men.'

'I cannot abandon the family business,' Edward said, smiling. 'And besides, I am not yet ready to settle down!'

'Who talks of settling down?' George said, mock-affronted. 'Just because we do not go willy-nilly on leaky boats to foreign climes? We do not need to go to the world, for this is London, Edward. Here the world comes to *us*.'

'That I cannot argue with,' Edward said. Somehow the

drinks were finished. Sam fetched another round. 'I would have liked to remain longer,' Edward admitted. 'I do not like ships, as you both well know.'

'Seasickness still?' Sam said.

Edward shrugged. 'It passes after a while,' he said. 'The laudanum helps.'

Sam's eyes shone greedily, and he took a bottle of Godfrey's Cordial from the pocket of his jacket.

'I don't mind if I do,' George said, reaching for it. They all extracted their handkerchiefs and soaked the cloth with the cordial, then breathed it in deeply. Edward's head swam pleasantly. Somehow it was his round then. The conversation grew louder, the smoke heavier, the air warmer. Then they were outside, swaying pleasantly, the night beckoning. Down to the Albion they went, where a waiter recognised these were men about town, and seated them right away, and brought over acceptable wine. They ordered beef tongue, and fried eels, and turtle soup. Sam sipped the broth and George scoured the underside of the shell – he had always been good at digging out the morsels. Edward partook more leisurely, enjoying the company, and thinking of his voyage yet to come. For this while, though, it was good to simply be amongst friends.

The Albion was a lively establishment. Tobacco smoke filled the air and flower girls moved between groups of drunken patrons, an offer unspoken but proffered. A singer with her petticoats showing broke into a lewd rendition of 'Ta-ra-ra boom-de-ay' as a group of men in the corner, of a low class, sailors or porters, cheered her on, their glasses raised.

'A smart and stylish girl you see!' the singer cried. She

had more verve than aptitude. 'A belle of good society! Not too strict, but rather free, yet as right as right can be!'

'Hoorah!' the men shouted. Edward saw the two flower girls he had met earlier enter the Albion. They cast about them, and the plain one's eyes met his.

She winked.

'Never forward, never bold,' the singer cried, 'not too hot and not too cold, but the very thing, I'm told, that in your arms you'd like to hold!'

Everyone cheered and joined in the refrain, 'Ta-ra-ra boom-de-ay! Ta-ra-ra boom-de-ay!'

'Excuse me,' Edward said. He rose and went to the latrines, and when he had finished his business and was adjusting his garments saw that the flower girl had followed him and stood watching him with a calculating expression.

'You seem lonely,' she said.

'I...'

She shook her head.

'I get lonely too,' she said.

She had a rather lovely Irish accent, he thought.

She took his hand. He didn't struggle. She led him out the back, to a small walled garden. It was dark. They were not alone there, but no one paid them mind. Edward felt her closeness, her heat. She pressed against him, her hands reaching below, and he felt his face grow warm and his thoughts flow sluggishly. He thought of those long days to come at sea.

He reached for her. She was right, he thought. He was lonely. It had been a while. She pulled down his trousers. He fumbled under her garments. Her breasts were full. She took him by hand and eased him inside her. He gasped, and his breathing came hard. He held her against him as he thrust, her back to the wall, his hands on her buttocks. It was over quickly.

He stood there feeling a little deflated. She eased him out and rearranged her clothes.

'What's your name?' he said.

'Mary.'

She looked at him curiously. Why did he ask? He reached in his pocket. He pulled out a gold pocket watch. It had been a Christmas gift from the firm one year to all employees. The name Feebes was etched on the underside of the casing. 'Would this do?' he said. The girl, this Mary, looked at him.

'Money,' she said.

'Look,' Edward said, scratching at the thin layer of paint. 'It's gold. Take it.'

'Five shillings,' the girl said.

'It's worth more than five shillings,' Edward said. 'Take it.'

The girl took it reluctantly. She put the watch to her ear.

'It works,' Edward said.

The girl nodded, touched Edward's cheek briefly with the back of her hand, and was gone.

Edward adjusted himself and re-entered the Albion. He couldn't see the flower girl. Sam and George watched his return with knowing grins.

'Where to, then?' George said.

'I know just the place,' Sam said. 'Shall we?'

'If Edward's business is concluded...' George said, and he and Sam both burst out laughing.

Edward shrugged, discomfited.

'We can go,' he said.

They settled their bill. It had been a simple transaction, Edward thought. That was all that life was, when it came down to it. A column of emoluments and a column of expenditures, running side by side until the inevitable moment when they had to add up: a final sum only God Himself, in His infinite wisdom, could reckon. Hence a final reckoning. And a man had to keep clean accounts.

He followed his friends with no further thought. They swayed slightly now, and the night took on a sickly sheen, the faces in the crowds ghostly and the horses themselves, as they passed, seemed insubstantial.

Flames flickering, their feet sank in manure, and the soot from the endless, rising cloud of ash settled on their clothes and on their faces and in their hair. Edward loosened his coat. They hurried through, and were rewarded with the sights and smells of Leicester Square in moments, the jaunty hotels cheek by jowl with the newly built Alhambra music hall and Wyld's Great Globe. Edward had been inside it once before, shortly after it opened. They had climbed up the ramps on the inside of the giant Earth and looked upon its features in miniature, its rivers and mountains, volcanoes and jungles. It had been a great draw when it opened, but now it seemed all but empty, with no one queuing to go inside, and dirt collected at the toll door.

On they went, not stopping, on to Piccadilly, and there they halted before a grand Egyptian temple, where torches burned upfront, illuminated the rising columns that supported the great entrance into shadow, over which stood two pharaonic figures carved in stone, gazing down upon the entrants, filling the air with a sense of theatre and mystery.

See The Two-Headed Nightingale! said the sign. *The African twins, Milly and Christina, born into slavery, only five years old, whom nature has linked by an indissoluble band, yet have a most pleasing and attractive appearance, and sing in two voices under the direction of one mind!*

'The freak show?' Edward said.

'They have elephants, too!' George said.

The barker, who had been crying for attention, came to regard them, his moustache waxed and his gloves yet white.

'The poor children's parents remain slaves on a North American plantation,' he told them with an air of great sorrow, 'and so their benefactor, Mr Thompson, has taken to exhibiting the conjoined twins solely for the purpose of raising the funds to enable the emancipation of their parents.' He was clearly following a script. 'The better feelings of humanity, as well as the natural impulse of curiosity, are therefore to be jointly gratified by their inspection! For you, only two shillings, gentlemen, but you must hurry, for the performance is about to start.'

He extended a gloved hand hopefully, and the three of them pooled their coins and deposited them into his waiting palm. He ushered them inside.

The Egyptian Hall, though well known to Edward, seldom held the same show twice. In its cavernous depths the visitors milled, fascinated by anything and everything that was on offer. In the middle of the great hall, the animal enclosure drew the largest crowds, to admire a skeletal giraffe, two elderly elephants and a similar pair of zebras, while nearby the snake charmer stood engulfed in a sleepy, recently fed python, and let people pet it for a penny a pop.

All about them men sold candied nuts and brandy-balls,

spice cakes and crumpets, coffee, hot wine and sherbet. Some of the acts stood alone, others had a barker to draw them a crowd. Edward passed a skeletal man and a bearded woman and a dwarf smoking a pipe. At the end of the hall, on a raised stage, stood the little girl twins, singing sweetly. George, in particular, was taken with the sight, and gazed on them in wonder, his mouth hanging open; while Samuel helped himself to a packet of nuts and stood munching on them contentedly.

Edward felt a headache coming on. He had drunk more than he should have. He was a man seldom given to drink. He had acted rashly with the Irish girl. He had not even used a skin, nor had she asked, so quickly was the transaction concluded. Eels, tongue and turtle meat sloshed unpleasantly in his stomach, which rumbled in dissent. The noise grew too noisome. The air was fetid. He bade a hasty farewell to his friends and staggered outside.

'Not here, man!' the barker said, and pushed him roughly. Edward fell into the muck, rose to his knees, and on his knees he retched.

He felt better then. He wiped himself down as best he could. He hailed a cab and let it carry him to Mrs Seacombe's, where he fell on his bed and was asleep in moments.

3

IN THE MORNING, WASHED, SHAVED, DRESSED AND SOBER, he managed a small breakfast and considered the previous night. It had been a good night on the whole, he decided, out with the boys. He put it out of his mind, drank two cups of the tepid coffee (nothing like Spain, he reflected ruefully) and gathered his few belongings. He had learned to travel light, in the course of his employ with the House of Feebes.

It was a short walk to Euston, and he boarded the Liverpool train with enthusiasm. This steam locomotive, a sleek thing of polished metal, thrummed with power as Edward found his carriage. It wasn't long before they departed the station, and shortly thereafter London's fetid atmosphere was replaced with the fresh air of the countryside. Soon it was hard to imagine a city had ever been, as England's green and pleasant land, as the poet, Blake, had so aptly put it, appeared in all its rainswept glory. Though he was not much for poetry himself, Edward was nevertheless an educated man. He could recite appropriately from Shakespeare, had a smattering of Byron, a line or two of Milton's, and possessed some additional notion of Virgil and Ovid.

There were six of them in the compartment, three each way. The hot air was foggy with tobacco smoke. A tea trolley went by, followed by a cart of newspapers and books. Rain patterned the window. Edward had a tea and crumpet and purchased that morning's edition of the *Illustrated London News*. Not much there: the ongoing war in the Crimea, the ongoing rebellion in China, a daring gold robbery on a train from London Bridge (this he pursued with interest), and a report on the devil's footprints appearing all across Devon (this he also read with interest). His companions in the carriage made conversation but Edward covered his face with his hat and dozed. When he woke he felt better, and outside he could see the gentle landscape had changed into a nightmarish vista of dark satanic mills, and he realised they were passing Birmingham.

He dozed again, and some hours later woke up refreshed to find the train approaching Liverpool at last. The city was engulfed in the smoke and fog of industry, with constant fires burning and ships congregating on the Mersey and along the docks. He left the train and ambled into town, looking with some regret at the Adelphi, which did not fit the purse of a clerk, and so made his way to the Feebes counting-house on the north side. It being closed he admitted defeat, and after asking for directions found the Admiral's Inn, not far from the docks, and with a cold wind blowing in from the river hurried inside. He was glad then for the fire, and for a small drink of port and a dinner of pie and mash.

The next morning he went to the docks and boarded the boat that took him to the steamer.

★

The *Wanderer*, laden with mail bags and industrial products for sale in the Americas, and laden also with passengers, servants, crew and assorted luggage, steamed out of the Mersey and into open sea. Edward, not a first-class passenger, found his accommodation agreeable enough, though he had to ascend two staircases in order to reach the uppermost deck each time he craved fresh air. There were only two berths in the cabin, the second being unoccupied. When he opened the porthole there was plenty of fresh air and light. He resigned himself to another long voyage. He passed an hour reviewing the most recent financial figures from Lima. He could see why his uncle had sent him. Moens had written from Lima. He said production on the guano islands was reducing, and the government tardy in paying the loans extended to them by the House of Feebes. Edward supposed he would have to find out the truth of it for himself.

He climbed on deck and watched as Ireland appeared slowly in the distance: green hills and mist, he thought. Green hills and mist. It was dark by the time they reached Queenstown. He went to the saloon, where dinner was served promptly: cold mutton, gooseberry pie and cheese, with a serviceable Madeira. Introductions were made around the table. Edward found himself seated with two planters from Trinidad, who complained bitterly of the economic situation: the home government having outlawed slavery, they were forced to pay free labourers.

'It's bad enough they freed the slaves,' the first one, a Mr Falconer, said, 'but then they go and pass the Foreign Sugar Bill!'

A Miss Grimshaw, who drew Edward's eye almost

immediately, petted the terrier in her lap and confessed ignorance of the topic. Mr Pettigrew, the second planter, said, 'The government has allowed the importation into Great Britain—'

'And Ireland,' Mr Falconer said.

'Of slave-grown sugar,' Mr Pettigrew said. 'Which means we cannot compete, dear lady! For how can we compete when we must pay a wage while others don't? It's all in the margins. You understand—' he appealed to Edward. 'You are a finance man.'

'It's true,' Edward allowed. 'It is a bind.'

'A bind, man? It is a travesty!' Mr Falconer said.

Miss Grimshaw – *really* quite fetching, Edward thought – bit her bottom lip and said, 'But surely slavery is a moral wrong, gentlemen?'

She was tall and well made, her waist slender and bust well rounded, Edward thought. He evaluated her favours much as he would on a counting sheet. Complexion very fair and clear; cheeks rosy, nose aquiline. Her lips were red, her teeth white. Her chin did not please him.

'Then is it moral to allow this unfair competition?' Mr Falconer said, trying to appeal to the lady's better nature. 'All we ask for is a fair shot.'

Miss Grimshaw nodded. 'Yes,' she said. 'I see.'

The conversation turned to other subjects. The food was cleared away. The planters lit cigars; Colonel Haassum a pipe. He was a distinguished-looking Dutchman, travelling with his young daughters to the West Indies, to assume governorship of the islands of Saint Martin and Saint Barthélemy. The daughters themselves were well behaved.

The colonel had spoken little up to that point. Now he suggested a game of chess.

Edward, not being much of a chess player, sat back and watched as the colonel played first Mr Falconer and then Mr Pettigrew, defeating them both. Edward's attention was half on the game, half on the enchanting Miss Grimshaw in her black silk dress.

'Do you, too, travel to the West Indies?' Edward asked.

She shook her head. 'Only as far as Madeira,' she said, 'on account of my father.'

'Your father?'

'He is in our cabin, resting,' she explained. 'He suffers from consumption. The climate in Madeira is beneficial to his health.'

'I see.' Edward tried to mask his disappointment. Miss Grimshaw smiled, then said, 'And yourself, Mr Fibs?'

'Feebes,' he said. 'It's Feebes.'

She blushed – prettily, he thought.

'I do beg your pardon,' she said.

'Think nothing of it.'

'Where do you travel to?' she said.

'To Panama first,' Edward said. 'Then I must go overland and board another ship to Peru.'

'Peru!' she said.

'Indeed.'

'But what is in Peru, Mr Feebes?'

Bird shit, he thought but didn't say.

A fortune, he almost did say.

Both of these one and the same.

'Some financial matters of my firm,' he said.

'Such a long way!' Miss Grimshaw said. She looked wistful. 'I wish I could travel.'

He felt sad for her then, shackled to her sickly father, bound for Madeira. For himself more, because he would be deprived of such pleasant company. They played a few hands of cards and then each went to their separate cabins – Edward somewhat regretfully.

By mid-morning the next day all the Irish had got on board, most of them in steerage, and bound for a new life in Argentina. He did not see much of them. Once in open waters Edward's seasickness returned. He spent a couple of days in his cabin, and when he emerged the weather had turned warmer, the sky no longer grey, and one afternoon he saw a whale in the distance. He dined, conversed and played games of whist and backgammon. A week later they reached Madeira, and said goodbye to Miss Grimshaw, her ailing father, and the dog. After that they turned towards the Americas and began the ocean crossing.

Two weeks later, and having changed to his light clothes during the voyage, the *Wanderer* made anchor in Barbados. Edward thought it pretty, and very hot. Many of the women were so scantily clad as to expose a great deal of skin. The porters carried everything on their heads. He bought a pair of light trousers for a dollar in a white man's shop. Then Grenada, also English, and a fight on board, where Mr Falconer, in great temper, complained to the captain of the poor attitude of the servants, who did not attend him, and the two men near came to blows. More islands, then, and more and more black faces, and a litany of complaints from the white men, of the sugar plantations going to waste, and of the coffee plantations sure to follow in ruin. In Jamaica he saw black soldiers and several churches. He changed there for a faster steamer, the *Santa Rosa*, which carried him at last to Panama.

This was uncharted land for Edward. He only knew his Uncle Henry's stories: traversing the isthmus in a native canoe, through the murky waters of the Chagres river and underlying swamps, a slow, miserable journey of some days.

But that had been the old days. The *Santa Rosa* arrived, not in the dilapidated Fort San Lorenzo of Uncle Henry's tales, but at the new port town of Colón. Edward was hardly an inexperienced traveller. His Spanish was more than passable and he had spent time on the continent on behalf of the House of Feebes.

This did not prepare him for Colón. The port town rose out of the island on which it sat and extended to the land on which the brand-new railway terminal sat. Yankee voices filled the busy streets, the civil buildings were lavish and the shops crammed with goods. An air of busy enthusiasm and enterprise hung in the saloons and the new hotels. It whispered *gold*.

Here were prospectors heading to California. The Americans funded and built the railway, someone in the Custom House told Edward as he inspected his bags. Expending workers on the construction of the track the way one would use up livestock. Migrants, coolies, slaves and anyone who could be utilised was used, and where they died there they remained, and the land claimed them.

The teller shrugged in the telling. There were no cemeteries here to remember people who didn't even have names. The ticket was twenty-five dollars. Edward was relieved to find it waiting for him in the hotel. The cost of his travel was covered by the firm.

He was glad to be on dry land again. The heat was very strong. He went down to the hotel lobby and found himself in the company of Irish immigrants, burly Yankees sporting guns, and Spanish-speakers with features new to him, a mix of indigenous, European and African. This was the New World, and something loosened in Edward when he smelled this new air, for it was nothing like what he'd experienced before.

The next day he caught the train to Panama City. There the port was busy with ships and the streets again filled with Yankee twang, and ships bringing gold, and men spending their money. It was a rough sort of town. He spent but two days in the Hotel del Istmo, kept by a German, and then boarded the *Bolivar*.

It was a former whaler, in poor condition. He was much seasick on the voyage, which for the most part hugged the coast. He saw but little of Colombia and Ecuador.

At last, some three weeks later, he arrived in Lima.

4

SHE WAS THE SORT OF GIRL BLESSED WITH GOOD LOOKS but cursed with a sharp mind. One did not go easily with the other, Edward felt. In time her beauty might fade and then only her mind remain, when it could be put to good use organising dinner parties. Right now the combination was distracting. Worse, she was a socialist.

'I beg your pardon?' Edward said. He wasn't sure he heard right. They were seated for dinner at the Salazars, in their home off the Plaza Mayor. The Salazars were an old family, going back to the time of the Conquest, with roots in Spain. They had land holdings outside Lima, and the youngest brother, Felipe, was board member of the Banco de Lima, and tight with Moens. He was important to the Feebeses.

'A mutualist,' the girl said. 'Have you not read Leroux? Our society, based on profit, is a monstrosity of inequality. Instead we should all work together, with the shared use of resources and—'

'Do you mean, like a co-operative?' Edward said. The girl's eyes lit up.

'You've read Robert Owen?' she said.

Edward straightened the edges of the napkin on his lap.

'A wealthy industrialist,' Edward said. 'I confess I do not understand his methods.'

'You can't argue his success,' the girl said. 'Owen proved that by running his cotton mill in New Lanark for, not despite of, his workers. Education, housing, pay! What is industry if not the sum of its workers?'

'What do you advocate?' Edward said, amused. 'A revolution, like in France? Or like that German fellow, Marx, extols?'

'Exactly!'

Her name was Sofia Salazar. She was very passionate. Also, rich. The Salazars were not in government so much as behind it. Edward had had a busy few weeks in Lima. He thought he was beginning to understand the lie of the land.

'I know nothing of these matters,' Edward said. 'I am not a wealthy man myself. But I believe that if I work diligently and acquit myself well then I can progress, both economically and socially. That is only fair. Success or failure are down to me and me alone.'

'Then you are just another individualist,' Sofia said with distaste.

'I suppose I am,' Edward said.

'And yet what is your labour, Mr Feebes?' Sofia said. He was a little surprised she was allowed to speak so freely. In England she would be considered quite rude. But he had to remember he was no longer in England; and the girl's brothers, all elder to her, were indulgent. She was rich, there was that too. The rules of social niceties need not apply to those born into social privilege. There was a hint of Indian blood in her. It annoyed him how much it attracted him to her.

'I am a clerk,' he said.

'And what is that?'

'I work with numbers,' he said. 'I see the flow of profit and loss, I chart its course, make sure it flows correctly. Take your nation, for instance—'

'For instance,' she said, and smiled a small smile.

'The government of Peru depends on the mining and shipping of bird guano to Europe,' Edward said.

'You can say shit,' Sofia said.

'I beg your pardon!'

'L'odeur de l'ordure dure où l'or dort,' Sofia murmured.

'The stench of shit lingers where gold sleeps!' her brother, Felipe, overhearing from his end of the table, said and roared with laughter. The table shook, wine glasses shivering.

'She's a keeper, our Sofia,' he said.

She wasn't that, Edward thought. But she was a looker. Dark eyes, dark hair, a lovely complexion. But she had a mind of her own. Perhaps he should look upon it differently, he thought. Different rules applied in high society. And he, though a Feebes, was lowly yet. Perhaps he should not dismiss her so quickly.

'The birds'... excrement,' Edward said, 'is of tremendous benefit as fertiliser in England. And Peruvian guano is the best in the world.'

'The best!' Felipe said.

'My firm extends credit to the government,' Edward said. 'Not to put too fine a point on it, Miss Salazar, we *fund* your government.'

'You are but the brokers!' she said, outraged.

'We pay in advance, at agreed upon rates,' Edward said. 'We are in effect lenders.'

And, he thought but didn't say, he was beginning to suspect the Peruvian government was running behind on its debts.

'And look what you've done with the money,' he said, rallying to his point. 'The new public buildings, the civic works. Lima truly is a jewel of the Americas.'

Grey, overcast and humid, with streets too narrow, he thought too but didn't say.

'You make nothing,' Sofia said. 'Not even the shit you profess to sell on our behalf out of kindness. It is Peruvian labour and Peruvian industry that enriches Europe, and what use is the money if it does not benefit the people?'

'You may as well give it to the birds,' Edward said, tired now of this exchange. 'For they are the producers of your shit, not you.'

Felipe laughed so hard his wine spilled.

'Liberate the birds!' he said.

'Oh, shut up, Felipe,' Sofia said. But her lips twitched, almost in a smile. Edward counted it a point in his favour.

'You speak as all Englishmen speak,' Sofia said. 'All the ones here in Lima, anyway.'

'I came to work,' he told her. 'I am a worker. What do *you* do, Miss Salazar?'

'Complain,' her brother said. He finished his wine. 'Shall we adjourn to the smoking room, gentlemen? I have some fine Por Larrañaga cigars only recently arrived from Cuba.'

The men rose. Edward followed suit. He nodded to Sofia.

'Miss Salazar,' he said.

'Perhaps we can continue this discussion another time,' she said, surprising him.

'I would like that,' he said.

Her lips twisted again, in what was now definitely a smile.

'Then until later, Mr Feebes,' she said.

'They're running out of guano,' Moens said flatly. His bald head shone with sweat. His breath smelled of brandy and it was only eleven o'clock in the morning. The man was a disgrace, Edward thought. 'That's the long and short of it.'

'How can you run out of guano?' Edward said.

Moens patted his forehead with a crumpled handkerchief.

'The birds are upset,' he said.

'The *birds* are *upset*?'

'Or whatever you want to call it,' Moens said. 'The... balance of nature, or what have you. They are simply not producing at the required rate.'

'And you know this how?' Edward said.

'A lady naturalist who did a survey,' Moens said. 'Mary something. Mary Stephenson. Comes from a trading family.'

'A lady scientist?' Edward said.

'She seemed well read,' Moens said. 'In any case, she counted the nests, up and down the country. All the birds that fly to take a dump over the islands, begging your pardon. Each nest produces around a dollar fifty worth of guano, she figured. You need thousands and thousands of birds to turn a profit, and we do. Or we did. I guess the mining operation unsettles them.'

'But that's absurd!' Edward said.

Moens shrugged. 'Is it any more absurd than growing rich off of their by-product?' he said.

'Well, can nothing be done?' Edward said. 'A sort of… a redress of the balance of nature, and so on?'

'I am not a scientist, Mr Feebes, begging your pardon,' Moens said. He smirked a little when he called Edward that. A needling man, gone to waste but still poisonous. When Edward was a lowly clerk, Moens ruled the counting house. 'A Feebes is not a Feebes until his name is on the ledger,' he used to say. He resented not being granted seniority. He remained a clerk. Edward suspected his uncle sent Moens to Lima just to get him away. He had been a good clerk, but now the numbers weren't adding up and Edward wasn't convinced by the story of the balance of nature. Birds crapped. It's what they did. They had done so, moreover, for thousands of years over the Chincha islands of Peru. The source of Peru's wealth, the source of his own family's fortunes. The Inca had mined guano on the islands, but the Inca were gone, and Britain needed fertiliser and was willing to pay handsomely for it. Top dollar, as the Yankees said. Something in the soil of Britain was no longer viable. Perhaps the factories and the crowding and the subsequent overproduction of food. Perhaps, as Moens had put it, the balance of nature had been put out of joint.

It didn't matter. The guano worked like magic. It made crops grow. And so the merchants took this small-time operation in Peru and turned it into a global trade. The stuff empires were made of. Nothing must be allowed to get in the way of that. Profits *had* to remain at the acceptable level.

'How long?' Edward said.

Moens mopped his brow. He sipped his brandy. He said, 'Five, six more years, maybe. I think.'

'You *think?*'

'Do not shoot the messenger,' Moens said. Something unpleasant came into his eyes; it was never far from the surface. 'Go there yourself,' he said. 'Take a look. *Mr* Feebes.'

'To the islands?' Edward was startled. 'What in God's name for?'

Moens barked a laugh. 'Don't like to get your hands dirty? Can't say I blame you. It's a foul place. Still, if you want to see how the chicken is made you have to go to the slaughterhouse, don't you.'

'I am going for a coffee,' Edward said. The office windows were closed and the air too hot and too still, and Moens' breath, and his shiny visage, turned Edward's stomach.

'Nothing for me, thanks,' Moens said, and laughed.

Edward turned his back on him.

Nearly a month in Lima now. He still wasn't sure what to make of the place. The sea was grey, the sky likewise. The air was humid. No slaves were sold in the slave market anymore, not since Castilla had assumed power again earlier in the year. The people came in all shades but the upper class were white. The houses were new but the roads were unpaved. A lot of money flowing through here, but how much of it stuck he still wasn't sure. Felipe Salazar complained the foreign merchants robbed Peru, kept all the money to themselves. Well, the Salazars were ones to talk. The government lived on borrowed money, much of it the Feebeses'. They shovelled guano onto the ships that sailed to Europe. They built palaces and parks. Edward had tried chewing coca but he didn't like it much. Some sort of stimulant. No money in it. The locals were surly. There was a river, the Rimac. It smelled. Edward stuck close to the old part of town, the one Francisco Pizarro himself designed. Now there was a man. A conqueror. Defeater of the Inca, founder of this City of Kings. He had laid down the foundation stone for the great cathedral, had designed the Plaza Mayor, had built the Viceroyalty Plaza – the Casa de Pizarro!

So much gold, Edward thought. And all that Inca gold flowed out of the Lima port to Spain for centuries. By the time the British ventured out to the Americas what were they left with? Bird shit, that was what. And they turned *that* into gold. He needed a coffee. He poured some laudanum mixture into his handkerchief and breathed. That helped. He didn't know the truth of it yet but he would. It was all in the numbers. It would be there. Moens wasn't helpful but then, Moens wouldn't be.

His head hurt. He needed coffee. He passed a tailor's and a Dutch merchant's shop and a street stall selling tamales. Some sort of Inca food. The meals in his boarding house were strictly European. He went to the café, which was French. Dr Steinmeier, the German, was sat at his usual table. Edward came in and sat down.

'Heinrich,' he said.

'Edward. It is good to see you.'

He signalled to the waiter, who came over promptly. Edward ordered a coffee and a small pastry. He unfurled the napkin. Lima put him out of sorts and he couldn't say why.

Something about the muggy air and the murky quality of light. Something about the way the earth seemed to tremble, as though the city's foundations were unsound. Earthquake country. And he didn't like the river.

'How goes your business?' he said.

'We are making good progress,' Dr Steinmeier said. He was a very large man with a degree from Leipzig and terrible Spanish. 'The new villa in Miraflores is half-complete and the workers are satisfactory.'

'You have been here a while,' Edward said.

'Three years. And always building. I can't complain.'

'You like it here, Heinrich?'

The German considered. 'It is a fine place,' he said. 'It could be finer. My wages are good. In two more years Miraflores will become a district of Lima and perhaps I will purchase a house there myself.'

'You do not miss Germany?'

Dr Steinmeier laughed, then touched his breast. 'Germany is here,' he said. 'Always here.'

'I must confess myself still in the dark in regards to the greater picture,' Edward said, 'concerning Peru.'

'Ah, my friend,' Dr Steinmeier said. 'Who of us can be said to understand her? She is a political creation, as all modern states are, an amorphous new thing imposed upon an old order. It is, ultimately, just another land for us to make a profit out of. Isn't that why you are here?'

Edward thought of Sofia Salazar's words. The Salazars were of Spanish blood but they were no longer Spanish – they were Peruvian. And their blood was mixed, this much was clear – everyone in this country for more than two generations had that *infusion* of native in them. To her,

Edward and the others were foreign parasites. He grew hot at the thought, though whether from anger at Sofia or some other, deeper emotion she elicited in him, he would not yet be drawn to say.

'Are you concerned of the morality involved?' Dr Steinmeier said, amused. 'Your firm benefits this country, Edward. You provide the funds to the government to look after the people. Without you, where would Peru be?' He bit into a pastry, then laughed suddenly, crumbs spraying.

'Excuse me,' he said. 'But you say, without Peru there is no House of Feebes? Yet I say, without the House of Feebes, there is no Peru!'

Edward sipped his coffee. It was good coffee. He said, 'I have been going over the ledgers. Without going into specific figures, I can nevertheless say you are not entirely wrong. The amounts that Feebes & Co. lend as advance against guano profits are considerable. Indeed, I had not realised quite how much before I came here.'

'You were based in Spain, correct?' Dr Steinmeier said.

'Cádiz, yes. Cloth and so on.' He felt suddenly defensive. 'It was the original line of business for us Feebeses.'

'But you are what, a cousin?'

'A second cousin,' Edward admitted.

'Not in the line of inheritance, as such, then,' Dr Steinmeier said.

'What is your point, Heinrich?' Edward said.

'That you have been given an opportunity, Edward,' Dr Steinmeier said. 'You are clearly trusted. Valued. You *are* family.'

'Yes,' Edward said.

'Instead of worrying what pretty Miss Salazar thinks of you,' Dr Steinmeier said, and he smiled at Edward's sudden blush, 'you should think of how you can use this opportunity to your advantage. You are not – romantic notions aside – going to settle in Peru, make a bunch of babies and retire as Vice President of the República. You are going home. Back to Europe and civilisation. And you could go back a clerk, or you could go back a man of prospects.'

'I appreciate all that,' Edward said.

'I thought you did,' Dr Steinmeier said. 'But it doesn't hurt to be reminded.'

They played a few hands of cards and the conversation turned to other topics. Edward remembered to ask Dr Steinmeier about Mary Stephenson, the lady naturalist Moens had mentioned, and Dr Steinmeier promised to ask around after her. It was only when Edward got up to leave that Dr Steinmeier grasped him by the wrist, so Edward had to bend down, close to the German's face, to hear his parting words.

'Be careful, Edward,' he said.

Edward was startled but tried not to show it.

'Careful?' he said quietly.

'Where there's money there's turbulence,' Dr Steinmeier said. 'Just a word to the wise, my friend.'

Steinmeier let go and Edward left the café, but he was shaken.

What did Steinmeier mean? Moens? The Salazars? Something else? He reached for his pocket handkerchief and put it to his face, but when he inhaled there was no swelling of relief. He took out the medicinal bottle and realised it was empty. His hands shook. He had brought extra supplies with him from England, but he realised now they had run dry. Well, it was no matter, he thought, steadying himself. There would be a drug store somewhere nearby.

5

'No, I'm sorry, I'm afraid we're all out,' the proprietor said. 'Even in diluted form.' He was an old Spaniard. Edward stood in his shop. A young Peruvian boy stacked shelves in the background with evident indifference.

'But you can't be,' Edward said. 'Where can I go to get some?'

'It's a supply issue,' the proprietor said. 'There are some farmers in the lower Andes trying to grow the poppies commercially here, but I don't know that that's viable. We have to get our opium the way everyone does, from India. So what we get here is strictly limited. I'm really very sorry.'

'But you *do* get some?' Edward said. He found that he was sweating. This was not a problem he had anticipated. He only really used the laudanum for seasickness, didn't he? There had never been an issue in Cádiz or London with getting hold of some.

'A limited supply, when the trade ships dock,' the proprietor said. 'Most of it goes to the hospital.'

'The hospital? Why the hospital!' Edward said.

The proprietor looked at him in concern.

'For the patients,' he said.

'Of course,' Edward said. 'Of course.'

His hands shook again, and he felt hot and cold. He just needed a breather, that was all. The inside of the shop was too hot. The ceiling was too low. He felt crammed in.

'You have nothing?' he said.

'What there is that isn't bound for the hospital goes to the coolies,' the proprietor said.

Edward looked at him in incomprehension.

'The coolies?' he said.

'The Chinese fellows,' the proprietor said.

'Why them?' Edward said.

'Keeps them docile,' the proprietor said. 'It's a cheap way to get them in line. You can get plenty if you go to the islands.'

'The islands?'

'Would you like to sit down, Mr Feebes? You seem quite flushed. I can give you something for the symptoms. Some coca leaf, a glass of sherry, perhaps, to steady the nerves? For medicinal purposes, of course.'

'I do not need wine,' Edward said. 'Are there coolies in town?'

'In town? Only a few,' the proprietor said. 'These fellows, they come to work on the plantations or in the guano mines. On account of you can't keep slaves anymore. I'm sorry.'

'It is fine,' Edward said stiffly. He marched out of the shop. Damned Godo! he thought. His heart was beating too fast. He took deep breaths, hands on his knees, right there in the street.

'Mr Feebes!'

Her voice was like a clear bell in the darkness. Edward

straightened and beheld Sofia Salazar, leaning out of a carriage.

'Are you feeling all right, Mr Feebes?'

'It is nothing,' Edward said. 'A little discomfort...' He felt foolish, under her bright gaze. 'There is this medicine I sometimes take,' he said. 'For my stomach and such.'

'Laudanum?' She was watching him thoughtfully. 'We have plenty in store at home,' she said. 'My grandmother takes it for her pains. Would you like some?'

'Oh, don't trouble yourself,' he began to say, then noticed again his shaking hands. So did she. 'I mean, if it isn't too much bother...' Edward said, hating his weakness. Knowing Sofia Salazar saw it in him too.

'It's no bother at all!' Sofia said, laughing. 'I am on my way home now. I could give you a ride.'

'What would people say?' Edward said.

'They would say I am a kind and benevolent mistress, Mr Feebes,' Sofia said. 'And one, furthermore, whose generosity extends even to a lowly English clerk. Besides, my Aunt Maria is in the carriage with me, so rest assured we will be suitably chaperoned. Your... modesty is perfectly safe.'

'Then how can I refuse,' Edward said. He climbed into the carriage, and nodded to Sofia's Aunt Maria, who looked at him with disinterest and went back to her knitting.

'We have just come back from the port,' Sofia said. She seemed in a good mood. 'We picked up my new dress for the ball.'

'The ball?' Edward said.

'The President's Ball!' Sofia said. 'At the palace. It's tomorrow night. You are going?'

'I have not been invited,' Edward said, stiffly.

Sofia frowned. 'Moens should have told you,' she said. 'For the House of Feebes is always represented.'

'Yet he has not,' Edward said. His opinion of Moens plunged even further. This was evidence, if more evidence he needed, of the man's hostility. Moens, Edward now realised, clearly saw Lima as his own private fiefdom. He resented the arrival of a real Feebes. Resented – or was he afraid of what Edward would uncover?

'You *must* come,' Sofia said. 'For you to not appear would be an insult to the government – one from which you would not have quickly recovered, Edward. It is a good thing I ran into you! Though I am sure Moens merely forgot to mention it.'

'Of course,' Edward said.

'You have suitable attire?' Sofia asked.

'I do.'

'Naturally,' she said. 'You must have nothing but the latest fashions from Europe.'

Edward thought of his modestly tailored suits and decided not to disenchant her.

'Tomorrow night?' he said.

'There will be dancing,' Sofia said.

'Dancing!'

'Do you dance, Mr Feebes?'

The smile she offered him was full of promise.

'When the occasion demands,' he said.

'We are here,' Sofia said. They had not travelled far. The Salazars' house stood on its own, with a well-kept front and a clean-painted façade. The carriage stopped, and Edward helped Miss Salazar, and then her aunt, to disembark.

'How gallant,' Sofia Salazar said.

She seemed much more amenable now, Edward thought, than the last time at dinner. He said, 'I fear we exchanged some harsh words on our previous meeting.'

'Nonsense, Mr Feebes!' she said, laughing. 'It is stimulating to talk to someone new here. I hope you did not take it to heart. I grow so weary of the same old men speaking the same old things. No one takes me seriously here.'

'Then you do not think I am a...' he searched for words. 'A *leech* upon the body politic?'

Her lips twitched in a smile he was growing accustomed to.

'I have not said that,' she said.

'You all but implied it last time,' he said.

'If the shoe fits...' she murmured, then burst out laughing again.

'Your *face*!' she said.

He felt his cheeks grow red.

'Come,' Sofia Salazar said. 'Let us take coffee in the parlour. Aunty, will you inform my brothers that Mr Feebes is here?'

Her aunt grunted something in reply and vanished inside. Edward followed Sofia into the large, comfortable house, past silent servants and polished silver. Old Salazars glared down on him from dark oil paintings hung on the wall. They had come on the ship with Cortés, they seemed to say. They had fought alongside Bolívar. They *were* Peru, and there will always be a Salazar here; long after any Feebes has gone back to the Old World.

'Ah, the medicine,' Sofia said. 'Wait for me here, I will only be a moment.'

She left him in the sitting room and so he sat. There were European papers months out of date. He read about the war in Crimea. It seemed very far away. Sofia returned with a bottle, unopened, cherubic children smiling on the label. *Ayer's Cherry Pectoral*, it said, for colds and coughs. Sofia handed him the bottle.

'Thank you,' Edward said, genuinely moved. He saw compassion in her eyes and was ashamed. He took the bottle and rose.

'I will only be a moment,' he said.

He didn't want her to see him like this. He withdrew to the corridor and quickly opened the bottle and soaked his handkerchief. When he put it to his face it was like a blissful vapour wafting into his very soul, calming and soothing. For a moment, the feeling was all-consuming. Then he lowered the cloth and wondered what he had been anxious about before. His hands were steady and his breathing calm. Moens was just an irritation, some accounting irregularity Edward would easily solve. He was even amused now by the man's childish behaviour. Of course Edward would go to the President's Ball – he was the Feebes man in Lima, he *was* Feebes. As for Miss Salazar, with her smart mouth and saucy eyes, *she* was no match for Edward, either. He pocketed the bottle and returned to the sitting room. A service of coffee and cake had materialised in his absence. The aunt had returned, meanwhile, and sat demurely in a corner, still knitting, but peering out intently from under, every so often, like a watchful guardian. She put him in mind of a large sea bird scanning for fish.

'Are your brothers within?' Edward said.

'Out on business, it would seem,' Sofia said.

'The work of trade and governance never stops,' Edward said, a little pompously. Sofia regarded him thoughtfully.

'You seem much recovered,' she said.

'I am. Thank you.'

'Don't mention it,' she said. 'Mr Feebes, I have a question to put to you.'

'Oh?' he said.

'Yes.' She glanced at her aunt. Moved to the settee Edward was on, and perched modestly enough on the end of it, yet close enough that he was so aware of her proximity, and the smell of her perfume, and her sweat. 'It is about my Good Works committee.'

'You have a Good Works committee?' Edward said, bemused.

'Well, yes.'

'I see.'

'To support the poor and disadvantaged in our society,' Sofia said. 'We distribute literature, and hope to build a school.'

'Literature?' Edward said.

'And hope to build a school, yes,' Sofia said. She moved a little closer. The aunt coughed, then fell silent. They paid her no attention.

'My brothers help, as do several others,' Sofia said. 'With donations and so on.'

'Yes,' Edward said. Her lips were so red, her eyes so piercing. She had turned her full attention on him and the effect, he thought, was rather paralysing.

'I have been trying to speak to Mr Moens,' Sofia said. 'The House of Feebes, I feel, could well prove the decisive, um, *element* in going forward with our plans. With a charitable donation, I mean. But Mr Moens claims he cannot authorise such expenses on his own volition. And writing to the London office has as yet to produce response.'

'I see,' Edward said, for he was indeed beginning to see. 'But Miss Salazar, I cannot—'

'Can't you?' she said, speaking softly, and moving closer, if by a mere inch or two, across the settee. 'You *are* a Feebes.'

'Miss Salazar, I am sure your committee does great works—'

'Good Works,' Sofia said.

'*Great* Good Works,' Edward said, 'but I am simply not authorised!'

'You are all the same!' Sofia said, and stood, moving away from him in one lithe motion. 'Think of the poor, Mr Feebes! Those who have nothing, while your firm profits!'

'I think of nothing else!' Edward said. He stood up too. 'I will see you at the ball tomorrow night, Miss Salazar.'

And he took his leave with some alacrity.

6

THE NEW GAS LAMPS AROUND THE PLAZA DE MAYOR were being lit as he made his escape. He did not trust Sofia Salazar, he realised. Did not know what her true intentions were. He trusted no one in this town: certainly not Moens, and none of the Godos, or the other Europeans all jostling each other to get in on the guano fortune. Didn't trust the Peruvians, either, of course. Them least of all. Were they really going to default on their loans? The thought was unthinkable.

The problem, the way he saw it, was that there was too much money. The Peruvians were spending it like there was no tomorrow. Spending *Feebes* money, on their palaces and, and... *gas lamps*? They cast a gloomy glow in the murky half-light. He mopped his face. The humidity. Talk of putting in tram rails next. Modernising. But what happened if the money ran out? If the birds stopped shitting? There was no *prudence* here. Lima was rich – for now. But if the money stopped flowing... then the Peruvians would be in the shit. No money, no salaries, no progress, and before you could say 'by your leave', you had an economy in ruins and a country with a bunch of half-completed civic palaces and a lot of hungry – angry – people.

Which wasn't his problem, but it was a problem for the House of Feebes, one to carefully consider. One way or another he'd have to find the truth of it for himself, Edward decided. He'd have to do as Moens suggested, and go to the islands. He would also like to track down this lady scientist who counted nests.

He looked around him. It was dusk and the sun had all but set. He was walking along the Rimac, a river that smelled unpleasant, though nothing like the Thames. Its water was greenish-grey. There were no gas lamps here and the bank was muddy and grass grew thick.

There were people milling about, of the lower classes, mostly, natives and so on, though the atmosphere was not unfriendly. All manner of furtive business was conducted near the bridge and couples strolled off, with the approach of darkness, into the bushes. Edward could smell open fires, cooking meat, tobacco smoke, cheap perfume. He turned his back on the river and watched the city as it rose ahead of him, its grand mansions, the president's palace, the enormous basilica of San Francisco de Jesús. Smoke rose over the city, too, and its lights glowed in the dark, making it seem truly a City of the Kings, as though it were shrouded in mist and gold.

He wanted it all, at that moment. The gold, that obdurate Miss Salazar, the *power*. Edward could see it now, if only he could plot the right course, make the right decision. His uncle retiring and he ascending to the top chair on the top floor, to command the House of Feebes for the next generation. Shipping, banking, trade, munitions! A *global* firm, for a new, global world. So rich they could print their own money. This was what he wanted, craved, when he watched Lima, thinking how small it really was, and how he could devour it.

'Excuse me, mister, do you have the time?'

'The time?' Edward said. He reached for his pocket. He'd picked up a cheap silver watch in Liverpool to replace the one he'd thoughtlessly dispensed with in Covent Garden. 'Why, yes, it is around s—'

He didn't quite get the chance to finish. His interlocutors, he noticed with some surprise, were three monks, Franciscan, clad in blackish-grey habits and with somewhat roguish faces. This was not unusual – Lima crawled with monks, and many of them were ruffians in nature – and he had assumed they had come to the river bank to hire a cheap prostitute or get drunk in peace, away from their superiors.

What *was* unusual, however, was that one of the brothers, with rather a nasty, determined – one may even go so far as to say an *ugly* expression – grabbed Edward roughly by the arm and *twisted*, rather painfully; and the other monk, holding a burlap sack, raised it and expertly, as though landing a fish, dropped it onto Edward's head and tightened the string like a noose.

As Edward tried to struggle, the third monk landed a hard fist in his stomach and Edward doubled over in pain. The monks caught him swiftly, one on either side, and carried him away, as though escorting a drunk, perhaps one of their own, back to the safety of the cloisters. Edward tasted blood and smelled rotting fish. The blood was his, the fish, perhaps, the previous occupants of the burlap sack. He gagged.

The monks hissed between themselves; sibilant words Edward could not make out. He could not escape their grip; it was like iron. Mud underfoot turned back to stone. He heard people, carts, horses. He kept hoping, surely, someone would notice, someone would raise the alarm. The watch! he thought. The night watch! Were they not paid for and maintained by credit extended by Feebes & Co.? And yet nothing, and the sounds grew dim, the land sloped, he heard a frog croaking, or perhaps only imagined it, and then the monks speaking again, in low voices, and the sound of a grate removed, metal creaking, and he was pulled, pulled through a narrow entrance and down, down.

Hell awaited him below, he knew it then, with shocking certainty. Something wet fell on his back. Things scuttled underfoot. The monks spoke in low voices. The walls were close, the ceiling low. He crouched as they walked him to his doom.

Why? he thought. For what possible reason? He had done no one any harm. He was but a lowly clerk, of a good reputation, he had not even yet started a family. Did they want to rob him? But if so they could have done it on the bank of the Rimac.

He tried to run. He turned, caught one of them unawares, pushed forward, and tripped on an extended foot. One monk laughed and another cursed. They pulled him up.

'No more of this, please,' one of them said.

They led him on. Through deep underground tunnels and caverns, the air dry, and here and there he heard the rustling of ancient bones. He knew where he was. He had not been long in Lima but he had heard of the catacombs beneath.

At last they stopped, and shoved him to his knees.

'No, please,' he told them. 'Please, don't.'

Silence. There was no more speaking. He heard them shuffling, rearranging around him. Ready to strike.

He closed his eyes.

'O God, who knows us to be set in the midst of so many and great dangers,' he prayed. His lips moved almost soundlessly. He heard metal whisper against metal as one monk drew a blade. 'That by reason of the frailty of our nature we cannot always stand upright.' He wanted to weep. Weep for all he'd done, weep for all he hadn't yet achieved. He began to cry. 'Grant us such strength and protection, as may support us in all dangers and carry us through all temptations! Through Jesus Christ, our Lord.'

Amen.

But no help was coming, and one monk held his shoulders as the other placed a blade upon his neck. It would be over quickly, Edward thought. At least there would be that.

'Well, finish him!' he heard one of the monks whisper.

'What's that?' one of the other two monks said.

Edward listened.

An ethereal moan filled the catacombs.

A shiver went down Edward's spine. The blade on his neck moved away.

'What is it?'

He heard a monk mumble a prayer in Latin. The sound of moaning, terrible and ghostly, came again, closer this time. Edward clenched his teeth, trying to stop himself from voiding his bowels in fright. Everyone knew, he thought. Everyone knew the catacombs were haunted.

'It is El Torturador!' one of Edward's captors cried.

The blade clattered to the floor. The moan came again, the eerie voice echoing from the walls.

'Santa Madre de Dios!' another of the monks cried. Edward heard his captors turn tail and run. Their sandalled feet slapped against the stone floor, the sound growing weaker as they vanished back the way they came.

Edward was left alone.

Alone with the ghost.

He didn't dare move. The moan came again, low and loud, more like a growl.

Then Edward realised his hands were free.

He reached up very slowly and removed the burlap sack from his head.

An elderly monk, in the same Franciscan habit as Edward's would-be executioners, stood in the open entrance to what proved to be a small subterranean alcove filled with human skulls. He had not seemed to have noticed Edward at all. One possible reason for this, Edward saw, was that the monk's habit was pulled over his waist, exposing his genitalia, which the ancient monk was very busy fondling, all the while emitting blood-curdling moans. No doubt he came down to the catacombs for some privacy. As Edward watched, the monk emitted the most terrifying cry of all, and then went limp. He wiped his hand on his habit and pulled the cloth down modestly around himself, then blinked and looked about as though awakening from a pleasant dream.

'Please,' Edward said. 'Help me.'

The monk turned in fright and saw Edward. He gave a shrill cry of alarm, and vanished with alacrity back the way he came.

Edward slumped, his back to the wall.

His mouth tasted of bile, his head bloomed with remembered pain. The burlap sack lay on the floor. A lantern lay on the ground by the entrance, still mercifully burning, where one of the kidnappers must have dropped it in his flight.

The horror of his situation hit Edward then and he whimpered.

But he was still alive.

He craved water then. Water, and light and air. He looked around him. He was in a small alcove and all around him lay the dead.

He was too numb now to fear them. Skeletons lay in stacks. A shelf full of skulls overhead, the dead staring at him mutely. *They* didn't care for the troubles of a Feebes, they seemed to say. To them the profit and the loss had been concluded long ago, the numbers added into sums which lost their meaning. No one remembered who they were, what they had done. Had they loved, had they hated? Did they fight in the War of Independence? The catacombs had been closed since 1826. Were these all heretics, natives or Jews, put to the screw and the rack by the Inquisition? So many of those unfortunates were buried down here. Unlabelled bones, that's all they were. Edward was a modern man. He believed in sums, not ghosts. Still. He thought – he'd better get out of there before his abductors came back to finish the job they'd started.

Never trust a monk, he thought. He pulled himself up.

He realised he was not seriously harmed, just shaken from the ordeal. He wobbled on his feet, reached out to steady himself, and found himself gripping a skull.

The skull was yellowed and old; its teeth were bad. Whoever it was had been down there a while, and was too late to try out modern dentistry. Edward let it fall. The skull rolled on the floor and came to a stop against the wall. Edward picked up the lantern, glad it had not gone out. Its flame wobbled and the smell it gave out was rank. He went out of the alcove the way the old monk went. He found a narrow corridor, with more skeletons laid in hollows in the walls. He followed it and came to a hall where piles of bones simply lay on the ground, skulls and femurs, rib cages and spines, and hands without measure. What had they held, these dead? Did they pick up a pen and write a confession? Paint blasphemy on the walls of a public commode? Did they hold sword or gun, did they hold a loved one, tilled a field, picked coca, chopped garlic for supper? He couldn't know, and all he knew was that he had to get out of that silent mausoleum before he became one of them too. He crossed the hall and went down another corridor, searching for stairs, but all he could find were two turnings, one leading left and one right.

He went left, and along another corridor, and more skeletons and skulls, and through a hall of bones and on, and on, and the torch spluttered, and he thought it would go out. The thought of being trapped there underground terrified him.

'Stop right there!'

Edward froze. He was afraid the kidnappers had come back for him. Then he saw the approaching light and a

Franciscan monk again, this one heavy-set, with sunken eyes, who hailed him.

'How did you get in here!' he said. 'The catacombs are closed!'

'You have to help me,' Edward said. 'I was taken here against my will and now I'm lost.'

The Franciscan frowned, then came closer. He shone his light on Edward's face.

'Yes,' he said. 'They do that, from time to time.' He shook his head at this apparent folly. 'Come along, then,' he said.

Edward followed the Franciscan. Along corridors and up hewn-stone stairs. Until at last they reached a door, which the Franciscan unlocked with a large key, and through it, to the outside.

Air! Fresh air! Edward drew in a shuddering breath, and looked up at a sky filled with stars. For once it wasn't too cloudy. All the constellations seemed polished anew. He wanted to hug the Franciscan. The monk relocked the door.

'Don't go wandering in there again,' he said. Then he set off and vanished into the dark of the basilica.

7

THINGS WERE BECOMING CLEARER TO EDWARD. IT WAS all in the numbers, ultimately. He splashed water out of the bath. Steam rose into the air. The ledgers sat on a bath tray before him, along with a hot cup of tea. When he had got back to Mrs Walker's hotel at last, the old widow – much respectable if plain, the mixed-blood wife of an English merchant who had succumbed to illness of a mysterious nature some years back – made much fuss over him and his bruises, and ordered the servants to draw a bath. Mrs Walker, though native to Peru, had been married long enough to Mr Walker to know the correct way of preparing English tea, a fact for which Edward now gave much gratitude. He stared thoughtfully at the sugar.

His study of the ledgers revealed a host of small errors. Those, he was sure, were not by malicious design but simple incompetence, but added together they formed a large piece of the irregularity of which his uncle had concerns. The rest, however, was not as easy to uncover. The sums involved were large, and skimming, he had to surmise, was easy. In fact, he calculated, purely as a working hypothesis, some 10 per cent set aside for the inevitable siphoning off of money

SIX LIVES

by clerks and middlemen. The secret of business, his uncle
once told him, was to find the right people, who would
skim just enough off the top. *That* could be allowed for.
That could be factored in.

And yet there was a hole. He had been circling it, this
absence, for all this time, like flotsam round a drain. He
needed to be careful not to fall in.

He shuddered. That had been close, the encounter with
the Franciscans. He would have nightmares about the
catacombs, he knew. When he closed his eyes, skulls grinned
at him from their shelves. He sipped his tea. Mrs Walker's
hotel was an acceptable establishment, providing long-term
accommodation to respectable gentlemen. Besides Edward
there was a Mr Schlotke, of Hamburg, a timber salesman;
Mr William Turner, partner of Turner, Marriott and Smith
of Arequipa and Valparaiso, who was in Lima for a couple
of weeks only, but a regular visitor; and Samuel Gibson, a
one-eyed ship's captain, now retired.

Edward splashed in the bath and examined the columns
of numbers in the ledger before him. Yes, things were
becoming clearer. He sank deeper into the water and closed
his eyes, but the sensation was unpleasant, as though he
were trapped again in the catacombs; and so he opened his
eyes and rose from the bath. He felt very tired then. When
he at last made it to his bed sleep overwhelmed him almost
at once. In his dreams he was chased around by grinning
skeletons, while Sofia Salazar writhed provocatively
in the arms of a wizened old monk who bore Moens'
face.

*

'What happened to you?' Moens said upon Edward's entrance, the next day, into the office. 'You look like...' He made a rude gesture. His cronies, who were sitting around him as they always did at that time of the morning over brandy and cigars, dutifully laughed. Edward felt the resentment rise inside him, but he tamped it down and smiled as though Moens' crude jibe had been a witty remark; as Moens himself no doubt imagined it to be.

'A slight accident on the riverbank,' Edward said. 'I fell and slipped in the mud.'

'You should be careful on the Rimac after dark,' Moens said. 'I should have mentioned that to you.'

'Speaking of things you forgot to mention,' Edward said. 'Tonight's President's Ball—'

'Did I fail to mention it?' Moens said innocently. His cronies guffawed. 'Well, it is no harm done, Mr Feebes. It is merely a function, one of many I must drag myself to in my service of the firm.'

'I believe it would have been seen as a slight had I failed to make an appearance,' Edward said stiffly, and Moens laughed.

'Don't overestimate your worth, Edward,' he said; not perhaps entirely unkindly. Though Edward did not see it this way. He made little time in the office, his main intention having been to confront Moens. Shortly he bade them a stiff goodbye, and went to the coffee house, where Dr Steinmeier was seated at his usual table.

'Edward!' he said, rising in alarm. 'What happened to you?'

Edward sat. He told Dr Steinmeier of the previous night's

events over coffee and pastries. When he had finished, the good doctor nodded thoughtfully.

'A lucky escape,' he said.

'You could certainly say that again,' Edward agreed.

'A lucky escape!' Dr Steinmeier said, and then burst out laughing at his own childish jape. Edward smiled despite himself.

'I am made of sterner stuff than they think me,' he said. 'I *am* a Feebes.'

'Indeed you are,' Dr Steinmeier said, recovering his composure. He filled his pipe. 'But still. I did tell you to be careful. You and I are civilised men, and it is easy to forget, sometimes, that this land is not. You don't even know if those men really were monks, though it would not surprise me. Half the flotsam and jetsam of the old Spanish dominions seek refuge in the vows. It's three square meals a day and a dry roof over your head.'

Edward dismissed it with a wave of his hand.

'It will be taken care of,' he said.

'You should think of leaving town for a while,' Dr Steinmeier said. 'Just in case. Which reminds me. I tracked down that lady scientist you were asking for. This Mary Stephenson.'

'The naturalist,' Edward said.

'Yes. She was last seen in Ica, in the south. I'm told that on her last visit to Lima a month back she had expressed interest in viewing the Candelabro de Paracas.'

'What's that?' Edward said.

'A giant etching on the side of a hill, in the shape of a candelabra, or perhaps a cactus. It's very unclear. Some say it was put there for the benefit of pirates, for it can really only be seen in full from the sea.' Dr Steinmeier shrugged. 'She might still be there, or she might have moved on.'

'I shall bear it in mind,' Edward said. 'Thank you. Will you be at the ball tonight?'

'Naturally. I shall see you there?'

Edward smiled.

'Naturally,' he said.

Evening made Lima almost pretty. Edward, dressed in his finest suit, still kept an eye out for the turkey-buzzards. These birds, gallinazos, the locals called them, looked like black widows wearing a devil's red mask. They were everywhere in the city, feeding on carrion, going wherever they could smell the rot of dead things. In that, they provided so useful a function as to be declared protected birds, to be neither killed nor threatened. They watched from the rooftops as Edward's carriage arrived at the palace.

There were many dignitaries already there, the horses jostling and the cab men lashing with their whips and arguing with each other as the horses relieved themselves and the guests alighted. Edward was glad to escape, and made his way inside, past the soldiers at attention and the musicians getting ready and the president's welcoming committee, who checked his invitation was in order before allowing him into the ball proper. There, the great and the good of Lima mingled as servants glided by with trays of drinks and finger foods. In the distance, Edward could see President Castilla, with his full head of black, luxurious hair: he had only just become president again, having defeated former president Echenique in the Battle of Arequipa. Echenique was now in exile in New York.

This was the problem, Edward reflected. The House of Feebes dealt directly with the government of Peru, but what did you do when the government kept changing? Business could not be allowed to be derailed based on political instability. At least the new president needed the guano money just as much as the old one did. He saw Felipe and Sofia Salazar.

'Edward!' Felipe said. He shook Edward's hand warmly. His face glowed with the warmth that wine brings. 'How are you, please?'

'I'm well,' Edward said, reminding himself that Felipe and Moens were close. Could he trust any of them? He didn't know. The Salazars were old money. They did not care who wore the presidential sash. It was always thus with the old families. Power moved between them like a cricket ball between players.

'Mr Feebes,' Sofia said.

'Miss Salazar.'

'Would you care for some wine?' she said. 'It's from Chile.'

She hailed a servant and Edward accepted a glass.

'To your health,' he said.

'And to yours.'

Felipe watched the two of them shrewdly. Edward could see the calculation in his eyes. A match between the house of Feebes and the Salazars would serve the latter well, he thought. And he could not but admit a certain desire for Sofia.

'. . . Excuse me?'

He realised Felipe had been talking. His gaze wandered from Sofia's bust up to Felipe. The man watched him in amusement, but his eyes were cold.

'I must go converse with Mr Bergmann, of Templeman and Bergmann,' Felipe said. 'I trust my sister to your keeping, Mr Feebes.'

'I shall look after her well,' Edward promised. Sofia smiled around her glass.

'Do you care to dance, Mr Feebes?' she said.

'Would *you* care to dance, Miss Salazar?'

'I would indeed.' She curtseyed. They disposed of their drinks and joined the swirling couples on the marble floor.

The music soared; the drinks flowed; the great and the good conversed and schemed and conducted business; Sofia was a nimble dancer and Edward did his best to keep up.

It was when they paused to rest that he heard a commotion outside, and shouting, though it was hard to make out in the music. Then the figure of a young man, dressed in dusty uniform, burst through into the hall, followed urgently by guards. He held something in his hand – a small round object, like a perfume bottle. He raised it above his head. His eyes were wild.

'Viva Vivanco!' he cried. 'Muerte a Castillo!'

He threw the object. Edward acted without thinking. He tackled Sofia and brought her to the ground and lay on top of her. There was the whoosh of an explosion. The musicians stopped abruptly and in the sudden silence all Edward could hear were screams.

He was painfully aware of Sofia's body beneath him. Of her warmth and the press of her flesh. She looked into his eyes and there was something there he had not seen before: a sort of longing.

'It should have been an anarchist,' she whispered.

It made no sense to Edward. He leaned forward, the better to kiss her. For a moment she let him. Then she broke the contact and pushed him gently away, and rose to her feet. He followed a moment later.

In the middle of the dance floor the marble was fractured. The young man was not dead, but his hands were burned and he was the cause of most of the screaming. He was being detained by the guards, who were not being gentle. The revellers watched, none seemingly hurt. President Castillo, on the other side of the room, watched with his lips pursed.

'Who is Vivanco?' Edward said.

'He is an enemy of Castillo,' Sofia said. 'Also my second cousin once removed.' She frowned. 'He is in exile in Chile, I think. Clearly, he wished to send a message.'

'You people are all mad!' Edward said.

'It's just politics, Edward,' Sofia said. She looked wistful again.

'You mustn't take it *personally*,' she said.

8

He was glad to leave Lima at last. The city walls rising at his back, the sea ahead. His only companion was Guido, a gruff, mustachioed native of mixed blood who had been in the Feebeses' employ ever since the Lima House was first established.

It was hot. Edward mopped his brow, felt pit stains spread under his arms. Ships jostled in the harbour, their sails down, looking like restless gulls. The road turned south, away from city and harbour both, away from all signs of habitation. This was desert country.

It made Lima seem so puny, he thought. The games of Salazars, Castillos and Vivancos so childish. Here there was only the desert and the sea, eternal under the beating sun, indifferent to these ant-like humans and their petty feuds and funny-money markers. It was a slow journey, past Miraflores and Chorrillos, then through a large sugarcane plantation. Edward mopped sweat and breathed laudanum. Then at last, some hours later, to a river. They followed its contours, and Edward beheld the ruins of the vast pyramid of the temple of the Sun. These were the first Inca ruins he had seen. He stopped and stared a while, at this St Paul's of the desert, while Guido smoked a small hand-rolled cigar.

An empire was here once, and stretched across vast distances and was rich besides. And now it wasn't. And Edward thought of the House of Feebes, which could by itself be, if not an empire, then the banker of one. For all empires needed money, and if he played his cards right the House of Feebes would be his. They crossed the river over a handsome stone bridge and rode through another sugar plantation, and at last reached the village of Lurin, in a temperate valley in which the great god Pachacamac was once worshipped.

They spent the night at an Incan tambo, a large way-station built with stones, and managed by a dour-faced Ichma man and his wife. It was another reminder to Edward that these were Inca roads he was traversing, and he felt ill at ease falling asleep within their old habitat. He didn't know much about the Inca. Stories of blood sacrifices and all that. He slept fitfully and was cold in the night. Birds flew overhead, numerous beyond count, and three islands rose in the ocean, and the birds rained excrement upon those lonely outcrops of rock, and their shit turned to gold and shone in the sun, and men in bowler hats knelt down before it on the shore and offered prayers.

'Time to go.'

'What? What?' Edward said.

'Time to go,' Guido said. Edward sat up. It was dark. 'Travel while it's cool,' Guido said.

They set off under a dismal moon and too many stars. They rode along a sandy road, a short distance from the sea, and the air was filled with the sound of breaking waves.

The world lightened gradually. They stopped in a small village with little vegetation and houses made of sticks and mud, drank water and continued on their way, until they crested a low hill and Edward beheld another green valley, planted with maize and sugarcane. In the village of Mala they stopped at the tambo and bolted down their dinner. Guido disappeared to visit a girlfriend that he kept there, or so he said. Edward paced a while, dazed by the heat and the distance he had come. Lima was a world away now, England but a dream he once had. He felt as though he had fallen off the map of the known world. He took a few drops of laudanum and fell asleep listening to the roaring of the sea.

Sunlight and distant shouts woke him, and he staggered out to see the conductor of the post, riding in from Lima on his way to Cuzco. Edward took breakfast with the conductor in the post house, of cold beef and chocolate, and he and Guido joined the mail for the next leg of their journey. On they rode, to Cerro Azul, a small fishing village with nothing much, Edward thought, to recommend it. It was too hot to ride but he did not want to tarry, and Guido acquiesced with some muttering. They waded through a shallow river in the valley of Cañete, then past sugarcane plantations and along the rocky shore until they came to a small, lonely house in the sands, where they had fresh water and Edward was overcharged for a small loaf of bread and some oranges. He rested there a while. The sun was growing low in the sky and so they rode on though it wasn't much cooler, and came at last to Chincha Alta.

The islands, which were his destination, were almost within reach. He watched the merchant ships sail sedately beyond the shore, and supped on a good meal and drank a measure of pisco, the local liquor, and his sleep was deep and untroubled.

In the morning he felt a reluctance to go on. He set Guido to take him to the Inca ruins. This proved elucidating, if hot work, for the ancient Inca had built palaces and temples in this valley, and Edward felt himself alone amidst them (alone but for Guido, who didn't count), and wished he had with him one of those Daguerreotype machines by which one was able to take a life-like image – what Sir John Herschel called a 'photograph'. Had Edward been an artist he may have considered drawing the extensive ruins, but his talents did not lie in that direction, and his mind, attuned as it was to the profits and the loss, was busy calculating the annual income collected in such a valley, and the cost of the building works, and how much the upkeep of the place must have been. He was, indeed, so sunk in his reverie (in his dream *he* was the tax-collector), that he did not notice when they were no longer alone, and was indeed quite startled when he heard a cheery 'Halloo!' come booming at him from the shadow of a tall tower.

This, it transpired, came from a rather small white woman, conservatively and appropriately attired, and holding a parasol. She was accompanied by two native companions, a man and a woman, and had set herself a comfortable-looking camp there in the ruins, with a small table and a picnic basket and a bottle of pisco that was half-full.

'Why, hello,' Edward said, when they had climbed down to her place. He took off his hat. 'Edward Feebes,' he said.

'Why, you are an Englishman!' the woman said. She

extended her hand for a shake, startling Edward. When he took her hand it was callused, her grip strong. 'Mary Stephenson,' the woman said. 'Formerly of Queenstown, currently of no fixed abode.'

'The naturalist!' Edward said.

'You've heard of me?' She seemed amused.

'My firm brokers the sale of guano from the islands,' Edward explained.

'I see.' The woman considered. 'Care for some brandy?'

'Only a drop,' Edward said. 'Thank you, yes.'

Miss Stephenson poured. The pisco was strong but smooth. It polished off the edges of the day.

'I met with one of your staff,' Miss Stephenson said. 'A Mr... Moens?'

'John Moens, yes.'

'I did not much care for him,' Miss Stephenson announced.

Edward smiled.

'I share the sentiment,' he said. 'Besides, I rather suspect he tried to have me killed.'

'Indeed?' Miss Stephenson, Edward noticed, didn't seem unduly surprised. 'They do that way here,' she said. 'All those recent battles have been quite the nuisance for my work.'

'I was hoping to talk to you about that,' Edward said. 'Your work.'

'Yes? But it is just birds,' Miss Stephenson said.

Edward laughed. '*Just* birds?' he said. 'They are the source of a fortune, Miss Stephenson.'

'You refer to the guano,' she said, frowning. 'I do not approve of guano, Mr Feebes.'

'How so?' he said, taken aback.

'Its use for agriculture is one thing, Mr Feebes,' Miss Stephenson said. 'But you and I both know that is not the *only* commercial use one can put bird... excrement to. Do we not?'

'I'm not sure to what you are referring, Miss Stephenson...'

She smiled thinly. 'But I think you do,' she said. 'Bird guano contains a high concentrate of potassium nitrate, Mr Feebes. That is the main component of gunpowder.'

'But Miss Stephenson!' Edward said.

She shook her head. 'Do not play the wide-eyed innocent with me,' she said. 'You and I both know the use to which these exports are put. The money the trade generates is beyond considerable. But where does it go? What good use has been made of the millions and millions of pounds which the guano has raised? For Peru as a nation, hardly any! Yet individuals have enriched themselves, and much money has been spent in powder and balls, in cannons, rifles, swords and in iron-clad men of war.' She shook her head again. 'Thank the Lord it is depleting,' she said.

Edward, despite his protestations, was aware of the use Miss Stephenson mentioned. It troubled him not, for the House of Feebes were mere brokers, and the end use of the product was hardly their concern. Fertiliser or gunpowder, both grew flowers of a sort. But her final pronouncement arrested him.

'*Depleting?*' he said, in some alarm.

'I told your man Moens all this,' Miss Stephenson said. 'It is a blessing, really.'

'How do you mean, Miss Stephenson?'

She shrugged. 'The natural balance of the birds' environment has been disturbed,' she said. 'Shall I put it crudely? There are less birds, and those that remain no longer poop over the Chinchas as much as they once did. The shipping and industry puts them off, I think. The islands have centuries of deposits on them. But they have been worked steadily for decades now, Mr Feebes. Sooner or later, you will run out of guano.'

'But that is terrible,' Edward said.

'On that,' Miss Stephenson said, and smiled that thin smile of hers, which he was quite growing to detest, 'we are both agreed. Though perhaps not for the same reasons. Care for another drink?'

'No,' Edward said. 'Thank you. I must be off.'

'Then have a safe journey, Mr Feebes.'

'And you, Miss Stephenson. Tell me…' as though it had just occurred to him.

'Yes?'

'How long?'

'How long what, Mr Feebes?'

'How long before the guano is depleted?'

'I don't know,' Miss Stephenson said. 'A few years. A decade maybe, if you're lucky. But of course, there might be other guano islands out there.'

'Of course. Well, goodbye.' He touched the brim of his hat and turned on his heels.

'Come, Guido!' he said.

They rode at night, Edward not wishing to remain in Chincha Alta any longer, and further calculating in his head the truth or otherwise in Miss Stephenson's words and in Moens' books of accounts. He was troubled, and only the tincture of opium helped alleviate his mood, though his stock of Ayer's Cherry Pectoral was – like the guano, perhaps – fast depleting.

The ride was pleasant, through thick vegetation, and after some eight leagues they arrived in Pisco, a small town built in the Spanish way, and with many churches. There were ships moored offshore and business being conducted in the Custom House. Edward sought accommodation with the postmaster, and slept soundly. He took a leisurely breakfast, washed and shaved, and by the time he was done Guido had returned to inform him the ship to the islands was waiting.

9

HE COULD SMELL THE ISLANDS BEFORE HE SAW THEM. The stench of excrement, rank and acrid, caught in the back of his throat. Dry-dust bird shit blowing in the wind, slushed and processed bird shit mixed with water and sieved, it blew on the breeze and Edward heaved over the side of the ship, feeling sorry for himself, and wishing he had never come. Then the islands came into view, one after the other: three lone, miserable-looking heaps of volcanic rock thrusting out of the ocean like obscene gestures, a dark cloud of birds weaving above them like a storm: gannets and petrels, pelicans and Inca terns.

And all around the islands were the ships.

He had not appreciated the scale of it until then: barks and packets, clippers and frigates, and one small kettle-bottomed boat that, Guido told him, dated back to Wolfe's expedition to Quebec in 1759. She now served as transport for the fleet. Nearly a hundred ships floated there on the sea.

He saw the *Calhoun* and the *Intrepid*, the *Webster* and the *Nyack*. Some of those ships had been in those waters for months, Guido told him. Waiting their turn at the loading docks, their sailors growing restless and idle in turns. Which is where their own vessel, the *Liberty*, came in. This barge was laden with supplies, from fishing line and tackle to cards, board games, bottles of pisco, books and other reading materials, needle and thread, razors and mirrors, fresh meat and produce, and everything else the stranded ships might need. The owner of this vessel, a wiry young Irishman, was named William Grace, of Cork; as he explained it, he had come to Peru to work in agriculture, but soon discovered a more lucrative form of employment.

'There she is,' he said now, pointing to a curious-looking wreck that lay between the North and Central Islands. 'Home.'

'I beg your pardon?' Edward said.

'The shop!' Grace said. 'We're set up there with supplies, me and the missus. It's a captive market, what with all the ships. And the margins are huge. In a few years I hope to make enough to go to New York.'

'Why New York?' Edward said, bemused.

'It's Ireland,' Grace said simply. 'Just without the bullshit.'

It wasn't anything Edward could argue with, so he didn't. He threw up his lunch overboard, and watched enormous shoals of sardines dart below the surface of the water. They fought over his lunch and it made him retch again but there was nothing left. He breathed more laudanum and saw a pod of whales in the distance, rising enormous out of the calm sea of the Bay of Pisco, then descend back to the depths. The *Liberty* sailed on, serenely, and the islands grew close, and the sailors from the nearby ships shouted greetings at Grace, who waved back cheerfully.

As they came closer, Edward began to discern features on

the barren islands. Houses, bamboo shacks and tents were dotted around, and the tiny figures of men who toiled in the intolerable heat on heaps of dung. Their destination was North Island, and the little barge cut slowly through the water towards that inhospitable grey rock from which the unlikely fortunes of the House of Feebes were made.

They made a landing on a small pebbly beach, the *Liberty* discharging Edward, Guido and supplies. Grace waved them off and sailed towards his wreck; Edward watched as the *Liberty* moored there and began to offload supplies.

He turned with a sigh and regarded his present home. The cliffs towered above him, and the air was choked with dust. Huge canvas pipes ran down from the top of the cliffs and onto the docks, where a ship called the *Wasp* was currently stationed. Chinese workers overhead sent down bags of guano. They slid from on high and down the chutes, making an almighty racket, and piped on to the top of the deck of the *Wasp*, where the sailors cursed and carried them into the hold. The ship sank slowly, slowly, down, bowed by the weight of the tonnes of guano, the waterline rising until the ship could hold no more. Edward watched the sacks slide down; he watched them piled high; he watched them carted. Each sack with a value attached, each ship a floating treasure chest of birdshit gold. And like the Spanish treasure fleet of old, these ships, too, bound for Europe, were beset by dangers on all sides. There were pirates out there, Edward knew, who would rob guano ships as happily as anything to command the waves. Then there were storms; reefs; negligence and acts of God. In all of this, the ledgers dictated that some ships and some cargo were destined to be lost, and that loss had to be calculated and accounted for on the balance sheets. This Edward understood, but it was good to have it confirmed, and the fleet that awaited the loading and departure reassured him. Say twenty-five ships drowned, then still seventy-five made it through. And even on the ones that were to be inevitably written off, the House of Feebes was insured, so it was no real loss bar the lives of the sailors.

Lives, after all, were the cheapest commodity: and he saw evidence of that in the coolies that slaved on top of the dung heaps, encouraged by the overseers with their whips if they stepped out of line. These men were promised pay to come here. Their transportation and housing and feeding all cost. If they died before fulfilling their contract, then that was regrettable. But there was no shortage of coolies. And more would be brought.

As he thought this, he saw a commotion above. One man, starvation thin, had roused himself in a desperate bid for freedom. He yelled as he ran, clutching a shovel. He saw Edward on the beach below. Something maddened came into his eyes then. He threw the shovel. It arced in the air, tracing a short parabola before beginning its descent. Edward watched in horrified numbness as the shovel shot through the air towards him. He took a hurried step back and the shovel stung the sand harmlessly a mere foot away from him and stood there, vertical. The man high above screamed in despair and ran to the edge of the cliff just as two gunshots rang out. The man's scream cut short and his body fell like a sack of guano and hit the ocean with a splash.

'Ah, Mr Feebes,' a man said. He came down to the shore. A dapper little man, in a good suit, and a sportsman's tan, and a rifle slung casually over his shoulder. 'Apologies for that, sir. I hope you are not greatly inconvenienced.'

Edward, still shaken, gestured helplessly. He held on to the shovel for support.

'No,' he said, after a moment. 'Not at all.' He attempted a smile. 'Makes a handy walking aid, what?' he said, lifting and planting the shovel in demonstration.

'Quite, sir,' the other man said, smiling. He extended his hand for a shake. 'A pleasure to make your acquaintance. It has been a long time since a Feebes honoured us with his presence.'

Edward shook the proffered hand warmly.

'Major Boyd, I presume?' he said.

'Indeed, sir. Was your journey pleasant?'

'It was – is – enlightening,' Edward said, and Major Boyd laughed.

'I am sure,' he said. 'Come. Let me settle you, then I'll show you around. I hope this unfortunate incident won't deter your otherwise good opinion of us. We run a tight operation, but these suicides are a constant problem. Do keep this shovel as a memento if you wish. We are all eager for a good report back to Mr Henry. '

'You know my uncle?' Edward said.

'He hired me, sir,' Major Boyd said. 'A fine man, and a fair one.' He whistled. Two emaciated men appeared. They looked beaten by life and overseers. Major Boyd barked orders. The men, uncomplaining, went to pick up Edward's bags, as more men appeared to carry the supplies. Major Boyd lit a pipe and escorted Edward up the slope. Edward moved slowly, leaning on the shovel like a walking stick. He had taken quite a liking to it.

'How do you control them?' Edward said.

'The carrot and the stick, sir,' Major Boyd said. 'Opium if they behave themselves, and the whip if they don't.'

This made sense to Edward; and his heart began to beat faster when he heard opium mentioned. It was what the old shopkeeper back in Lima had told him, too: that the drug was brought in to control the coolies.

He saw them everywhere now. Small, bent men, mostly young, insect-thin and coughing. Many wore dirty scarves over their faces to protect themselves from the ever-present guano dust. There were angry red welts on their naked backs, and they moved lethargically, helplessly, with a sense, Edward felt, of the absurd. These men had come here in search of a life that they were destined not to get. The very act of coming here had robbed them of a future. They would die here, and they knew it, but there was no escape, the sea around their prison holding them in, and their masters working for higher powers: the Peruvian government and the House of Feebes. *They* were the true source of Edward's would-be fortune. The workers Sofia Salazar was so fond of referencing. They were the means to an end: to dig guano out of the mountainous layers where it lay, to dig through the centuries of that dark gold, to process it and to ship it elsewhere.

He followed Major Boyd to the small settlement on the peak, the hotel and staff quarters, and watched the workers below and their bamboo tenements, and the ships all around the island awaiting their turn at the dock.

The hotel was small and basic, but adequate. Major Boyd poured them both a drink.

'It is a beautiful view,' he said.

It really was. Edward could see for miles, to the mainland and the strange Inca inscription on the hill, which did indeed look a little like a candelabra. He saw Central and South Islands and the mining operations there, and the coolies crawling like ants. He sipped his drink. He mopped his brow. He said, 'I need to see your account books, Major Boyd.'

'Of course,' Major Boyd said. He studied Edward. 'This is why you came?' he said.

'Partly.'

'We send copies on the regular to the office in Lima,' Major Boyd said.

'I saw.'

'You suspect a discrepancy, Mr Feebes?'

Edward examined his glass. It was empty. He poured himself another.

'Should I be suspicious, Major Boyd?' he said.

The major examined his hands. He had very clean nails, Edward saw.

'Well,' Major Boyd said slowly. 'It depends, I suppose.'

'Depends on what?'

'On what numbers you have.'

Edward smiled. 'You record the number of sacks, tonnage and so on, I assume,' he said.

'Of course.'

'Mr Boyd,' Edward said. 'May I be frank?'

'I would like that,' the major said.

'You can't steal anything here but shit,' Edward said. 'No money changes hands. You could, however, under-report a certain percentage of production to be sold locally, on the side. To someone with a boat?'

'I suppose.'

'And you could make money selling the coolies their medicine or luxuries, on which you could levy a tax, on top of a healthy margin—'

'I suppose.'

'Even run whores, on occasion, for the sailors, or what workers aren't already too ill or dying.'

'All of these things are possible,' Major Boyd said.

Edward shrugged. 'You'd need a partner, though,' he said. 'Moens? No, don't answer. All this is a fraction of a percentage at best. Part of the—'

'The profits and the loss,' Major Boyd said. 'Yes. Your Uncle Henry was clear on this from the beginning.'

Edward nodded.

'Is production down?' he said.

'No, sir. Not for now.'

'Show me the operation.'

They rose. It was hot and dusty outside. Birds circled overhead. Major Boyd handed him an umbrella.

'For the shitting birds, sir,' he said.

Edward watched this mountain of guano, and the men digging it, and he thought it could go on forever. He said, 'How long?'

'Sir?'

'How long?'

The major hesitated. 'Maybe five years at full capacity,' he said. 'Ten good years overall. Maybe ten more bad years after that.'

'How many men?'

'We have around three thousand at a time,' the major said. 'But there's a lot of... turnover, as you saw. We spend ten thousand men a year, perhaps?'

Edward considered. Ten good years. A hundred thousand workers had to die before the profits slackened. He wondered what Sofia Salazar would say. His head spun, from the heat and the drink. He needed air. He took a step and then another, to the edge of the cliff. Something churned in the sea below. His vision swam, then focused, and he saw the corpse of the man who had earlier jumped, bobbing in a water dark with his blood. Creatures were feeding on him, ripping the body apart, maddened by the blood.

Edward turned away from the sight.

He said, 'Show me where you give them the opium.'

He lay on the cot in the shade of the bamboo roof, his muscles relaxed and heavy and his mouth slack, the shit shovel leaning against the wall.

The pipe sat beside him. A doctor had gently administered the medicine, the flame heating up the precious resin so that Edward could inhale its bitter fumes. His mind felt sharp. His body felt like it was floating.

He could see it all then. The numbers made sense at last. Moens' greedy little scheme, no doubt with the help of the Salazars. Skimming money off the top and making extra on the workers – no doubt he had a hand, too, in procuring the coolies in the first place, and collecting a fee on that. It hardly mattered. Edward would submit his report and Moens would be replaced, perhaps with someone more trustworthy, perhaps not. A margin of loss for corruption was always factored in.

More important was the question of the future. He had learned something on this journey. The guano wouldn't last.

The House of Feebes must make arrangements, divest some of its assets – into banking or insurance, perhaps, or extend its stake in the munitions business, which was already flourishing.

The question he faced, Edward supposed, was a moral one. To terminate the arrangements now would leave the House of Feebes exposed. Moreover, the Peruvians would merely hand over the brokerage to another firm. So nothing he could do would stop the mining operations on the island, or the usage of the indentured workers who were little more than slaves. And what would Sofia Salazar say of that? Would she harangue him, and speak of the rights of those who do the labour? He suspected that, deep down, she was more clear-headed than that. She must know her own fortunes rose and fell with the price of guano. What would she do, when the mines ran out of shit? What would they all do, Castillos and Salazars, when the well of their wealth ran dry?

It was not on his conscience. He lay back. The doctor applied the pipe to his lips again and Edward inhaled. He thought of his future, and was carried aloft into a wonderful and well-deserved dream.

PART TWO
MEMENTO MORI

ANNIE

1912

10

Annie woke with a cry of terror, pushing black water away from her as she drowned. In her dream she had been a man voyaging across the sea from the Americas to England.

She sat up, clutching at memory to replace dream. She never knew her father. Her grandmother had spent time in London, years earlier, and came back pregnant and with a husband in tow, a Murphy of Kilkenny who may or may not have been the baby's begetter. It was all rather murky in Grandma Mary's stories, who had liked to sit up late drinking gin and brandishing a pistol, and whose only gift to Annie before she died was a cheap pocket watch with peeling gold paint around it and the name *Feebes* engraved, which some English gobshite had swindled her with in exchange for services rendered, she said. The baby she carried in her womb from England, born in Cork, was Annie's mother, Katherine, who lived just long enough to accumulate a record for vagrancy, loitering and immorality of the usual sort, get knocked up and die giving birth to Annie. As for the Murphy her grandmother married, he took off to fight in the American Civil War when Katherine was seven, and was never heard from again. It was not uncommon for men at the time to go fight in America, reasoning that the experience thus gained could be used for the future fight for the liberation of Ireland from the English. But anyway, this was how Annie found herself at the age of twenty-six, unmarried, pregnant and alone, living in Grandma's old house and wishing she could get the hell out of Cork.

No wonder she was having nightmares, she thought. She framed the composition: faint light coming in from the high window, illuminating the bed but leaving the rest in darkness, so that it looked as though it were floating in a black sea. Herself: sat up, face illuminated, pale and wet with night sweat. Press the shutter, release and hold.

Gunshots broke the stillness of the night. She tensed, but they were far away, and followed by shouts, and wild laughter, and the sound of glass smashing on the pavement, and running feet. The running came close and then someone rattled the door handle.

'It's me! Annie, it's me! Let me in!'

'Jesus, Jamie!'

She unlocked the door. He burst in and grabbed her in his arms, laughing, smelling of sweat and smoke and whiskey.

'Lock it, quick,' he said. 'I've got the bobbies after me.'

'When don't you, Jamie!' she said. He swirled her round and let her go. She locked the door. 'What did you do?' she said.

'Robbed an Englishman in the harbour, Annie.'

'Is he dead, Jamie?'

He grinned, looking like a lunatic.

'Dead enough,' he said.

'You goddamned idiot!'

He touched her belly tenderly.

'It's for the baby, ain't it,' he said.

'You idiot,' she said again, affectionately. 'Be quiet, now,' she said.

They waited, unmoving now. She heard them come, no longer hurrying. Men with boots that trod the ground. On they came. She willed them to go on and go away.

Their steps slowed. She heard their voices. Cold and low. A truncheon drawn, so softly, like a feather trailing against a wall. She shivered. She felt so full of life. So much damned life inside her. She heard the coppers knock on doors.

'Hide,' she said.

Jamie was ahead of her. He went into the cellar. Grandma's old smugglers' cove, where Jamie now kept the things he stole down in the harbour. The knock came on her door. She didn't answer. The knock came louder. Next they'll break it down, she knew. The constables. She went and opened it.

'Annie,' the policeman said.

'Tom.'

Dark-haired, unsmiling, white as a worm.

'We know he's in here,' he said.

'What did he do?' Annie said.

'Killed a man.'

'What kind of man?'

Tom shrugged. 'An English sailor,' he said.

'Not much of a crime,' Annie said. Bolder than she felt.

'A *navy* sailor,' Tom said.

'Oh.'

'Yeah. May we come in?'

'Listen, Tom, you won't hurt him much, will you?'

He pushed her aside. Went in, his men behind him.

'Come out, Jamie!' he said.

'Screw you, Tom!'

She heard it then. They all heard it. A gun being primed. The old shotgun she kept downstairs.

'Jamie, don't do anything stupid!' Annie screamed.

Tom said, 'He's been doing stupid his whole life.'

The constables spread out, against the walls.

'Please don't hurt him,' Annie said.

'Go outside, Annie,' Tom said.

'No.'

'Get out!'

'Don't talk to her like that!' Then the floor exploded upwards, wood flying as the shotgun blast tore through it.

'Jesus Christ, Jamie!' Annie screamed. How drunk *was* he? she thought. She touched her face. Something wet, and a pain blossomed. A chip of wood cut her, she thought. She put her hands on her belly.

'I'll be outside,' she said.

She stood shivering under the stars, the neighbours' windows with the blinds twitching. Charlie-Next-Door and his drunken mum. She wanted to shout abuse at them all. She didn't. She could hear the constables moving inside. Heard the shotgun go off again, then a crash, then Jamie's scream.

He screamed for a while. Then he stopped. She waited in the cold. When the door reopened the men came out. They dragged Jamie behind them. Their truncheons were slick with blood.

'Oh, Tom,' Annie said.

'Sorry, Annie. Had to hurt him some.'

'I can see that.'
'Have a good night.'
'You too, Tom.'
They pulled Jamie along. His eyes were too swollen to
see much.
'Jamie,' Annie said. 'Jamie!'
There was no response. They put him on the back of a
cart tied to a pony. The pony shat on the road. Annie said,
'Aren't you going to clean this up?'
'Not tonight, love,' one of the constables said. Then they
left, going downhill with their prize.

She made a half-hearted effort to tidy up but it was useless.
She brewed a pot of tea and sat up in the kitchen and leafed
through old White Star Line brochures. Sleek steamers
floated in pale blue seas, a glorious sun behind them. *Swift
to the goal!* the adverts said. Just buy a ticket, board the
ship. These monsters of the sea: double and triple-screw,
Teutonic, Britannic, Majestic, docking at these grey shores
and sailing to Shanghai, Hong Kong, the Azores, Boston
and New York! Every day people boarded those ships in
Queenstown, sailed across the ocean, landed in a world
where everything was possible, everything was new again.
All she needed was the money to go. She tried not to
think about Jamie – gorgeous, adorable Jamie with his dark
puppy eyes and his ready smile, so hard to resist in the night,
whispering promises: how he loved her, how he wanted to
marry her, how they would be so happy together, living here
in Grandma's old place. The nights were cold and Jamie was
warm, and when he wasn't there she ached for his touch.

But it did not mean she believed a word out of his stupid mouth, for he *was* just a boy, taking up nationalism less from fervent belief than as a handy excuse to beat people up when they all got together and they all got the chance: a few drinks, a bit of trouble, a lot of good times. *Jamie* didn't want to go to New York. What would he do there? he said. This was his home, right here, with her. Her and the baby. The damned baby. She touched her belly. Jamie was going to propose. That's what he kept saying. Get her married under the eyes of man and God, so that she didn't end up like those unfortunate girls, as they called them, working on her back in the Monto in Dublin. It was that or the convent, and Annie wasn't about to end up in either. She supposed she might have married Jamie, if it came to it. But it had seemed like just another one of his dreams, which he wove for her in the night, in the bed, and she knew in her heart of hearts he was sooner or later going to end up dead or in prison. So here she was, her prophecy fulfilled, and she didn't feel one damn way or the other about it. This was just how it now was.

That was how it was always going to be. A candle burned on the table before her. She framed the image: a lone young woman with a cut on her face, sitting at a wooden table, the light illuminating her within a sea of dark. Press and hold. Were all her photographs going to be like that?

They were, she thought, unless she changed them.

'You're late,' Lady Julia said. She wore her habitual black. With her austere white face unlined above it she looked like a widowed china doll.

The shop wasn't much to look at from the outside. A sign said *Montmorency Photographic Studio, Lady Julia Montmorency, Proprietor.* Her husband, Sir John, had died in the Belfast dock strike of 1907 – fell off his horse while policing. He'd had a fondness for law, order, the King, booze, cigars and unwed women of a certain age, not necessarily in that order. Wagging tongues said he hadn't so much fallen off his horse than collapsed on top of one of those unfortunate girls in a kip on Amelia Street, but that was loose gossip for you, it could go anywhere. Lady Julia, bereft of husband, and with a fortune either squandered or never to have existed in the first place, retreated to Cork, where she kept a house, and opened the studio, turning her never quite respectable society hobby into a moderate business. Tongues wagged and people talked, but Lady Julia, whose only companion now was the Lord, was deaf to it, or indifferent. An enlarged photograph of Sir John hung on one wall and looked down on anyone entering the premises.

'I'm sorry,' Annie said. 'It won't happen again.'

'See that it doesn't,' Lady Julia said. She clasped her hands before her and nodded twice in a rapid fashion. 'You must go to Blarney,' she said. 'You have an engagement at Mahoney's, while I must tend to portraiture at the Lord Mayor's. You will take the No. 2 Brownie, stand and flash. Look after them well, for any damages will be docked from your pay. Remember, you represent the studio in all your interactions. Carry yourself with composure and do not embarrass me. Am I clear?'

'Very,' Annie said. 'My lady, how do I get there?'

'Joe Doyle will take you,' Lady Julia said. 'Make sure he does not idle in the village over drink. He is a sensible enough lad when sober, but you couldn't whip the Irish out of him if you tried.'

Annie bit her lip but refrained from answering. She nodded.

'Good girl. Now go! The dead wait for no man. Or woman.'

'Yes, my lady,' Annie said.

She collected the equipment from the storeroom. For a moment she ran her hand fondly over the older devices: an Abraham bellows camera with glass plates, a Knight Daguerreotype machine, a collection of hand-made tintype cameras of all shapes and sizes that Lady Julia had amassed over the years. Annie liked the tintype machines, which were simple and reliable. But for the clients, newer was always better, and so she collected the Kodak Brownie and carefully wrote it out in the record book. She went out and found Joe Doyle leaning against his horse cart, chewing on a blade of grass.

'Hey, Annie,' he said.

'Hey, Joe.'

'Heard about Jamie,' he said. 'I'm sorry.'

She smiled and touched him lightly on the shoulder.

'Thanks, Joe,' she said.

'It's not right, what they did to him,' Joe said.

'It's not.'

'Still.' He reflected. His eyes were blue and guileless. 'I suppose Jamie didn't make it easy for them.'

'He did not,' Annie said. Thinking, he did not make it easy for her, either.

'Let's go,' she said.

'It's going to rain,' Joe said.

'So?'

He shrugged.

'Just saying.'

It was like saying the Earth went around the sun, she thought. She thought again of the brochures. Of how they showed her blue skies without a cloud in sight, a hot sun shining down. She thought of beaches and orange groves.

'Let's go,' she said again. She put the equipment in the cart and got on herself.

'Right you are,' Joe said.

11

IT RAINED. THE RAIN FELL ON THE NARROW ROAD AND over the green hills. It fell on sheep and badger holes and foxes. It fell on tiny weathered white-stone farmhouses, on ancient hedges, on crows and chaffinches and bees. It fell with an indifference to the little cart and to its morbid destination, or to the tiny dreams of those who rode inside. The rain gave not a fig for Annie's wishes and desires, or for her unborn child's. And it most definitely, Annie thought, didn't care a jot for Joe Doyle, who drove the horse with cheerful goodwill, doing his best impression of John McCormack as he whistled 'Mother Machree'. Time passed, because that was what time did, and rain fell, because that's what rain did. And here she was, wishing time went faster and rain fell less or not at all, and what good was wishing anything unless you took control of your own life and made the wish come true? Which was why she knew, suddenly and with an aching clarity, that she was going to buy a ticket for the steamer to New York, and there was not a thing in the world she would let stop her.

She sat then and enjoyed the rest of the ride, the slow

rhythm of the clop-clop-clopping of the horse and the swaying of the cart, and the fog settling gently on the hillside. Then she heard a loud *honk!* and something large and impossibly fast came up behind them, making an almighty racket, and passed almost within touching distance of the cart. The horse neighed in fright and Joe said, 'Whoh, whoh!' and Annie looked and saw a black automobile, and a good-looking, black-haired man driving it. Their eyes met and he smiled. Then the monstrous thing shot forward, overtook the cart and vanished ahead, raising dust in its wake.

'Jesus!' Joe said. The horse, panicked, gradually settled back. Annie gazed after the automobile. She'd just been granted a small vision of the future, she realised. God, who moved in mysterious ways, had done this, and she could not take it lightly, for it was a sign, meant only for her. She settled back again, resolved, and didn't speak until they reached the village.

'Through here,' the man from Mahoney's woollen mills said. Joe had pulled up the cart on the side of the road, let the horse loose in a ground of pasture, and gone to the pub. Annie carried the equipment inside and followed the Mahoney employee. Carpeted floors swallowed sound. The light was dim. The room was at the end of a long corridor. A woman in black stood outside, holding a handkerchief twisted into knots. She looked up when Annie approached.

'I'm sorry for your loss,' Annie said.

'He was a good man!' the woman said. 'A good man!'

Her breath smelled of sherry.

'This way, please,' the man from Mahoney's said. He pushed the door open. Annie went in.

The dead man lay on the bed, wearing his good suit, his hair neatly combed. His pallor was untouched but his lips had been dabbed with just a touch of rouge to make them lifelike. It was a very nice job.

'What happened to him?' Annie said. 'Was it an accident?'

'Oh, no,' the man from the mills said. 'He just dropped on a shift.'

'He had a bad heart,' the woman said. 'A bad heart, but he was a good man!'

'Something to remember him by,' the man from the mills said. 'We were all very fond of Terry.'

'My Terry!' the woman said. She splashed sherry into a glass on the side table and drank greedily. Annie didn't blame her. She looked at the light. She would need to use the flash, she thought. She didn't like using the flashlight powder. No wonder Lady Julia was worried about nationalists stealing chemicals. The stuff was dangerous. She began to set up.

'How would you like him?' she said. 'It should be naturalistic. Sitting up or...' She reconsidered. 'Perhaps in repose is best after all,' she said.

The woman burst out crying and left the room. The man from the mills looked uncomfortable. 'I thought Lady Julia would come,' he said.

'I am but her extension,' Annie said. Lady Julia liked her to say that. Annie was little more than another piece of equipment, as far as Lady Julia was concerned. She saw the man's worried look and tried to smile.

'It will be fine,' she said gently.

She moved around, setting up. The camera, the light, figuring out the angle. The man lay on the bed in repose. It was quiet. She set up the flash lamp, carefully. She had a scar on the underside of her left hand to remind her to be careful. Lady Julia had several. She looked through the camera, moved it back a little, adjusted the lens.

'I require quiet,' she said.

'Of course.'

The man from the mills left the room. Annie took a long, quiet breath. She released it slowly. The light flashed, bright and terrifying. The dead man in the bed was illuminated in the sort of holy glow that Moses must have felt on Mount Sinai in the face of God. Annie took the picture. She took several more, refilling the flash lamp each time. From outside it must have looked demonic, the flashes of light, the burning smell, the dead man on the bed.

Memento mori. She packed her equipment away, opened a window. The smell of fresh rain came inside.

'All done,' she said.

'Thank you,' the man from the woollen mills said.

'Lady Julia will of course have the final say,' Annie said. Mollifying him. He nodded.

'Thank you,' he said again. 'He will be missed, our Terry,' he said.

'I know,' Annie said. 'I'm sorry.'

She hurried out. She hated it when they grieved. She just wanted to take the picture.

She found Joe at Corkeran's, in the shadow of the castle. The automobile that had passed them earlier was parked outside. She spent a moment looking at her reflection in its polished surface. Her own, too-serious face stared back at her. She went in to Corkeran's. Joe was nursing a pint of Beamish on the bar.

'How was it, Annie?' he said.

'You know how it is, Joe,' she said. 'A job's a job.'

'It gives me the creeps, Annie,' he said. 'Hey, you want a drink?'

'I'm good, Joe.'

'We can go if you want,' he said.

'Finish your pint first,' she said. 'I won't tell Lady Julia.'

'You're one of the good ones, Annie,' Joe said.

She let it fly past her. She took a seat at the bar. Looked around the room. Not that many places to go in Blarney unless you were going to work at the mill or kiss a stone. Corkeran's served beer downstairs and had rooms to rent upstairs for those who were visiting. She saw a face attached to a dark-suited figure in the corner. The face looked familiar, somehow. He noticed her watching him and raised his head, a mocking smile forming, and she knew who he was then. She went over to him.

She said, 'You nearly drove us off the road earlier.'

'That was you?' His smile remained, and he looked her up and down, appreciatively. He had big city clothes. He had a big city attitude. He had an Englishman's voice. 'That would have been a shame...' he said. He took out a slim case, gold, and extracted a cigarette before offering it to Annie. She declined. The man put the case away and lit his cigarette. His lighter, too, was gold. He took a breath of smoke and blew it out with evident enjoyment. He looked at her through the smoke.

'John Savage,' he said. 'And you are?'

'Annie Connolly,' she said. 'What do you do, Mr Savage?'

'Please,' he said. 'Call me John.' He toyed with his gold lighter and eyed Joe Doyle at the bar. 'I'm in business,' he said.

'What sort of business?' Annie said.

'Shipping, logistics. Finance. I came to look at Mahoney's.' He shrugged. 'I live in London.'

'No kidding,' Annie said.

'You ever been?' he said.

'I'm just a girl from Cork,' she said.

'I don't think you're a just anything,' he said, giving her another appreciative look. He was a funny one, she thought. It was like he was trying a little too hard.

'What *do* you do, Annie Connolly?' he said.

'I photograph dead people for money.'

If she'd hoped to shock him, she was disappointed. His eyes opened a little wider and so did his smile.

'My,' he said. 'You're full of surprises. Care for a drink?'

'I'm not drinking right now,' Annie said.

'Oh? Why not?'

Then he glanced at her belly, lost some of the smile and said, 'Married?'

'No.'

'I'd like a child,' he said. 'Of course, I'd need a wife first.'

'Why can't you get a wife?' Annie said.

Savage shrugged. 'It's not that easy, finding the right girl.'

'How hard can it be?' Annie said. 'For a fancy man like you?'

'You think I'm fancy?'

'Too fancy for Cork,' she said.

He laughed.

'I'm just fancy enough, Annie Connolly,' he said. 'How about you? Will you marry me?'

It was her turn to look him up and down.

'I don't even know you,' she said.

'Does it matter?'

'It should.'

He shrugged.

'I have money,' he said.

'You seemed to imply as much already.'

'Well, now it's stated.'

'You're English.'

'With Irish roots.'

'You live in England,' she said.

He opened his eyes in mock innocence. He had very expressive eyes, she thought.

'Is that so bad?' he said.

'To some.'

'And to you?'

Annie had to laugh.

'You aren't serious, are you?' she said.

'I'm always serious, Miss Connolly.'

'To me, then,' she said. 'England does not appeal.'

'You prefer Ireland?' he said.

'I would like,' she said, 'to go to America.'

'America!' He was mock shocked. He did everything mockingly, she thought. She watched his eyes. The way they darted to Joe Doyle on the bar. Joe was a good-looking guy.

'I see how it is,' she said.

'You do?'

She touched his hand.

'I do,' she said. 'And you're trying too hard.'

He did lose the smile then.

'I'm afraid I don't understand what you're suggesting, Miss Connolly.'

'I am not suggesting anything,' she said. 'But you can find Joe over there most nights in one of the pubs around the English Market in town. If you're interested.'

'Why would I be interested?' John Savage said.

Annie shrugged. 'Because that's how God made you, I suppose,' she said. 'And He made Joe the same. Now, if you wouldn't mind, I'd like to go for a ride in your automobile. We can discuss your marriage proposal on the way.'

He looked at her for a long moment, weighing her up.

'Hidden depths, Miss Connolly...' he said. Then he smiled again, with only slightly narrowed eyes, and stood and extended his hand to her.

'Your horseless chariot awaits, my lady,' he said.

12

THE FIDDLER STRUCK HIS BOW AND WILD MUSIC FILLED the smoky hall of the Palace of Varieties. It was late into the string of acts. A strongman came and did the things that strongmen always do. A troupe of dancers in kimonos flashed long legs. A comedian told off-colour jokes, a singer sang songs, a clown clowned. The lights grew dimmer, the smoke thicker, the atmosphere bawdier. Couples formed and vanished into dark corners. A sailor was getting his sail polished by a dockhand in the stalls. Furtive men in furtive groups exchanged pamphlets and plotted sedition. Another Friday night on St Patrick's Quay.

'I need a man and I'm not fussy!' Lily said, laughter spilling around her. She was a little drunk. 'Come dance with me, Annie! Come dance!'

Annie, sober and miserable with it, framed the sad clown on the stage, the spotlight, white make-up, the darkness of the backdrop. The clown foundered in a dark sea. She froze the image, the shutter clicked, if only in her mind. The clown face suspended, still, reminding her unpleasantly of all the corpses she had had to shoot. Memento mori. It was good business, nothing more.

She checked Grandma's gold watch. It was nearly midnight. She traced the faint outline of *Feebes* etched on the metal. A relic from another era. What would she call the baby? She thought of Jamie, locked up in the city gaol. How many times had he been there? This time, she thought, he wasn't coming back.

'Come on, Annie!'

She let Lily draw her by the hand. The clown mercifully took his bow, giving up in the face of the fiddler and the crowd. The music took over then, and it was anything goes. A drunk bumped into Annie, stared at her in confusion and threw up on her shoes.

'Get off!' She shoved him and he went flying, stumbled into a sailor who cursed and swung at him. The drunk fell.

'Hey, lay off him!'

The drunk had friends. The friends were drunk. Annie could sense where this was going. The sailor stuck up two fingers.

'Son of a bitch!'

The sailor laughed. The sailor had friends. The friends were drunk. Annie pulled Lily away.

'It's going to get—' she started to say.

Glass broke. The lads in the corner swapping pamphlets about resistance and revolution heard the bottle break too. They looked up from their political discussion. Annie saw them smile. The fallen drunk's friends went at the sailors. The sailors went at the drunks. The would-be revolutionaries waded in just for the hell of it. Annie pulled Lily along as another bottle whistled overhead, struck the wall and smashed. The fiddler stopped abruptly. No one cared. The air filled with curses, grunts and fists.

Just another Friday night on St Patrick's Quay.

'Oh, Annie, you're no fun anymore!' Lily said. They staggered out into cold air, the Lee flowing dark and the street lamps stuttering. Annie shivered. She said, 'I met a man today.'

'Aren't you fancy!' Lily said.

'He's rich,' Annie said.

'How rich?' Lily said.

'He has an automobile.'

'An automobile!' Lily said.

'It's a Wolseley,' Annie said.

She thought of the ride with John Savage back from Blarney to Cork. She had no idea motor cars could be so *fast*! It was terrifying and exhilarating all at once, the open roof and the sheer *speed* of the thing, going along that narrow road, scaring the birds. She loved it. She vowed then that when she got to America she, too, would have a motor car.

'Let's go somewhere else,' Lily said. She swayed on her feet. 'Somewhere with music.'

'I'm going home,' Annie said.

'What's gotten into you, Annie?' Lily said. 'Is it about Jamie?'

'Jamie's going to hang,' Annie said flatly.

'All he did was kill an Englishman,' Lily said.

'All he did,' Annie said, 'was kill an Englishman and get caught.'

Lily burst into laughter. 'There's just no luck to that boy,' she said. She wove her hand through Annie's. 'Come on,' she said. 'I'll walk you home. You can tell me more about this rich suitor of yours.'

'He's not my suitor,' Annie said. But she thought of John Savage, and the hidden longing she could feel inside him, under that layer of calculated indifference. They were kindred, in a way. He'd driven her back and let her out at the studio. She'd gone in and replaced the equipment she had taken. The Kodak film still had a few pictures left on it. Lady Julia was there, back from the Lord Mayor's. She chatted to Savage and seemed quite delighted by him. Lady Julia was a snob, in some ways, but she also had her independence. You could be independent when you were rich. Annie wasn't rich, so Annie's choice was either marriage or...

She wasn't sure yet. She didn't know how to get rich, other than to marry money. It was different in America. There you made your own luck. And everyone drove an automobile, and there was so much food you couldn't even finish it all.

She walked with Lily, hand in hand. They had known each other since they were children. She came with Lily when a boy knocked her up and she had to do something about it. Annie remembered the hard old woman who opened her door to them in the middle of the night. The dim light of a lamp and candles, the sweat and fear on Lily's face, the taste of sugared tea the old lady made them. She gave Lily something to make her sleepy. But Lily didn't sleep. Annie held her hand as the old woman went about the business. Then the blood. There was too much blood. Annie knew something went wrong. She helped Lily back, Lily wracked with fever. She'd recovered, eventually. But she could not have children, Annie knew this much.

'I love you, Lily,' she said.

'I love you too,' Lily said. They walked arm in arm, up the hill, the sound of their footsteps echoing in the fog.

The presiding judge was devoid of mercy. It was in his eyes. His wig sat like a nest of wasps over his head. The court was full, Jamie's aunt in black as though preparing in advance for the funeral. She had an embroidered handkerchief pressed to her face. Beside her sat Father O'Malley, who wasn't so bad as far as priests went. He was there to offer comfort and the Lord.

The Lord was not in evidence. Other evidence there was aplenty, presented by the Crown: to wit, a knife, the defendant's shoes soaked in the victim's blood, and witness testimonies.

'I saw him broad as daylight,' Agnes Pugh, the fishwife, said. 'I was gutting a flounder when I saw Jamie, I mean, the accused, engage in an argument with Able Seaman Williams, a lovely fellow, he liked my pickled cockles—'

There was a brief wave of laughter in the gallery. Agnes looked confused.

'You knew them both?' the King's Counsel said.

'I've known Jamie since he was a boy,' Agnes said. 'And of course, I know all the sailors round these parts, on account of my profession.'

Again, a titter. Annie hid a smile. There were always stories about London Agnes in her youth. She wasn't from around here. Which was all that needed to be said.

'Then what happened, please?' the KC said.

'I saw Able Seaman Williams fall,' Agnes said. 'And heard

an impact as a knife fell to the ground. It made a dull sound, like a silenced bell.'

'This knife?' the KC said, holding up the evidence.

'I couldn't say,' Agnes said. 'My eyesight is less keen than it once was.'

'But you made out the two men plainly,' the KC said.

'That I did.'

'Let it show the weapon was collected from the scene of the crime by the constabulary,' the KC said. He turned back to Agnes. 'Please, continue,' he said.

'Williams fell,' Agnes said. 'Jamie turned and ran. The able seaman had a satchel bag. When Jamie ran he had it in his arms.'

'You are sure of this?' the KC said.

'I am.'

Annie thought. Jamie had no satchel on him when he came to the house. So where was it? And what was inside it worth killing a man?

'Then what?' the KC said.

Agnes shrugged.

'People ran to Williams,' she said. 'But Williams was dead. Then the constables came. This is all I know.'

'Thank you, Mrs Pugh,' the KC said.

Annie had taken to wearing a looser dress. The pregnancy was new. She didn't want people to know. Babies changed everything. When they brought out Jamie he was wearing a suit. He looked good in a suit, she thought.

He looked at her. She couldn't read his eyes at all. Was he sorry? Was he proud of what he'd done? They were meant to have a life together. Now the life they'd made was hers alone. This tiny human growing inside her.

Outside the court, the rain drizzling, Jamie's aunt came over with Father O'Malley.

'The poor child,' Aunt Eithne said. 'The poor child!' She dabbed her tears. Father O'Malley patted her back.

'There, there,' he said.

There was no sympathy for Annie, she realised. No care as to *her* position. Aunt Eithne had never approved of the relationship. If she found out about the baby all hell would break loose. She would want it to grow up a Flynn. Well, Annie didn't know what will happen to the baby, but she wasn't giving it to Aunt Eithne. She mumbled something about the unbearable tragedy of it all.

'There, there,' Father O'Malley said. He patted her back. His hand remained a little too long, stroking. Annie moved away.

Back inside, Jamie's solicitor offered a final plea for lenience, and the King's Counsel, all but smirking, spread his arms as if to say, *Fate is inevitable.* Or so Annie thought, watching it all, and watching Jamie in the dock, and wondering, still; about Able Seaman Williams, and that missing satchel, and what Jamie was doing down in the harbour at that time anyway.

The gavel descended. That gave her a fright. The judge frowned in irritation. He was pastry-flour white under the wig. He tapped the gavel again, as though uncertain of its use.

'James Patrick Flynn,' the judge said, 'you are sentenced to the rope.' A cry rose in the gallery and the judge tapped the gavel again for silence.

'And may God have mercy on your soul!' he said.

13

HER NAUSEA CAME AND WENT. HER SKIN WAS AGLOW. Her belly protruded under the loose dress. She'd covered herself as best she could, but soon it would show. Cork City gaol under a grey sky, a grey stone castle, the wardens' boots against the hard floors, the jingle of keys, the slamming of doors. Jamie looked at her across the table. He was thinner, had a couple of missing teeth. He tried to shrug.

'Everyone knows he's a hanging judge,' he said. 'It was always going to be...'

He fell quiet.

She wanted to reach across to him, but she couldn't.

'Why did you do it, Jamie?' she said.

'You wouldn't understand.'

'Why?'

'It was for you! For us... For the baby.'

'How?' she said.

'Home Rule will never come to pass,' Jamie said. 'We will rise to fight for it. We will free Ireland. Or we will always be dogs for the English to whip at their will.'

'Where did you learn to talk like that, you damn fool!' she said.

'There are people, planning. Organising. That's all I am going to say. We will be ready. There will be a war, Annie.'

She stared at him. He wasn't smiling. She had him down as an easy-going lad. A good lay. Always up for some fun, always up for some mischief. But this? This was new. Did she not see it before, or was it that she did and didn't want to?

She could respect a man like that, she thought.

But she couldn't love him.

'What was in the satchel, Jamie?'

'Important papers. Information. Listen, Annie...'

All I do is listen to men talking, she thought.

'What?' she said.

'If you need help. Go see Eleanor Wallace. She's with... with the movement.' He coughed. He didn't look too well, she thought. But then, it wasn't like there was anything she could do about it.

'All right, Jamie,' she said.

'If it's a boy,' he said. 'Will you call him James Patrick?' He tried to smile. It didn't take.

'Of course, Jamie,' she said. 'Of course I will.'

'Are you pregnant?' Lady Julia demanded.

'Excuse me?'

'How irresponsible can you be, child?'

'I am not a child!' Annie said. She glared at Lady Julia. The older woman moved like a chiaroscuro, widow-black against the white studio lights.

'And yet you got yourself knocked up,' Lady Julia said.

'Don't lie to me, Annie. I knew you were hiding it. Hard to hide, though, as it grows.'

'*It?*' Annie said. '*He* will be a beautiful boy—'

Lady Julia sighed.

'Children are a prison,' she said, 'designed to keep women in chains. Sit down.'

Annie sat down.

'Well?' she said.

'You could take it to the convent,' Lady Julia said. 'That, or find yourself another husband to replace that Flynn of yours, but you'd have to be quick. Prospective husbands vanish like dew upon the morning when there's a baby in the picture.'

'I will make my own arrangements,' Annie said.

'Is that so? And what will you do for money, Annie? I do not need a pregnant assistant.'

'I am hardly your assistant!'

'It will not do,' Lady Julia said. 'You must cover it up better. You must wear looser clothes. You must powder your face, give it some pallor. You are too...' She waved a hand. '*Glowing*,' she said in distaste.

'I am as women have been since the dawn of time, Lady Julia.'

'But this is not the dawn of time, child! This is a new century under Christ, where many things are possible that were never possible before. The camera, Annie! The automobile! Perhaps, in time, even our right to vote! We are the way God made us, yes, but He made us with a brain to think, with hands to learn new skills, with hearts to yearn for more than what we have. You would throw it all away?'

'I would not,' Annie said.

'Good,' Lady Julia said. 'Then do as I instruct. Perhaps, with luck, it will be into the sixth month before it becomes too obvious. In the meantime, I have another job for you.'

'My lady?'

'Don't "my lady" me, child.' Lady Julia almost smiled. 'I dare say I see more in you than you see in yourself. Did I not give you this position? Did I not instruct you in the use of light and shade, of composition? There is a dead man down in Kinsale. Joe Doyle will drive you. You may spend the night there and claim it from expenses. Come back early. I do wish to help you, Annie. But children are expensive. You will not work once it is born. And I have spent too much, training you as a photographer, to let you go this easily. Put up the baby for adoption. It needs a father. It needs a family. Oh, take the Kodak again.'

'I would like to take a tintype machine, too,' Annie said.

'What for? You are not an itinerant, Annie. We do not take beach snaps for pennies. We are artists.'

'Just in case,' Annie said.

Lady Julia shrugged.

'As long as you record it in the book,' she said, 'and bring it back. Any damages will be deducted from your wage.'

'Of course.'

'Are you saving, Annie?'

'Saving, Lady Julia?'

'Saving money, for the hardships to come,' Lady Julia said.

'I try,' Annie said.

'I worry for you, Annie,' Lady Julia said.

Annie thought, I worry for myself, too, Lady Julia.

'Yes, my lady,' she said.

She went to the stockroom. She signed out the Kodak and a tintype machine she liked, a flash lamp and powder, chemicals and stock. She carried it all outside.

Joe Doyle leaned against the cart.

'Hey, Annie,' he said.

'Hey, Joe.'

'Let me give you a hand,' he said. He smiled shyly. 'On account of your condition.'

'Does everyone know!' Annie said.

Joe shrugged. 'Word gets around,' he said. 'You know how it is. Besides, your...' He blushed. 'You know. They're bigger.'

'My what?'

'Bosoms, Annie. Sorry.'

He carried the equipment into the cart. Annie started to laugh. She couldn't help it. All the tension, and the fear, about Jamie, the baby, the future – it all burst out of her, making her shake with laughter until she had to hold her ribs to stop them from aching.

'What?' Joe Doyle said. Then he, too, started to laugh.

'My... bosoms? My *bosoms*!' She roared with laughter until tears streamed down her face. Then she was crying, and Joe held her, saying, 'What's wrong, Annie? What's wrong?'

She buried her face in his chest.

'Everything, Joe,' she said. 'Everything's wrong.'

'Well, it will be all right,' he said. 'Everything will be all right.'

He helped her onto the cart.

'Keep your eyes on the road, Joe,' Annie said. A giggle escaped out of her, like a bubble rising to the surface of the water from a depth. She took a deep breath of air. Lady Julia was right. Annie didn't know what to do. She hadn't felt like this before. This... life, forming inside her. It was changing everything, changing her body. But she was still her, she thought. She was still Annie. She had the same dream, the same desire to stand on her own.

She thought of America. She needed money, because in everything in life you needed money, so she would have to take steps to acquire it. Lady Julia was right. It was the twentieth century, and everything was possible. One day she might even get to vote. She sat back, strangely comforted by that notion, and watched the road as Joe drove the horse on the road, out of town.

The rain rained and the fog fogged the green hills. A frog on the side of the road hopped into a puddle. It stared at the approaching cart with big, bulging eyes, as though the cart was a particularly large and juicy fly coming the frog's way. The cart swayed from side to side, Joe humming as he held the reins, Annie holding on, half-drunk on all that quiet. She would miss it, she thought.

She had been thinking more and more of the ties that held her and the roots that went deep into that dark, wet soil. She was a green shoot out of that earth, she thought, and now she flowered, pollinated by a bee named Jamie. Plants couldn't travel but they could die. And to live she would have to die herself: uproot herself from something that resembled peace to go elsewhere, across the sea. She would become someone new, she thought. Perhaps in her dotage she would sing old maudlin songs about the old country, and how much better everything was there. Perhaps everything *is* better when you're young, she thought. And maybe that was just a crock of shit for people who liked banal quotes.

The rain rained, but gently. The fog fogged the green hills. A goat wandered across the road, indifferent to the approaching cart, to Joe Doyle's singing, to Annie's vacant stare. It was as if the goat was the only one real, and Annie, Joe and cart were merely ghosts, things from the past drifting like smoke across an empty road. The goat chewed grass and stared.

Thatched stone-walled cottages, a church. The bell rang as they passed. As Annie watched, a silent procession emerged from the church, a priest in front, holding a chalice, and black-clad monks behind him, carrying a coffin. They chanted Latin. The cart rolled on. They passed a graveyard with the headstones broken and jutting out of the ground at angles, the grass grown over the graves. A barefoot child stepped out from under an ash and stared at them as they passed, chewing a blade of grass thoughtfully.

Did he even see them? Annie thought. She felt uneasy. The rain made sound disappear, Cork was long vanished behind them, and she felt as though she were drowning, going on some quest into the netherworld. The road crossed ponds swelling with water next, a fisherman with rod and wire stood on one bank and watched them pass. He waved. It seemed incongruous. Joe Doyle waved back.

'I liked your man,' he said.

'John Savage?'

'Him,' Joe said.

'He liked you, too, I think,' Annie said.

'Oh, that he did, he does,' Joe said.

'You'll see him again?' Annie said.

'Could be. Could be.' Joe brooded. 'It doesn't do, you know,' he said. 'A bit of fun and games and all is well and good, but a man needs a wife and babies to call himself a man.'

'You're still a man, Joe,' Annie said.

'Perhaps.' He brooded. 'Not everyone sees it that way.'

'I do,' Annie said.

'And you are leaving,' he said, giving her a sudden, unexpected smile.

'You know?' she said.

'Annie,' Joe said. 'Your face is a book even the village idiot could read. Him best of all, perhaps. It takes one to know one.'

She laughed suddenly. 'You're calling me an idiot?' she said.

'It takes one to know one,' he said, and laughed too.

'I'll miss you, Joe,' she said.

'I'll miss you too. Perhaps I'll follow you,' he said. 'There are so many Irish in America now it may as well be Ireland.'

Horses ran in a field on their left. Smoke rose from a stable. Annie heard the sound of hammer on metal, a man shoeing a horse. She wouldn't miss it, she thought. She was never a country girl. She wanted to hear the sea again, the cry of gulls, the ocean swell, the sound of the waves against the docks. A dog barked in the distance. All was well.

By early evening they had crested one last hill and in the dying sunlight they beheld the harbour of Kinsale.

14

'FELL IN TWO NIGHTS AGO,' THE CONSTABLE SAID. HE was young, with a blond moustache. A local boy in uniform. His name was Conor. 'Hit his head and went straight down.'

'Fisherman?'

'Yeah.'

Annie stared at the corpse. She seemed to spend her life staring at corpses. The water had done damage to Mr Brady. That was the deceased's name. By the time he got fished out of the Bandon he had swelled up, and some bits were missing. The smell was terrible but she was used to the smell. Joe Doyle wasn't with her. He was down one of the pubs near the harbour. Joe Doyle was just the driver. Nobody paid him to go near a corpse.

'And you want a memento mori?' Annie said.

The constable nodded. 'The fellows put the hat around and raised some money for the widow,' he explained. 'She is distraught, as you can well imagine.'

'I'm not sure what...' Annie said.

'I know he doesn't look the freshest, Annie,' Conor said. 'But you're the expert.' He gave her a shy smile. 'You did my

Aunt Mona, I don't know if you remember. And she looked terrible even before she died.'

Annie couldn't help but smile back.

'I remember, Conor,' she said. She stared at Mr Brady.

'I suppose,' she said. 'If we use a low light, and some powders...'

'See? I knew we were right to ask for you,' Conor said.

'You asked for me?' Annie said. 'Not Lady Julia?'

'She is a great photographer,' Conor said. 'Everyone says so. But she's lousy with this sort of stuff.'

Annie laughed. It just rolled out of her.

'If she could only hear you...' she said. 'I will do what I can.'

'Thanks, Annie.'

She examined the room.

'It is best we do it now,' she said. 'When do you bury him?'

'In two days.'

'You should bury him quickly.'

She started setting up. Conor helped her. They propped Mr Brady up. Annie put a cushion behind him. His skin was waxy and cold to the touch. She shuddered. She used her bag of powders. Touched up the man's face. A vision came to her as she worked. Mr Brady might have been lighter in life, but he looked like a beached whale now. The blood vessels in his eyes were broken. She drew eyebrows, smoothed his skin, made his lips redder. She put a single source of light in the room, behind the subject. A candle. She placed the camera directly in front of the bed.

'His head,' she said. 'It needs to stay upright. You will have to hold it, Conor.'

The constable flinched.

'How?' he said.

She showed him. They pushed the bed away from the wall. Repositioned Mr Brady as he rolled over and nearly fell from the bed. Once he was back in position she told Conor to hide behind the bed. She gave him black gloves to wear. She looked through the lens. Yes. She liked it. Conor couldn't be seen and his hands were mere shadows, holding Mr Brady's head up, giving him a life-like, defiant expression. There was something monstrous and noble at once in the composition. The man, not living, had nevertheless achieved a sort of dignity in death. She wondered what he was like in life. He must have been well liked, for his mates to go to all this trouble. But then again, they weren't the ones holed up in the room with a corpse.

'Hold him,' she said. '*Hold...*'

She took the photo. She snapped three times, but she knew she'd got it right the first time. Press and *hold*:

The corpulent, pale man floating on a raft in a sea of darkness. His eyes are open, staring into the lens. The light behind him casts him almost in a halo. He is alive, for just this moment and forever: to hang up on the wall, framed in tasteful dark wood, to be remembered.

'You can let go now,' she said. The head lolled to one side and Conor withdrew. He stood up, looking paler than before.

'I could do with a drink,' he said.

'Give me a moment.'

She packed up the equipment.

'Can you give me a hand with that?' she said.

'Of course.'

She was glad to be outside again. The cold sea air revived her. The taste of death in her mouth, coating her tongue. She saw the fishermen's lights bobbing on the water. A seagull cried in the distance. From one of the pubs came the disharmonious singing of 'The Rose of Tralee'.

'I'm staying with Joe Doyle's aunt, Deirdre,' Annie said.

'Yes, I know,' Conor said. He smiled again. He had an easy smile. 'Small town,' he said.

'They're all small towns,' Annie said.

They walked along the quiet houses. A horse neighed nearby. A cat watched them, curled up on flagstones. Deirdre let them in, smiled at Conor, made everyone a pot of tea. Annie put the equipment carefully away in the room. The brown wallpaper depressed her. Deirdre made small talk. The price of fish. The latest in the *Cork Free Press*. The suffragettes. The latest book she was reading – Conan Doyle's *The Lost World*.

'Dinosaurs!' she kept saying. 'Dinosaurs!'

'I'll go find Joe,' Annie said.

'Don't you worry about Joe,' Deirdre said. 'He can come and go as he pleases.'

'I just need some fresh air,' Annie said. 'I'll be back soon.'

'Just let yourself in, then,' Deirdre said, with an air of disapproval.

'I'll accompany you,' Conor said. 'If that is all right with you?'

'That's all right with me,' Annie said, smiling.

Deirdre watched them without making comment.

Outside again, Annie collapsed against Conor, laughing.

'Dinosaurs!' she said.

'She is a well-meaning lady,' Conor said, but he couldn't help laughing too.

'I just needed to get away,' Annie said.

'It is a nice night,' Conor said. 'I could show you the harbour—'

'The hell with the harbour,' Annie said. She pressed against him, feeling his heat. Her lips found his. He returned her kiss, as hungry as she was. She just wanted to forget for a little while. The drowned man, his bloated corpse, the house with the horrid wallpaper.

'You must know a place,' she whispered. She ran her hand down his front, felt him shiver. He took her hand.

Conor knew a place. A shack by the harbour, with fishing nets hanging to dry. The moon through the window. She fumbled with his belt. He ran his hands over her body. Stopped abruptly.

'You're pregnant?' he said.

'It just means I can't get pregnant again,' she said.

It must have been enough for him. She didn't give him time to think. She pulled him to her, into her. The moon looked down on her as she cried.

She thought, it was almost romantic.

She woke up with her body aching, the baby a strange feeling inside. Kinsale was so quiet, through the thin wall she could hear Deirdre snoring. A cock crowed outside. A dog barked. The first tendrils of light softly touched the window.

Annie needed a pee. She always needed a pee these days.

She didn't want to get out of bed. It was freezing outside the bed. She shivered as she removed the covers and shuffled quickly into her coat and boots. She went downstairs as quietly as she could. The stairs creaked. Joe was sprawled on the carpet by the fire, sound asleep. Annie let herself out the back to the outhouse. Peeing was a luxury. Her breath fogged in front of her, but the air felt fresh. She arranged her clothes, went outside and decided she didn't want to go back in. She stepped out onto the quiet street.

No one around. It was nice to be alone. The horizon lightened. She walked down to the harbour. The stars overhead, reflected in the dark sea, were winking out one by one as the sun rose. Boats pulled up on shore, fishing nets spread out, the fish already gutted and cleaned from the night's catch. Standing there, Annie could hear the town beginning to awaken. Doors opening and closing, dogs barking, the sound of a sweeping broom, of crates being brought outside, of horses stepping on cobblestones, waiting patiently as they were harnessed. She thought of breakfast, which Deirdre said she would provide for additional pay. Bacon and eggs and black pudding and kidneys and fish, potatoes and tea... Her stomach rumbled. She heard footsteps behind her but didn't turn. She was aware of another person approaching, stopping. Looking at the sea.

'Hi, Annie.'

A woman's voice, educated, rich. Annie turned. The woman who stood there was pretty in a businesslike way. She stared out at the sea, a smile that was not quite a smile on her face.

'Do I know you?' Annie said.

The woman extended her hand for a shake. 'My name is Eleanor Wallace,' she said.

Annie shook her hand, cautiously.

'Jamie mentioned you,' Annie said.

'Did he?'

'You're some sort of, what? Nationalist?'

'A Republican, yes,' Eleanor Wallace said.

'Freedom for Ireland,' Annie said.

'That's right.'

'What about freedom for me?' Annie said.

Eleanor Wallace looked at her in amusement.

'Is that what you want?'

'What you want and what you get are two different things,' Annie said. 'My grandmother used to tell me that.'

'Smart woman,' Eleanor Wallace said. 'So what is it that you do want, Annie? If I knew, then maybe I could help you get it.'

'She also told me not to trust strangers offering gifts.'

'I'm not offering a gift,' Eleanor Wallace said.

'Then what, Miss Wallace?'

'I'm offering you a job.'

Annie laughed. The sky was lighter now. Seagulls circled overhead, crying. A trawler went past slowly across the sea. The waterfront was filling up with people.

'Doing what?' Annie said.

'Doing what you already do,' Eleanor said. 'Take a few photographs.'

'You need a memento mori done?' Annie said.

'Not exactly. It's… a different kind of bodies.'

'In Cork?'

'Here. Could you stay a couple of extra days?'

'No,' Annie said. 'I'm expected back today.'

'Say you're not feeling well,' Eleanor said. She glanced meaningfully at Annie's belly.

Annie hesitated.

'Why should I?' she said.

'Do you support the cause?' Eleanor said.

'It makes no odds to me,' Annie said, and Eleanor nodded.

'That's what Jamie told us you'd say,' she said. 'It's a shame, Annie. You'll understand it one day. Why we plan to fight. We fight for you. But...' She waved it away, seeing the look that came into Annie's eyes. 'It doesn't matter. You must need money, don't you? And I need someone to take pictures. I'm happy to pay you.'

'What sort of pictures?' Annie said. 'Blue stuff?'

'So you've done it before?'

'I've been asked before. I don't. Lady Julia would never—'

But Eleanor shook her head. 'I am not asking Lady Julia,' she said. 'I am asking you.'

Annie hesitated, torn. She knew, or thought she knew, what sort of pictures Eleanor Wallace had in mind. She wasn't a prude, but she did not want to mix in with the Republicans. Then she thought of Jamie in prison, the baby inside her, the dream of a liner ticket to New York.

'What does it pay?' she said.

Eleanor Wallace said, 'Let me buy you breakfast.'

15

THE YOLK SPREAD OUT ACROSS THE PLATE. ANNIE STARED at the smear of yellow and put down her bread. She felt suddenly nauseous. They sat at the Castle, where Eleanor Wallace was staying. Fishermen sat around them drinking tea and smoking.

'His name is Feebes,' Eleanor said.

'Feebes?' Annie said, stirring. She fingered her pocket watch. It was an unusual name.

'Major General Edmund Feebes,' Eleanor said. 'Son of Sir Edward Feebes, who fought in the guano wars years ago. Or maybe he started them. In any case, a powerful family. Edmund is destined for Parliament. We would like to have something on him.'

'Is this what this is?' Annie said. 'A blackmail job?'

'I don't like to use that term,' Eleanor said. 'It's common.'

'You said nothing about blackmail,' Annie said. 'I don't need trouble, Miss Wallace.'

'It strikes me you're already in trouble,' Eleanor said. 'All you have to do is take a few pictures. What's the harm? No one will be the wiser. And you could use the money. Couldn't you?'

'I could,' Annie admitted. She pushed the egg around on her plate as she thought. 'What *do* you have on him?' she said.

'A mistress.'

'Here in Kinsale?' Annie said.

Eleanor smiled. 'As it happens.'

'I see. And the major general?'

'Due to visit her tonight.'

'I see.' Annie stared at the yolk. She picked a chunk of bacon and chewed. She made herself swallow. She sipped her tea. The tea was hot and sweet.

'This woman is… aware of your intentions?' she said. Her mind was suddenly made up. It was like Eleanor said. There was no real harm. And she needed the money. You had to do what you could to make it out in this world. Another one of her grandmother's sayings. 'Only, it would make it easier,' Annie said.

'As it happens, Mrs Doyle is a patriot,' Eleanor said.

Annie stared. '*Deirdre?*' she said.

Eleanor Wallace smiled.

'One and the same,' she said.

A lot of thoughts ran through Annie's mind all at once. She said, 'This job here. This Mr Brady who drowned. Did his friends really raise the money for—'

'It was an opportunity,' Eleanor said. 'It got you here, didn't it?'

'I suppose it did.'

'It's just a few pictures,' Eleanor said, as if that decided it.

★

If you were going to do a job, Grandma Mary always told her, you may as well do it well. Annie examined the room, with its awful wallpaper, the high window and the Victorian bed.

'Move the table,' she told Joe. 'Not there. Put it there. Push the bed a little way, like so. We need a light source. It is going to be dark. Maybe some candles.'

'Very romantic, candles,' Deirdre Doyle said. She seemed unbothered by all the fuss. To look at her, you wouldn't know she was mistress or rebel. She was just matter-of-fact. 'Where will you put the camera, Annie? I feel like a right Marie Lloyd.'

'All the world's a stage,' Joe said. Both women looked at him.

'What?' he said. 'I've got education.'

'That you have, boy,' Deirdre said. 'That you have.'

'The wardrobe,' Annie said. 'But we'll have to make a hole in the door.'

'And who's going to pay for that, eh?' Deirdre said.

'This is your contribution to the cause, I guess,' Annie said.

'As if I'm not contributing enough already,' Deirdre said. 'He's sweet, the major general, you know. I hate to do this to him. Poor Edmund.' She brooded. 'Still. It can't be helped. Will you make the pictures tasteful?'

'Tasteful?' Annie said.

'Yes, you know. Get my good side and all that.'

'What is your good side?' Annie said.

'The left.'

'It would be better not to get your face in the picture,'

Annie said. 'Just, you know. The act itself. And the major general's face, of course.'

Joe mumbled something under his breath, then fled the room when they looked at him.

'He's not wrong,' Annie said. 'You could do that.' She tried not to blush.

'Don't worry about me,' Deirdre said. 'This isn't my first dance. Joe! Get back here!'

'Aunty?'

'We need to make a hole in the wardrobe,' Deirdre said. 'For the camera.'

'Right you are, Aunty.'

They emptied the wardrobe first. This took some time. When it was all taken out there was just enough space for Annie to squeeze in. She asked for a stool. She put the camera on a stand. She used the tintype machine, not the Kodak.

'Could work,' she said.

'Let's try it out first,' Deirdre said.

Annie went in the wardrobe. She sat on the stool, her legs to the side. The doors closed. The lens touched the wood, engulfing the small hole Joe Doyle made. It was dark inside. It was hot. Annie felt her heart beat faster, her hands get clammy. She didn't like being in there.

She tried to calm herself down. She could feel the baby inside, growing, *being*. One day soon it will be a whole person. She wondered what it would be like. Would it be like her, like Jamie? Like her unknown grandfather, like her tragic mother? The present was not like the past, she thought. Things were different. This baby will be a twentieth-century baby, not a fussy old Victorian like her. The thought made her smile. She looked through the refracted lens, saw the bedroom, the bed, adjusted the camera's position just a tiny fraction, already composing the scene in her mind.

'Move the bed a little to the left,' she said. 'Put a candle on the side table.'

'What?'

She pushed the door open. Light and air greeted her as though she was a long-term prisoner suddenly released from her cell.

'I *said*, move the bed a little to the left,' she said. 'And we need to put the candle—'

'All right, all right,' Deirdre said. 'Hold your horses.'

At last it was done. They repaired downstairs for tea. Annie kept looking at Deirdre. Did she not mind? She seemed so unselfconscious. Perhaps some people were like that, she thought. Eager to be seen. Perhaps in another life Deirdre Doyle would have been on stage. Annie didn't know. She sipped her tea. She tried not to think about tonight.

Nine thirty. So quiet outside. She sat squatting in the wardrobe wishing she was somewhere, anywhere else. She'd had to telegraph Lady Julia from the post office to inform her of their delay in Kinsale. Lady Julia wouldn't be happy, Annie knew. But Lady Julia's happiness was not, currently, at the top of her list of priorities. She kept getting cramps. It was so hot inside. Come on, she thought. Come on! Get it over with.

Joe was down the pub – well, that was the story; he was skulking at the back of the house to be on hand instead, just in case. And Eleanor Wallace's people were watching the house, too. Annie didn't much care for Eleanor Wallace, she realised. But then, she didn't care for any of this. She sweated and waited. What was Deirdre *doing*!

Entertaining her guest downstairs. From time to time Annie could hear voices, Deirdre's laughter, the clinking of glasses. They were having a good old time down there, Deirdre and her beau. She wished they'd hurry the hell up. But Deirdre seemed to have all bloody night to get going.

Cramps again. She bit her lips, trying not to move. The heat made her nauseous. She focused on the camera, the view through the peephole, of the room, the bed, the sources of light. It would just about do. She tried to pass the time. Counted barking dogs. One, two, three barks. Four. Another one. Six. She lost count. She tried to calculate how much money she had now. She kept it under a loose floorboard in the basement. Enough for a second class ticket on the *Olympic*, enough to get her to Boston or New York, enough to live a while. Not enough to make a future, though. She needed more. She needed enough to reinvent herself, become something other than Annie Connolly of Cork. There was no point going somewhere if you were still going to be yourself when you got there.

Ten, eleven, twelve barking dogs. So hot. The cramp shot up her leg. She tried to shake it without moving. It was a nightmare. The clinking of glasses, Deirdre's lewd laugh. She could murder the damn woman. Twenty-one barking dogs, twenty-two, twenty-three.

Steps coming up the stairs.

She froze. The door banged open. She heard them, Deirdre and this Feebes. The sounds disgusted her.

'Oh, darling,' Edmund Feebes said. 'Oh, darling!'

Annie heard clothes being removed, loud kissing, a groan, a giggle, Deirdre saying, 'Major General, stand to attention!'

For a moment they came too close to the wardrobe. Annie steadied the stand as the wardrobe shook.

'Come to bed, Edmund,' Deirdre said. The bodies moved away. Annie let out a soft breath of relief. She looked through the lens, adjusted position. She could see them clearly enough, Major General Feebes with a pot belly and hairy buttocks. When he turned in profile she saw he did have a magnificent moustache. He was also painfully erect. Deirdre Doyle, meanwhile, had shed her clothes and was writhing provocatively on the bed. Annie hesitated, then pressed the shutter button.

She had to hope the pictures would come out. Eleanor Wallace was all softly-softly smiles and insinuations for the moment, but Annie knew a killer when she met one. If she didn't do the job, Miss Wallace would make sure *some* shit about Annie would get out. Not like she was in anyone's good books anyhow. She had only herself. Deirdre dropped to her knees, her back to the camera. Major General Feebes stood to attention like the captain on the deck of a ship going down fast. Annie pressed the shutter button. Edmund Feebes shuddered and cried out. It was all over fast. He sat on the bed. Deirdre stood and dabbed her mouth demurely.

'Rest awhile, my hero,' she said. 'But don't rest too long!'

The major general laughed, scratched his stomach and farted. He stretched out on the bed. Annie cursed.

Get him out of the room! she thought, furious. She took one last photo, the man and his naked companion. The sweat got in her eyes. She was desperate for a pee. Her leg cramped again. She nearly screamed.

'What was that?' Major General Feebes said.

'What?' Deirdre said.

'That noise.'

'I didn't hear a noise.' Deirdre stared daggers at the wardrobe. 'Probably a mouse,' she said.

Screw you, Annie thought.

She sat there, stewing. She couldn't wait much longer. She had to get out. Her leg spasmed.

'What was that!' the major general said again.

'Let's go downstairs,' Deirdre said. 'I need a drink.'

'But we just got here,' the major general said, pouting.

Deirdre reached across and held his limp member in her hand. She gave it a couple of experimental tugs.

Jesus Christ and all the angels, please don't, Annie thought.

'Well, maybe a small drink,' the major general conceded.

Annie didn't dare breathe for relief. She watched as Edmund Feebes got up ponderously from the bed. Deirdre looked directly at the camera. She mouthed 'Be quick', then escorted the major general out of the room. As soon as the bedroom door closed Annie pushed the wardrobe door open. She took in big gulps of air.

A knock on the window. Then another one. She went over. Joe Doyle, chucking pebbles at the glass.

She opened the window.

'You've got to get me out of here,' she said.

'Keep your voice down!' Joe said. 'Throw me down the camera, Annie.'

'There is no way the camera leaves without me,' Annie said.

'Then jump, I'll catch you.'

'You must be crazy, Joe. Tell your aunt to get him out of here!'

Joe shook his head.

'Hold on,' he said.

'Where are you—'

He vanished into the dark. What was he *doing*? She could hear Deirdre and the old boy downstairs. Getting rowdy again. She didn't have long. She had a feeling Edmund Feebes was soon going to get his second wind. *Not* something Annie wanted to be a witness to. She shuddered.

'Here!' Joe said. He appeared out of the dark, holding a ladder.

'You've got to be kidding,' Annie said.

Joe put the ladder against the wall.

'Hand me the camera and climb down,' he said.

'You've *got* to be kidding,' Annie said.

'I think they're coming back up!' Joe said.

Annie had never moved so fast. She grabbed the camera and tossed it out of the window. She shut the wardrobe doors. She shimmied out of the window and onto the rickety ladder, which barely held. She grabbed the sides for dear life.

'Shut the window!' Joe said.

'What?'

'Shut the bloody window!'

She reached to close it. Teetered at the top of the ladder. Somehow she did it. She reached for a hold on the ladder again and descended just as the bedroom door opened and Deirdre and Edmund tumbled back in. Annie slid down the ladder the rest of the way. Her palms burned. She could hear them going at it upstairs.

'I don't even *care* about Home Rule!' Annie said.

'Don't say that,' Joe said. 'Come on. Let's get out of here.'

He led her out through the back gate. Across the road a black automobile was waiting. Eleanor Wallace was in the driving seat.

'Did you get it?' she said.

'The pictures need developing,' Annie said.

'Get in,' Eleanor said.

'What? Why?'

'I'll drive you back to Cork.'

'Better than staying in this dump any longer,' Annie said. She slid into the passenger seat. Joe handed her the camera.

'I'll take back the cart tomorrow, then,' he said.

'You do that, Joe.'

Annie sat back. She closed her eyes. She was suddenly very tired.

The car engine started. As if from a great distance, Annie heard Eleanor speak, but whatever she said was lost to her.

'Just drive,' Annie said. 'Just drive.'

16

'IT'S SO BEAUTIFUL,' LILY SAID. SHE SIGHED. THEY WERE standing on the pier, looking at the sea and the ships calmly sailing.

'How are you and John getting on?' Annie said.

'Oh, like a house on fire,' Lily said. 'He's sweet, really. And, well... It would be nice to live in London. He has a big house there. Servants, too. Can you imagine having servants, Annie?'

Annie couldn't.

'In America no one has servants,' she said. 'And everyone is free.'

'You talk such rubbish sometimes, Annie,' Lily said. She laughed. 'Of course they have servants. You're either rich or you're a servant. If I marry John, I get to be rich.' She stared out at the sea. 'Or at least wealthy,' she said.

'What's the difference?' Annie said.

'Rich is like... You can do anything,' Lily said. 'Wealthy, you're just comfortable and have a few servants.'

'That still sounds nice,' Annie said.

'It really does,' Lily said.

'So will you do it?'

'I don't know, Annie! Do you think I should?'

'I think he's a good match,' Annie said. She thought of John Savage, with his easy, mocking smile and his fast automobile. He had kind eyes and a sadness that lurked under the exterior. 'He's nice,' she said.

'Nice is good,' Lily said. 'Nice is more than anyone could ask for. I just wish he, you know. Could do some of the other stuff.'

'Some people just don't,' Annie said.

'We've been talking it over,' Lily said. 'We can make accommodations. He has his friends, and I could have mine. As long as we're both discreet. It's different in London. It's bigger. And we'd have lots of things to do that a man can't do on his own. He *needs* a wife. All those dinner parties, and the opera, and, and…' She shrugged. 'I will be a society lady,' she said.

'You also need a child,' Annie said. 'A family's no good without a child.'

'We were talking about that, too,' Lily said. She took Annie's hand and squeezed it, and they didn't speak again for a while, but gazed at the open sea, one looking to England, the other to America.

Anywhere, anyway, but here.

This was a feeling that stole over generations, Annie thought. There had been other people before her who stood on the shore and watched out to sea and thought, there had to be something else out there. Maybe something better. Who got on ships and went to wherever *there* was: London, Boston, Lima. There were Irish people everywhere, it sometimes seemed: anywhere but Ireland. And yet the ones who stayed behind wanted it back for themselves so passionately that they were willing to fight and die to keep it. She didn't say any of that to Eleanor Wallace, of course.

Eleanor said, 'This is the room. What do you think?'

'I think once was enough,' Annie said.

They were in the Royal Victoria, upstairs. Eleanor was chewing Turkish Delight. She waved the bag at Annie.

'You want some?'

'No, thanks.'

'You look very pregnant,' Eleanor said.

'I feel very pregnant,' Annie said.

'Well, it won't be like last time,' Eleanor said. 'Look.' She pointed out features. The bed, the electric lights, the concealed hole in the wall.

'Come,' she said. She took Annie out of the room and through a locked door into a supply closet.

'See?' she said.

Annie did. It was dark, comfortable, and adjacent to the bedroom Eleanor had set up. There was already a stand for the camera, which would face the hole and be able to take pictures with ease.

'Why do you need me?' Annie said. 'Get any pier-side photographer.'

'Why, I need you because I have you,' Eleanor said. 'It's just a job, Annie. No one is asking you to swear an oath of loyalty to the Republic. You need money, don't you?'

So that was that: the hotel room in the Victoria and the camera set-up, and whoever Eleanor Wallace could ensnare within. All for the cause. Which Annie fully supported, as long as she didn't have to live in this new Jerusalem Eleanor and her co-conspirators were going to build here, just as soon as they finally got rid of the English.

She took the money. She wasn't going to stick around for much longer, anyway, she thought. She had her ticket for the ship now. It was all arranged. She'd leave and never look back. That was the mistake her grandmother made. She didn't stay away. Something brought her back. But there wasn't much tying Annie down anymore.

She knew the day would come, but still she hadn't quite prepared herself. It was a grey, overcast day. Jamie looked faintly silly standing on the gallows in the gaol. He was thinner, and his hair, which was once so black and luxurious, now looked matted and old. *He* looked old. His eyes kept shifting over the small crowd until he found her, standing at the back, and for a moment he smiled.

It almost broke her heart.

When the trapdoor opened, Jamie dropped. The heavy knot of the rope fitted around Jamie's neck snapped the bones cleanly. The hangman knew his job. There was no suffering. The body dangled there in the air for a moment, legs twitching. Then they lowered him down. Aunt Eithne sobbed into a handkerchief. Annie saw them all through a film of mist. She must have been crying. She saw Eleanor Wallace and the men from the Brotherhood in the crowd. They'd sent Jamie to his death, Annie thought. To get whatever papers were of such importance in Able Seaman Williams's satchel bag. Annie didn't care anymore. Aunt Eithne found her and hugged her.

'The baby...' she said. 'The baby!' She burst into tears again.

The body was removed and the rope separated from the man. There was no one to pay for a memento mori. But Annie framed it all the same: the pale face diffused now of its suffering, the hair at rest, the arms neatly folded. The head at an unnatural angle, but that could be fixed, with some care and attention, and the background arranged without jailers or executioner. A nice grey sky. It was going to rain. In the haze of light he looked at peace.

'Goodbye, Jamie,' Annie whispered. 'And goodnight.'

'I can't keep you on in your condition,' Lady Julia said. 'I am sorry, Annie. I tried to tell you.'

'But, Lady Julia...'

The studio, in gloom. Sir John glaring down from his photograph on the wall.

'So much time and effort that I put into you, all wasted!' Lady Julia said. 'And now look at you. A baby, Annie? And no ring? It's... It's unseemly.'

'Lady Julia, I just—'

'Here,' Lady Julia said. She pushed an envelope into Annie's hands. 'It isn't much,' she said. 'But more than you deserve. I did all that I could.'

'Well, screw you, Lady Julia,' Annie said. 'No offence and all.'

For a moment she thought the old lady was crying.

'I'll miss you too,' Lady Julia said.

★

The baby grew bigger and bigger inside her.

Eleanor Wallace and the mayor lay together in the bed in the Victoria. Annie wasn't supposed to be there but she was. She took a picture. Eleanor turned to the concealed hole and smiled.

Alone in her house, the baby kicked and Annie woke up crying without quite knowing why.

It couldn't go on like this, she thought.

Something had to change.

'Since it is your intention to enter into the covenant of Holy Matrimony,' Father O'Malley said, 'join your right hands, and declare your consent before God and his Church.'

He beamed at the assembled guests. Stained glass windows high above, and candlelight, the smell of incense, the women in their fineries and the men in Sunday suits, and Joe Doyle leaning against a wall, watching with a sad and longing look only Annie saw.

'I, John Ebenezer Savage, take you, Lily Elizabeth Counihan, to be my wife. I promise to be true to you in good times and in bad, in sickness and in health. I will love you and honour you all the days of my life.'

Lily, resplendent in white on this, her wedding day. There were not many people there. A handful of English visitors here for the wedding, on the groom's side. Lily's aunt and mother, relatives and friends on the other. John

Savage looked at his bride-to-be as if wondering if she were going to change her mind. As if she would, Annie thought.

'I, Lily Elizabeth Counihan, take you, John Ebenezer Savage, to be my husband,' Lily said. Her voice quivered. She looked very pretty standing there, Annie thought. The baby kicked just then, as though sensing the excitement. 'I promise to be faithful to you in good times and in bad, in sickness and in health, to love you and to honour you all the days of my life,' Lily said.

'What God joins together, let no one put asunder!' Father O'Malley said.

Annie felt hot and heavy. She just wanted to go outside, to get fresh air. The couple exchanged rings. Gold, and gold. Only the best for the newly-weds. Annie still didn't quite understand what John Savage worked in. Not rich, Lily said. But wealthy.

'Let us pray,' Father O'Malley said.

'Hey, Annie,' Tom, the constable, said.

'Tom. I didn't know you'd be here.'

They were at the Palace of Varieties for the reception. There was definitely no God there. The place was crowded and smoky, and big band music filled the air. Dancers on stage were boys and girls with long legs, bare arms and not much else. One girl did the fan dance.

'Keeping the peace,' Tom said.

'Really?'

He laughed. 'I'm off duty,' he said.

'I didn't know you knew John.'

He shrugged. 'I'm here for Lily,' he said. 'We used to go steady for a while. You didn't know?'

'You dark horse!' Annie said. 'She never told me!'

'Well, it wasn't anything,' Tom said. 'It's the groom invited me, though. I almost arrested him a couple of times when he was being too indiscreet. Nice guy, though, so I always let him go.'

'He contribute to the Widows and Orphans fund?'

'Something like that. You want to dance, Annie?'

It was her turn to laugh.

'Look at me,' she said.

'You look fine to me,' he said. 'You look more than fine.'

'I'm pregnant, Tom. In case you hadn't noticed.'

'It's just a dance,' Tom said.

He took her hand, and they danced amidst the swaying bodies as the band played on.

'Annie, look! Annie, look!'

Lily, with her diamond ring and gold ring both. She beamed drunkenly. Her husband was making out with Joe Doyle somewhere in the shadows. Tom, the constable, was gone. Annie liked him well enough. And taking Jamie in wasn't his fault, it was just his job. But you had to draw the line somewhere.

'They're gorgeous, Lily.'

'Will you come visit me in London?' Lily said.

'I don't think so, love.'

'I know.'

Lily hugged her. She started to cry.

'I hope I did the right thing!' she said.

'Are you happy, Lily?'

'Happy? I suppose I am.'

'Then yes,' Annie said. She kissed her on the cheeks, held onto the hug, then pulled away.

'I have to go,' she said. 'I'm beat.'

'All right, Annie. I will see you.'

'Yes,' Annie said. 'I will see you.'

17

ANNIE WOKE UP WITH A CRY OF TERROR, PUSHING BLACK
water away from her as she drowned. In her dream she
had been a man voyaging across the sea from the Americas
to England. She sat up in the bed, the dream, recurring,
fading now. She listened to the house. Nothing stirred. She
was alone, just her and the baby. She felt it now, moving,
stretching, restless. Its little feet kicked against the womb.
She put a hand on her belly, soothing it. A boy or a girl?
She thought a boy. She got up, wrapped herself warm.
Shuffled into the kitchen. Wan light pushing in through the
dirty window. Someone should clean the glass, she thought.
No more Jamie to come bursting in. No more constables
to chase him. The street outside was so quiet. She was so
sick of the quiet, she thought. She was so sick of lonely
shores and cold winds, houses where the foundations
slowly rotted, of fence posts bleached with saltwater, of
fields where sheep feasted on grass grown from the bones of
druids and dead saints. She wanted modernity, she thought.
She wanted lights, laughter, noise. She wanted to drive in an
automobile!

She went from room to room, restless, the baby inside

her restless too. She wondered what it would grow up to be. So far it was living. She knew this was not always the case. But so far everything seemed fine. She was fine. The baby was fine. She was repeating herself. Was that bad? How much was too much repetition? She wanted to break free from it, do something new. To get away. Instead she went down to the basement.

A rug on the cold floor, the colour of old, dried blood. Like someone was shot on top of it with a pistol, and slowly left to bleed to death. Old china cups and plates covered in dust, sitting on cabinets of unvarnished wood. As though someone had gone to all the trouble of making the cabinets, then lost interest just before the finish. It suited her grandmother, all of that. Dead flowers in a vase. A painting of sheep in pasture on the wall, unsigned. It wasn't very good. Some old man in Queenstown gave it to her grandma once. Why, Annie didn't know. She liked coming down here, though. The floor above was still splintered wood, since no one repaired it, but the shotgun Jamie used was taken away by the constables. Annie went to the empty fireplace. Grandma used to sit there sometimes, late at night, when she could be bothered to light a fire. She read – trash, mostly – and drank and sometimes talked to herself. Sometimes Annie sat with her. Now the hearth was cold and had been for a long time. Annie reached inside the fireplace, withdrew the box with plates and prints. She put it on the low table and sat in the old chair Grandma had used. She opened the box.

There was Agnes Pugh, the fishwife, in bed with Mrs Smith, the bank manager's wife. And there was Joe Doyle with an English sailor, and there was Lily with an English soldier, and there was Eleanor Wallace with the mayor. It was just dirt. Annie looked at it in distaste. She had felt soiled by doing this work, but it was a means to an end. She gathered together the photographs and put them in the fireplace, and tossed a match into the pile.

They burned so quickly, like something ending. She stared until there was only ash.

Something moved inside her. A sudden pain. Then wet.

'Oh, hell,' Annie said.

The pain was more frequent now. She'd walked out as she was, into the cold night, feeling almost preternaturally calm. She knocked on next door's. Charlie's mum answered, bleary-eyed, fag in mouth.

'Oh, love,' she said.

She sent Charlie-Next-Door out. Annie went back to the house. The pain again, shooting through her. She heard the automobile before anything else. Then the door. Lily and John Savage, soon to be of London, still of Cork.

'It's here?' Lily said.

'It's here,' Annie said.

Lily sat with her. She held her hand. Rain pattered against the window.

'What are you thinking about?' Lily said.

'A ship on the ocean,' Annie said. 'Moving on the waves.'

'We'll call him Edgar,' Lily said. 'If it's a boy.'

'That's a nice name,' Annie said.

A knock on the door. Charlie-Next-Door burst in, with his mop of dirty blond hair and running nose. He grinned shyly.

'Did you get the midwife?' Lily said.

'I got what I could at this hour,' Charlie said. 'I mean, Mrs Dolan's down in Queenstown visiting her daughter, and Francine's passed out blind drunk listening to records.'

'Do I have to do this on my own, Charlie?' Annie said. 'Jesus, you're as useless as tits on a nun.'

'I got the next best thing,' Charlie said, and he grinned in that idiotic way of his, which Annie didn't like one bit.

There was a knock on the door.

'Hello...'

Another wave of pain coursed through Annie's body, and then Eleanor Wallace came into the living room, looking brisk, looking efficient, and looking mostly sober.

'What are you doing here?' Annie said.

'You need a midwife,' Eleanor said.

'So?'

'So I have some experience, as it happens.'

'Jesus,' Annie said.

'Just relax,' Eleanor said.

'Don't tell me to relax!'

'Baby won't be out for a while yet,' Eleanor said, sitting next to her. 'Charlie, why don't you go back to your mum. Lily, make us all some tea. John—'

'Yes? Yes?' he said. All mockery gone, he looked as nervous as a wash rag ready to be squeezed.

'Make a fire,' Eleanor said. 'It's freezing in here.'

'Right you are,' John Savage said.

Annie lay back. She closed her eyes. She could hear them moving all about her, getting busy like bees in a hive. She hated all of them suddenly.

She wished they would all go away.

Another wave of pain. She gritted her teeth. This wouldn't

go on forever, she thought. Eleanor Wallace's cold hand on her brow.

'This is what women do,' Eleanor said. 'We give birth. Your child will be free in his own country, Annie.'

'Screw you, Eleanor,' Annie said.

'Push! Push!'

'Shut up!' Annie screamed.

The baby was coming. It wasn't making it easier for her. She was on all fours, her guts loose, the smell nauseating, the fire too hot, Eleanor too bossy and Lily too timid, and John hiding in the kitchen – a small mercy, at least. This wasn't men's work, she thought, because men could never handle it.

'I can see the head!' Lily said.

'Keep pushing!' Eleanor said.

'Shut... *up*!' Annie screamed.

But she pushed all the same. She had no other choice. And the baby kept coming, and coming, and—

'It's a boy!' Eleanor Wallace said. Annie could barely see for the pain.

'What are you doing!' she said.

'I'm just going to pull out the placenta,' Eleanor said.

'You what—'

She didn't scream but Eleanor *pulled* and something wet and bloody plopped out of her and fell on the floor where it joined all the other fluids. Eleanor held a knife. She cut the cord. Annie heard a baby suddenly cry. The sound felt so alien in that old room. For a moment she had an unbearable desire to laugh. Then she felt something small and warm on her chest as Eleanor placed the baby there.

'Let him feed,' Eleanor said.

An overwhelming rush of something she couldn't quite put a label to washed over Annie. The tiny thing nestled against her, helpless and infinitely fragile.

Where did he come from? she wondered. How was it possible that lives just came, out of nowhere, just as they were so quickly snuffed out? She had taken too many photographs of the dead. Now she tried to frame this scene in her tired mind. Virgin and Child, in Repose. The baby's tiny lips found her nipple and fastened. A rush of something that might have been love washed over her, almost breaking her against some distant shore. She closed her eyes.

'Just give me a moment,' Annie heard herself say. 'Just give me a moment before you take him away.'

18

SHE WATCHED THEM LEAVE, AND WAVED GOODBYE FROM the pier as Mr and Mrs Savage, accompanied by their newborn son, boarded the ferry to England. Annie was crying, but she didn't know why. Lily with the baby carriage, a bag full of rubber nipples, feeding bottles and tins of Cow & Gate Milk Food, advertised as the best health insurance policy for Empire children. Edgar would be an empire child, Annie thought. He would enjoy all the privileges and benefits of being English, well-educated and rich. She had to give him the best shot at life, and that meant letting him become a Savage.

She watched the boat. Seagulls cried overhead. A grey, drizzly sky. Her breasts ached, missing the tiny child she barely got to hold. She'd have to express the milk soon. Her whole body felt different. But it would come back, she knew. And perhaps she could have other children, later, when she was ready.

She turned her back on the ship as it started to slowly sail away. She looked on the city, grey homes under a grey sky, peaceful, content: or so it seemed. Somewhere in Cork Eleanor Wallace laid down plans, somewhere the English soldiers were keeping guard. In the studio, perhaps, Lady Julia was seeking to train a new apprentice. Somewhere a man lay dead, waiting for his photograph to be taken in memoriam. A cleaner would be sweeping the Palace of Varieties from last night's excesses. In the woollen mills of Blarney the workers would be milling wool. A sense of calm engulfed her then. The thought of a new world and a new life filled her with a promise that kept her afloat. She turned back, and the ferry was small against the horizon, and then it vanished entirely. Annie let the tears flow. They would stop in time.

'Hi, Jamie,' she said. She laid the wreath of flowers on his grave. Black earth, white stone, a grey sky. She longed for sun.

'His name's Edgar,' she said. 'I'm sorry I didn't name him like you wanted. But he was never really yours. You'd have had to stick around for that.'

No one else around. The cemetery was quiet. A bird chittered on a branch.

'It's for the best,' Annie said. Telling him, or herself, she didn't really know. 'And now you can have Ireland all to yourself, forever.'

Jamie didn't answer. She wondered how long he'd rot down there before there were only bones.

'I'm leaving,' she said. 'I have enough money to make a new life. I might start a pub, over in America. I have the feeling there'll be a lot of thirsty Irishmen there.' She tried to smile, for his benefit. 'I'll call it Annie's,' she said.

She reached for her pocket watch to check the time but,

of course, it was no longer there. She'd given it to Lily to give to Edgar one day, when he was older. Something to remember her by. She didn't need that stupid pocket watch anymore anyway. It was just one more tie to a life she was determined to leave behind.

'Goodbye, Jamie,' she said.

Joe Doyle was where he always was when she needed him most. Leaning back against his cart, smiling, a blade of grass between his lips. He looked up when he heard her coming. Charlie-Next-Door's mum looked out through the blinds, saw the two of them and shut the blinds closed.

'Hey, Annie,' Joe said.

'Hey, Joe.'

'One last ride, right?' he said.

She smiled. 'Why, you'll miss me?'

'Yeah,' he said. 'I will.'

Then she was hugging him, for the first time, she realised. First and last.

'I'll miss you too, Joe. I'll miss you a lot.'

'Well,' he said, when she released him. 'I could always come visit sometime. I heard they have ice cream machines in New York on every street, in any flavour you could ever want. Can you imagine such a thing, Annie?'

'No,' she said, laughing, 'no, I can't.'

'Just send me a postcard,' he said. 'When you get there. Just to let me know you're safe.'

'I will,' she said, both of them knowing that she won't.

'Well, we should go,' Joe said. 'Don't want to miss the tide and all.'

'She isn't docking for another two days,' Annie said. 'But you're right. Here.'

She put the keys in his hands. He looked at them a long moment.

'Are you sure?' he said.

'I'm sure.'

'Here,' he said. He gave her an envelope. She didn't need to look inside to know it had the rest of the money. She put it away. She had squeezed as much out of Cork as she ever could.

'Look after the old dump for me, will you?' she said.

'I'll love it,' Joe said. 'I never had a home of my own.'

Annie didn't say anything to that. She got on the cart. The horse clip-clopped sedately along the cobbled street, up the hill and down again, until the city ended and the green world began.

'I'd like to come back as a moss,' Joe said. 'So green and soft, so green and soft. To lie upon an ancient trunk and be. No thought, no sound but the rain...' He stopped, looking startled.

'That's nice,' Annie said. They were two hours out of Cork. All that water, reflecting the sky. She thought she'd miss it, at last, once it was no longer there. In the distance a man was digging potatoes out of the dirt. A farmhouse and smoke rising from a chimney, a woman scattering seeds for her chickens. In the other direction, the shadow of a gaunt fisherman pulling in nets. This is how the land was, this is how it would always be. Under all that skies her people lived upon the land, fed on it and fed it in their turn. Caught between ocean and land, islanders adrift in a cold, biting wind.

'I must have heard it somewhere,' Joe said.

The road wound up and down and around. A dog barked in the distance. The horse moved with the same patient, even walk, pulling the cart, Joe and Annie tiny under all that sky. Clouds shifted overhead, made shapes Annie couldn't read. Portents of a future. She thought about the baby. He will be happy, she thought. He will have everything.

She thought about the ship. It would be docking in Cherbourg about now.

'How does it go?' she said.

'What?' Joe said.

'The rest of the poem.'

'I don't know,' Joe said.

Annie shrugged. She felt suddenly free, unburdened of her past. The miles went past. They caught the ferry to Great Island, the ferryman dour, his face as lined as a cobweb. She paid the toll. Crossed running water.

Gentle hills and the final stretch, the horse pulling more laboriously now, until at last they reached the top of the final rise and she beheld Queenstown down below, along the slope and on the harbour, gaily painted houses and the beginnings of a grand cathedral, only half-built, rising over the town. They had been building it for over half a century and it was still not finished. Below this house of God the shipyards, and out on the cold grey sea the prison on Spike Island and the garrison on Haulbowline. They rode down the steep hill to the city below.

She felt the first tremor of excitement rise in her then.

The cold grey waves against the gaily decorated pier, and the offices of the White Star Line right there.

'I'm going to stay the night, go back tomorrow,' Joe said.

'I can get you a room,' Annie said.

'I have an aunt in town,' Joe said.

'Another Doyle?'

He smiled. 'There is always a Doyle,' he said. 'Besides, I thought I might wave you off. Someone should.'

'You don't need to,' she said.

'No,' he said. 'I know I don't.'

She smiled as she got off the cart.

'This is the place?' she said.

'This is it.'

'All right.'

Annie went inside. The Rob Roy Hotel on the waterfront. The wave of music hit her as soon as she walked through the door. The air was thick with a miasma of smoke, sweat, spilled beer. Bodies pressed against bodies, moving to the wild music of the band. It could have been midnight in there. There was no sense of time. Someone grabbed her arm, twirled her around, another pushed a glass of Murphy's into her hands. She was half drunk by the time she got through the throng.

'The room? Yes! Upstairs!' the woman who ran the place shouted over the noise when Annie finally found her. 'You won't get much sleep tonight, love, sorry!'

'That's all right!' Annie shouted back. 'I'll sleep on the ship!'

The woman grinned.

'That's what they all said, too!'

Annie went upstairs, to the small room the size of a cupboard. It won't be any larger on the ship, she thought. She stowed her luggage and went back down. By the time she got there Joe Doyle was already at the bar, looking like he too was going to America. She went and joined him. He raised his glass to her.

'To Annie Connolly,' he said. 'Our dearly departed. Who lived, and laughed – if not often – and loved, though perhaps too much. You weren't long for this world, and too good for it. Rest in peace.' He raised his glass high, and was joined by all the other mourners in the bar, and all the people that they mourned.

'To Annie!' Joe Doyle cried.

He was met with a roar as everyone cheered and drank. This was it, the vigil for those who were to cross the big water, never to be seen again. An American wake. The barman poured whiskey. Annie drank, the liquid burning her throat. Stupid warmth spread through her. The music rose, the bodies swayed, and the party would have gone on forever. Annie thought of caverns deep in the hills, where tiny men and women lived and lured the traveller into a great feast and dance that never ended, that went all through some eternal night as outside the decades passed unbidden. She forgot everything, for the dead carry no memories with them beyond the dark sea. Another drink and then another. She could go on forever.

She woke with sunlight burning a hole through her head. She groaned. A warm male body on the mattress beside her grunted something unintelligible and rolled over. Annie crawled out and threw up into a bucket. She felt a little better after that.

She had no time to wash. She ran a wet cloth over herself and dressed hurriedly, picked up her gear. She went downstairs, stepping over prone bodies. The barman was asleep at the bar. Annie stepped outside. The sunlight hit her. The biggest ship she'd ever seen nestled in the sea between the harbour and the islands. Damn but she was beautiful. A monster of the deeps risen, a creature so majestic it could cross oceans with no more effort than it took a woman to cross the road from one side to the other carrying her shopping. Annie's heart beat faster. The promenade thronged with people. A brass band played. A priest offered heartfelt prayers. Kids kicked a ball down the street. Porters carried luggage. Passengers lined up the deck of the ship, watching Queenstown. Hundreds of them, from England and Europe and the Near East, they came from all over to take this voyage of a lifetime, to seek out a new home, a new world, where they could remake themselves and be something new; something that was never seen before.

Annie smiled. From a vendor on the waterfront she bought a pair of tinted glasses. She put them on against the sun.

Then, carrying her luggage, she made her way up the gangplank and onto the titanic waiting ship.

PART THREE

THE COUNTRY HOUSE MURDER

EDGAR

1933

19

THE SOUND OF A SHIP'S HORN, ECHOING UNCANNILY through the peaceful English countryside, jolted Edgar at the car wheel. It conjured up images of an ice-strewn sea, of malevolent shapes looming in the fog. Then an open-top Crossley, honking loudly, passed him on his right, its passengers laughing gaily, and the notion was dispelled. He watched the vehicle vanish off into the distance, and with a somewhat forlorn sigh returned to his uneasy thoughts.

It was the summer of 1933 and, being of sound mind and sound body, if suffering somewhat of a nervous disposition brought about in the aftermath of a doomed love affair, from which he was still recovering, the young Edgar Waverley (as he now went by that name), twenty-one and not unhandsome, had accepted an invitation extended by an Oxford friend to spend a long weekend in the luxurious confines of Feebes Manor.

The manor, in the Devon countryside, was renowned far and wide as an architectural marvel, extensively rebuilt and renovated in the neo-Gothic style by the well-known philanthropist, Sir Edward Feebes, in the 1870s. A deeply devout man, it was said, Sir Edward followed the teachings of the Oxford Movement, to whom the Gothic was not only, as Augustus Pugin wrote, 'a return to the faith and the social structures of the Middle Ages', but in fact the only style suitable for Christian worship. The family had made its money some time past in the lucrative guano trade in South America, from which it got out just in time before its inevitable collapse. It had since spread out into banking, shipping and insurance; though it had reached an apex of wealth during the Great War, when it was singularly and spectacularly successful in the munitions trade.

An invitation to Feebes Manor, therefore, was a much coveted social engagement, and Edgar, though in his private thoughts about wealth was increasingly leaning towards the somewhat heretical teachings of Engels and Marx, was acutely aware of its significance. It would be an opportunity to meet and mingle with some of the finest in the land and in the wider Empire, those of a high social standing – people, in other words, who could help advance one's career. Though he was born a Savage, and comfortably wealthy, his father, John, died shortly after Edgar was born, in circumstances never entirely explained, and following the collapse of his financial dealings. Edgar's mother, Lily, eventually remarried, to the dependable and not unkind James Waverley, a man of many good qualities but not, unfortunately, a man of great affluence. Edgar had won his place in Oxford, but it was expected that he would make his own way in the world henceforth. A weekend at Feebes Manor should go, he felt certain, towards assisting in that course of action, should he but play his cards right.

The question of his future was much on Edgar's mind just then. He was in his final year in Oxford, and reading

History, which provides great insight into the past but offers little immediate reward going forwards. A job in the Civil Service, perhaps in the Foreign Office – something to do with the management of Britain's imperial domains. A posting in the Near East might suit him, he thought. He had spent some time in Egypt the previous school break, helping on an archaeological dig in Abu Simbel, under Mallowan, then went by felucca down the Nile to Cairo. He found the city exciting, and when the hot days settled into warm nights he frequented the cafés and bars where expatriates from all across the world met to conduct business. He found that he could blend in; that people liked him, on the whole; and that if he listened quietly he could hear more, perhaps, than was anticipated he would. Later, on his return to Oxford, he was approached one grey morning by a man in a trilby hat as he sat drinking coffee alone at the Cadena. The man pulled up a chair and sat down without being invited. He placed his hat on his lap and regarded Edgar with some evident interest. Edgar watched him back, curious and unwilling to be rude. The man reached for a pouch of tobacco and a pipe. For a moment he paused.

'You do not smoke?' he said.

'No,' Edgar said.

The man nodded. He lit his pipe and puffed out smoke with a contented air, and put away his pouch of tobacco.

'Drink?' he said.

'Socially.'

The man nodded again.

'Coffee, though, of course,' he said.

'Of course.'

The man signalled the waiter, who hurried over with

a cup already prepared. They knew this man here, Edgar thought.

'Thank you, Rudolph,' the man said.

Edgar waited. The man took a sip of coffee, nodded to himself, and put down the cup.

'Any other vices?' he said.

'Excuse me?'

'Everyone has vices,' the man said. 'The question is, what are yours?'

Edgar shrugged. He tried to hide his discomfort.

'Who are you?' he said.

The man smiled. He drew in smoke. Exhaled. Took a sip of coffee.

'I understand you have only recently come back from Cairo,' he said.

Edgar considered the situation he found himself in. The pieces were fitting together rapidly. He had met one man like this in Cairo, a gregarious Englishman, who said he was with the Joint Committee of Cotton Trade Organisations, whatever that was. He bought everyone drinks but never got drunk. He laughed at everyone's jokes but watched everything without any humour in his shrewd eyes. He had noticed Edgar watching him one evening, laughed, and said, 'You're a dark horse, Edgar,' and left shortly after. Edgar had almost forgotten him, until now.

'Yes,' Edgar said.

'You met many interesting people?' the man said. He brushed ash from the brim of his trilby.

'I suppose,' Edgar said.

'Meet any Germans?'

'A few.'

They were all over Cairo, the Germans. The old ones, with their Prussian eagles, and the new ones with the swastikas.

'Baron von Bolschwing,' the man said. 'Ring a bell?'

Edgar nodded.

'Yes,' he said. 'I met him.'

The man leaned across now. His eyes were harder somehow.

'Tell me about him,' he said.

So Edgar did. He did not know von Bolschwing well, had not liked the man, but observed him. He had been floating around in the same social circles as Edgar, one of the new Nazis, what Edgar heard one of the others refer to contemptuously as May Lilies.

'He was on his way to Palestine, I think,' he told the man now. He told him everything he knew and remembered, not embellishing, giving clear, concise reportage, the way he would write a history report.

The man in the trilby hat nodded thoughtfully when Edgar was done. He had taken no notes, but Edgar thought he remembered everything. He asked a couple of follow-up questions, then subsided. He rose abruptly, left exact change on the table to account for two coffees, and shook Edgar's hand.

'Thank you,' he said.

With that he was gone. It had been a strange, momentary episode, and Edgar was all but certain that the man was from the Secret Service. He gripped the wheel of the car, concentrating on the dark road. He had packed evening and leisure wear, toiletries and a couple of volumes from Tacitus's *Historiae*. He did not expect he would have much time to read. The car, a Hornet, wasn't his. It was a loan from a close friend, the same one, in fact, who so badly affected Edgar's current disposition, for only the previous night they had both agreed it was finally over between them. This was not the first love of Edgar's life, nor, he thought, would it be his last. There was something wonderful about being in love, and a part of him, too, relished the secrecy that had to accompany a love of this nature, which could not be made public. Love, to Edgar, was a complex system of agreed-upon signals, of clandestine meetings and unseen departures. As Tacitus long ago observed, the illicit has an added charm.

And though Edgar knew that he must, surely, sooner or later fall in love again, a part of him grieved this final parting, for this friend was very dear to him, and perhaps in another life, another time, they would not have had to hide themselves from the world.

Nevertheless, Feebes Manor beckoned, and with it a weekend promising to be filled with delightful company and sparkling conversation, excellent food and wine and comfortable lodgings, which would make quite a change from his cramped college accommodation and otherwise frugal sustenance. And, whatever else, it was a chance to get away for a while, for which he was grateful.

The car handled well on the country road. The air smelled agreeably of summer, and in the distance birds called and brooks rushed, and trees rustled their rustly leaves. Tacitus, who had something to say about most things, was silent on the benefits or otherwise of nature. He was more concerned with power and its abuses, which was also much on Edgar's mind. His father's death, though he did not remember him, impacted him greatly. He was born rich, or so he was told. Then the riches went away, and he and Mother went through several homes, each shabbier than the last – the last being even without a servant. The union between Lily and the kindly Mr Waverley restored a semblance of normality the young Edgar much needed. Once more there were clean, pressed sheets, wood beside the fireplace, hot porridge and tea in the mornings, roast beef and potatoes for lunch. James Waverley worked as a junior solicitor in the City, specialising in the dull but dependable field of commercial contracts, of which there were plenty. When he took little Edgar with him into the offices, Edgar found himself in the company of men of power, of riches. Men who needed people like his adoptive father to set their agreements amongst themselves in ink and parchment. James Waverley, Edgar realised, had a *proximity* to power, but not power itself. It was wealth that ruled the City, and there were those who had money and those who worked for the men who did.

Mr Waverley – Father – saw no wrong in this arrangement. He was well-regarded, even liked, and provided for his family. If he was disappointed that Lily never gave him a child of his own he gave no sign of it. He treated Edgar kindly and raised him as his own.

It wasn't, the young Edgar thought, *fair* that Father should be working for the rich, or that others should be poor, the way Edgar and Mother had been poor. Something did not sit right with him, though he found it difficult to put it into words.

There was church, of course, and the admonition that no man can serve two masters, those being God and Mammon. But the church was richly decorated and collected its worshippers' offerings, which always included James

Waverley's tithe. He explained to Edgar that it was like a tax. Edgar asked what a tax was. James laughed and said a tax was the money one had to pay to the government so it could go about its business, and that taxes were as old as time and as inevitable as death itself. This led to a broader explanation of finance, which took in banks, inherited wealth and, inevitably, the importance of commercial contracts. Edgar did not quite understand all of what Father was telling him, but it seemed to him it boiled down to the basic notion that some people collected the money and other people paid it.

The question of fairness, Father explained, seldom if ever came into it. Being kind, he had left it unsaid that fairness was in essence a childish notion, but Edgar got a sense of it even so.

None of this was foremost in Edgar's mind growing up, but it niggled. He was a quiet, watchful child, recognised that in himself and accepted it. He had few friends, but a few were all he felt he needed. He was not unhappy. He did well in his studies, was adored by his mother, spoiled by his father, and destined to the bar. It was a cause of some disappointment to Father when, on getting into Oxford, Edgar elected to read History instead.

But history taught him that there had always been rich and poor. Some men were kings and others were slaves. This was merely the nature of humanity, and it often made for exciting reading, in the comfort of the Bodleian and away from the bloodshed and horror that accompanied the acquisition of wealth. That this wasn't *fair* seemed indeed a childish notion, one he still carried within him, but then he discovered the writings of Gaius, Fourier, Owen and Marx.

The idea that others had found so exciting, of creating a new, more equitable society, Edgar found exciting too, almost exhilarating. And the men who set out to create such a new society, people like Lenin and then Stalin, were far from childish dreamers but men of action, not afraid to shed blood for the cause. There were others in Oxford at that time with similar notions and feelings as Edgar, students who formed communist circles and societies and the like. But Edgar avoided them, and did not share his emerging views with others. He was not committed one way or the other, anyway. There was too much of the English in him, he felt. Staid, respectable, he was a man who would make a capable administrator, not a fighter for workers' rights.

The moon hung in the sky, the car drove as if by itself along the road, and then he beheld the stately home rising in the distance, its many turrets, chimneys, attic dormers and gables forming a jagged and curious skyline above the imposing building that squatted there in the darkness like a huge and somewhat hostile toad. The house was lit, and the electric lights did not so much dispel the Victorian gloom that clung to that edifice as somehow accented it, as though drawing the eye, and the mind that beheld it, to contemplate the vanity that riches can buy. Edgar felt quite nervous. Which was no doubt the intention. To approach here, the buildings whispered, you must yourself be powerful, moneyed, well-connected. The Feebeses had become so rich off guano that Edward Feebes's descendants could purchase their way into peerage. Now Henry, 1st Baron Feebes, sat as MP in London, where he was also chairman of Feebes Bank. His father, Admiral of the Fleet Edmund Feebes, a corpulent and amorous man, died in service in the Great

War, not so much going down with his ship as going down on a Parisian prostitute, or so rumour went. Edgar drove to the gates, which were open, the name *Feebes* inscribed upon them in elaborate wrought-iron and the requisite Gothic typeface. He thought somewhat uneasily of the gold watch in his pocket, which similarly, though less elaborately, had that same name engraved upon it. How it came into his possession he wasn't sure. An old family heirloom, Mother told him. A dear friend of hers had wanted him to have it.

It was a cheap watch. Edgar had had it appraised. Still, he kept it, and kept it wound and showing the correct time. Why, he couldn't quite say. Mother had seemed quite emotional when she gave it to him, just before he went to Oxford. He smiled fondly when he thought of Mother.

He drove slowly through the gates and into the grounds.

20

'Welcome to Feebes Manor, Mr Holmwood,' the butler said. He stood stooped and regal, holding the car door open for Edgar. 'Oh, I do beg your pardon!' he said. 'You must be Mr Waverley?'

'Yes,' Edgar said, feeling very self-conscious. 'Roddy couldn't come at the last moment, but I was told that—'

'Yes, yes, of course,' the butler said. 'It was all arranged. The baron is eager to make your acquaintance. Mr Holmwood always speaks so highly of you.'

Edgar blushed. The butler, taking no notice or, at any rate, doing a good job of appearing not to, said, 'Most of the other guests have already arrived, sir, and are taking refreshments in the Lima Room.' He clicked his fingers. Two other servants, standing under the awnings, hurried over.

'Your bags, sir,' the butler said. 'They will be placed in your room. You will be staying in the El Torturador room. It is on the second floor. Very comfortable accommodation, sir, I can assure you. Mr Holmwood always stays there when he visits.'

'El Torturador?' Edgar said. He had some Spanish, and a good ear for languages. 'The torturer's room?'

'The old Mr Feebes named most of the rooms, sir,' the butler said. 'I believe it was the moniker given to the ghost of an old monk in Lima. The old Mr Feebes was very taken with that story, for whatever reason.'

'I see,' Edgar said, not really seeing and not caring all that much, though slightly spooked. The whole place had that macabre feel about it, as if a murder was to take place at any moment. 'Well, the Lima Room, you said? For the refreshments and so on?'

He spoke a bit abruptly. He immediately felt bad. Butlers had that effect on him.

'Indeed, sir. Let me escort you,' the butler said, not taking offence. He turned and Edgar followed him. Up the stone steps and through the imposing doors, and into the manor. He could hear voices raised in conversation in the distance, and the sound of glasses clinking together. His mood lifted. Above his head the oil portraits of ancient Feebeses stared down on him. Edgar stopped to examine a superb portrait of Sir Edward Feebes. A youngish man, at the time – the discreet plaque underneath the painting said it was commissioned in 1865. Edward was tanned, with thoughtful eyes. He held a handkerchief in his hand as though afraid of letting it go.

'It's by Arthur Hughes,' the butler said.

Edgar stared at him blankly.

'The artist,' the butler elaborated. 'He was what you would call a Pre-Raphaelite.'

'Excellent work,' Edgar said. 'Excellent.'

'And this,' the butler said, moving smoothly on and drawing Edward's attention, 'is the late, and much lamented Admiral of the Fleet Edmund Feebes.'

Edgar stared at the photograph, in sepia tones, of a large, jovial-looking man in uniform.

'It was taken by Lady Julia Montmorency,' the butler informed him. 'The famed female photographer. She was truly a credit to her gender, don't you think?'

Edgar looked at the photograph.

'Marvellous,' he said.

The butler smiled.

'I am glad you think so,' he said.

'You are a connoisseur of the arts?' Edgar said.

'One always tries to better oneself,' the butler said.

Edgar nodded. He followed the butler. More oil paintings. More Feebeses. They multiplied like birds over a coastal island.

'The Lima Room, sir,' the butler announced.

They arrived at a large, comfortable-looking space, with a fire blazing merrily in the fireplace, for though it was summertime, nights in the country could be cold. All faces were turned as Edgar made his entrance. The assembled guests held drinks aloft, and their lively conversation had momentarily stalled.

'Mr Edgar Waverley,' the butler announced, then silently withdrew.

Edgar could see all their faces: some curious, some indifferent, others calculating. Then they all turned back and conversation resumed. As though his appearance never happened, or was of no consequence, or was merely filed away for later use. A servant materialised with a tray of drinks. Edgar gratefully accepted a glass of wine.

'It's a Mouton Rothschild,' a trim, energetic-looking man said, coming over. '1900 vintage. Not first class, but very acceptable. Their vintage in recent years has been below par, I'm afraid. Hello. I'm Henry Feebes. And you are Edgar. I have heard good things about you.'

'It's a pleasure to meet you, sir,' Edgar said, shaking Baron Feebes's hand. 'And thank you for having me. I must admit I feel awkward, considering it was only at Roddy – I mean, Mr Holmwood's – instigation that I was to come – I mean, as his companion—'

He stopped talking. Baron Feebes smiled affably.

'Nonsense, man,' he said. 'You are more than welcome. Please! Drink, have a smoke, dinner will be called shortly. We will talk again.' He patted Edgar on the shoulder and went to speak to a young, elegantly dressed man by the fireplace. Edgar turned to watch the young man, arrested by his good looks, when he was interrupted by the arrival of a formidable lady in a flowing gown, a glass of wine in one hand and a lit cigarette in the other. She wore thick rings on her fingers and gold bracelets on her arms. Her earrings were diamonds. She examined Edgar the way one would a fascinating new dish they were being served.

'And what, pray, are you?' the lady said.

Edgar introduced himself.

'You're Mrs Edna St James,' he said. 'The novelist.'

'But of course,' the lady said, though she turned pink with pleasure at being recognised.

'I very much enjoy your books,' Edgar said. '*Murder on the Zambezi* I thought was wonderful. And *Death Catches the Train*!' He decided to lean into it. Compliments never hurt anyone, he'd found.

'I'd say you are even better than Christie,' he said.

Mrs Edna St James beamed at him in delight; though

he noticed her blue eyes were cold, and more appraising; and that she was not, perhaps, quite as drunk as she first appeared.

'Dear Agatha!' she said. 'We are best of friends, we really are. We are members of the Detection Club together, you know.'

'The Detection Club?' Edgar said.

Edna St James waved a bejewelled hand. 'A new literary society, for only the best and most prestigious of us humble practitioners of the art of the detective story,' she said. 'Christie and I are members, as are Chesterton – of course – Freeman, the Coles, Sayers...' She frowned at the last name, then waved it away. 'Funny Dorothy,' she said. 'You are an aficionado, Mr Waverley?'

'Oh, very much so,' Edgar said. In truth he liked the relaxing simplicity of the mystery novel, which did not put undue demands on one's concentration, being concerned primarily with the convoluted but comforting machinations of plot. People were always getting bumped off in those mystery novels, but there was never anyone to mourn them when they went. They were just convenient corpses.

He didn't say that to Mrs Edna St James. He just smiled in what he hoped was an endearing sort of way.

'What brings you to Feebes Manor, Mrs St James?' he said.

'Oh, do call me Edna,' she said. As though he had passed some kind of test. 'I come often, don't you know. Always such a delight, these little gatherings. One never knows the sort of people one might meet. I see you have recently been to Egypt.'

This caught Edgar off-guard. Edna St James regarded him innocently, anticipating his reaction. Edgar forced a smile.

'How could you tell?' he said.

'You just confirmed it!' she said, laughing. 'It was a guess. You have a deep tan, but it is peeling slightly, which suggests a recent sojourn in the sun. You clean your nails but your hands show calluses, not the sort of thing one expects on an Oxford scholar. It makes one think of archaeology, which *is* a suitable activity for one, however. I would have guessed Iraq, but Egypt is more romantic, and you do strike me as a romantic, Mr Waverley.'

Her eyes sparkled. Her glass was empty. A servant materialised and refreshed her drink. Edna St James paid him no attention. Her hungry focus was on Edgar.

'How did you know I was from Oxford?' he said.

'You arrived in Roderick Holmwood's car,' she said. 'I was watching. It was an easy inference.'

'You are very good,' Edgar said, in genuine appreciation. Edna St James waved it away.

'A cheap parlour trick, my dear, I assure you,' she said.

'You have been to Egypt yourself?' Edgar said.

'Recently, as it happens,' Edna said. 'I was thinking of setting a novel there.'

'Perhaps we crossed paths,' Edgar said.

'I'm sure I would have remembered you, darling,' Edna said.

And I, you, Edward thought.

'Of course,' he said now, 'I imagine our gracious host has many interests in the Levant himself.'

Edna St James burst out laughing.

'What did I say?' Edgar said, feeling his face grow hot.

He had felt himself so grown up and sophisticated up to this moment. But her laughter made him think he was not.

'Dear boy!' Edna said. 'A third of the ships sailing down the Suez Canal right at this moment belong to the House of Feebes, and another third is insured by them!' She hiccupped laughter, took another sip of her glass, and gazed at Edgar over the rim with her kohled eyes.

'Interests indeed,' she said.

'Why am I here?' Edgar said. He felt so small just then. 'Why me, amongst you all?'

She waved a hand. 'Don't take this the wrong way,' she said. 'But if it weren't for Roderick you wouldn't even make it through the gate.'

Edgar understood. It stung less than he thought. Honesty, he appreciated.

'We all play our musical chairs before the great and powerful,' Edna said. 'All of us are scrabbling in the dirt.' She'd lost her smile. Underneath it she seemed older and more sad. 'But you're a scrappy one,' she said. 'You strike me as a scrapper. Perhaps you'll measure up.'

At that moment Edgar hated her. Hated them all. It wasn't *fair*, and that knowledge made him angry. He wanted to burn down the whole damn edifice. Manor and peerage both, and the entire rotten system that held them up above him. Instead, he forced a smile. He raised his glass.

'To your good health,' he said.

'That's the spirit,' Edna said. 'Now, if you'll excuse me, darling creature that you are, I really must circulate. Perhaps we shall talk more at dinner.'

With that, she patted him on the hand and turned. He caught her looking sideways, and with apparent ill-concealed contempt, at a gentleman who stood apart from all the others, his back to them, who was intent, it seemed, on studying a painting, of a king at a dinner party surprised by an apparition.

The king and guests were fabulously dressed, the dishes gold, their jewellery a fortune in precious stones and metal. Yet they all looked uneasy.

21

'IT'S *BELSHAZZAR'S FEAST*,' SOMEONE NEARBY SAID. 'BY Rembrandt. The story is that Edward Feebes won it at cards from the Earl of Derby. Hello. I am Edith. And you must be Edgar Waverley.'

Edgar turned. A small, thin woman with hair cut short into a bob stood there puffing on a cigarette. She had long fingers, nicotine-stained, the nails bitten to the quick.

'You know me?' Edgar said. Wondering, uneasily, if everyone there did; and if so, why.

'I make it my business to know people,' Edith said.

'Yes? And what business is it of yours?'

He had not meant it to come out that hostile. He felt rattled. The man who had been observing the Rembrandt painting turned then and saw Edgar. He watched him quizzically for a long moment, then slowly smiled, with a mouth full of gold and silver teeth. It was an unpleasant smile, and filled with unhidden malice. And it made Edgar quite afraid. The man nodded amicably, then turned back to the painting.

'I am a journalist,' Edith said. Edgar was relieved to find

she had apparently taken no offence at his abruptness. 'You were involved in the publication of a student pamphlet in Oxford denouncing the rise of Adolf Hitler earlier this year. Were you not?'

'I was,' Edgar said, surprised. 'I feel Nazism is reprehensible, a threat to all of Europe.' He thought of the new Nazis he'd met in Cairo. 'Perhaps the world, though that may sound overly sensationalistic. But a threat to the stability of the Empire, at any rate. I merely provided an analysis—'

'Yes, yes,' Edith said. 'I read it. It was thorough.'

'Thank you.'

'Not all British people share your views of the new order in Germany,' Edith said. 'Edward, the Prince of Wales, for one. Lord Rothermere of the *Daily Mail* for another.'

'And they are wrong,' Edgar said stiffly.

Edith shrugged. 'Let me ask you,' she said. 'Your… analysis, as you call it. You are merely concerned for the Empire?'

'How do you mean?'

She smiled. 'You move quietly through the world, Mr Waverley, yet you leave interesting ripples in your wake. You are friends with all kinds of people. Members of the October Club, for instance?'

'I am not a member!' Edgar said. More forcefully than he perhaps intended. The October Club was a discussion group, nothing more. But most of its core members were dedicated communists.

'I did not say you were.'

'I just attended some lectures. H.G. Wells…'

'Wells is an oaf,' Edith said.

'Where are you from, anyway?' Edgar said. He couldn't place her accent.

'Vienna.'

'Then what are you doing here—oh. You are Jewish?'

She smiled without much joy.

'Nazism may not be a threat to your Empire just yet,' she said. 'It's certainly a danger to my people, though.'

'I'm sorry.'

'It isn't your fault. You are sympathetic to the cause of the workers?'

'Where are you coming up with all this?' Edgar said. He did not like being quizzed like this; did not like that she knew so much of him. He felt exposed under her gaze. 'I'm really very sorry, but I find you quite rude, Miss...?'

'Hoffman,' she said. She looked at him with disconcertingly watery eyes. 'I am sorry I make you nervous. I am merely curious. It is my job.'

'Are you working now?' he said.

She smiled.

'Aren't you?' she said.

He felt he had given her too much, too quickly. He tried to mentally regroup.

'I do beg your pardon,' he said. 'I was just feeling out of sorts.'

'It's understandable,' she said. 'This place, this luxury... It is not regular fare for the likes of us.'

'That it isn't,' Edgar said, smiling.

She was fishing for something, this Edith Hoffman from Vienna. But what?

'Perhaps we shall speak again,' Edith said. She turned to leave.

'Wait,' Edgar said on impulse.

'What?' Edith said.

'That man over there. Examining the paintings. Who is he?'

And he glanced again, uneasily, at the man. He still had his back to them. His hair was greasy and thin, his shoulders bunched under the cheap jacket, as though contemplating some terrible violence he was keen to unleash.

Edith followed his haze. A moue of distaste passed her face. She could be pretty in better light, Edgar thought uncharitably. He appreciated women's looks, if not their attraction. There was an exciting vitality in men that he simply could not find when studying a woman.

'He is a thug,' Edith said. She seemed disinclined to discuss it further.

'I feel I should know.'

'What information will you trade for it, Mr Waverley?' she said.

'Trade, Miss Hoffman?'

'That's how it works, you see,' she said, smiling again. He felt drawn to her then and didn't know why. It was a novel feeling.

'What do you wish to know?' he said.

'Tell me something true,' she said. 'Something secret.'

He felt afraid.

'When the hunger march passed through Oxford,' Edgar said, 'I went to bear witness. I saw the man, Abe Lazarus. The union organiser. I spoke with him, briefly. He... He inspired me.'

'You are a member of the Communist Party?' she said.

'No,' Edgar said quickly. 'I did not join.'

He had been tempted. Felt ready to do so. But some innate caution held him back.

'Good,' she said. 'You shouldn't.'

He looked at her, confused, then put it out of his mind. 'Tell me who this man is,' he said.

She looked at the man under the paintings.

'His name is Earl Cody,' she said. 'He is a Pinkerton.'

'A Pinkerton?' Edgar said.

'An American strike breaker. The Pinkertons, they're a detective agency over there. He worked for them. Got kicked out, somehow,' Edith said. 'How you get kicked out of that mob I do not know. You have to be pretty bad, I guess. He made his way over here... Now he works for Baron Feebes.'

'Works doing what?' Edgar said.

She shrugged. 'Someone has to do the dirty work,' she said. 'For others to keep their hands clean.'

She touched him on the shoulder, lightly.

'We'll speak again,' she said. 'I like you.'

He was left alone, once again uncertain of his place there. Then a bell rang, and the butler re-materialised, much like Bela Lugosi in *Dracula*, which Edgar had gone to see in London at the Empire in Leicester Square, and announced that dinner was now to be served in the dining hall.

Candelabras gleamed. White linen shone, it was so clean and fresh. The silverware sparkled. Edward Feebes, dead these many years, watched approvingly from the high wall. Servants glided like silent ghosts. Wine was decanted. Aromas rose, of beef, suet, and creamy sauces.

'Please be seated,' Baron Feebes said.

Edgar found his place. A card bore his name. To his left

should have been Roderick (and who was he seeing that night instead? In whose arms did he seek solace?) but that was not to be, and he saw a handsome young man, of a dark complexion, seated there instead. The man wore a crisp suit with a fabulously folded pocket square, his hair was cut short, with a neat, almost military line at the back. His eyes were very pretty, his teeth white and even. He smiled easily. He smiled right now, and extended his hand for a shake.

'Ernesto Salazar,' he said. 'And you are?'

'Edgar Waverley,' Edgar said.

'A pleasure to meet you, Edgar,' Ernesto Salazar said. He was roughly Edgar's age, but so much more self-possessed. He clearly belonged here, and in places like this. He spoke English well, with only the hint of a soft, foreign accent. He wore a gold Cartier watch.

'I look forward to the snails,' Ernesto said companionably. 'Uncle Henry's new chef, Pierre, used to be at the Regent Palace Hotel. His cooking is quite exquisite, I am told.'

'Uncle Henry?' Edgar said.

'Baron Feebes.'

'Oh. Of course.' He felt foolish.

Ernesto smiled. 'I think of him as my uncle,' he said. 'Though we are not related. Our families have done business together for a long time.'

'You are from Peru?' Edgar said.

'I am!' Ernesto said. 'Though I was raised near Madrid, for the most part, where my family has an estate, and took my degree in Cambridge.'

'I'm an Oxford man, myself,' Edgar said.

'You must be Roddy's friend, yes?'

'I am,' Edgar said.

'Good old Roddy,' Ernesto said. 'An excellent family, the Holmwoods. Ah, pardon me,' and he turned to exchange pleasantries with the woman to his left. Edgar, realising without too much surprise that the conversation had abruptly ended, studied the rest of the table. Across from him was Edith Hoffman, and she was sat next to the novelist, Mrs Edna St James. They were engaged in conversation. From time to time they glanced his way. Once, Edna said something and Edith laughed. Wine was poured. Still the seat to the right of Edgar remained empty.

The baron, Henry Feebes, at the head of the table, said, 'Ah, there you are at last, Earl.' A shadow fell across the table. The man who had been so studiously examining the paintings loomed over Edward. He nodded to the baron, then sat down. The baron raised his glass.

'To a wonderful weekend!' he said.

'Hear, hear!' Ernesto Salazar said, returning the toast. The others all joined in. Edgar sipped the wine. It was agreeable.

The man on his right – Earl Cody, the Pinkerton – did not acknowledge Edgar. He attacked his food ravenously and intently, as though he were battling a mighty foe. The snails, swimming in garlic butter, came and went, as did the oysters, foie gras and whitebait. A soup of cauliflower and cheese was pleasurable, though the man Cody looked at it with evident distaste. Edgar felt quite at a loss sitting there. He should have been making a good impression, he knew. Attempting to forge valuable connections, people who could make introductions into a world he did not belong in, yet wished to enter. He listened to Ernesto Salazar and the woman to his left. The lady was Irish, of the Wallaces who so distinguished themselves during the Civil War fighting on the Irish side. She was from Cork, she said (at this Edgar's ears pricked up, for he knew vaguely that his mother had roots there), but living in Belfast now. Her name was Emma. She seemed rather charming, and the soft lilt of her accent reminded him painfully of his mother's voice. The main course was a whole roast goose, deer with red wine and shallot sauce (Edgar had a small slice, and had to spit out the shotgun pellet that was inevitably still embedded in the meat), potatoes cooked with cream in the French style, and a side of sautéed green beans. There was more wine.

'Is it true you are a communist, Miss Hoffman?' Ernesto Salazar said. Edith turned and smiled pleasantly.

'Don't believe everything you read,' she said.

He laughed.

'It is all the fashion on the continent, is it not?' he said. 'We have this problem in Peru now, too.'

Earl Cody said nothing; he glared at them both with his lips bloodied from venison, his eyes moving between them as he chewed.

'You do not believe in the rights of the workers, Mr Salazar?' Edith said.

'I believe they are paid to do a job,' Ernesto said.

'Paid fairly?'

'What is fair, Miss Hoffman? Men should work in this world. Whether it is in the factory or in the field, or shovelling manure. Work is work.'

'And what is it that you do again, exactly?' Edith said.

For a moment the pleasant smile slipped from Ernesto Salazar's handsome young face.

'There are those who labour and those who work,' he said. 'Without men like me there would be nothing for your workers to do. I *create* wealth, Miss Hoffman. It trickles down, as it should. I am a fair man. It is a fair system.'

'Indeed...' Edith murmured. But she seemed disinclined to pursue the argument further.

'Your workers, they are well treated?' Edgar said curiously. Ernesto turned to him, as if only now seeing him there.

'Well treated?' he said. 'They are like family!'

A strange sound escaped into the conversation. Edgar turned to its source, and was startled to see the American, Cody, his face red, bits of meat and specks of wine on the table before him, gasping for air.

It took Edgar a moment to realise Earl Cody was laughing.

'Family...' Cody said. He seemed to find it too amusing to speak. Baron Feebes watched from the head of the table.

'Enough of this, Earl,' he said.

'Family!' Cody said, his body shaking in mirth.

'I said, enough!'

The American pushed back his chair. He stood up, glaring malevolently at the assembled guests. They shied from his red, rage-contorted face.

'You ain't nothing but dirt,' he said. Then he stalked out.

'An amusing chap,' Baron Feebes said. 'A dreadful lack of manners, but he has his uses. Shall we proceed to dessert?'

'Certainly, sir,' the butler said – the last remark apparently made to him. He signalled, and more food began to arrive.

'Ah, an excellent sorbet,' Ernesto Salazar said. Edgar dipped his spoon into his own confection. It was lemony and refreshing.

'Delicious,' Edith said.

'Quite so, quite so,' Edna St James said.

'Very nice,' Emma Wallace said.

Edgar did not venture an opinion; and no one seemed to care enough to ask.

They ate their sorbet, followed by a course of cheese.

'A wonderful meal, Henry,' Edna St James said when the plates were cleared away. 'My compliments to your chef.'

'It is quite the murder mystery party,' Edith said. Edna St James smiled thinly. The baron laughed.

'I rather hope not!' he said. 'Shall we retire to the library? I have brandy and port waiting, and cigars for the gentlemen. And let me say once again how delighted I am to have you all here.'

They all nodded. Edgar felt they were not guests but convicts, bound in invisible shackles, but what tied each and every one of them to the power of Feebes he could not know nor articulate. He mumbled his thanks and rose with the others. A forced cheer, a gaiety mimed was upon them.

He shuffled with the others to the library.

22

A FIRE BURNED IN THE FIREPLACE, TURNING THE CLOSED confines of the library suffocatingly hot. Leatherbound books that had never been cut open lined the floor-to-ceiling shelves. Brandy and port were decanted and waiting on the low tables. Comfortable armchairs were scattered across the carpeted floor. A gold shovel hung over one wall. A box of Romeo y Julieta cigars sat open on one table, next to a cutter and matches. The butler stood silently, like a waiting owl, besides the drinks tray. He poured out measures and handed them to the assembled guests. He clipped cigars.

Edgar accepted the drink reluctantly. He felt heavy and befuddled, the unaccustomed meal (he was usually a frugal eater) and wine combining with the heat to make him feel out of sorts. He waved away the offered cigar. Baron Feebes and Ernesto Salazar were already smoking with great enthusiasm. They were seated by the fireplace.

A couple of men who Edgar had not yet been introduced to stood chatting together under a painting of three barren islands surrounded by ships. From overheard conversation he knew them to be Colonel Green, latterly of the 20th Lancers regiment, now retired, and a Mr Jacobs of Hong

Kong – a banker of some sorts. Both men seemed ill at ease in the gathering, and had kept their distance all evening.

The three ladies present – Edna, Edith, and Emma Wallace – sat at one sofa against the far wall from the fire, clutching their drinks and chatting quietly.

Finally, the American, Earl Cody, sat alone in an armchair in the shadows, in a sort of reading nook. The lit tip of his cigar glowed when he drew on a smoke.

Edgar hesitated, not sure where to turn. He saw the room in tableau, each figure bent under some unseen weight, anchored and tethered to Baron Feebes as he sat at ease in his armchair, smoking his cigar and drinking his brandy. Edgar didn't know where to sit. He stood there, feeling helpless.

'You. Oxford man.'

It was the American, his voice thick with drink. Of course it was him, Edgar thought. It was always going to be him.

Earl Cody leaned forward. For a moment his face passed into the light. The manic hatred that had so animated him earlier had left his face. He seemed tired and withdrawn, bags under his eyes, the hand holding the cigar almost imperceptibly shaking.

'Sir?' Edgar said politely.

'Come here.'

Edgar hesitated. He was aware of the others, watching, pretending not to. The hatred they were too afraid to show but which poured out of each and every one of them towards this man.

He went over.

'Sit.'

Edgar sat.

'Enjoying the party?' Cody said.

'Very much so, sir.'

Cody laughed.

'Have a cigar,' he said.

'Thank you. I don't smoke.'

'Have a cigar, boy!'

Cody clicked his fingers. The butler hurried over, a freshly cut cigar extended. Edgar took it. The butler applied a match. The thick smoke filled Edgar's mouth and he coughed. The butler withdrew.

No one was watching them. They were studiously avoiding the two of them, Edgar thought. It was as though they were in their own private bubble.

'Why do you hate them so?' Edgar said.

'Hate?' Cody contemplated the lit end of his cigar. 'They're not worthy of hate, boy. They are merely...' He waved a hand and let it fall. 'Pieces.'

'Pieces?'

'To be used when needed, then discarded,' Cody said. He heaved himself out of the chair with some effort.

'Have you seen the gardens?' he said. 'They really are magnificent.'

'It's night-time,' Edgar said.

'Let's get some air. Indulge me. You might learn something.'

'Very well,' Edgar said stiffly. He made to put the cigar away.

'Bring that with you!'

The American stalked out of the library. Edgar followed. Only Edith looked up when he left. She gave him a quizzical look. He shrugged.

It made him feel better, though, that she checked.

He left the room. Along corridors and carpets and servants gliding out of sight at his approach. Following the malevolent figure of the American and the stench of his cigar.

At last they reached doors that opened onto the outside. Fresh, cool air and the smell of fresh flowers. It was a balm to Edgar's senses. It felt good on his face, the air, after the hellish heat of the library.

'Do you know me?' he said to Cody. 'We haven't been introduced.'

'Your name is Edgar Waverley,' Cody said, not bothering to even look at him. 'You were illegitimately born, in Ireland, to a Miss Annie Connolly, current whereabouts unknown. You were adopted by Lily and John Savage. Savage died by suicide after defrauding his partners of a significant sum of money. You were blissfully unaware of this information until this moment. Sit down.'

Edgar sat. He felt light-headed.

'My mother,' he said. The words wouldn't come. His mother was his mother. Not...

'Be a man about it,' Cody said. He turned his face to Edgar then. Shoved it close, his breath reeking of brandy and cigar. 'Everyone comes from somewhere.'

Edgar couldn't take it in. Yet things fell into place despite themselves. His father's mysterious death. His mother's dear friend who'd given him the... given him...

He fumbled in his pocket, took out the old gold watch.

'It was hers,' he said, surprised.

Surprised, too, at how calm he felt.

Everyone had to come from somewhere, after all.

Cody took the watch and turned it over. The light from inside the house caught the gold and the inscription.

'Feebes?' Cody said. He grunted.

'What?' Edgar said.

'Huh.'

Cody gave him back the watch. He seemed to have lost interest.

'Can you walk?' he said.

'I'm not a child.'

'Good. Then stand up.'

Edgar did. His legs held. He'd think about it later. Not now. Maybe not for a long time, he thought.

Cody ambled down a garden path. It was dark. Edgar followed him. He felt compelled.

'You know why you are here?' Cody said.

'I was invited... My friend, Roddy...'

He felt the weakness of his reply immediately.

'You know why they are all here?' Cody said.

A weekend away... festivities in the countryside... dinner, drinks, some hunting in the morning, perhaps... He'd never hunted, he wasn't a proper gentleman...

'No,' he said, defeated.

'To look at them you'd think them simple,' Cody said. 'You'd think me simple, too. Or the old colonel from the Lancers, say. Or the lady who writes mystery books and wears too much perfume. That skinny Jew girl, or the banker from Hong Kong, or the industrialist from Peru, or that Irish lady who don't talk much. They're all... known. They are the face that they show to the world. And you believe it.'

Edgar didn't know why they were there. The American

was a brute. Yet he seemed melancholy. Cody said, 'But you should never believe it, Edgar Waverley of Oxford, who doesn't yet know what he wants to be when he grows up. You should never believe it, because people are not, and never are, *simple*. And for every face they show the world there is one they keep for themselves.' He shrugged. 'It's my job to uncover it,' he said. 'That secret face.'

'Why?' Edgar said.

'Because then it can be used against them,' Cody said.

They'd reached some sort of hedge maze and there they stopped. All was quiet. Edgar wondered uneasily if they would go into the maze. He was afraid to follow Cody further into the dark. But the man had stopped. He smoked his cigar, mopped sweat from his brow. Edgar's cigar had gone out. He stared at it for a moment, confused, then dropped it in revulsion on the ground and trod on it.

'It's a waste,' Cody said.

'What did they do?' Edgar said. 'What do you have on them?'

Cody smiled. He shook his finger in Edgar's face.

'No, no,' he said. 'That's their business.'

'Then what's mine?'

Why had he spoken? He stood stock-still. He thought he heard a rustle in the maze. A squirrel, most likely.

'You are, or were until recently, at any rate, friends with Roderick Holmwood,' Cody said. 'Heir to the Holmwood fortune. And by friend I mean that you were fucking.' He stared at Edgar. Edgar stood still.

'I don't care, in particular,' Cody said. 'In case you were wondering. And no one cares about you at all. Holmwood, though… He's a useful man to have something on. So. Now the baron does.'

Edgar steadied himself. A silent, deeply buried anger was rising through him. He kept it in check.

'Then what?' he said. 'Why are you telling me this?'

'The baron lands the trophy fish,' Cody said. 'But sometimes he lets me keep the minnows. How much money do you have?'

'What? I don't have money, man, I'm a student!'

'I don't need much,' Cody said. 'Ten pounds should do it.'

'Ten pounds! I don't have that kind of money!'

'Then get it,' Cody said. 'What do you have on you now?'

Edgar fished out his wallet. 'I have two pounds and five shillings,' he said.

'That will do, to start,' Cody said. He looked bored now. Edgar stared at him. He felt he was somehow living in a nightmare.

'But this is all I have,' he said.

Cody just waited. Edgar wanted to kill him very much just then. He handed over the money.

'That'll do,' Cody said. 'Remember one other thing, kid.'

'What's that?'

'When someone shows you who they really are – believe them.'

He patted Edgar on the shoulder. Then he walked away, and melted into the dark.

Damn him! Edgar thought. Damn him to hell! He began to shake. The night was so very dark and yet he felt unseen eyes watching. He leaned against a tree. He was suddenly sick. It came out of him, the horrible food and the sickly wine and that brief rancid taste of the cigar in his mouth. It all came out and down on the roots of the tree.

'I'll fucking kill him,' he said.

'Who?'

He jumped. It was Mrs Edna St James, her face in the moonlight different to her party face. Sad, a little lost.

'Nobody,' he said.

'Earl Cody?' she said. 'I often wish… Yes.'

'What do you owe him?' Edgar said. 'What do they have on you?'

She looked into his face, searching – searching for something. What, he didn't know. Whatever it was, she didn't find it. She sighed.

'Nothing,' she said. 'You are being dramatic, child. Drama is more my department, don't you know?'

'I am not a child,' Edgar said. At that she smiled.

'That you very much are, still,' she said. 'But what you will grow into… Well, that could be interesting. Walk me back to the house?'

'Of course,' he said. He tried to wipe himself down. He made a sorry sight, he thought. She looked at him and shook her head.

'I've seen worse at these parties,' she said.

Edgar nodded. He offered her his arm. Edna St James took it and they walked back together slowly. The house towered above them, mock-Gothic, indifferent. Too big for anyone to live in but a statement of permanence, of wealth. He hated them all just then. He realised, with some surprise, that it wasn't going to fade this time. Something had changed in him. He wondered how one learned to live with hatred.

23

WHEN THEY GOT BACK TO THE LIBRARY THE EVENING WAS winding down. The fire in the hearth burned low. The baron had retired to his quarters. The Irish lady, Emma Wallace, was playing chess against Colonel Green, who was losing. Edith Hoffman was missing, as was Ernesto Salazar. Mr Jacobs, the banker, was quietly reading a book.

The silent butler appeared with two glasses on a silver tray. Edna St James took one. She nodded to the other.

'Drink it,' she said. 'It helps.'

Edgar drank. His head swam.

'It has been a long day,' he said.

'It will be better tomorrow,' Edna said. 'They do a good breakfast here.'

Edgar tried to smile. It felt brittle.

'I think I will retire now,' he said.

'I think I will too,' Edna said. 'Goodnight, Mr Waverley.'

'Goodnight, Mrs St James.'

She nodded. She touched his arm lightly.

'It gets better,' she said. 'We humans, we have an immense capacity to heal.'

It sounded like a cheap line from one of her cheap novels. Edgar shook his head and left.

He went up the stairs to his room. Too tired to bathe, he washed his face in the sink, rinsed the taste of puke from his mouth. He felt feverish. All he wanted was to sleep, but his mind was full of swirling, unconnected images: the shadowy form of a woman, the mother he didn't know; his adoptive father dying by his own hand; Roddy, naked in the moonlight, smoking a fag by the window after the last time they made love; the bloodied, brutalised face of the brute, Earl Cody.

Edgar fell on the bed. He was asleep in moments.

When he woke up it was dark. His head hurt indomitably. Something had woken him. He stirred uneasily. What was it?

A faint sound he'd heard, filtering into unsettled dreams. A scream.

That was it. A scream.

He listened. All was quiet. No. Someone moving out there, fast and muffled, steps up the stairs. The stairs creaked. Nothing in the corridor. Then a door closing with a soft hush.

Then it was silent. It was the dark before dawn. He wanted nothing more than to go back to sleep.

Instead he stood up. He wobbled, then found purchase.

It was definitely a scream, he thought.

He listened but there was nothing. No one else had woken up or, if they had, they went back to sleep.

Foxes, maybe. Foxes made a lot of noise.

But the feet in the corridor, the door shutting?

It wasn't his business.

Go back to bed, Edgar.

What kind of a person goes back to sleep? he asked.

A sensible one, his ghost-self answered.

A coward, Edgar answered himself. To move in this world you have to stand for something.

Fool's errand, boy, his ghost-self said. But knock yourself out.

Thanks. I think I will.

He went to the door. He stepped into the corridor. He padded along, his bare feet making no sound. Did the person he heard take off their shoes?

He went down the stairs. The stairs creaked.

No light. He went cautiously. Heard nothing.

No servants, too early even for them to wake up to prepare the house. The house felt cold. Feebes Manor, this pile of architectural kitsch, this pious monument to avarice. He went down the stairs, holding on to the banister. A corridor below, doors leading to rooms. He needed a candle, a light. Something. He staggered in the dark.

There. The library. He recognised roughly where he was. The door was open. The blinds were drawn. The fire had died in the fireplace, only embers still glowed. He tried to see in their light. His foot hit something heavy and soft. He stumbled, lost his balance and fell.

He cried out when he hit the object. He fell on it with a soft whoomp, his fall arrested by... Arrested by...

His mind shied from what it was, what he knew it had to be.

A soft human body, slick with something Edgar knew just then, with certainty, was blood.

He scrabbled to get away from it, every inch of him screaming at him to flee. His ghost-self laughed at him.

Didn't I tell you? Nothing good comes from screams in the night.

Screw you, Edgar answered himself. The corpse moved under him, huge arms, a big belly, swaying like the sea. He fell from it and onto the floor, crawled on hands and knees to get away. Something hard and sharp hit him then. He bit back a curse, felt for it, found a long handle. He stood up, picking up the object, breathing heavily.

The overhead electric light came on abruptly.

A young servant girl stood facing him. Edgar looked down, saw the corpse of Earl Cody, his brutal face brutalised and bloodied, just like in Edgar's dreams.

He looked at his own hands.

Saw he was holding a gold shovel.

Then the maid screamed.

'I came in to prepare the fire, and he was... he was...' The girl swallowed back sobs. 'I saw the body on the floor and Mr Waver... Mr Waverley was standing right above him, covered in blood, holding the... the...'

'The shovel,' Colonel Green said.

'The shovel, yes. It always hangs on the wall, it belonged to the old Mr Feebes, they always show it off to guests, they call it the—'

'The golden shit shovel,' Colonel Green said. 'Yes, we all heard that story more than once.'

'I didn't do it,' Edgar said. He was sitting in an armchair. 'I didn't do it!' He stared at their faces. 'May I have a cup of coffee?' he said. 'And some aspirin? My head is killing me.'

At that the servant girl began to cry again and Edgar immediately regretted his choice of words. Baron Feebes, who stood glowering by the window, nodded to the butler.

'We could all do with some breakfast,' he said.

No one seemed unduly upset that Earl Cody was dead. No one but the maid, at least. And she was just scared, she wasn't *sorry*. Edgar looked at the assembled guests one by one. They looked sleepy, harassed, confused. But none of them was sorry for the loss.

'A nice croissant,' Edna St James said. 'With raspberry jam. I find it does wonders for one's energy in the morning.'

'I could murder a fried breakfast, myself,' Emma Wallace said. 'This is all very upsetting, you understand.'

'You must have seen bodies before,' Edna said. 'During the Civil War and so on.'

'Ah, well, the fight for *independence*,' Emma Wallace said. 'Well, one does see things, of course.'

'Or helps them happen?' Edna said.

Emma Wallace smiled, for just a moment, then shook her head.

'It was so long ago,' she said.

'Yet you will have the north,' Edna said.

'Edna, let's not do this now,' Emma Wallace said. She looked at Edgar. He realised it was the first time she had paid any attention to him.

'Are *you* all right?' she said. 'You must have had a terrible shock. Get this man his aspirin!'

'It was only a shock if he didn't do it,' Colonel Green said. 'If you ask me, he looks guilty as hell.'

'I've already *told* you, I found him like this!' Edgar said. 'I heard a noise, I came downstairs, and I stumbled over the damn body!'

'There's no need for strong language, I'm sure, Mr Waverley,' Mr Jacobs, the banker, said.

Ernesto Salazar, who was pacing restlessly up and down the room, smoking a cigar, stopped and waved the cigar at them.

'None of us are safe here, man!' he said.

'How so?' Colonel Green said.

'If this madman killed Cody, who knows who else is on his... his assassination list? Good god, it could have been me right there!'

'Why?' Emma Wallace said. 'Whatever did *you* do, Ernesto?'

She turned a smile on him. There was nothing sweet in it.

'You know what I mean, Emma!' he said.

'I am sure that I don't.'

'I will have coffee also,' Edith Hoffman said. She was sitting apart from the others, her face pale. 'An aspirin, too. I'm afraid I find this whole affair distressing.'

'Poor girl,' Colonel Green said, sounding sincere. 'Well, an Englishman has a right to be considered innocent until proven otherwise. And I myself agree with Mrs Wallace, a good breakfast will do us all a world of good.'

Edgar stared at them, trying to think. He knew he hadn't killed Cody. Hadn't, as much as last night he'd wanted to. So one of the others in the room had to be the killer. He thought in horror of what this could mean for him. It could kill any hope he had for a decent career. Or worse. Imprisonment? Hanging? He had to prove his innocence!

'I will call my man,' Baron Feebes said, evidently reaching a decision. 'I have a man for this kind of thing.'

He spoke of this the way others would of the man who took out the rubbish.

'Let us adjourn to the dining room,' the baron said.

'What of the body?' Edna St James said.

'Well, it will still be there when we've finished, won't it!' the baron snapped.

'Of course,' Edna said. She seemed cowed. 'I wasn't thinking.'

'It really is a terrible inconvenience,' the baron said. 'A very useful man, this Cody. One should always strive to make oneself useful.'

With this eulogy concluded he turned and left. The others followed. Edgar gave Edith Hoffman a pleading look. She looked back in what seemed like pity, then shrugged.

'We had better… adjourn,' she said.

Edgar almost smiled.

They all sat around the same dining table as before. The servants served coffee and tea and fresh juice. The oranges were from Seville. Eggs and bacon and devilled kidneys, sausages and mackerel and black pudding. Edna St James nibbled on a croissant. Edgar drank coffee and tried to think. He couldn't shake the dead man's face from his mind.

The man had only moments before been alive. Earl Cody, a drunk and a bully, had threatened him so casually – that was what had really hurt. He did it only because he could.

And yet the vitality of the man was unmissable, and Edgar wondered what had made him what he was: who were his parents, what was his childhood like, how did he grow up to be the man he became? For once he was a newborn babe, the first soul in all of creation to emerge from the womb. Then, in a snap of the fingers, a mangled corpse on the floor. No thoughts, no dreams, no fear. What *did* he fear, this Earl Cody? Everybody was afraid of something.

'You look pensive, Mr Waverley,' Edna St James said.

Edgar shook away the maudlin thoughts. He said, 'I was just reflecting how this is not quite like it is in the books.'

'My books?' She looked at him in some amusement.

'For instance,' he said. 'Yes. I mean, the awfulness of it, the violent taking of a life. It is like...' He tried to think. 'In the books it always makes sense, it's a puzzle to solve. But when you see it...'

'Death is distasteful,' Edna said.

'Exactly.'

'Which is precisely why we skim over it,' Edna said. 'It is tragic that a man should die but it is delightful if it is merely to provide a mystery. In real life murder is seldom complicated. It is done for love, or hate, jealousy or greed, and if a woman is to be murdered it is almost always by the husband. This is not the material of which book advances are made, Mr Waverley. My colleagues and I at the Detection Club – I think I mentioned it to you last night? – we feel a strong moral sense. We are as outraged, if not more so, at senseless murder than your average man on the street ever is. But our job is to entertain first, to make death seem almost palatable, like a game of draughts by the fireplace. I've seen death before. It's never pretty.'

'I saw so many die, side by side,' Edith Hoffman said. Her voice was hollow. 'The Nazis are murdering my people back home, and no one lifts a finger.'

'I saw the corpses of my countrymen and women lying in the gutter,' Emma Wallace said, 'murdered by British soldiers, their blood soaking into the dirt.'

'People die!' Colonel Green said. 'No one dies a *natural* death, Mr Waverley. Something or other always kills you in the end. You don't like it? Tough break, I say. You think like a boy, but you must be a man. You must know death. Don't you agree, Ernesto?'

'Eh?' The Peruvian looked startled. 'I don't read those kind of novels,' he said. 'I find them silly. What were you discussing again?'

'Boor,' Edna said, but she said it quietly.

Edgar looked at them all again. Trying to discern, the way a Poirot or a Holmes might, which one of them was guilty. He had the sense then that they were all murderers, that they had all taken a life before, and done it casually. Edna in her fiction only, perhaps. But he was not so sure about the others.

It made him afraid. Yet he realised that a part of him liked the feeling; it kept him sharp. He attacked his breakfast, so far untouched, with a new hunger. The eggs just right and the yolk so yellow, and the sausages made of Baron Feebes's own pigs. They were delicious.

He said, 'Where were you all when the murder took place?'

'We don't know when the murder took place,' Edna said.

'Who was last in the library last night?' Edgar said.

'I was reading a book,' Mr Jacobs said. He spoke so little

that Edgar was vaguely surprised to hear him just then. 'One of Mrs St James's, in fact, *Memento Mori*. Rather good, I thought. When I had finished and bid goodnight only Mrs Wallace and Colonel Green were still there, locked in a mighty battle across the chessboard.'

'We finished our last game shortly after,' Emma Wallace said. 'I won. Then went to bed.'

'As did I,' Colonel Green said, looking sheepish. 'Separately, I mean, of course.'

Emma Wallace smiled a small smile. Edith Hoffman muttered, 'I could hear them through the wall. My room is adjacent to the colonel's. They were… quite loud.'

The colonel blushed. Emma Wallace's smile grew wider.

'I was in bed,' Edith Hoffman said. 'Throughout the night.'

'As was I,' Edna St James said.

'As was I!' Ernesto Salazar declared. 'I retired early, thinking we would be grouse shooting this morning.' He looked annoyed.

'So everyone was asleep,' Edgar said.

'What else would we be doing, man?' Ernesto said. 'You are the one with blood on your hands!'

'I didn't kill him!'

'So you keep saying.'

'Perhaps no one killed him,' Mr Jacobs suggested. They all looked at him in surprise.

'The shovel could have fallen off the wall,' he said. 'Hitting Mr Cody as he stood underneath it. It is heavy, it hit him on the head and he fell, smashing his face further against the floor…' He looked wistful.

'It would certainly make life simpler,' Emma said.

'Absurd!' Colonel Green said. 'Waverley is clearly a murderer! No offence, sir,' he said to Edgar.

'I didn't know him well enough to kill him,' Edgar said. At that, the others exchanged amused glances.

'Oh, I think you did,' Emma Wallace said. 'It doesn't take long, with old Earl, you know.'

'Before you want to kill him,' the quiet Mr Jacobs said.

'Did the world a favour,' Ernesto Salazar muttered.

'Enough!' It was the baron, his hand slamming against the table. Glasses rattled. 'He was *my* man, *my* property! And no one breaks *my* things without my say-so. Do not think his death changes our arrangements.'

They all looked down then.

'Of course, Baron,' Ernesto Salazar said, as eager to please as a frightened puppy. 'One did not mean to suggest—'

'Do not play amateur detectives,' Baron Feebes said. 'I have a man for this kind of thing. He will be here shortly. As for you, Mr Waverley...' He turned a baleful glare on Edgar. 'I am a generous host,' he said, 'but you will find me a fearsome avenger should this be your handiwork. Am I clear?'

'Very much so,' Edgar said.

'Good. Porridge?'

'I am quite full, but thank you.'

'I love porridge,' the baron said.

'Perhaps a little, then,' Edgar said.

'Good man.'

Porridge duly arrived.

Edgar duly ate.

24

THE DEAD MAN STILL LAY, UNDISTURBED, ON THE library floor. He looked worse now, the face waxy, the blood drying and the smell growing as bad as a Victorian sewer someone had forgotten to brick over. Whatever sins he had upon his conscience, whatever dreadful deeds he had committed when alive – and who knew just how long the list went? Edgar wondered – they troubled him no more. The dead bear no more responsibility in the world of the living, he thought. It is those who remain who must deal with their shit.

Edgar stared at the corpse of Earl Cody. Willing it to speak, willing it to tell him what happened. No, not tell *him* – tell *them*. His hands shook when he thought of what could happen. It would ruin everything. It didn't bear thinking about.

Who murdered you, Mr Cody? he said, speaking to the dead. The dead don't answer, as a rule. Edgar's first thought – when he could think rationally again, after finding the corpse – had been that someone was trying to frame him (to use the parlance of the sort of novels Mrs St James wrote). He had examined that thought over breakfast, however

– turned it over and over again in his mind – and he had to conclude, however reluctantly, that it did not hold up. He had been sound asleep in his bed when the murder happened. It was the noise that woke him up, and that mysterious sound of a door being shut – proof enough that one of his fellow guests was behind it.

But no one had *expected* him to go and investigate. No one could predict he would have had a bad sleep, or felt the need to go down, or that he would have stumbled over the corpse, or got hold of the murder weapon…

Anyone could have responded to Cody's scream. It just happened to be Edgar.

Which left, what? The others, all six of them. He discounted the baron. He had the strong feeling that if Baron Feebes wanted someone gone, they would be gone, and not making a mess on the man's own library floor. Whoever did this, in fact, did not merely strike at Earl Cody – they struck at the House of Feebes itself. For if Earl was the baron's instrument, and the six guests all suborned to his will in some way, then murdering the baron's own man in his *own home* was tantamount to a declaration of war.

One of them was still not entangled enough, not so fully under the thumb of Feebes as to submit meekly. *One* of them killed Cody in revenge.

But what if there was more than one? He felt his thoughts spinning out of control. What if two or even more of them had worked in tandem?

But no – he had heard only *one* set of footprints, only *one* door shutting. Only one of the six killed Cody.

Who, then?

Take your pick.

'You seem deep in thought, dear boy,' he heard a voice. Looked up to see Edna St James, smiling benevolently, smoking a thin cigarette that smelled of cloves. 'Wonderful stuff,' she said, 'Colonel Green has them shipped from Malaya. I can read your face, Mr Waverley. You are trying to work out a puzzle.'

He smiled at that, feeling self-conscious.

'Am I that transparent?' he said.

'No. Just young. And,' she said, 'in quite the predicament. I have been thinking much as you have been, of course. Trying to fit together the pieces of the puzzle. I do not believe you did it. You have kind eyes.'

'I doubt that would hold up in court,' Edgar said.

'Court?' she laughed openly. 'None of this will end up in *court*, Mr Waverley. None of this will ever be *public*. Too many reputations are at stake. But justice... can still be served. How about if you and I team up? Try to solve this little mystery together? Unless, of course, you think I did it.'

Edgar rose to his feet. He had been sitting there staring at the corpse for too long. The golden shovel, used nearly a century ago by some poor soul to dig up precious excrement half the world away, still lay where he dropped it. Nothing in the room had been disturbed.

'You could have,' he said.

'I was fast asleep, Mr Waverley,' Edna said. 'As you should have been.'

'Did you hear him?' Edgar said. 'Did you hear anything?'

'No. I am a sound sleeper. So what do you say?'

'The baron told us not to play amateur detectives.'

She looked at him in amusement.

'Do you always do what you are told?' she said.

'I thought he had sway over you,' Edgar said.

Edna St James considered.

'The baron has power,' she said. 'Influence. It is not a, how do the Americans say it, a one-way street. We feed off his power more than he does off us. It is nothing more than a mutually beneficial arrangement.'

She sounded like she was trying to convince herself.

'Why does he need you at all?' Edgar said, curious. At this she didn't smile.

'I am famous,' she said. 'Influential. In my own way. I move amongst commoners and royalty, read by station porters as I am by sheikhs. I am welcomed in places many wouldn't be.'

'I apologise,' Edgar said.

'You spoke out of ignorance, so I will accept it,' she said. 'But you would be wise not to underestimate me, or the others.'

'All right,' he said, accepting it. 'Then tell me about the others. What are their uses?'

She smiled again. She stubbed out the cigarette in the ashtray and steepled her fingers (a little theatrically, Edgar thought) as she considered.

'There's Colonel Green,' she said. 'Retired military man. The Butcher of Amritsar, they still call him.'

'That was *him*?' Edgar said, appalled. He had heard of the Jallianwala Bagh massacre. Indian protesters were herded into a square with only one way out and, once penned in, the British soldiers opened fire. The dead numbered in the hundreds. 'He gave the order?'

'And never lost a wink of sleep over it, the way he tells it,' Edna said. 'The Feebeses used their influence to exonerate him, and now he's theirs. Not that Britain could have admitted wrongdoing in the matter, but anyway. Colonel Green would have done for Earl quite happily, I think, though perhaps with less mess.'

'He was blackmailed, too?'

'That I don't know,' Edna said. 'Colonel Green is the baron's man, but perhaps… I do know he loathed Cody all the same.'

'There's Mr Jacobs, then,' Edgar said.

Edna shrugged.

'A banker,' she said.

'Bankers don't make good murder suspects?'

'They make great murder suspects,' Edna said. 'I had a banker as the killer in *The Deadly Cost of Murder* a few years back.'

'I haven't read that one yet.'

She shrugged again. 'Oops,' she said.

'What did Cody have on him?'

'I don't know what dirt Cody dug about anyone here,' Edna said. 'That's their business.'

Edgar rubbed the bridge of his nose. He felt a headache coming. He said, 'Any of them could have done it, then.'

'Sure. Including me, or you.'

'What about the Austrian girl? Edith?'

'She's a communist,' Edna said. 'You should stay away from her. She's trouble.'

'You don't like communists?'

'I don't like the girl.'

It was Edgar's turn to shrug. They were just passing time, and with every moment that went by his future shrank. He said, 'The Irishwoman.'

'Emma Wallace. Yes. She runs guns for the IRA.'

'Really?' He looked up, curious. 'What is she doing here, then?'

'There's money in guns, Mr Waverley.' She looked at him in what was half amusement and half pity. He resented the look. Like he was a child. Naive.

'The baron?' he said.

'Money has no nationality, Mr Waverley. It has no loyalty, no flag. It is the thing whole in itself.'

'All right,' he said. He tried to think who was left.

'Ernesto Salazar,' he said.

'Ah,' Edna said. 'That handsome son of a bitch. Yes. Now, he makes a good suspect.'

'You think he did it?'

'I think if he crawled any further up the baron's backside he would give our gracious host a hernia,' Edna said. 'Is he capable of murder? As sure as eggs is eggs, as the fellow says, Mr Waverley. Yes. My money would be on him... He is a nasty piece of work, that one.'

'This is all just speculation,' Edgar said. 'We need a way of figuring this out. Perhaps we can construct a timeline of the events. Who was the last person to see Mr Cody alive?'

'I believe that was you,' Edna said. 'I saw you both talking by the maze. You then said, "I'll kill him" – with a swear word I won't repeat.'

'You heard.'

'I did.'

'It sounds damning,' Edgar said.

'It does.'

'But I did not kill him! I never saw him again!'

'Let's take a walk,' Edna said. 'Retrace our steps, as it were. Perhaps we'll find something. A clue.'

'I am beginning to suspect clues only happen in novels,' Edgar said.

'You wouldn't be wrong, Mr Waverley,' Edna said. 'In real life the murderer often walks away free, unless he happens to be found standing over the corpse while holding the murder weapon.'

She wasn't smiling now.

He said, 'You think I did it. You actually think I did.'

'I think it's possible,' Edna said. 'In life the simple explanation is often the right one.'

'But you're still going along with my attempt to prove otherwise?'

She stood up.

'Why not?' she said. 'If nothing else, I am grateful to whoever did it. I hated him too, Mr Waverley. I often dreamed of doing the deed myself. Come, let us partake of the outdoors for a while. Who knows what clues we may find and, if nothing else, at least we can enjoy the sunshine.'

Edgar followed her along the corridor and to the outside. It seemed to him a week since he had first arrived here, but it had not even been twenty-four hours. In that time he had had his illusions about his lineage and family shattered; his innermost secret exposed and contemptuously exploited; his shoes ruined by his own vomit, and then the final indignity, stumbling over a corpse. There was dried blood on his hands he could not scrub off. He felt more alone than he had ever felt in his life. And the only thing that sustained him now, he realised with some surprise, was the hatred

Cody had kindled in him and blown into a full, roaring flame.

It was not even Cody he hated, but the whole goddamned edifice that had made an Earl Cody necessary. This parasitic world of wealth and privilege that he could never have, this edifice of Feebes in which the current baron was merely the latest in a line of... of... leeches... His thoughts wandered. Something about leeches. The good thing about leeches was that you could squish them, sooner or later. And all that blood they'd sucked would come right back out again... His fingers were bunched uselessly into fists. He made himself relax. It was sunny outside and the air smelled fresh when he got further away from the manor. Ernesto Salazar and Edith Hoffman were both on the veranda, smoking, he with a cigar and her with a thin rolled up cigarette. Ernesto scowled. Edith gave Edgar a quizzical look, then turned away and continued blowing smoke in silence. Co-conspirators, perhaps. Or maybe they had just had sex. Or they were just waiting out the time.

In the daylight, the maze looked less impressive. It was just a hedge, trimmed to within an inch of its life by some hidden gardeners, every green leaf accounted for and in its place. In the daylight, Edgar could see the tree where he threw up, and some footsteps in the soft earth, deep and heavy, that could have been Cody's.

'What are we looking for?' he said.

'Maybe nothing,' Edna said. 'Maybe something. You were both talking, then he walked away. This way.' She pointed.

'Yes,' Edgar said, remembering how the American seemed to just melt into the darkness. In the daylight his passage was more noticeable. Footsteps, then thick ash on the ground near an elm, where he must have stood and smoked for a while. They followed it further, around the maze – 'There!' Edgar said.

He pointed to the cigar stub on the ground, next to a fountain in which naked marble nymphs frolicked with water running down their bosoms. Edna bent down, scooped up the cigar and smelled it.

'So?' Edgar said.

Edna nodded very seriously.

'It's a cigar,' she said.

Then she cracked up. Her laughter sent a blackbird flying up in alarm, and Edgar, surprised by the unfamiliar feeling, felt the laughter bubbling out of him, escaping at last in a series of bellows. He laughed until his sides hurt.

'It's a... a *cigar*!' he said.

Gradually it faded. When it did he felt sad.

'What do we know?' he said.

'Not much. When he left you he came here. He smoked on the way. He dropped his cigar.'

'Was he alone?'

'I am not sure,' Edna said. She pointed to the ground. Footprints, possibly. Too faint, Edgar thought, to know for sure who they belonged to. And even if you could – then what? Anyone could have come here, at any time. But still—

'Who was not in the library when we got back last night?' he said.

'Edith and Ernesto,' Edna said promptly. 'But Cody was not murdered last night, Edgar. Whoever he met here didn't kill him. Or, well, they might have, but only much later, and not here.'

'Oh, it's impossible!' Edgar said.

Edna shrugged.

'We're just passing time,' she said.

'Where do the footprints lead?' Edgar said. But he already knew, even as Edna said, 'Into the maze.'

'Of course.'

She smiled.

'Shall we?'

'And get lost?' he said.

'If you do, cry out,' she said, still smiling, 'I'll come to your rescue.'

25

EDGAR WENT INTO THE MAZE.

At the first turn he was separated from Edna. She went left. Edgar went right. He didn't know what he was looking for. A clue, he supposed. Had Cody arranged to meet someone by the fountain? Or had they found him there, confronted him, perhaps? Edith or Ernesto. The others had been inside. The maze walls were high. He couldn't see outside. It was surprisingly quiet, too. He took a step and paused, something on the ground bothering him. When he looked down he saw it was a dead blackbird, its body flattened in the dirt, feathers caked in blood, its eyes blind. He swore in surprise and backed away.

From somewhere in the distance he heard Edna call, 'Are you all right, dear?'

'I'm fine!' Edgar shouted back. But he was shaken. He knelt beside the dead bird. A fox had killed it, perhaps. How could he tell? It was another murder, and just like Earl Cody's, there was no easy way to solve it. *Had* there been a fox? He thought uneasily of his sense the night before of something moving in the maze behind the hedge as he and Cody spoke.

Had someone been standing there, listening to them?

He stepped over the dead bird and kept exploring the narrow paths of the maze. He took each turning, not sure anymore if he was near the centre now or on the outskirts.

It was getting hot and there was no shade. He blinked sweat from his eyes and thought he saw something then: snagged on the hedge to his left was a small piece of white cloth. He pulled it out, spread it and discovered it was a handkerchief, monogrammed with the letters ES.

Ernesto Salazar.

He pocketed the handkerchief and kept walking, slowly now. Here he found something unexpected. There was a small hole in the lower part of the hedge, and he got on his hands and knees and peered through it. He saw it led to a secluded little spot in the hedge itself, just big enough for one or two persons to fit in. He crawled through. Inside he was completely hidden from the world. A blanket had been laid down on the ground here. It smelled peculiar. He felt around with his hands and found something pushed into the branches. He pulled it out and realised it was a rubber. It had been used. He threw it away, disgusted, then wiped his hands on the blanket. A picture had begun to emerge in his mind. He'd seen enough. He crawled out and stood, supporting himself on the hedge, as he thought.

Ernesto and Edith had both been absent from the library the previous evening. They had not seemed particularly friendly towards each other, in Edgar's brief acquaintance with them. But people did not need to like each other to screw each other, as Roddy once told him.

Edgar kept walking. He looked for anything else but

couldn't find it. He heard voices, and realised that he was near the outer wall of the maze.

'It will be bad for us,' the first speaker said. It was a man – Mr Jacobs, he thought. The Hong Kong banker.

'Hold your courage, goddamn it,' the second speaker said. A woman – Emma Wallace. 'This will be handled quietly.'

'Not if the stupid boy did it! There will have to be policemen, a trial. It could end up in the *newspapers!*'

'Feebes owns the newspapers, Ezra.'

'Not all of them,' the man replied. 'And he has enemies. They will use it against him.'

'So?' the woman said. 'We don't owe him. The Feebeses are nothing but new money people. They're little more than merchants.'

'Merchants rule the world now, Emma! Our connection can't be exposed – too much is at risk as it is!'

'You handle your side of the deal, Ezra. All you have to do is keep the money moving. I will handle the guns.'

'We could be done for treason!'

'Really, Ezra, you are making too much of this. Hold your nerve and it will all be cleared away. What was that?'

Edgar froze. He had moved, and when he pressed against the hedge the leaves had very softly rustled.

'Is there someone there?' Emma said loudly.

Edgar didn't dare move.

'Probably a squirrel,' Mr Jacobs said.

'Let's go back in the house. Say nothing more of this.'

Edgar heard Mr Jacobs mutter something, but it was too soft this time for him to hear. The two moved away.

Edgar waited. When he could hear them no longer he began to try to make his way out of the maze. He kept turning but getting nowhere, and then, turning one more time, found himself stumbling straight into Edna.

'Did you find anything?' she said.

'How do we get out of here!' Edgar said.

'Oh, it's easy,' she said. 'I'll show you.'

'What did you find?' Edgar said.

'Nothing but a dead bird,' Edna said. 'I think a fox got to it.'

He followed her, took one right turn and then another and then, somehow, they were out again.

'It really isn't very large,' Edna said.

26

ON A DAY OF SUMMER, IN THE YEAR 1933, BEING OF sound mind and sound body, if suffering somewhat of a nervous disposition brought about in the aftermath of the discovery of a corpse, and being the chief suspect in its murder, an experience from which he was fervently hoping to one day recover, the young Edgar Waverley (as he still went by that name), twenty-one and not unhandsome, though somewhat more bedraggled of late, and with bloodied hands, lumbered slowly and reluctantly towards the luxurious confines of Feebes Manor.

The manor stood there in its splendid isolation. Its army of servants moved, unseen, behind the walls. In the kitchen cooks barked and under-butlers scurried, maids rushed and valets valeted. No one dared touch the slowly decomposing corpse still lying in the library, nor scrub the stain of dried blood, though someone did thoughtfully open a window to let out the worst of the gaseous air. The corpse, one Earl Cody, formerly of the United States of America and latterly of Great Britain, an empire on which the sun, as they said, never set, did nothing. Death, Edgar reflected, would do that to a man.

Large and busy in life, malevolent of spirit and full
of spite as he was, this former agent of the Pinkerton
Detective Agency and one-time instrument of the House
of Feebes, who had an evident genius for uncovering the
secret misdeeds of others, had sadly concluded his final
investigation and ventured forth into the unknown. One
could not take blackmail material with them into the Great
Beyond, of which Plato himself, in his *Apologia Socrates*,
wrote, that to fear death is to think one is wise when one
is not. And though no one knows whether death is the
greatest of all blessings to man, yet men fear it as though
they already knew it to be the greatest of evils.

And why Edgar was suddenly thinking of Plato, who
was himself dead and buried these two thousand years and
more, he couldn't tell. He felt rattled.

His mind buzzed with possibilities, accusations and
demands as he approached the manor. The smokers were
no longer at their post. A hush had fallen over Feebes
Manor, not of mourning (for there was no one to mourn
the passing of Earl Cody) but of a nervous anticipation.
A fragile equilibrium, post-mortem, had been established
in the intervening time since the discovery of murder. But
sooner or later, Edgar knew, it was to be irrevocably broken.

This shattering of equilibrium, this breaking of the peace,
false as it might have been, was heralded just then by the
appearance of a column of dust far in the distance. As it
grew nearer, Edgar saw that it was caused by a black car,
as small as a beetle in that distance, which rode, in some
unseemly haste, towards the manor.

As the sound of the engine became apparent to those
inside, the guests began to emerge one by one.

First to appear was Ernesto Salazar, wearing dark shades and scowling as he clipped and lit a fresh cigar. Behind him came Emma Wallace, holding a martini. She looked coolly at Edgar, then at the approaching car.

Jacobs came next, followed shortly by Colonel Green. Both men stood shoulder to shoulder and watched as the small black car, slowing down now, came to the gates.

Last and seemingly reluctantly came Edith Hoffman. She watched the car come in through the gates and up the driveway. Her face was pale. She came to Edgar and took his arm.

'We should talk,' she said quietly.

'I was hoping to speak with you, too,' Edgar said.

'Not here,' she said quickly. 'Let's go inside.'

The car stopped. The butler materialised out of some hidden passage, just in time to hold open the car door as the driver climbed out. He was an unassuming man in a black suit and a sober tie, and he wore a trilby hat. He raised the hat in greeting at the assembled guests, and Edgar recognised him then: it was the same man who had approached him some time back to question him on his activities in Egypt.

'It's a pleasure to have you back with us, Mr Harker,' the butler said. 'Even under such trying circumstances.'

'Good to see you again, Reginald,' the man in the trilby hat said. He took a small satchel bag from the car. 'Is the baron inside?'

'In his study, sir. He is awaiting you.'

'And the corpse?'

'In the library, sir.'

'An unpleasant business, Reginald.'

'Yes, Mr Harker.'

'We shall try and clear all this up, what?'

'Indeed, sir.'

'Well, lead the way.'

'Certainly, sir.'

Edgar watched as the man in the trilby hat ascended the steps. Harker studied each of them in turn, but didn't stop. When his eyes met Edgar's the man in the trilby hat merely nodded in recognition, then passed on, into the cavernous inside.

'Who is he?' Edgar said.

'Harker?' Edna St James said. She had been quiet all this while. 'Something in the Secret Service, I believe.'

'I see,' Edgar said.

'Balderdash,' Ernesto Salazar said. 'He's with the Foreign Office.'

'I thought he was with Scotland Yard,' Colonel Green said.

Edgar felt Edith Hoffman pull on his arm again. Her fingers were bony, her grip surprisingly strong.

'We'll talk now,' she said.

He acquiesced and followed her indoors. She led him to an alcove under a flight of stairs. It felt a little like being inside a confession booth.

'I don't believe you did it,' Edith said. 'But it looks bad for you, Edgar. We need to think of a way to help you out of this.'

'Where were you last night?' Edgar said. 'When the others were in the library.'

'What business is it of yours?' Edith said.

'You were in the maze, weren't you?' he said.

'What if I was?'

'Did you confront Cody?' he said.

'Like you did?' she said. 'I heard you saying you would kill him.'

'So you *were* there!' Edgar said. It came out accusingly, he realised.

'If you must know,' Edith said.

'With the man Salazar?'

She smirked. 'We were fucking,' she said. 'Does that shock you?'

'But he is loathsome!'

'A few years ago there was a fire in one of his factories,' Edith said. 'Over a hundred workers died. One day I will slip Mr Salazar a fatal poison in his coffee and watch him die. But in the meantime...' She shrugged. 'Ernesto's a good lay,' she said.

'One or both of you spoke to Cody that night,' Edgar said.

'So what?' Edith said.

'So...' He didn't know what to say. She was right, he thought. It was meaningless.

'Earl was still alive last night,' Edith said.

'One of you must have done it,' Edgar said doggedly. 'But why? What does he have on you?'

'Nothing,' she said. 'He has nothing on me.'

'Then why...'

She shook her head. 'You are grasping at straws,' she said. 'What we need to do is try to figure out how to help you.'

'Why would you want to help me?' Edgar said.

'I see potential in you, Edgar,' she said. 'You are currently the worst kind of man – you are aimless. But a man can be pointed in the right direction and be of use. I sense you're searching for a purpose. A target. I sense your values are true. It's why I came here, you know. To meet you.'

'Did you?' he said, startled.

'To assess you for myself,' she said. 'We've had our eye on you for some time now.'

'We?' Edgar said.

'There is a movement in the world,' Edith said. 'Of workers, for the workers. I am speaking of socialism, Edgar.'

'You are... I mean... What can *I* do?' he said. It came out plaintive, he thought. She gave him a pitying look.

'All you can do,' she said, 'is your part. But first we need to get you out of this mess.'

Her pitch caught Edgar off-guard. He tried to rally.

'The only way to help me is to find the real killer,' Edgar said.

Edith said, 'That won't do any good.'

'Why not?' Edgar said.

She looked at him, her eyes pale and merciless, then shrugged.

'Oh, what the hell,' she said. 'It's because I killed Earl Cody. I did it to protect you.'

It was as sorry a group of specimens as one could expect who assembled later that day in the library, where Earl Cody's corpse had mercifully and at last been removed. The murder weapon was hung back on its place on the wall. The blood scrubbed off the floor by servants who must have had names, but no one had bothered to find out. Servants, like children, were best seen but not heard.

No one felt sorrier for himself, perhaps, than Edgar Waverley, née Savage, who sat somewhat apart from the others, as though on trial. From Edna he got a sympathetic look. From Edith, a stare that held within it calculations he could not account for. The others glanced his way occasionally, then looked away. They gave the strong impression they wished for the whole sorry ordeal to be over with.

The man in the trilby hat came in then, accompanied by the baron. Harker, if that was his real name, had interrogated each of them over the intervening hours, as the sunlight of late afternoon lingered, painting the skies a pleasing palette of yellows and reds, then faded into the bruised blue-and-black of early evening.

When Edgar was called in, in his turn, he was determined to say little. The man in the trilby hat nodded, but did not acknowledge their previous acquaintance, and neither did Edgar. The baron, standing by the window, turned and glanced at Edgar without much interest. In the sunlight he was short and squat, turning to fat, and his hair was thinning. He looked less than impressive.

'This is the Waverley boy,' he said. 'Friend of Roddy Holmwood. He was the one standing over the corpse.'

'I see,' Harker said. He turned his full attention on Edgar then. 'You say you discovered him by accident.'

'I heard a cry and decided to investigate,' Edgar said. 'I wish now, fervently, that I never left my bed.'

The baron snorted.

'Woke us all up!' he said.

'Did you have reason to kill Mr Cody?' the man in the trilby hat said.

'I... no.' Edgar hesitated. He glanced the baron's way.

'One of the guests says they saw you arguing with Mr Cody late last night,' Harker said. 'Harsh words were exchanged.'

'I did speak to him,' Edgar said. 'But I didn't even know the man!'

'Baron, would you mind?' Harker said. The baron glowered, then shrugged and left the room.

'You can speak freely now,' Harker said. 'I am a friend.'

'I do not think I have any friends here,' Edgar said.

Harker smiled.

'You are not wrong,' he said. 'But you had best tell me the truth, Mr Waverley. Only I can help you now. If I choose.'

'We spoke,' Edgar said. 'He threatened me.'

'With what?'

Edgar felt himself blushing.

'Some indiscretion,' he muttered. 'Like I said, I didn't even know him!'

'He knew you, though,' Harker said. 'I found this when I searched his room.' He took out a small brown envelope.

'You searched his room?' Edgar felt so foolish. Of course. He should have done that himself, they must have searched everyone's rooms. He really was an amateur, he thought. Stupid. Stupid!

'What is it?' he said.

'The negatives of some candid photographs,' Harker said. 'Of an act illegal in its nature.'

'Did the baron...?'

Harker shook his head. 'No,' he said. 'He did not see these. I expect they were meant to blackmail your friend, Mr Holmwood. You were incidental.'

'I am ruined,' Edgar said.

'Perhaps. Tell me, Mr Waverley. Do you love your country?'

'Of course,' Edgar said, startled.

'You would serve her? You would lay down your life for king and country?'

'Gladly.'

'I thought as much. You strike me as a competent young man, who could go far in the Service.'

'The Service, sir?'

'The Secret Service,' Harker said. 'You will be graduating Oxford soon. In need of employment. We need good men. If you choose, you will officially become a part of the Foreign Office. With training you could become useful. I had my doubts when we first met, though we have been monitoring you for some time. But you have shown your mettle here, Waverley. You identified a threat, and you took care of it. You got your hands dirty, and in my line of work, that counts for a lot. Of course, your execution was poor. But those things can be learned.'

'You think – you think *I* murdered him?' Edgar blurted.

Harker smiled again. 'Come, come, Mr Waverley,' he said. 'There is no need for pretence between us. And as for these negatives – there is not one reason for them to see the light of day, is there?'

He took a lighter out of his pocket. A flame flickered into life. It licked hungrily at the small brown envelope, traversing it until it blazed. Harker threw the burning matter into the fireplace.

'There,' he said. 'That's that.'

That was earlier. Now Harker came in, the baron in his

wake, and he stood in the library and looked coolly at the assembled guests.

'You might be wondering why I have gathered you all here,' he said.

'Not really,' Ernesto Salazar said. 'Get on with it, man.'

Harker nodded.

'I have interviewed each of you,' he said, 'and searched all your rooms—'

At this there was a collective pouring of outrage, which Harker ignored.

'And I have built a picture of what transpired,' he said. 'When one looks into a person's murder, it is dangerous to be swayed off the clear path by the temptation of clues and puzzles. They are more often than not a mere distraction. For instance, two witnesses heard Mr Waverley argue with Mr Cody the night before the murder. But Mr Waverley was seen shortly after in the library, which Miss Wallace, Colonel Green and Mr Jacobs can all attest to.'

'True, true,' Mr Jacobs said. Emma Wallace nodded.

'There is, also, the matter of the footsteps Mr Waverley thought he had heard on the stairs, but could not be sure of. And of a door being softly closed.'

'Yes!' Edgar said. He had all but forgotten that.

'It was merely Miss Wallace, returning to her own room after a night spent in, ahem, another's,' Harker said.

Colonel Green smirked. Emma Wallace looked down demurely.

'And you did not hear the scream?' Edgar said.

'*I* heard plenty of screams,' Edith Hoffman said, looking at Emma and the colonel pointedly. 'And the colonel does make the most outlandish sounds.'

'Now, listen here!' Colonel Green said.

'Enough,' Harker said. He spoke quietly, but his voice carried. They stopped, and watched him, ready to pass sentence.

'First and last,' Harker said, 'I examined the corpse itself, as well as the instrument of its demise.'

'The shit shovel,' Ernesto said.

'It was not strongly affixed to the wall,' Harker said. 'A fact which has now been remedied. Here is what happened. You were all in your beds—'

'Or other people's beds,' Ernesto muttered, to some laughter.

'While Mr Cody, a known drunk, had stumbled into the library in the early hours of the night, no doubt searching for a drink. Alcoholism is a curse that afflicts many, and I wish devoutly one day it will be gone from the world.'

'Amen,' Ernesto said, toasting him.

'Mr Cody stumbled in the dark and hit the wall,' Harker said. 'The marks on the left side of his body are consistent with this hypothesis. He caused such a ruckus that he cried out in pain – the same faint scream Mr Waverley must have heard.'

The others looked Edgar's way. He looked away.

'The impact of Mr Cody's collision with the wall unfortunately caused the shovel hanging overhead to come loose from its position,' Harker said. He sounded so reasonable, Edgar thought. 'The shovel fell and hit Mr Cody on the head, causing a major injury. Mr Cody then fell, further hitting his head on the floor, in what proved to be the second, and sadly fatal, injury. I am satisfied this was nothing more than an unfortunate accident, and can find no one at fault but for the servant, perhaps, whose task it was to ensure the proper hanging of the shovel on the wall.'

They sat in silence.

It was, Edgar thought, an expedient solution. And an expedient solution, he was fast learning, was better than the truth. It was a harsh lesson to have to learn; and he felt as though another piece of his soul had detached itself and floated away.

'Well, good riddance to all that,' Ernesto Salazar said. 'I will take my leave early, if that is acceptable to you, Baron?'

'I suppose you should all bugger off,' the baron said. 'Thank you, Harker, for helping untangle this knot. I trust the corpse and so on –' he waved his hand vaguely.

'Will be taken care of, of course,' Harker said.

'Good man. Good man.'

One by one they said their thanks and their goodbyes and left. One by one down to the front, where their luggage already sat, packed by the servants. They spoke little as they left.

'We will talk again,' Edith Hoffman said.

'Yes,' Edgar said.

She reached out for him, hesitated, then went to join Ernesto in his car.

'I booked us a table at Rules,' Ernesto told her. 'With some oysters and a bottle of Moët on ice.'

'My hero,' Edith said. Ernesto gunned the engine. The slick little Bentley roared to life and sped away from the manor. Edgar watched it go.

'It was not a very *satisfying* solution,' Edna St James said. She came and stood beside him. 'But I suppose it will have to do.'

'I suppose so,' Edgar said.

'Goodbye, dear boy,' Edna said. 'Perhaps we'll meet again another time.'

'I hope so,' Edgar said. He meant it. 'And thank you for your kindness.'

She shook her head, then left too. The others went past Edgar, barely acknowledging his presence, all but for Colonel Green, who said, 'I had you down for it, Waverley.'

The butler, who had been hovering, came to usher Edgar to his car. He handed him his bag.

'Thank you, Reginald,' Edgar said.

He got behind the wheel. He thought of Edith, who had heard Earl Cody blackmailing him; who went and spoke to the man after, and lured him, on some pretence, into the library, where she had brained him with the shovel. It was her he had heard running up the stairs and into a bedroom. She must have been more than a little taken aback that, having gone to such trouble to protect Edgar, he had blithely walked down and got himself entangled in the murder. Now he was tied to her. And now, too, he knew, he would be tied to Mr Harker, the man in the trilby hat. And he thought of Jesus, who said that no man can serve two masters. For either he will hate the one, and love the other; or else he will hold to the one, and despise the other. And which to choose, he thought. Which to choose.

'Drive safely, sir,' the butler said.

Edgar felt the engine wake and thrum, and he put his foot on the accelerator and his hand on the clutch, ready to go.

'Do you know, Reginald?' he said. 'I don't think I will.'

PART FOUR

THE SPY

VASILY

1964

27

CARS BEEPED THEIR HORNS IN THE DISTANCE, A SOUND so embedded into the background of the city that he barely noticed it anymore. But they were driving on the main road. No car would come by here, and no one would think to notice him. When the end comes, Edgar Waverley once told Vasily, it comes at you so fast you never see it. But this wasn't how it was supposed to end for *him*!

Not like this. Not lying in a garbage dump in the alley behind the Balmoral Hotel in Cairo, his blood slowly seeping into the dirt.

Or maybe, he thought, this was how it was always going to end.

Take a look at your life, Vasily, old boy, he thought. A rat chattered as it came to check out what all the commotion had been about earlier. Its nose twitched as it smelled the blood. Vasily tried to scream at it, to tell it to go away. Nothing much came out. The rat seemed to shrug. I'll catch you on the next turn of this merry-go-round, it seemed to say. No hurry.

No, Vasily thought. This was definitely not how it was supposed to end. People thought this was what the job was like, all shootouts and car chases, like in that Bond picture he went to see a couple of months back at the Metro on Soliman Pasha Street with Henrietta Feebes, the one where Honor Blackman wore that blue bikini. It was the sort of movie the censors would never have allowed into Russia, and rightly so, but still, he enjoyed it. He wished then that his job had been like in the movie, but the truth was it was mostly bureaucracy, and paperwork, and he was never in any real danger. For one thing, he was posted to a relatively friendly country and, for another, he wasn't an illegal or anything like that, not an *agent* – those poor bastards put their lives on the line, but for him, he was a case officer; if anything went south he'd just be deported politely by the Egyptians back to Moscow.

So how did he get himself into this mess!

His vision was becoming blurry. Someone was bound to come by sooner or later and find him. It wasn't too late to call a hospital, or the hotel doctor – the hotel *did* have a doctor on call, didn't it? Yes, it did, he thought, Dr Sharawi, of course, a good doctor even if he was an Egyptian; he spoke beautiful French and the European guests trusted him implicitly. Which had been useful for Vasily, who'd put the good doctor on his payroll, one of the very first local agents he'd recruited when he got to Cairo. You couldn't have enough agents, not in Cairo. It was, as Edgar told him back in Moscow just as he was leaving, a hub of second-rate spies.

The Englishman had said it kindly. For Vasily, at that time, any assignment outside Moscow sounded wonderful. He'd spent years studying at the Institute of Foreign Languages in Leningrad, hiding within its high walls the old czarist army barracks where Vasily was to be fashioned into a proper agent of the KGB. For the first year it was seven a.m. wake-up and a run around the freezing courtyard, followed by a dress inspection. Any deviation, an unshaved cheek, a loose button, would result in punishment like the loss of Sunday leave. Then breakfast and classes. He studied English, German and a concentration in Arabic, for he had it in his mind from the beginning he might like to serve in the Middle East. Often as a child he had dreamed of Egypt and its pyramids, spending hours staring at the postcards that had fallen out of the old German Baedeker in his grandmother's house.

Sitting by the fire, hearing the wind outside and the howl of wolves which he might have just imagined, he was taken to flights of fancy as a boy. In that time, too, he had fallen under the spell of *Timur and his Gang*, the story by Arkady Gaidar about the boy, Timur, who together with his friends worked in secret in their village to help the needy, such as the families whose men went to fight in the war; and they faced up to the hooligans who threatened the peace of the village. There was a hint of romance too. He had liked that. He wanted to be just like Timur – Timur in his secret world, moving unseen as he helped the people.

Vasily had been an idealistic boy, good at sport, bright for his age. A little solitary, perhaps. His father went to fight the Nazis and never came back. After that, a new spirit animated Vasily. Before, his world had been small, contained and safe. His father's absence had opened a wound in the dome of the sky, and through it he could see now the vast forces that animated creation, great powers indifferent to human suffering, a wind blowing that could flatten the entire world. The Great Revolution was the first step in humankind's effort to halt, even reverse that chaos. To bring about a new and better world. Vasily wanted to help. He wanted to make himself useful.

He joined the Komsomol at fourteen and became leader at his school. After the Great Patriotic War was over he lived with his mother and his brother Ilya in a small, crowded apartment in Leningrad, sharing the bathroom and kitchen with three other families. His mother got a job working in a farm machinery factory. A friend of his father's came by one day, and shook Vasily's hand solemnly. He had brought with him a tin of black caviar and a loaf of rye bread. It was the first time Vasily had tried caviar. He discovered he liked it. The man had been in the NKVD with Vasily's father. He listened to Vasily with a quiet intensity, treating him like an adult.

'Do you know what you want to do when you graduate from school?' the man said.

Vasily said, 'I want to follow in Father's footsteps. I want to join the Ministry of State Security.'

The man clapped Vasily on the back.

'Keep up your studies,' he said. 'Get good grades and good reports from your teachers, that is the important thing.'

Later, Vasily had to lie there in the dark as his mother and the man made love behind the thin privacy screen. All around him people snored, farted, talked, in the kitchen Tovarisch Sidorov brewed tea, at the kitchen table Tovarisches Babikov and Oborin played chess. Vasily lay on his back and dreamed of his future. It did not escape him that not everyone could get caviar, that the man (he tried not to listen to the sounds the man was making behind the screen) was privileged in some way over the rest of them in the apartment. But he justified it in his mind that the man served his country and the revolution, no doubt putting his very life in danger. And besides, wouldn't it be nice to be one of those who could get caviar himself? With this he fell asleep.

The rat was back. Eggshells with rotting yolk baked on top of discarded sardine tins. Time passed and Vasily, lying on the garbage heap, felt it move. Where were the Zabbaleen when he needed them? Even rubbish didn't go to waste in Cairo. Someone would find him. He just had to hold on till they did.

How naive he had been. It was before the truth about Stalin came out. That was... when? He had started at the Institute by then. The man, that friend of his father, visited them every so often. He took a shine to Vasily, and put in a good word.

Stalin... They were all shocked, first at the death, the entire world in mourning. The great leader, silenced. Then whispers of Khrushchev's secret speech at the 20th Congress, denouncing the former leader. Word leaked: of Stalin's atrocities, the Terror, the millions in the gulags, the savagery of the secret police. Was that when Vasily first began to have doubts? No, it couldn't be. He had been a loyal cadet, his studies were going well, not just languages but espionage work in general – he enjoyed the shadowing exercises on the streets of Leningrad, tailing and being tailed in his turn and trying to shake off the people who followed him. He learned to use ciphers and codes, the stuff Henrietta Feebes once called 'all that James Bond shit'. If she only knew... Of course, everyone in Cairo already assumed he was a spy, it was just that they didn't care. The Soviets were a friendly power to Gamal Abdel Nasser, valued guests and advisers in Egypt, suppliers of rockets and planes. No door in Cairo was closed to him. He wasn't like those illegals who had to assume some dead child's identity, and send messages to their operators from a hidden radio transmitter in the dead of night. He had wanted to be one, at first. But his career path, as it turned out, lay elsewhere.

Three years ago he was newly arrived – fresh off the Tupolev, as the long-term staff on the ground called it. Not his first plane ride, that had been to Paris, where he spent six months in the Sorbonne, masquerading as a student while making contact with left-wing groups, getting some field experience and improving his French. He had enjoyed Paris, its festive air, how freely everyone spoke, shouted, sang, danced, made love. He listened to jazz and read novels in the Série Noire from Gallimard. The students he met were filled with revolutionary fervour, wanting to tear down the bourgeoisie structures of post-war society. If this was what being a spy was like, he thought, drunk on freedom and cheap red wine one night outside an English-language bookshop popular with leftists in the Quartier Latin, then he had chosen well.

When his time there ended he was recalled back to Moscow, a shock of grey, the air subdued. His apartment was a horror of concrete in a newly built workers' block, cold and run-down. The baby – they had had the baby by then, he and Svetlana – the baby was colic. Sveta was tired, her face wan. She never complained. They'd met his second year at the Institute. A strong, sensitive woman. He had been madly in love. Now he got up every morning and made his way under cold grey skies to Lubyanka, where he shared an office with Alexei Ivanovich, an old acquaintance from back at the Institute, the two of them minor functionaries of the KGB machine, awaiting orders. They passed the day reading other people's mail and dreaming of their next assignment.

One day Edgar popped his head in through the door. Vasily met Tovarich Waverley during his first year at the Advanced School in Moscow. Waverley was already a legend in the KGB, of course. The Englishman had risen to the very top of the British Secret Service, all the while passing information back to Russia. He had been recruited before the Great Patriotic War and was a true believer, never accepting payment for his work. He was uncovered by the CIA in the mid-fifties, who alerted their British counterparts. Waverley managed to escape via Beirut, and received a hero's welcome once safely in Moscow. After his debriefing he was given a small apartment just off Gorky Street, along with a small KGB pension.

After that grand public reception, though, Waverley was neither wanted nor trusted, for one should never trust a spy. He cut a mostly lonely figure in those days. It was only due to the intervention of Alexander Shelepin that Edgar was given the task of speaking to the recruits at the Advanced School, to share some of his experience with them. He had taken a liking to Vasily, for whatever reason.

Perhaps it was because, of all the recruits, only Vasily seemed to value the older man's stories. The others looked on the Englishman with suspicion, and often made fun of his halting Russian, sometimes even within earshot. Vasily thought it was disgraceful. The man was a hero. He had put his life in danger every day for twenty years for the revolution.

'Vasily!' Edgar said. 'Permission to come inside?'

'Edgar,' Vasily said. 'It's good to see you!'

Alexei, too, stood up. He formally shook Waverley's hand.

'It is an honour, tovarich,' he said.

'Nonsense,' Edgar said. 'Please. You are the true... What is this you are studying?'

Vasily and Alexei exchanged guilty glances, for spread on their shared desks were photographs of a decidedly lurid nature, which they had been admiring at their leisure.

'My, my,' Edgar said. 'I see they have you boys working hard defending Mother Russia.'

'Her name's Galina!' Alexei said. 'She's the mistress of a member of the State Committee for Standards and Product Quality Management. We're intercepting his mail on suspicion of improper conduct, tovarich.'

'Quite the lady,' Edgar said.

Alexei quickly pushed the nude photographs back into their envelope.

'Sorry, tovarich,' he said. 'We are just doing our jobs.'

'I understand,' Edgar said. 'Vasily, may I have a word?'

'Of course, Edgar,' Vasily said, pleased. He followed the Englishman out to the corridor.

'Perhaps we could take some tea in the canteen?' Edgar suggested.

'I would like that,' Vasily said. They fell into step together, just as they had back in the Advanced School, often taking walks together in the pleasant countryside outside Moscow where the KGB school sat.

'This is not what you had hoped for, I take it,' Edgar said.

'I will do the work I am assigned,' Vasily said. 'But you are right, of course. My place is in the field, just like you were!'

Edgar laughed gently.

'I worked at a desk much like this one for most of my service,' he said. 'I read people's letters just as you do now. I was never in any danger, and it was seldom very exciting, do you know. Nor am I sure that I achieved anything... But enough about me, Vasily. I have no doubt your assignment will come soon. I just worry that you are too much of a romantic still.'

'Is that bad?' Vasily said with a smile.

'It is in this line of work,' Edgar said. 'It is no use telling ourselves fairytales when all we do is dig in the dirt. You must see your work for what it is. You must see clearly.'

But Vasily, just then, did not pay any mind to the older man. The Vasily of the moment, however, and all too late, saw Waverley's meaning.

It was just too bad that this moment of clarity came while bleeding to death in the hot Egyptian sun.

28

Vasily blinked sweat and tears of pain, heard the distant honking of the taxis, the shouts of hawkers, an argument breaking out beyond sight between two men. The rat was back again, joined by a friend. They watched Vasily in enraptured fascination.

'Shoo,' he tried to tell them. 'Shoo.'

But the words didn't come. Every breath hurt. He'd broken ribs. There was a knife in his side, he thought. It stemmed the bleeding somewhat. How long before one bled to death? He should know this. He had studied this at the Advanced School. He never even got to kill anyone, not in the line of duty anyway. They had people to do this kind of wet work. Career spies didn't murder people. Career spies did paperwork and tried to make friends and occasionally blackmailed them.

What was he doing three years ago?

Cairo. The embassy. Yuri Gagarin.

Right.

Everything was new and exciting when he first landed in Cairo back in '61. He couldn't get used to the heat, the traffic on the roads, the colours. Moscow had been grey and utilitarian. There was order in Moscow. Here cars zigged and zagged around donkey-pulled carts, children running across the road, people crossing every which way, and he was astounded by the sight of the women in their fashionable Western clothes, and the men in suits and ties or in Arabic dress, the lights of this big, cosmopolitan city, its bars and casinos, the smell of the sheesha pipes, the cries of the mosques to prayer. His grandmother's Baedeker had nothing on the real Cairo, or so it seemed to Vasily just then. He quickly realised the Arabic he learned was not Egyptian Arabic, and set to learn the dialect, all the while, of course, carefully maintaining the pretence that he spoke none of it.

'Be dumb,' Edgar had counselled him, back in Moscow. 'Learn to be overlooked, and let them underestimate you – to their detriment.'

Vasily had presented himself to the ambassador. Vladimir Yakovlevich Yerofeyev was a professional diplomat, who'd served with distinction in Turkey, Britain and France. He had looked at Vasily with cursory interest, shook his hand and welcomed him to the Soviet mission. The embassy itself sat in Dokki, across the Nile from downtown. When Vasily arrived the whole place was a construction site. They were building a new, grand embassy as befitted the Soviet Union and its increased presence in this new, United Arab Republic. It was not even a decade since Nasser led the revolution that brought down King Farouk and ushered in a new age to the ancient kingdom. Nasser embraced socialism, and he looked to the Soviets to help him with his military ambitions in the region. He'd even nationalised the Suez Canal, dealing a major blow to the British who were Egypt's one-time paymasters.

'We must cultivate Egypt,' the ambassador told Vasily and the assembled men of the rezidentura. 'With our help she could become a shining beacon of socialism in the Middle East. Do not attempt heavy-handed approaches to Egyptian high-ups. Do not engage with the local communist party. We have a hold here now, and I do not need you mucking it up. Tread softly, gentlemen.'

Later, the men of the rezidentura sat in the rezident's office over vodka and cigarettes.

'The truth of it,' Tovarich Kirpichenko, Vasily's new boss, said, 'is that we hardly need to, what did the ambassador call it, use "heavy-handed" tactics with these Egyptians? Our men infiltrate every level of the army and government here. We train them, we provide them with weapons, and the colonels and generals willingly share most things for a bottle of good whiskey. No, Vasily. What I need you to do is turn your focus to the other Western forces who meddle in Egyptian affairs. This place is riddled with diplomats and spies. Bring me someone I can use, not now but further down the line. Use your good looks if a woman presents herself, use persuasion if you meet a fellow traveller, or blackmail if the opportunity presents itself. You will be based out of the Balmoral Hotel downtown. Many foreigners stay there. Make friends. Make yourself popular. You can ride?'

Vasily said that, yes, he could ride. He had learned back when they were still living in the countryside, before Leningrad, before his father went away to war.

'Good. Life here revolves around horse riding. Perhaps you could go to the races. They are very popular. I do not care much for horses, myself. And I am too ugly to seduce a duchess.' He laughed, and the others joined in.

'I have a wife in Moscow,' Vasily said. The others turned and looked at him. One smirked.

'Moscow is Moscow,' Kirpichenko said. 'This is Cairo. And you must do what you must for your country.'

The others all laughed. Vasily resented them. He was glad he would not be based out of the embassy. His cover was as a trade delegate. He even had an expense account. He intended to use it.

The Balmoral, when he arrived there, was a hub of unimaginable luxury. His head spun. The porter carried his suitcases to his room. It was early evening, the heat of the day dissipating into a pleasant warmth, and a faint breeze over the Nile cooled Vasily's face. There was an electric fan in his room, an enormous bath, soft carpets. From his balcony he could hear the noises of the city and the clinking of glasses and the laughter and chatter of guests as they assembled for what he soon learned was the traditional twilight gin and tonic.

This custom, much favoured by the British, could easily go on for three hours, following which they were all loose-tongued and merry, and ready for their meals. Nothing happened early in Cairo. The days were too hot and the nights were when things came alive. Vasily shaved, washed, and dressed in his finest suit. He examined himself in the mirror.

He cut a dashing figure, he thought to himself. He was thinking of growing a moustache. His eyes, he thought, were his best features. Pale blue with a hint of grey, the colour of Lake Baikal. Sveta often told him she fell in love with his eyes. His hair might be thinning slightly. He had to admit that. Not enough to worry him, not yet. He should seek out a good barber, get a more fashionable haircut, more Western, he thought. Though he was still a Soviet official, a junior member of the trade delegation, nothing more. But still. He could give out the impression of a man on the make, a man given, after all, to trade and international business more than he was to revolutionary ideals. Just a *person*, to put it another way.

He put a comb through his hair, splashed Aqua Velva on his cheeks, nodded to his reflection and jauntily left the room. That night he dined in the hotel restaurant, sitting by himself, quietly watching the other diners and trying to make out their connections and interactions.

'Learn first,' Edgar had told him. 'The tools of the spy are people. Know them before you attempt to use them.' Edgar had the air of a man who knew what it was like to be used. For now Vasily sat there, enjoying his steak and his glass of wine, rare luxuries that would be rare no more, not as long as his assignment here lasted. It made him feel strange. In Russia, only the Nomenklatura – the elite – had access to luxuries. Yet here he was, simple Vasily, with more than even members of the Politburo could have. Or so it seemed to him.

'Hello,' a voice said. A man stood over him, smiling pleasantly, indicating the unoccupied chair across the table. 'Mind if I join you? Daniel Pikorski, I work for Feebes Bank. Transportation and logistics insurance. How do you do? You must be the new Soviet spy.'

He laughed, clearly making a joke. He had an American accent. Vasily forced a smile of his own.

'Please,' he said. 'Do sit down. I am Vasily Sokolov.' He used his cover name. 'Soviet Trade Delegation,' he added.

'I thought you guys always travelled in groups,' Pikorski said, sitting down. He indicated to the waiter, who hurried over with a new bottle of wine. 'It's rare to see a Russian alone.'

Vasily shrugged. 'I don't know why that should be so,' he said.

'I merely mean... No, never mind,' Pikorski said. 'I like to meet the new arrivals, Vasily – can I call you that? Vasily? Call me Daniel. I have been here two years now, living out of the Balmoral, do you know. I can't bear the thought of having my own place. The amount of staff you need to maintain those stone piles! I prefer coming and going as I please. I assume you do too.'

He smiled. Vasily smiled too. He wondered what the man's game was. Was he looking to turn Vasily? Was he CIA? Alternatively, was he looking to defect, and measuring out who he thought was a Soviet agent? Either way the man was a fool, to make an approach this early on and in public. Unless he was just what he appeared to be, a bored banker looking for a new drinking partner.

This was the problem, Vasily reflected. You just couldn't tell. Everything could be false or everything could be real. Or something in between. Edgar had said much the same to him in Moscow.

'Your suit, is it Russian?' Daniel Pikorski said. 'It looks uncomfortably hot. I recommend linen. Remind me, and I will give you the name of my tailor. The man can work wonders with material.'

'I'll be sure to do that,' Vasily said. He indicated to the waiter. The man came and cleared his plate away. Vasily stretched and took a sip of the wine. It was good wine.

Pikorski took out a silver cigarette case and proffered it to Vasily.

'Thank you,' Vasily said. He took a cigarette. Pikorski fished in his pocket, came out with a gold lighter. He lit them both up.

'A bank, you say?' Vasily said.

'Feebes Bank,' Pikorski said. He blew out smoke. 'It's one of those old, family-owned British firms. Had an office here for many years due to the Suez Canal, of course. I came on board in the Hong Kong office. I went to Harvard business school, you see. Did three years at Chase Manhattan, then got headhunted to Feebes. I talk a bit British now, don't let that fool you.' He winked. 'Cairo's fun,' he said. 'You'll like it here, Vas.'

Now Vasily was more than a little confused, not sure if he was being propositioned or set up. And being called *Vas*? This was a new ignominy. There was just something about Pikorski that didn't add up. He'll look him up tomorrow, he thought. Though of course Pikorski's story will check out.

'What do you do here?' he said.

'I can show you around, old man!' Pikorski said. 'Listen, I was just with some friends at the bar when I saw you sitting here. Why don't we take this wine with us and you can join us? I'll introduce you to everyone. How about it?'

Vasily thought quickly.

'Sure,' he said. 'Why not.' Pikorski smiled, like a hunter who'd just collected a trophy. Vasily followed him to the bar, the waiter following with the wine in its bucket. They went to a table by the window. Three others already sat there, two women and a man.

'We're quite an international gathering,' Pikorski said. 'This is Dirk Müller of International Rakete, he's working on Nasser's new missiles.'

'Hello,' the young German said. He shook Vasily's hand. 'Pleased to meet you.'

'This is Stéphanie Bernier, of the Compagnie financière de Suez—'

The woman wore her hair short and had a brisk, no-nonsense manner.

'Hello,' she said.

'And this is my good friend and employer, the Honourable Henrietta Feebes.'

Vasily stared. The girl was roughly his age, with an easy, assured poise that must come, he thought, from a life of luxury. Her eyes were hidden behind expensive, dark sunglasses. When she smiled it was like the sun slowly rising over the pyramids (an image he was yet to see, but which he had since come to associate with her).

'Please,' she said, 'call me Henrietta. These titles are so… *feudal*, don't you think?' She turned that smile on him. He found himself standing there at a loss.

'And you are…?' she said.

'Vasily Sokolov. Soviet trade d—'

'Of course,' she said. 'We were told you were coming. Replacing old Volkov, aren't you?'

'You're well informed,' he said.

'Trade is the life blood of capitalism, Vasily,' she said. The others laughed politely. Vasily shrugged.

'The Soviet Union must act within a world at odds with our ideals,' he said. 'But we are not at war, and we have much to offer.'

'Nasser certainly seems to think so,' Stéphanie said.

'Your firm,' Vasily said. 'Was it not the Suez Company, before Nasser nationalised it?'

'*You* are well-informed,' Stéphanie said.

'And you are now a banking and investment firm?' Vasily said.

'We are indeed,' Stéphanie said. 'Make no mistake, Mr Sokolov. Our business here is business. None of us are here to see the pyramids.'

'Though they are quite a sight,' Pikorski said.

'Neither am I, Miss Bernier,' Vasily said. 'I too am here for, as you say, business.'

'Then we shall all get along famously!' Pikorski said. 'See, I told you he'd fit right in. Where shall we go tonight? The El Cohara casino? The Havana?'

'How about a nightclub?' Stéphanie said.

'The Arizona? Skyrockets?'

They fell to discussing plans. Vasily watched them, felt a kind of excitement he had last felt in Paris. Here were young people, much like himself, free to go and do as they pleased. He tried to push the thought away. But the more he did the more did Moscow loom in his mind, grey and depressing, somehow.

'Well, Mr Sokolov?' Henrietta Feebes said. 'As you are the guest, we must leave the decision to you.'

'Please,' he said. 'Call me Vasily. These titles are so... *feudal*, don't you think?'

She laughed. He found that he liked making Henrietta Feebes laugh.

'Very well, Vasily,' she said. 'Where would you like to go?'

Vasily smiled.

'I'd like,' he said, 'very much to see the pyramids.'

That was a good night, he thought as he lay bleeding. Though the bleeding had almost stopped, he realised. He tried to move. Pain shot through him. No. He would not try that again. He felt groggy and his mind wandered, unanchored in time. A good night, yes. They had taken a taxi to the place where Cairo abruptly ended. They were all a little drunk at that point. Pikorski negotiated with some Bedouins, and before Vasily knew it he was sitting on top of a camel, swaying dangerously under the moon and the stars, riding across the desert. The pyramids rose under the night sky, ancient and majestic. They took his breath away. They dwarfed Stalin's Seven Sisters, or so it seemed to him then. They were nothing like the Hotel Ukraina or the Ministry of Foreign Affairs or the Kotelnicheskaya Embankment Building.

They had stood here in the sands for thousands of years. Before capitalism, before communism, when men made themselves gods and slaves died for their glory.

He saw the Great Pyramid of Giza and his mind swirled.

Then Henrietta Feebes said, 'Let's climb it.'

Vasily followed her as though bewitched. He stared up at the huge stone structure. The steps were more or less even. Henrietta didn't wait for him. She hauled herself over the first step, reached for the next. In moments she was above him, moving like a spider on a wall.

'You're mad!' he said, laughing.

'Come on!' Pikorski said. He followed Henrietta.

Stéphanie touched his arm. 'We've done it before,' she said. 'It's fun.'

She began to climb. Vasily tried it himself. It was easy going at first. He caught up to Stéphanie, then overtook her.

'Hey!' she said.

Henrietta was above him, moving fast. Vasily overtook Pikorski, who was taking a rest, breathing heavily, hanging there between heaven and earth. When Vasily looked down, the ground was very far away. He could see Cairo spread out beyond the desert, a great big beast alive, glowing with all the lights in the world. It might have been a second-rate assignment, he thought. It wasn't Washington or London or Berlin. But he would make it his own. He would show those bastards back in Moscow what he could do!

'Almost there!' Henrietta shouted, high above him. Vasily strained, moving as fast as he dared, the ancient stones holding as they had for untold centuries. Still he couldn't catch up with her, and then, with a cry of triumph, she reached the top ahead of him. He climbed the last few steps and collapsed on the narrow summit.

'It's worth it,' Henrietta said, 'for the view.' He heard her laugh, then the click of a lighter. She drew deeply on a cigarette.

'An ugly dawn,' she said, 'but a beautiful day.'

Vasily sat up. He could see all of Cairo from here, maybe the world. Henrietta offered him her case. Vasily took a cigarette and let Henrietta light it. Her hand touched his briefly, then withdrew. They smoked in silence, sitting on top of creation.

29

His mind wandered. It had been a good night. His memory played tricks on him. Did they stay up there all night, and in the morning watched the sunrise, and the mail plane from Alexandria flying low overhead? He might have dreamed it. He had tried to kiss her, just the once. Henrietta pushed him away gently, smiling.

'It won't be like that,' she said. 'But we will be friends.'

Somehow he knew she was right.

'Besides,' she said, 'I think Stéphanie likes you.'

Stéphanie… *He* didn't think she liked him. Now he still couldn't make his mind up if she ever did. He remembered one night, about six months later. They were in the hotel. The window was open, and Stéphanie was by the window, her naked back to him, smoking a cigarette. Vasily was in the bed, watching her watching the world outside.

'I worry about Daniel,' Stéphanie said. She turned and looked at Vasily. 'He is not like us, Vasya. You and I understand the rules of this game. But Daniel, he is different. He is sensitive. He still has… ideals, I think.'

'He's a banker, Fanny,' Vasily said, 'for crying out loud.'

'I just don't want him to get hurt, that's all,' she said. She stubbed out her cigarette and came to sit on the bed.

'You won't try to *trap* him, will you?' she said.

Vasily laughed. 'I told you,' he said. 'I'm just a trade delegate.'

'A Soviet trade delegate with a permanent room at the Balmoral and an expense account,' Stéphanie said. 'Old Volkov never made much of a secret of it, you know. I think it worked in his favour. He just sat at the bar every night and waited for someone to come. He figured sooner or later someone would.'

'Well,' Vasily said, pulling her down to the bed, 'communism *is* in the right, and there are enough people in the West to think so, too. Why wouldn't they wish to help the revolution?'

'After Stalin?' she said. 'Maybe a few less people do.'

'I don't want to talk politics,' he said, drawing her close. He went to kiss her.

'You didn't answer me,' she said.

'What was the question?' he said.

'If you were going to trap Pikorski.'

'What would the KGB need with a banker?' Vasily said. 'Besides, I get all my information from a very beautiful agent of the French Service de documentation extérieure et de contre-espionnage.'

She laughed.

'Do *you* ever think of defecting to the West?' she said.

'Why, are you offering?' he said. He wasn't sure now what game they were playing. She lay very close to him. He could feel her heat.

'I know some people,' she said. 'If you were interested...'

Vasily kissed her.

'I love my country,' he said.

'They have bugs here, don't they,' she said. 'I don't mind if they listen in.'

She nestled into him, and then they didn't speak at all for a while.

'Report, Tovarich Sokolov,' Kirpichenko said. They sat in the secure room at the embassy.

'I am embedded in the ex-pat community centred around the Balmoral Hotel,' Vasily said. 'So far I have refrained from using active measures' – this being the current euphemism for attempts at recruitment, blackmail or undue influence of all sorts – 'in favour of gaining trust and a greater understanding of the social circles operating in the small Western community—'

'You sound like a sociologist,' Igor Saakashvili said. He was a dour Georgian and a middling operative, the sole but inevitable representative of Department V. His job was to dream up contingency plans for assassinations and sabotage. At any given moment he was ready to carry out a sniper attack on Nasser, to poison the water of the River Nile, or blow up the pyramids in a false flag operation. In Vasily's humble opinion, Saakashvili was a useless piece of shit, but that didn't matter. Every large rezidentura had a Department V operative in the office, and as long as he *stayed* in the office then Vasily had no problem with him.

Ignoring Saakashvili, he said, 'I have identified one potential asset for recruitment which I am currently evaluating.' He didn't mention his suspicion that Pikorski was CIA. 'I am cultivating several high-placed sources in the shipping and banking industries. I am also looking at gaining trust with the West German scientists currently assisting the Nasser regime on their rocket programme—'

'We have those well in hand, Vasily,' Kirpichenko said. 'I find these ex-Nazis distasteful, myself, but... we're in effect the ones bankrolling the military here. Concentrate on the others. There are not as many Americans here and the tide is in our favour, but make no mistake, the Americans will be angling to sooner or later gain influence back in Egypt – if we let them. There are diplomatic staff, and the American University is just crawling with CIA operatives. I want to see some results soon.'

'We could blow up the Aswan Dam,' Saakashvili said.

'We're the ones *building* the Aswan Dam, Igor,' Kirpichenko said.

'I'm just saying,' Saakashvili said.

'I'll get on with it, boss,' Vasily said.

The rat was talking to Vasily now. It had the voice of a CIA debriefer. What happened then, Vasily? *Did* you get on with it? Did you produce *results*?

It depends, he wanted to say. Three years ago. Kirpichenko. He wasn't a bad boss. A professional. What happened in '61?

Vostok 1. He remembered that night...

They heard it on the radio first. Yuri Levitan on Radio Moscow broke the news: Gagarin was in orbit. The Soviet Union had launched the first man into space.

Vasily was in the bar at the Balmoral. Everyone was. For

that whole day it didn't matter who you were and where you were from. Everyone gathered at the bar, listening to the radio, hoping for news. They looked up at the skies, and couldn't imagine there was a man up there, orbiting the Earth. Then the nail-biting moments as the cosmonaut re-entered Earth, the fear that it would all go wrong. How could the censors approve this? But already Vasily knew why. This was momentous. Even if Gagarin never came back, he had made it into orbit. The first human in space was a Soviet! He had felt such a swell of pride that day. The Soviet Union had shown the world what it could achieve. They made history!

They all drank vodka that night. Nothing else would do. Then the next day, on the news. Gagarin had landed safely. He was paraded as a hero through Moscow. There was a formal invitation from the embassy, as befitted a civilian trade delegate: the ambassador hosting a party for valued guests. Vasily guessed this was to be repeated across the world. The Soviet Union showing off its medals. Anyone who was anyone was invited.

Vasily dressed in his finest new suit. When he arrived at the embassy, the taxi driver of course smoking through the open window and honking his horn at anyone who dared get in his way, he realised how minor he was in the machinery of things. Expensive black cars with their uniformed drivers blocked the road. He saw Henrietta Feebes step out of a limousine accompanied by the Foreign Minister, Mahmoud Fawzi. Fawzi was a career diplomat, not a politician. He served under the former king and now he was close to Nasser. For the rezidentura he was white gloves approach only. Photographers snapped photos.

Henrietta Feebes smiled for the cameras. She and Fawzi vanished inside.

'Just drop me off here,' Vasily told the driver. He handed him notes. He walked through the queue of cars. No one was going to take *his* photo. Inside there were waiters circulating with trays. Food and drink. Musicians played Shostakovich. He saw Ambassador Yerofeyev chatting to the American ambassador. Pictures of Yuri Gagarin and the rocket going into space adorned the walls.

'I heard he landed in a potato field,' Saakashvili said, passing him by. 'Had to ask an old lady and her granddaughter to use the phone to call Moscow. Scared the shit out of them.' He wandered off.

'Hello, Vasily,' Stéphanie said. She materialised beside him, holding a glass of champagne. 'How decadent,' she said.

He kissed her on the cheek.

'Stéphanie.'

'I'd like you to meet my friend Rusty,' she said. A handsome German in a suit, a twinkle in his eye, extended his hand for a shake.

'Wolfgang Lotz,' he said. 'A pleasure. Please, call me Rusty. All my friends do.'

'Vasily Sokolov,' Vasily said.

'I heard you ride horses,' Lotz said.

'Sometimes,' Vasily said.

'You should join us at the club. Sometimes,' Lotz said.

'I would like that,' Vasily said. He studied Lotz with interest.

'What do you do, Mr Lotz?' he said.

'This and that,' the man said. He had this easy smile...
Vasily didn't like him.

'Mr Lotz is independently wealthy,' Stéphanie said.

'Aha.'

'Excuse me,' Lotz said, 'I see my old friend Lieutenant
General Mahmoud of the air force wishes to have a word
with me. No doubt about the bottle of good whiskey I
owe him! Stéphanie, always a pleasure. Mr Sokolov, I look
forward to seeing you soon. Come to the club! Goodbye,
goodbye.'

'What does Mr Lotz really do?' Vasily said.

Stéphanie smiled. 'No one knows for sure. He's an ex-
Nazi. Wehrmacht, so I'm told. Lots of them about in Cairo.
But Rusty's not a bad one as far as they go. Mad about
horses. Friends with all the generals – *they* all love horses
too.'

'Horses and whiskey?' Vasily said.

'And whores.'

Vasily watched Lotz thoughtfully. He looked like a
playboy. He could be a spy. Bundesnachrichtendienst or
Mossad, who the fuck knew. Or he could just be a rich
playboy who liked riding horses. That was the problem in
Vasily's line of work. You had to assume no one was exactly
who they said they were.

'He does *look* like a Nazi,' he said, and Stéphanie laughed.

There was vodka. There was caviar. There was music,
and he and Stéphanie danced. Vasily went outside and lit
a cigarette and watched the feluccas on the Nile. He didn't
need to turn to know when Henrietta Feebes came to stand
beside him.

'It's a lovely night,' she said. 'You must be pleased. About Gagarin, I mean.'

'It's incredible,' Vasily said. 'Somehow it makes you feel so big and so small at the same time.'

'We can go into space, but we still fight each other here on Earth,' she said.

He said nothing to that.

'My family,' Henrietta said. 'There has always been a paradox at the heart of our existence, ever since old Henry Feebes opened our Lima branch in 1822. By the middle of the last century my great-grandfather, Edward, had amassed a fortune from the exploitation of bird guano in Latin America. We have profited from others' misery, Vasily. But at the same time, our power and influence have served to help the world, to open new trade routes and contribute to the economy and well-being of many more people than we have ever exploited.'

'I don't believe that,' Vasily said, and she smiled.

'You think me silly,' she said. 'But this is at the heart of our warring ideologies. Money can help people, Vasily.'

'And it can destroy them,' Vasily said.

'My father, you know, he died some years back,' Henrietta said. 'A heart attack, though my brother James always suspected poison. There was a woman my father was seeing for a time, a Mrs Hoffman. James always resented her. A strange woman. Rather thin. Lives in Brighton now, I think. Do you think she poisoned him?'

Vasily shrugged.

'Were you and your father close?' he said.

She considered.

'No. Not really,' she said.

'Your brother, he is the baron now?' Vasily said.

'Yes. Yes, he is.'

'He must be very powerful.'

'He has his club,' Henrietta said. 'He hasn't much of a head for business. I don't know why I am telling you all this, Vasily. Perhaps I am a little bit drunk.'

'You are lonely, perhaps,' Vasily said. He felt lonely too just then. He thought of Sveta and the baby, and whether they had gone to the parade, to see Gagarin. He felt a pang of sadness and he tamped it down. This was his job. They will understand it one day. He looked up at the sky again.

'Do you think one day there will be other people up there?' he said.

'People,' Henrietta said, 'satellites like your Sputnik, who knows what else? Perhaps it will get so crowded we wouldn't even be able to see the stars.'

'My,' Vasily said. 'You *are* melancholic today, Miss Feebes.'

She laughed. 'Don't call me that,' she said. 'You make me sound like an old maid.'

'You're the furthest thing from it,' he said gallantly.

'I know. I will see you later, Vasily.'

She hesitated, looking at the Nile, then left.

When Vasily turned around, Daniel Pikorski was there.

30

THE SUN MOVED IN THE SKY. STILL NOBODY CAME TO HIS aid. How could that even be, in a city like Cairo, where one was never alone? There was always someone watching. It had just taken him a while to figure out who they were.

When he did, it made his name.

But first there was Opal.

'There are many kinds of courtship and seduction, Vasily,' Edgar had told him once, his second year at the Advanced School. 'The bloom of first love, the fumbling passion of adolescence. There is the ritual of mutual attraction, the pretence and counter-pretence of observing every mannerism on the surface, yet sending subtle signals to each other. A sort of speaking in codes. It is a dance, and when it is at last consummated it is not yet over, though some fizzle out quickly. Others last into a marriage, almost—'

'We are talking about recruitment, now?' Vasily said.

Edgar sighed. 'You must learn not to be so bloody blunt,' he said.

'Sorry.'

'You can force a man to become a source,' Edgar said. 'Blackmail him, have power over him. This is true in any relationship. Others may be more like a fling, even a transaction. They'll come to you, wanting money, wanting something they don't have. Your average spy is probably in middle age. He drinks too much. He is single or divorced, and at any rate unhappy. And he has money troubles. This is as true for the Western spy as for the Soviet. Keep an eye for men like these, present yourself, and they will make themselves available for a price. Just never mistake the exchange for true love.'

'I'm not sure I understand you, Edgar...' Vasily said.

'A true source,' Edgar said, 'what you'd call a *spy*, Vasily, will only come willingly. He will do it for reasons that you may well never understand. It would be ideology, only ideology is never a true enough explanation. You could say faith, but the truth is even I, having been one, cannot say for sure. A true spy, like true love, is a rare and wonderful thing, and seldom encountered in the wild. He is worth waiting for, and when you see him, hold your nerve. It is a courtship, Edgar. It is a dance.'

'Who recruited you?' Vasily said, discomfited.

Edgar smiled.

'A dear woman,' he said. 'A dear and ruthless woman, who saw me for what I was long before I saw myself. She runs a bookshop in some English seaside town now... I want you to have this.'

He reached in his pocket and brought out an old, battered pocket watch on which the gold paint was peeling. Edgar felt it with his fingers, as though trying to smooth the metal.

He handed it to Vasily. It felt warm to the touch. At the base of the watch, in faded letters, was the name Feebes.

'An old family heirloom,' Edgar said. 'But I have no children, and I find I have no use for it. I don't know why I kept it with me all these years. Sentimental, I guess. I'd like you to have it.'

'Thank you,' Vasily said, touched. 'I really couldn't, Edgar.'

Edgar shrugged.

'I don't need it,' he said.

Vasily slipped it into his pocket.

'What's Feebes?' he said.

'An old family,' Edgar said. 'They rose to power with the empire and as the empire fades their power does too. I was never sure how my mother got this. I had it evaluated in London by a watchmaker on Bond Street once but he couldn't tell me much beyond that it was a cheap but sturdy construction, and that a small number of them were etched and plated on behalf of the House of Feebes for its employees back in the 1850s. It is only worth a few quid, even now.'

'I will cherish it,' Vasily said—

Why was he thinking about the stupid gold watch now? He didn't even have it anymore. He'd given it to Soraya.

Where was the rat? He hadn't come back. Vasily missed the rat all of a sudden. The thought of not having any company at all was terrifying. He didn't want to die alone. Real spies, agents, they died in violent ways. Executed. The Egyptians hanged the ones they caught. The Soviets shot them. The Americans used the electric chair. But case officers died in their beds, surrounded by family. This just wasn't *fair*. He wasn't supposed to be here!

'Tell me about Opal,' Saakashvili demanded one night. They were working late in the rezidentura.

'That's none of your business, Igor,' Vasily said.

'Is he a man? A woman? Where does he get his material from?'

'You know I can tell you none of that. Why don't you go back to making plans to assassinate Nasser?'

'Why would I want to assassinate Nasser?' Igor said, confused. 'But I have plans in place for when the American president visits Cairo.'

'You want to assassinate the American president? Also, why would he ever come to Cairo?'

'I don't *want* to assassinate him,' Igor said. 'It's my *job* to have a *plan* for it, Vasily. Are you stupid or something?'

'How would you do it?' Vasily asked, interested despite himself.

'Bomb at the airport,' Igor said. 'Sniper on stand-by.'

'How are you going to get a bomb into the airp— Never mind.'

'It's easy,' Igor said. 'Egyptians have lax security.'

'You'd start World War Three if you carried out an assassination on Kennedy,' Vasily said.

'I don't make that kind of decision,' Igor said happily. 'Now, tell me about Opal.'

'Opal is just a source.'

'I just don't see it,' Igor complained. 'You're a nobody, Vasily. A little KGB rat from Leningrad who didn't do well enough at the Advanced School to go somewhere exciting like Washington. Cairo is where they dump second-rate people – myself excepted, of course.'

'Why are you excepted?' Vasily said.

'I'm very good at my job,' Igor said.

'Then why were you assigned to Cairo?'

Igor shrugged. 'I just needed to lie low for a while.'

'Why, who did you sleep with, Semichastny's wife?'

Semichastny was chairman of the KGB. Their boss. Vasily only saw him once, when he came to the Advanced School.

'His secretary,' Igor muttered.

'Is that a punishable offence?'

'He is apparently very fond of her. Who knew!' Igor said.

'You could have married her,' Vasily said.

'She was already married.'

'Ah.'

'Tell me about Opal.'

Vasily dropped the casual tone.

'Why?' he said. 'Why do you need to know? Who are you going to tell? Do you work for the Americans, Igor?'

'What? No!' Igor said, alarmed. 'Just making conversation—'

'Got you!' Vasily said. He started to laugh. 'You should have seen your face,' he said.

'You bastard.'

'Don't ask me about Opal again,' Vasily said. 'Or I'll tell Kirpichenko.'

'Bastard,' Igor said. But he fell quiet after that.

'Igor was asking about Opal,' Vasily told Kirpichenko. 'How much do you trust him?'

'How much do I trust *you*, Vasily?' Kirpichenko said. He looked annoyed. 'How much do *you* trust Opal?'

'He gives us good material,' Vasily said.

'Good but low grade,' Kirpichenko said. 'If I was a suspicious person I'd say it was the sort of material meant to build confidence in a source without really giving anything away.'

'What are you suggesting?' Vasily said.

'I'm not. I'm telling you,' Kirpichenko said. 'He needs to prove himself. Give us something real.'

'He is a long-term prospect,' Vasily said. 'A few more years, he will move up, he will have more access. We've got to play the long game here.'

Kirpichenko shrugged. 'Sure,' he said. 'That's one possibility. But Moscow is telling me to cut him loose. If he isn't genuine, Vasily, then he is trying to play you.'

'He's genuine,' Vasily said.

'Then let him prove it.'

'I'll see what I can do.'

'What about that girlfriend of yours, though?' Kirpichenko said.

'Who?'

'Henrietta Feebes. She is connected. Is she useful?'

'She's not my girlfriend.'

'Then bloody make her your girlfriend.'

'I don't think she goes that way,' Vasily said. 'She wants to do business in Russia, though.'

'Yeah? I'm not in the trade delegation, last I heard.'

'We can offer her preferential treatment. Build the connection that way.'

'I'll kick it upstairs,' Kirpichenko said. 'Her dad was in

Parliament, her granddad was something big in the navy.'
He sighed. 'I suppose she's best handled at a distance,' he
said.

'That's what I figured, too,' Vasily said.

'Well, get lost then, will you? Come back when you have
something real for me.'

This was it, he thought miserably, sitting at the bar at the
Balmoral. *This* was the fine art of spying. Rooting through
garbage hoping to find a bone the rats hadn't gnawed on so
much already that it still had some meat left. This wasn't the
Rosenbergs or Klaus Fuchs, smuggling nuclear plans under
the Americans' nose. Even Edgar Waverley, high up as he
had been in MI6, what real material did he ever procure –
what *difference* had he ever made? And next to them, Vasily
was just an errand boy with an allowance.

'Hey,' Pikorski said. He came over and sat down, smiling
that smile that was sardonic or boyish, depending which
way the light fell on it. 'Bad day at the office, Vas?'

He motioned to the waiter, who hurried over with a
bottle of Dom Pérignon.

'Expensive,' Vasily said.

'Business is good,' Pikorski said. He touched Vasily's
hand lightly. 'How have you been?'

'Fine,' Vasily said. 'It's just hard to make new business,
you know? Egypt wants to buy all the weapons for that war
they're going to have, but I don't sell guns, I sell...'

'Tractors,' Pikorski said.

'Right.'

'Moskvitch cars.'

'Right.'

'Red Moscow perfume. Zorki cameras. Smirnoff vodka.'

'There's real money there, Daniel.'

'I know,' Pikorski said. 'I have been talking to Henrietta. She is interested. Well, not in tractors. But luxury brands. Vodka, perfume, furs. She thinks they could do well on the British market and in the Far East.'

'Doesn't help me, though, does it?' Vasily said gloomily. He drank the French wine but it just tasted like fizz.

'What *do* you need?' Pikorski said.

'Something better than good, Daniel.'

'Bosses giving you trouble?'

'What boss doesn't?' Vasily said.

'I understand.'

'Do you?' Vasily said. '*Do* you understand?'

'I said I understand, Vasily!'

For just a moment the mask of affability slipped, and Vasily got a glimpse of the real Daniel Pikorski.

Or did he? This was the problem in this line of work. You could never really tell.

'All right,' he said. 'All right. Let's not talk about work.'

'Want to hit the casino tonight?' Daniel said, jovial as ever, the mask – if that's what it was – firmly back on.

'I thought I might stay here and drink,' Vasily said.

Now Pikorski genuinely smiled. 'My,' he said. 'We really *are* feeling sorry for ourselves tonight. You want misery? I have a better idea than the hotel. Come on.'

'Where are we going?' Vasily said.

'You'll see.'

'It's a surprise, is it?' Vasily said.

Daniel looked over his shoulder at Vasily and grinned.

'It's a birthday party,' he said.

31

IT WAS A TWO-STOREY HOUSE IN A FASHIONABLE neighbourhood, with many private cars parked outside. An Egyptian guard with a machine gun stopped them from coming in until he could check their names on a handwritten list.

'Is this very common, here in Cairo?' Vasily said.

'No,' Pikorski said. 'Indeed it is not. But then again, this is not a very common sort of party.'

Evidently satisfied, the guard – a member of the secret police, the Mabahith, if Vasily was any judge – passed them to a house boy who escorted them inside. Here some thirty men and women sat in groups, chatting in English, German and Arabic. An elderly man, with thin white hair that might have once been blond, and watery blue eyes that looked like frog-filled ponds, approached them, accompanied by his very blonde, somewhat younger wife.

'Ah, Daniel, Daniel,' he said. His voice trembled. 'Heil Hitler, Heil Hitler!'

'Good evening, Professor von Leers,' Pikorski said. 'Frau von Leers.'

'Always a pleasure, Daniel,' the woman said, kissing him

warmly on both cheeks. 'And who is this handsome young man?'

'Vasily Sokolov,' Daniel said. 'He is a good friend.'

'Any friend of Daniel's is a friend of ours. Come in! Come in! Would you care for a drink?'

'I wouldn't mind…' Vasily said. He shot Pikorski a withering glance. It was returned with a guileless smile.

'Whiskey?'

'Thank you.'

Vasily accepted the drink. He felt he needed it. What the hell had Pikorski dragged him into? He looked around the room. He saw familiar faces.

There was General Murtaji, commander of the Arab forces in Yemen. There was Wolfgang Lotz, the charming German he had met who had such an interest in horses. And there was Pikorski's friend, Dirk Müller of International Rakete, who had come climbing the pyramids with them that night long ago.

'Colleagues, friends!' Professor von Leers said in his reedy voice. He struggled to hold up his glass. 'It is a joy to have you all here, tonight, as we celebrate this occasion.'

'What occasion?' Vasily said.

'Oh, you just wait for it,' Pikorski said.

'I would like, therefore, to raise our glasses—'

They all did, promptly.

'To the birth of Adolf Hitler!'

'It's Hitler's *birthday*?' Vasily said.

Pikorski kept his smile fixed and raised his glass in a cheer with all the others.

'To Hitler!'

'What the hell, Daniel?' Vasily said.

'Come here,' Daniel said. He grabbed Vasily by the sleeve and pulled him outside, onto the veranda.

'You see them in there?' he said.

'I see them.'

'But you don't *see* them, Vasily. Perhaps because your superiors are so much more interested in getting their hands on some hot CIA asset, or French at a pinch. That there, that's Otto Skorzeny, formerly of the SS, who is wanted for war crimes across three continents. He escaped from prison in '48. He now trains Egyptian commandos, while dreaming of establishing the Fourth Reich in South America.'

Vasily sighed. He felt disappointed.

'I do see Skorzeny,' he said. 'You can't miss him with that old duelling scar on his face. We have a file on him. We have a file on all of them, Daniel. That's Dr Heim over there, the Butcher of Mauthausen. Dr Death, they used to call him. I also heard Martin Bormann, Hitler's personal secretary, passed through Cairo last week on his way to Argentina. So fucking what? The war is over. These are sad old men, Daniel. No one cares about the Nazis anymore. What I don't understand is what you are doing in their company.'

'Senior Egyptian officers come here,' Pikorski said, piqued. 'So do the German rocket scientists. It's a place where they feel comfortable. Where they can speak openly. It is *useful*, Vasily.'

'For the Americans or the British, perhaps. Or the Israelis. But I need more than this, Daniel.'

Daniel sighed.

'I will see what I can do,' he said.

'Can we get out of here now?' Vasily said.

Daniel downed his drink.

'Sure,' he said. 'Let's go to the casino.'

The Casino Havana was the sort of place men went to play dice and drink too much and meet women whose love was charged at reasonable rates. The light was dim enough to hide the stains, neon-bright enough to chase away the gloom. The drinks were cheap. They stood by the roulette wheel and watched the players. An elderly Englishwoman kept betting on red.

'Why do you really go there, Daniel?' Vasily said. 'To see those old Nazis?'

'Because I hate them,' Daniel said. His voice was even. He stared at the roulette wheel. 'I hate them more than it is possible to put into words, Vasily. I go and I smile and I drink with them, and I think of all the ways that they could be killed. All the horrible ways.'

'And they accept you?'

'I am a banker, Vasily. And these men are always in need of money.'

'Red wins,' the croupier said. 'Red wins again. Well done, Mrs St James.'

The woman whooped delightedly and pushed the chips back on red.

'Spin it again, François!' she said.

'Is that his name?' Vasily said.

'I don't think so,' Daniel said.

'I could help you kill one of them,' Vasily said. 'If you liked.'

'You would?'

'If it was someone no one would really miss. I don't like the Nazis either, Daniel. My father died in the war—'

Lying in the sun on the garbage heap, Vasily remembered the stupidest thing he'd ever done.

Going off-book. Going *rogue*, as the movies called it. But there had been something so exhilarating about the idea, too. No one would know. And it was to bind him and Pikorski together forever. Pikorski, who was young and unassuming, a grey banker, Harvard-educated, so clearly CIA but... It took Vasily months to figure it out. Never sure if it was him making the overture or if it was Pikorski. Not sure who was trying to use who.

To understand, for instance, that some companies did not really exist, and some were fronts. That funding had to be diverted, washed, rerouted, hidden. That Feebes Bank, old, respectable, immoral, with branches in the Far East, was perfectly situated to help finance and supply an American war that wasn't officially happening in Laos – as a for instance. CIA operations in South-East Asia that went from training guerrillas to running its own airline, with a profitable side-hustle in opium – as a for instance. They even called the damn airline Air America. And for all this, one needed a bank. And one needed a banker.

'So why are you here?' he asked Daniel, once, long after they had ceased to pretend to each other, after they had kidnapped Heinz Krug just for the hell of it. 'What went wrong?'

And Daniel smiled, and said, 'Why should anything have gone wrong?' and wouldn't be drawn on it. But he had fucked up somehow. And he ended up in Cairo, where they sent only the inexperienced or washed-up. Vasily knew this much.

He was getting good, solid material off Opal. Nothing earth-shattering, but solid. And when Opal passed Vasily the material on Air America – some flight routes and refuelling stops, hand-drawn on a map, even if the routes had been abandoned by the time Moscow processed them – it had made Vasily's name. He even got a telegram congratulating him from Lubyanka. And *that* had made Kirpichenko ease off.

'Are you sure you want to do this?' Daniel asked. They were sitting at an Egyptian café by the harbour, smoking a sheesha pipe and drinking small, bitter cups of coffee.

'You ever kill anyone before, Daniel?' Vasily said.

Daniel shook his head. 'You?' he said.

'No.'

For some reason that made both of them crack up. Maybe it was the tension. Vasily took out bunched-up photographs held together with a rubber band. He fanned them on the table.

'This is the guy I was thinking of,' he said.

'Oh? Why him?'

'He's one of the Nazi scientists from Peenemünde. Heinz Krug. He runs a munitions company, with an Egyptian shell company in Munich to transport supplies for Nasser's rocket programme. He comes to Cairo regularly.'

'I know who Heinz Krug is,' Daniel said. 'Feebes Bank has been involved in the munitions business for a long time,

Vasily. And I have been in Cairo long enough. My question was, why *him*?'

'Honestly?' Vasily tapped the photo distractedly. The man in the picture looked as average as they came. Late forties, well-fed, with small eyes. He could have been anyone. 'I just don't think anyone'd miss him.'

Their plan, if Vasily could even call it a plan, now that he reflected on it, and he had time to reflect, what with dying on top of the rubbish heap, as it were, and all that, wasn't overly complicated. Krug was worried for his security – the German scientists were drawing unwanted attention from the Mossad. But a friendly call from his current partners arranging a quiet trip to Cairo, to discuss financial arrangements, with security provided – well, that was just business.

Daniel made the initial approach. It was important, he stressed to Krug on the phone, that there should be no trail or notice of the meeting. He should discuss it with no one, and make his way to Cairo by an informal channel. This came in the form of a cargo plane out of a private airport outside Munich, the cost to be paid for by Krug in cash, to be reimbursed on arrival. They would pick him up in person. Vasily used a contact at the air force, a general who, like most generals, was amenable to suggestion if it were prefaced with the offer of a few bottles and a handful of cash, to get them access. There was no passenger on the manifesto. As far as anyone else was concerned, Krug simply left his office in Munich one day and vanished.

'Mr Krug? A pleasure to meet you.'

They shook hands, then bundled him into the car. They bought it third or fourth hand – a Mercedes. Which they both thought was funny for some reason.

'I do not like coming to Egypt,' Krug said. 'I think people are trying to kill me.'

That made it even harder for Vasily and Daniel to keep a straight face.

'What people?' Daniel said.

'You know what people.'

'Oh, those people.'

'Where are we going?' Krug said. 'I thought you booked a suite at the Balmoral.'

'Sure,' Vasily said. 'But the meeting is not at the Balmoral. Security and so on, Mr Krug.'

'Of course. Of course.'

'You had a good flight?' Vasily said. He was behind the wheel.

'Very uncomfortable.'

'Would you care for a drink, Mr Krug?'

'A drink?' Krug said. 'What kind of a drink?'

Vasily took out a flask from his breast pocket. 'Just a little pick-me-up,' he said.

'No, thank you,' Krug said with distaste.

'Suit yourself.' Vasily put it back.

'You are not drinking?' Krug said.

'I'm driving,' Vasily said.

'Never stopped you Russians before,' Krug said. 'Where are we going? There is nothing here.'

'Not far now, Mr Krug,' Daniel said.

They came to the edge of a small industrial estate. Nothing

much was made there and the place was currently deserted. They drove in, and parked outside a small warehouse.

'This is very unorthodox,' Krug said.

'Is it?' Vasily said. 'No one is going to see us here.'

'But what is there to hide?' Krug said.

'Our business. Your business.'

'I don't see any other cars here,' Krug said.

'We're early.'

Krug stared at the deserted estate.

'No,' he said. 'I do not like it. Take me back.'

'It's a bit late for that, Mr Krug,' Daniel said. And now Daniel had a pistol pointing at Heinz Krug. 'Step out of the car quietly, please,' he said. 'Let's be civilised about this.'

'What is the meaning of this!' Krug said. But he knew. Vasily could see it in his eyes. For men like Heinz Krug, there was always someone who was going to show up with a gun sooner or later.

'Get out of the car, you bastard,' Vasily said.

Heinz Krug stared into Vasily's eyes.

'But why me?' he said. 'I was a nobody.'

Vasily smiled.

'Exactly,' he said.

Daniel cocked the gun. The sound was loud in the confines of the car. There was no other sound for miles around. There was nothing but desert.

Heinz Krug got out of the car.

32

THEY TIED HIM TO A CHAIR INSIDE AND STOOD OVER HIM with their guns. Vasily felt a bit foolish doing that. Heinz Krug just sat there, looking like he knew he was going to die, knowing there was nothing he could do about it, and feeling shitty about the whole thing. It was in his eyes.

'You son of a bitch,' Vasily said, just to try it on.

'You have to understand,' Krug said. 'I am going to be missed. There will be an investigation.'

'It won't go anywhere,' Vasily said. 'Neither will you.'

'Is this about the war?' Krug said. 'Who the hell cares about the war anymore?'

'Some people do,' Vasily said.

'Listen, I wasn't some monster,' Krug said. 'I worked in Peenemünde on the rocket programme, under von Braun. I didn't have a choice. We were just scientists. Engineers.'

'You used slave labour,' Daniel said quietly.

'I never saw any slave labour,' Krug said.

'You're a Nazi, Krug,' Vasily said.

'Everyone was a Nazi,' Krug said. 'It didn't mean anything. We weren't like those concentration camp guys.

No one ever put us on trial after the war. We were just trying to do our job.' He stared at them with those small, hopeless eyes. 'I'm a West German citizen,' he said. 'I demand you release me.'

'Enough,' Daniel said. He put the gun to Krug's head.

'Wait,' Vasily said.

'What?'

'Do it from further away. Otherwise you'll just get blood and brains all over you.'

'Oh, yeah. Good call.'

'Come on, guys,' Krug said. 'Enough's enough. Just let me g—'

Both guns fired at the same time. The body in the chair fell back, twisted, crashed to the floor. Pikorski went to stand over the dead Krug, then fired again at his head.

'Confirmation kill,' he said. Then, 'I don't feel so good—'

He bent over double and threw up all over Krug.

'Shit, Pikorski!' Vasily said.

'Oh, God,' Pikorski said. 'Oh, God!'

'Just let it out,' Vasily said. He patted him awkwardly on the back. 'Just let it all out—'

He jumped back as a second torrent of puke came out.

'What the hell did you *eat*?' Vasily said.

'I like Egyptian breakfasts!' Pikorski said. 'I like that ful medames they make.'

'You just puked up pureed fava beans? Jesus, Daniel!'

'And some hardboiled eggs,' Pikorski said.

'How many eggs can you *eat*!'

'I like them,' Pikorski said. Then, 'Shit!'

Vasily watched as the last of Pikorski's breakfast emerged.

The floor was smeared in blood, brain matter and mashed beans. Vasily thought he spotted some parsley, too, then wished he hadn't.

'Are you done?' he said.

Pikorski wiped his mouth.

'I think so,' he said.

'Let's have a drink,' Vasily said. He took out his flask, then remembered he'd crumbled sleeping pills into the whiskey, which was why he'd offered it to Krug earlier in the first place.

'We don't have a drink,' he said.

'*I* have a drink,' Pikorski said, scooping out a handful of tiny bottles from his pocket. 'I raided your mini-bar before we left.'

'I pay for this!' Vasily said. 'Come on, Daniel, I have to justify expenses.'

'Just pick one,' Pikorski said.

Vasily snatched two bottles without checking what they were. He unscrewed the first one and chugged it down.

'Some sort of crème de menthe,' he said. 'Tastes like mouthwash.' He shrugged and opened the second bottle.

'Whiskey?' Pikorski said.

'Gin.'

'Not bad. Let me catch up.' Pikorski unscrewed a tiny bottle and raised it.

'Na zdravie,' he said.

'Cheers,' Vasily said.

They drank.

Later, they poured acid on Krug's corpse.

★

Vasily tried to move again. He couldn't. It wasn't far now, dying. He was pretty sure of that. It was funny. He never expected to die. Not like this, anyway. When he did, he pictured it as like something out of a movie. The coffin carried through the streets of Moscow, the red hammer and sickle flags draped everywhere. A chest full of medals, his hair a distinguished white, his children and grandchildren by the graveside. When was the last time he even saw Sveta and the little one?

This was the *job*, he tried to tell her, the last time he was home. That awful concrete apartment and the grey skies and damp washing hanging everywhere. The child crying. The smell of boiled cabbage in the corridor. He couldn't wait to get out of there, he could admit that now. This was his *job*, Svetlana! If you wanted a regular worker, some nine-to-five guy, then you should have married one!

No, he told her, of course there weren't other women. How dare she even ask? She'd burst out crying, he stormed out, went for a long walk. He found himself in Gorky Park, stood in the queue for a beer from a kiosk. Queue once for the ticket, once for the beer. He sat on a bench and watched the Moskva flow beyond the trees.

Someone came and sat next to him. The man unscrewed a pocket flask and took a long drag and offered it to him.

'Vasily,' the man said.

'Edgar.'

They sat there and watched the river. Some kids were chasing ducks.

'There are concerns, Vasily,' Edgar said.

'Concerns about what?'

'This source of yours. Opal.'

'I don't know what you're talking about, Edgar.'

'Are you running your source, or is your source running you, Vasily?' Edgar said. 'This is what they are asking.'

'That's absurd.'

'Should we pull him out?' Edgar said, ignoring the reply. 'Should we put him on a desk in Lubyanka, to keep him out of trouble? Send him somewhere he can't make problems, a field office in the Congo, maybe? Or should we put a bullet in his head and just be done with it? This is what they are asking.'

'Edgar, what are you talking about?' Vasily said. 'I do good work in Cairo. Great work! My new network—'

'Yes,' Edgar said. 'Your new network. It is quite ingenious. They were impressed, Vasily. I can tell you that.'

'So they should be! I'm not some muzhik, Edgar. You tell them that. I'm a thinker.' The beer – and some vodka – was warming him up. 'Chernaya Gryaz,' he said proudly.

'Black Dirt,' Edgar said. 'Yes.'

'A treasure trove of information!' Vasily said. 'They should promote me. They're scared I'm coming for their jobs!' He laughed. Edgar didn't laugh. He patted Vasily on the shoulder and stood up to leave. He moved slowly, Vasily saw. As though in some pain. Edgar wasn't that old. But he did not look well.

'When are you flying back to Cairo?' Edgar said.

'Tomorrow.'

'Then goodbye, Vasily.'

He shook his hand. Edgar's skin felt clammy.

'Be careful,' Edgar said. He turned and left. Vasily watched him, a small lonely figure, vanishing into the distance until he was swallowed up by the fog.

He brooded. He had nothing to worry about! He was tense all through the evening, and when he lay beside Sveta in the narrow bed. But no one knocked on the door, no one disturbed their peace, and he fell asleep, and in the morning he said his goodbyes and went back to Cairo.

He would have given anything now to be back in Moscow. Back in that bed, with Sveta by his side, with the child sleeping, back... home. You never miss it until it's too late, he thought. Dying in the rubbish heap like some sad joke.

'Isn't it beautiful?' Henrietta Feebes said. She was back from a business trip abroad. They were on a boat, sailing down the Nile. A lot of English people there. An old Englishwoman who looked vaguely familiar was holding court on deck, surrounded by admirers.

'She writes detective stories,' Henrietta said, noticing his look. 'Old friend of the family.'

'It's beautiful, yes,' Vasily said, answering her earlier comment.

'You seem distracted,' Henrietta said.

'Your life, in the West,' Vasily said. 'It is good, no?'

'It can be,' Henrietta said.

'But you have poor people and rich people. You have injustice.'

'It's true. But that's the cost of freedom,' Henrietta said.

'What is freedom?' Vasily said irritably. He lit a cigarette. He felt ill at ease. He was supposed to meet a contact on the boat, someone from Henrietta's odd circle. But he hadn't spotted him yet.

'I don't know, Vasily,' Henrietta said. 'I don't know what your fucking definition of freedom is.'

'You seem also in a bad mood,' Vasily said.

'I might be leaving Cairo soon,' Henrietta said.

'What for?' he said.

She shrugged. 'It was fun for a while, but the office here is established and I could better advance the business elsewhere. Can I bum a cigarette?'

'Sure,' he said. He lit one and passed it to her.

'Thanks.' She leaned over the railing and he did the same. They were shoulder to shoulder, staring at the lights of Cairo passing by.

'*The Country House Murder*, yes, that was one of mine,' the loud old Englishwoman said, and barked a laugh, somewhere in her crowd. 'Early work, my darling. But then which of us didn't write one of those at some point.'

'You could come with me,' Henrietta said quietly.

Vasily blew out smoke.

'I am not always what I seem to be,' he said.

'I know what you are,' Henrietta said. 'You want to know what the West is like, then find out.'

'It's not that simple,' he said.

'But is it that hard?'

He felt her closeness. Wished it could be something more between them. He threw the cigarette into the river.

'Think about it,' Henrietta said.

'You know I will,' he said, wishing she hadn't spoken. He had his own plans.

She touched him on the shoulder, smiled and went to join the others. Vasily waited. Presently a man came over and stood beside him.

'You're the Russian?'

'Yeah. You're Doyle?'

'Call me Sean,' the man said. He gave him a smile. 'We have a cause in common, no?' he said.

'That we do, Mr Doyle.'

'I told you, call me Sean. We don't do titles, tovarich.'

'You want guns,' Vasily said. 'To fight the British.'

'Correct.'

'You can afford to pay?'

'We have money.'

'There are surplus guns and munitions that come into Egypt,' Vasily said. 'Not from us directly, but from Czechoslovakia.'

'I am aware,' Sean Doyle said.

'Some of it may be misplaced,' Vasily said.

'I'm glad to hear it.'

'You will arrange transportation?' Vasily said.

'Sure,' Sean Doyle said. 'We have pilots.'

'That's good. Well, I am sure we can work something out,' Vasily said.

'Good,' Sean Doyle said.

'Anything else?' Vasily said.

'Yeah,' Sean Doyle said. 'Think they got anything stronger to drink on this tub? Because I say we go find it.'

'Try the galley,' Vasily said. 'It's where they keep the top-shelf stuff. I'll catch up with you, all right? I need to... mingle.'

'Mingle away, my friend,' Sean Doyle said. 'We'll talk.'

'Sure,' Vasily said. He stared as the Irishman left. His uncle Joe was supposed to be some kind of a hero, died in the Civil War over there. IRA. They always had their hands out. Kirpichenko cleared it. It was a nice bit of triple-dealing. Selling the weapons through the Czechs to the Egyptians, and losing some of it on the side to help destabilise the situation in Ireland. Everybody wins.

You could come with me, Henrietta said. *You want to know what the West is like, then find out.*

He stared at the assembled guests. Cairo was small, when it came down to it. After a while it was all the same people, and always the same party. The German, Lotz, came and joined him.

'Rusty,' Vasily said.

'You look thoughtful, my friend,' Lotz said.

'I wonder what they see when they look at you,' Vasily said.

The German smiled. 'They see what there is,' he said. 'Nothing more.'

'A rich, idle German,' Vasily said. 'An ex-Nazi who loves horses, drinking and the company of top Egyptian generals.'

'I'm a sociable guy.'

'You seem to turn up everywhere I go, Lotz.'

'I guess you're a sociable guy, too,' Lotz said.

'I guess we both are,' Vasily said.

Lotz laughed. 'I like you,' he said. 'Come have a drink with us, Vasily.'

'I'm already drinking,' Vasily said. 'But I can't seem to get drunk.'

'You seem morose.'

'Just thoughtful,' Vasily said.

'Then I shall leave you to it.'

The German left.

Vasily thought.

He needed an edge. He had recruited no Western agents other than Opal, and Opal was still only giving him low-grade material. Solid, always. But not exciting. He needed to be creative. He wished there was a way he could have access to the entire city, somehow. To every embassy and safe house, to every bank and every den of vice.

What he needed, he thought, was a secret key to Cairo itself.

33

HE FOUND THE KEY THAT HE WAS LOOKING FOR, AND with it his inevitable promotion and the birth of the Chernaya Gryaz network, by waking up too early one morning. He had been drinking – he was out with Stéphanie at the casino the night before – and he woke up alone, with a splitting headache, and couldn't go back to sleep. He went down for a coffee. The air was cool. An hour later it will be unbearable.

He found himself wandering outside the hotel, coffee in hand, to the quiet alleyway in the back – the same one he was lying in now, in fact. The hotel's trash was out there: rotting food, crates and boxes, broken lamps, soiled towels, broken glassware and empty bottles, used cleaning products, empty toothpaste tubes – Vasily had never considered just how much waste a hotel produced every day.

He gazed at it, nursing his hangover, the coffee bitter when he sipped. Then he saw them, a sight he must have seen before, perhaps a hundred times, but never registered – the Zabbaleen.

First one donkey-driven cart and then another appeared in the mouth of the alleyway. The men driving them were bare-headed, dressed in trousers and shirts, and as they reached the mounds of trash they jumped off and began hauling everything onto their carts. Vasily watched them without thinking much of it at first, admiring the efficiency with which they moved, how quickly the trash rose upon the carts and vanished from the ground. The men, having finished, got back on the carts. The donkeys moved, and soon they would disappear back out of the alleyway and to wherever it was that garbage men went.

Vasily thought of all the garbage left out every day all over Cairo. Outside hotels and houses and offices, outside embassies – yes, that's where he saw them before, similar men collected all the rubbish outside the Soviet Embassy in Dokki—

Gears moved slowly in Vasily's brain. But they moved all the same.

'Wait!' he shouted. He dropped the coffee as he ran after the carts. The men turned their heads to watch, no doubt bemused by the sight of this European chasing them, perhaps uneasy, perhaps indifferent – 'Wait!'

The donkeys slowed, then stopped.

'Where do you take it?' Vasily said in Arabic.

'Sir? Is there a problem?'

'No problem,' Vasily said. 'I just...'

'Imbaba,' the older man driving the cart said. 'We take it to Imbaba, the trash.'

'You collect all over the city?' Vasily said.

'All over the city, yes, of course,' the man said.

'So what... what do you do with it?' Vasily said.

The man shrugged.

'You want to see?' he said.

'I... Yes,' Vasily said. 'I do.'

'Then you must come to Imbaba,' the man said.

Vasily would have laughed now, but there was hardly a breath left in him. It must have been a comical sight that early morning, the Zabbaleen cart and perched awkwardly upon it, the hung-over figure of one Vasily Sokolov, KGB. The men of the Zabbaleen seemed indifferent. The older man's name was Hani. The younger one, who was his son, was called Youssef. As they drove down the road, ignoring the cars as they moved at their own pace, Vasily became conscious of the emergence of other Zabbaleen vehicles, a whole procession forming as they approached the boundaries of Imbaba.

It was a poor neighbourhood, the sort of place he had never visited before, nor would he have but for that morning's spark of inspiration or madness. Here the alleyways were narrow and covered in dry mud. Washing hung from concrete balconies. Stalls on the street sold bread, newspapers, cigarettes, beans and spices. Men on motorbikes passed women carrying their shopping. A camel sat asleep under the awning of a bicycle shop where wheels hung on the wall. The cart, moving slowly, made its way deeper and deeper into the maze, and Vasily was carried aloft with it.

They came then to streets where garbage piled high. It was everywhere. Stacked against walls, sitting on pallets, strewn on the floor. Pigs ran rooting through the garbage. They passed a small church and then another. They came to an open field surrounded by crumbling buildings and open warehouses. Hani drove to a spot where men and women waited. The donkeys stopped. Vasily climbed down.

'Well,' Hani said, 'this is it.'

Vasily stared. There was industry here, order in the seeming chaos. The men came with the carts and the boys offloaded the rubbish. The women set out to sort the trash. All food waste went into one area where the pigs feasted on it. Metal went one way. Plastics another. Linen, cloth and weave went into yet another pile. Glass went somewhere else again. But even as he watched the mountains of garbage grew and were added onto, and he thought it would never be reduced to nought, for Cairo produced it quicker than the Zabbaleen could ever hope to clear it.

'What do you do with it all?' he said.

Hani smiled, the smile of a man taking pride in his work. 'Everything can be reused,' he said. 'Remade. The plastic we grind to dust and resell to the factories. The scrap metal to the factories again or to construction. The food, the pigs eat it all, and our wealth is in our pigs. The glass—'

'You're not Muslim?' Vasily said, surprised.

'We're Copts,' Hani said.

That certainly explained the profusion of churches.

'How does it all work?' Vasily said.

Hani studied him.

'Why do you want to know all this?' he said. 'Why do you care?'

'Maybe I want to buy something,' Vasily said.

'Yes? What?'

'I am not sure yet,' Vasily said.

Hani nodded. 'Would you care for tea?' he said.

Vasily wasn't exactly sure he wanted to eat or drink

anything in this place. But he said yes, of course. He followed Hani to an area outside one of the warehouses, where coals burned.

'Soraya, go to the baker, bring bread,' Hani said. A young woman turned and regarded Vasily with interest. Her dark eyes seemed to study him intensely.

'My daughter, Soraya,' Hani said. He gave Soraya a handful of coins. 'Go.'

'Very pretty,' Vasily said.

Hani ignored the remark. But Vasily found that he could not so easily put away the girl's image from his mind. He had been captivated with a single glance.

Steady, Vasily, old man, he told himself. Then laughed at his own folly.

Hani boiled the water himself. He added sage to the water, waited, then poured out two glasses which he placed on a copper tray. He placed the tray on a stool between them.

'Itfaddal,' he said.

Vasily took the tea. He sipped, nodded.

'Very good,' he said.

'You are Russian?'

'Yes,' Vasily said.

Hani nodded.

'You are a strange man,' he said, 'to follow us here. Where did you learn Arabic?'

'In Moscow,' Vasily said.

'Why would a Russian man need Arabic?' Hani said.

Vasily shrugged. 'To work in Egypt?' he said.

Hani inched his head. He almost smiled. Vasily was aware others were watching them, but keeping their distance.

'How does it work again?' Vasily said. 'You really collect trash from all over the city?'

'From everywhere.'

'Dokki? Zamalek? Heliopolis?'

'Everywhere. We pay...' Hani sighed. 'We must pay the Wahiya to collect. They were here first, so they got the licence. But the trash is ours. It is how we make our livelihood. Without us, there would be no Cairo.'

'What do you do with the paper?' Vasily said.

'Paper? We sell it. It gets turned into toilet paper or pulp, for the newspapers or books...' Hani shrugged. 'Why?'

It was then that it all came together for Vasily. A thought. An experiment. The girl, Soraya, came back with bread. Vasily accepted it from her. She smiled, as at a joke only she could see. She really was very pretty, he thought.

'Shukran,' he said.

'You're welcome,' Soraya said in English.

'You speak English?' he said, surprised.

'A little.'

'She goes to school,' Hani said. 'Sometimes.'

'Sometimes,' Soraya said.

'Go,' Hani said.

'Yes, Father,' Soraya said. But she kept smiling at Vasily as she went back to her sorting, joining the others. He could see the women talking amongst themselves as they glanced his way.

'So,' Hani said.

'I am interested in paper,' Vasily said. He had reached a decision. He would try it, he thought. His heart beat faster. It felt strange sitting there, between these people.

'We have plenty of paper,' Hani said.

'I am only interested in specific papers,' Vasily said. 'From specific places.'

'I see.'

'Can it be done?'

'Anything can be done, Mr Sokolov. But there are many families, each covering a different area. We do not always cooperate.'

'I believe I can smooth things over,' Vasily said. He took out his wallet. Felt eyes watching. Took out a handful of notes. 'Consider this an advance.'

Hani nodded. 'Very well,' he said. He pocketed the money.

Vasily bit into the bread. He took a sip of tea. He said, 'I will give you a list to begin with.'

Even now, even dying, he felt a swelling of pride. No one else had thought of this! People *looked*, but they didn't *see*. He did! He came back that day to the Balmoral with his hangover forgotten. He had a new spring in his step. Before he'd left Hani and the Zabbaleen they had an agreement in principle. And a list of targets. The French, West German, British and American embassies were first. The sensitive material would be shredded or destroyed on site, but it was worth a dig all the same. Then the hotels. He wanted every scrap from every room a foreigner stayed in. Then offices. Feebes Bank being just one of them. If his hunch was right, even if he only just got lucky *once*, it would all be worth it. He could barely sleep that night, in the excitement of it. He wouldn't tell Kirpichenko, not yet. He'd get results first.

He made some quick calculations. He was due to meet the Irishman, Doyle, the next day. He could divest some

IRA cash into this new project. He went to sleep dreaming about secrets, and of Khrushchev pinning a Hero of the Soviet Union medal to his chest.

Morning. Lunch at Lotz's new horse riding club. Then to Cinema Radio, where he met Doyle in a screening of *From Russia With Love*. A small satchel full of hard Western cash. He took a cab to the embassy, handed it over, minus the money he'd earmarked for Chernaya Gryaz. Then to meet Henrietta for drinks at the Diplomatic Club. Until recently it was the Mohamed Ali, but Nasser's revolution changed a lot of things. One thing it didn't change was the club's luxury. Vasily felt like a peasant going in there. Henrietta looked right at home. To her it had a mixture of the shabby and genteel. She kissed him on both cheeks and offered him champagne. She was with that old Englishwoman again, Mrs Edna St James. The old lady was quite inebriated by now.

'Do you remember that darling little man?' she said. 'What was his name. Waverley. Little Edgar Waverley. He used to come to the manor when you were small.'

'He was a spy, Edna,' Henrietta said patiently. Like she'd said it a thousand times. Vasily was startled. He tried not to show it. He knew Edgar must have known the family, how else did he get hold of that old watch? But of course he never mentioned it to Henrietta.

'A spy? Really? I never would have thought...'

'Mrs St James,' Vasily said politely.

The old woman blinked at him.

'Who are you supposed to be?' she said.

'Vasily Sokolov. We have been introduced.'

'Several times, Edna,' Henrietta said.

'A Russian? Are you a spy, too?'

'No, I'm in trade – I've already explained this,' Vasily said. The old woman smiled, and he saw something cold and sharp peeking from under the booze. She was toying with him.

'Not every Russian is a spy, you know, Mrs St James,' Vasily said, recovering his good humour.

'Do you play bridge?' she said.

'Bridge?'

'Yes. Do you play it?'

'I'm afraid I never had the pleasure,' Vasily said.

'I will teach you,' Edna St James said.

'I would love that,' Vasily said, 'but I just realised I have an appointment—'

'At this hour? Nonsense,' Edna St James said. 'Come. Sit. Can you shuffle cards?'

'Can I shuffle c— Yes?'

'Good. Then shuffle.'

Vasily stared at Henrietta, who was trying not to laugh.

'You need four players for bridge,' she said.

'You called?' Daniel Pikorski said, materialising from the bar. He smiled at Mrs St James.

'Edna,' he said. 'Always a pleasure.'

'Danny boy,' she said. 'My white knight to the rescue.'

They played cards—

Why was he thinking about the batty old woman? God, he would kill for a cigarette. He was lying on a pile of cigarette stubs, he was sure of it. He wished he could have had one last cigarette. Well, he supposed he had, he just hadn't known when he smoked it that it would be his last. It had been a fun night, anyway, playing cards at the Diplomatic Club, or would have been if it weren't for Pikorski cornering him in the bathroom and saying, 'I need more material, Vas. I need better quality stuff from you or they'll be asking questions!'

'I am not having this conversation now, Daniel!' Vasily had said. Pikorski seemed to want to push it, then changed his mind. They washed their hands in silence.

Damn but he could use a cigarette. He barely slept that night, after the club. He was early to bed and early to rise again, waiting for the Zabbaleen to arrive for the trash. He hitched a ride on the cart again, back through the narrow streets of Imbaba, back to the wasteland of waste that was its secret heart.

Then he saw the girl, Soraya. She turned and looked at him, and smiled; and something inside him fluttered, and he felt suddenly as free as a bird.

34

'WELL,' HANI SAID, 'THIS IS IT.'

Vasily stared at the piles on the ground.

'What is this shit?' he said.

'Everything from outside the places you asked for,' Hani said.

'But this is disgusting!'

Hani shrugged. 'This is what you asked for,' he said.

'I asked for the papers!'

Somewhere in the trash heap there must be papers, he thought. Sodden, disgusting paper, covered in cigarette ash and feminine hygiene products and broken glass and rotting food.

'Is that a fucking *syringe*?' Vasily said.

'People throw away all sorts of things,' Hani said placidly.

'This is no use to me!' Vasily said.

'You asked for the waste,' Hani said. 'The sorting work is extra.'

'How much extra?' Vasily said.

'It would take five women,' Hani said. 'This is a lot of waste.'

'You process thousands of heaps! You need *five* workers for this?'

He knew when he was being out-haggled.

Hani said, 'You could sort it yourself, of course. For free.'

'I'm not touching this shit!' Vasily said.

He stared at Hani. Hani stared back.

Vasily broke first.

'Fine,' he said. 'Here.' He thrust a bundle of notes at the Copt. 'I'll wait.'

'Soraya!' Hani said. 'Make our guest some tea. Then sort out his rubbish.'

'Yes, Father,' Soraya said. Still with that smile of hers. Was she mocking Vasily? She brewed water for tea. Vasily sat down on a rickety stool. An old man was already sat by the coals, a backgammon board at his feet.

The old man said, 'Do you play?'

'I can play,' Vasily said.

'Care to play, then?' the old man said. 'One pound a game.'

Vasily did a quick calculation, and figured he could win some of his money back. He smiled.

'Sure,' he said.

'Here's your tea,' Soraya said. When she handed it to him their hands touched briefly. He felt like he'd touched a live wire. She just kept smiling that damn smile.

'I want to live in America,' she told him. Then she went to the piles of trash and began sorting.

Vasily played backgammon with the old man. Vasily lost. He counted over the money gloomily. When he looked over to the piles the Zabbaleen women had reduced them to almost nothing.

'Another game?' the old man said hopefully.

'No, thanks,' Vasily said. He went over to the remaining trash. A much smaller, if sodden and dirty, pile of paper sat at his feet. He picked a sheet up, tried to read it, saw it was smudged and ruined. He said, 'These are torn and wet.'

'We could dry them,' Hani said, coming over. 'Clean them. The torn ones can be maybe joined together again. For a—'

'Price, yes.'

'We are poor people,' Hani said. 'But we do honest work.'

'Fine,' Vasily said. 'I don't care about the money. Here.' He took out the rest of the cash and pushed it into Hani's hands. 'I'll come back on Monday. I want everything by then. Collected, clean, sorted, and waiting for me. All right?'

'No Egyptians,' Hani said.

'What?'

'Your... interests. I will help you, but not against Egyptians.'

'I am not against... Sure, fine. I am not interested in Egyptian matters, Hani.'

'Then we have a deal.'

They shook hands.

'It is best,' Vasily said, as an afterthought, 'if I don't come back here too often. I'd like the material delivered to me. And the cash delivered to you.'

'I'll need someone I can trust,' Hani said.

Vasily nodded to where Soraya stood watching them.

'Send her,' he said.

Hani frowned.

'I will think about it,' he said.

'Monday,' Vasily said. 'I will come back. After that, we'll see.'

'What are you doing now, Vasily?' Igor Saakashvili said. He was sitting at his desk drawing a military parade on a large sheet of paper.

'Stuff,' Vasily said.

'Aha. Well, you're the master spy, Vasily,' Igor said, and he snickered when he said it, and he drew a soldier throwing grenades at a man with medals on his chest.

'What are *you* doing, Igor?' Vasily said.

'Planning an assassination.'

'What sort of an assassination, Igor?' Vasily said.

Igor shrugged. 'Just a plan to kill the president on the event of a public parade,' he said.

'*Nasser?*'

Igor shrugged again. 'Whoever's president when they tell me to put the plan into action.'

'No one is ever going to ask you to put the fucking plan into action,' Vasily said.

'Language, Vasily!' Igor said. 'I have children.'

'Do you?' Vasily said.

'Probably,' Igor said. He kept drawing. Vasily tried to ignore him. He waited for Kirpichenko. At last the door to Kirpichenko's office opened. The man himself peered out.

He said, 'Yes, Vasily?'

'A moment of your time, tovarich,' Vasily said.

'Come in. Take a seat.'

Vasily sat, clutching the satchel in his hands. His palms felt sweaty.

'Well?' Kirpichenko said.

'Tovarich, I have this.'

Vasily took out the first sheet and put it on the boss's desk. Kirpichenko picked it up, stared at it for a moment, put it down again. He said, 'What is it, Vasily?'

'The entire staff list of the French embassy,' Vasily said. 'With their internal extension numbers. And here, tovarich. There's this!' He took out a second sheet.

'This smells of rotten eggs, Vasily,' Kirpichenko said.

'Here, too,' Vasily said. He took out a smaller sheet, carefully stuck together, with some parts missing. 'A request from an Alain Garnier for a raise in salary.'

'Where did you get this?' Kirpichenko said.

'Tovarich, I called Mr Garnier on his extension, pretending to be from the Diplomatic Club. He confirmed his home address, at which point I conducted a similar operation on his trash. There are many empty bottles in his rubbish, and then there was this.'

He gave Kirpichenko the next sheet of paper.

'A letter demanding repayment of debt, from the El Cohara Casino. I spoke to the guard at his house. Mr Garnier is married, but the wife has recently left for Paris. I further conducted surveillance on Mr Garnier. Here is a photo, see?'

He put the black and white photograph on the table and stabbed at it with his finger. 'No wedding ring. I think he is ripe for recruitment. I would like to make an approach.'

'Where did you get all... this?' Kirpichenko said, his hand sweeping over the crumpled and somewhat smelly papers. 'The trash, Vasily?'

'The trash, tovarich!' Vasily said. He felt an enormous

sense of pride. 'And there is more. Much more! I am only beginning to explore the possibilities. With financing in place I could extend Chernaya Gryaz to multiple targets. Expand! Tovarich, we stand on the precipice of a gold mine here!'

Kirpichenko pursed his lips. He examined the papers, then pushed them in distaste to the side.

'Don't bring these here again,' he said. 'But clever, Vasily. Well done. The Zabbaleen?'

'Yes, tovarich.'

'Ingenious. This will have to remain compartmentalised.'

'All taken care of, tovarich.'

'Single point of contact?'

'Yes, tovarich.'

'Total deniability?'

'Yes, tovarich.'

'You handle the materials directly. Write me a weekly report. No active measures for now, Vasily. Leave the Frenchman – what was his name again?'

'Garnier.'

'Leave him alone. Let's see what your... fishing net hauls up next, shall we?'

'Of course.'

He'd never really intended to pursue the Frenchman anyway. It was just the lure he used, to show Kirpichenko what his network could do. The KGB hardly needed more agents in the DGSE, after all. The French secret service leaked like a sieve.

'Chernaya Gryaz, eh?' Kirpichenko said.

'Yes, tovarich.'

'Cute. You can go now, Vasily.'

'Thank you, Tovarich Kirpichenko.'

Vasily left. Outside, Igor was still making his assassination plans. He barely looked up as Vasily left. Vasily made it all the way to the toilets and only when he closed the door did he raise his fist in the air and whisper, 'Yes!' like he was a child. But he couldn't help it. He could see his entire future laid out before him now. The quick rise in the ranks, a couple more years in Cairo before a recall back to Moscow and a promotion, a year or two on desk then Washington, or some other plum assignment. As rezident this time.

There goes Tovarich Sokolov, they'd whisper. They say he was trained by that English master spy, Waverley himself. Sokolov, the guy who brought in Opal. The guy who built the most successful Middle Eastern network of the modern age. They say he has the ear of Khrushchev himself. Youngest KGB agent ever promoted to the rank of colonel.

They'd point as he passed. They'd be jealous and envious and aspire to be him. He could see it all.

He could see the future, and the future was so bright it hurt.

He would have laughed but, of course, he couldn't. The life was draining out of him fast. He had had such *hopes*! He supposed one could never tell the manner of one's death. He had hoped to live to be a hundred and die in his bed, but then he supposed that was just an idle fancy. He could be philosophical about it now. There just wasn't much time left.

The rat was back. Or was it a different rat?

His last meeting with Pikorski:

'I think someone is following me,' Vasily said. He had looked from side to side nervously but couldn't see anyone.

Pikorski laughed. 'You're getting paranoid,' he said.

'I'm telling you,' Vasily said.

'You think the bosses suspect anything?'

Vasily thought of Edgar's warning back in Moscow.

'Get me out,' he said.

'It's too early, Vas. They won't go for it.'

'My life is in danger!'

Pikorski sighed.

'I can ask,' he said.

'I won't be alone,' Vasily said. 'I want to take a girl with me.'

'Who doesn't want to take a girl with them,' Pikorski said. The ruthlessness behind his placid façade peeked out then. 'They'll want a real payout, Vas. What can you give them?'

Implicit in the question: You're just a second-rate spy.

'I'll come up with something,' Vasily said.

'Do that and we'll talk,' Pikorski said.

Damn the Americans and their effortless arrogance, Vasily thought. But he didn't want to go back to Moscow. He dreaded the greyness and Svetlana's touch. Standing in line for the baker's. The child he barely knew. Sooner or later they'd recall him. He'd get a desk job or a bullet, either way, the carefree life he had would be over. He wanted to be a *real* spy! Sean Connery with the girls in bikinis. Not... this.

Lonely men with drinking problems and not enough cash. Wasn't that the profile? No wonder they were watching him. But then he rallied. He really *was* a great spy, what with his new network and all. And he was crazy about Soraya.

'What *do* you do, Mr Sokolov?' she said.

'Please, call me Vasily. Soraya.' He liked saying her name.

'What is this for, what you do?' she said.

'As I told your father, I'm a commercial representative,' he said. 'I am just looking for an edge over the competition. Everyone does it, really.'

'Yes,' she said. She didn't sound convinced. But it was a good enough story. When she came to the hotel he barely recognised her. She'd done her hair, her dress was new, Western. She looked like any of the chic girls passing by outside in downtown. She turned heads.

She had handed him the latest papers. Clean, pressed, put together. He put them away. Said, 'Can I get you a drink?'

'I don't drink much, Mr Sokolov.'

'Please, please,' he said. 'Vasily. Vasya.'

'Vasya?' she said.

'That's what my friends call me,' he said, and smiled at her. She smiled back. The dress clung to her body so well. He was very conscious of it, of the way she moved.

'You like me?' she said, with a lack of embarrassment.

'Yes,' he whispered. 'Very much so.'

'I like you OK,' Soraya said. As though she'd just decided.

'Here,' Vasily said. 'I got you a gift.'

He took out the cheap pocket watch with the flaking gold paint. He gave it to her.

'An old watch?' she said.

'Antique,' he said. 'A family heirloom. I want you to have it.'

'You like me that much, huh?' she said.

'I like you,' he said helplessly.

And that was that. That was all there was to say. Lying here on the old broken trash, he felt himself become a part of it. Vasily Sokolov, which wasn't even his real name, who was born, had lived, had trained in his chosen profession, had travelled and seen some, if only a little, of the world. Who recruited Opal, or was recruited by him, who could now say? Who established the Chernaya Gryaz network, who loved and laughed and cried if only rarely, who once killed a man and once, just once, climbed the Great Pyramid and saw the whole world lying at his feet.

He thought of his confused final moments, coming out of the hotel, coming out here to see the trash men, but there was only one, a young intense man who looked vaguely familiar – one of those who hung out in Imbaba, who always stared directly at Soraya.

Vasily started on a greeting he never finished. The young man had a knife. He plunged it twice into Vasily's body, each blow making a soft whoomp sound. The world spun. The man stabbed him a third time, then ran away. Vasily staggered, fell onto the rubbish.

It was all so stupid, he thought.

A galaxy of stars spun overhead. There was nothing like the skies above the desert.

He saw the rat was back.

Vasily tried to say something, perhaps goodbye.

The rat's nose twitched, and then the lights went out.

PART FIVE

ZABBALEEN

MARIAM

1987

35

The lights waited. When the lights came on Mariam came alive, like the princess in the fairytale who slept until a kiss woke her. The lights murmured, calling to her, promising sweet nothings. Mariam loved the lights and the lights loved her.

The spotlights on stage had not yet been turned on, and the audience hadn't yet come in through the doors. Ticket sales had gone well, Enrique told her, they might even have a sold-out screening tonight. The marquee above the cinema said *Fantastafestival – Roma – 1987* in tired letters, and below, *Tonight's showing: Gladiatore 3000!*

Mariam sat in the dressing room, far nicer than anything she had had in Cairo, and looked at her reflection. The mirror was surrounded by bright light bulbs. The woman who did the make-up had come and gone. Mariam was alone. She waited. She waited to come alive.

There was a knock on the door.

'Come in,' Mariam said, in English.

A woman poked her head in through the door. She had long, curly brown hair and wore glasses in a black frame. She said, 'Miss Khouri? I'm Flavia. From *Cinema Nuovo*?'

'The magazine,' Mariam said. 'Yes. Yes, of course.' She felt self-conscious.

'May I come in?'

'Yes, of course. Please. I was told you were coming.'

Flavia smiled. She closed the door behind her. 'I'm sorry I'm late,' she said. 'Traffic was hell. Rome, you know.'

For Mariam, Rome was a confusion of noise and colour, the smell of garlic in olive oil, tiny compact cars, clean streets, people in fabulous clothes. It was a little like Cairo and yet nothing like it. Being here was like being in a fairytale. A line she needed to remember to say to the woman from *Cinema Nuovo*; it was the sort of line readers liked, it made her life seem like a dream. No one wanted reality from the girl on the screen. No one needed it.

Flavia brought out a notepad and pen. She sat down in a chair and tapped the pen on the notepad and smiled again. She seemed friendly.

'Whenever you're ready,' she said.

Mariam nodded. The lights went on in her head. She smiled sweetly, the same smile that captured Bobby Rhodes' heart in *Alligator Women* and Jack Palance's in *Ride 'em, Cowboy, Ride 'em Hard*.

'Shoot,' she said.

Just like Palance taught her. She liked saying it. It sounded American.

'Tell me about your childhood,' Fabia said. 'Let's start with that.' She looked at Mariam encouragingly.

Mariam took a breath.

'We were poor but happy...' she began.

★

One morning, when she was eight or nine years old, her mother took Mariam to the Egyptian Museum off Tahrir Square. She'd paid the full ticket price, and for some three hours she led Mariam by the hand around the ancient exhibits of their ancestors, for like many she liked to claim direct descent for the Copts from the ancient Egyptians. Mariam saw more treasure than she could ever imagine. Gold, which never fades and never changes, eternal as a sun, filled the museum, sitting behind display glass. Entombed with the fabulous brooches and headdresses, amulets and statues were the mummies and the canopic jars that held their viscera. The dead lay in the museum surrounded by their gold. Death and wealth, both unimaginable to Mariam at the time, became inexorably entwined in her mind. Later, on the street, Soraya bought her a rare treat, a plain feteer dusted in a thin layer of powdered sugar.

'You're a smart girl, Mariam,' her mother said. It was said not so much as praise. A statement of fact, perhaps, that wasn't quite an accusation.

'Yes, Mama,' Mariam said. She licked sugar from the corner of her lips.

'You do well at school.'

'Yes, Mama.'

'People can be so smart sometimes,' her mother said, 'that they are downright stupid.'

With that somewhat cryptic comment she took Mariam home. This was not too long after their sudden eviction from Imbaba to the foothills of Mokattam. Mariam did not remember Imbaba well, but she remembered the hasty, panicked voyage as they were forced to leave, how they packed the little they owned and left behind the world she knew to trek across the city to the new place. Here they had to erect makeshift tin huts from the refuse they had collected. Grandfather Hani was angry for a long time after the move.

At that time, too, the Ramzy family grew strong and more numerous, and used the move to the new territory to claim more of the traditional collecting routes to themselves. This led to conflict with her kin, the Khouris, and for a while things were tense, and scattered gunshots could be heard sometimes in the night, echoing in this new, lonely home.

Soraya no longer worked in the sorting of the rubbish. She took a job at the Balmoral, through the assistance of an American friend who had resided there for a time, and she held on to it with tenacity. She always had stories, though Mariam never knew how much to believe. Once, her mother told Mariam that her father was a Russian spy, another time that he was dead, or had defected to America, where he was waiting for them to join him. There had been various men in Soraya's life, including, for a time, a small, intense man who was a Ramzy, but he vanished one day, in something of a hurry, and it was rumoured he had killed a man.

Not that the police were likely to come to Mokattam. The Zabbaleen kept their own order, and a policeman was wiser than to come inside. On Sundays, Grandfather Hani took Mariam to the Coptic Orthodox church in St Simon Monastery. The church was situated in a huge cave, dug into the side of the mountain. It was there, under rough-hewn stone, that the Zabbaleen congregated, the hush of the stones allowing the singing and praying to rise and multiply.

Mariam loved it there, loved the amphitheatre seating that made her think, perversely, of being present at some ancient gladiatorial arena under Greece or Rome, and though the church was new it seemed timeless to her. Here, too, all differences were put aside, and the rival families would meet on holy ground to remember what united them. A shared faith, and a shared heritage, and though they saw themselves purely as Egyptians, Mariam was aware that more and more were leaving for Canada or the United States, especially since President Sadat came into power and made such departures easier. Every month a different family was gone from the congregation, and sometimes airmail letters would arrive, the letters scribbled small on thin rice paper, telling of their new, exciting lives in their new world.

Soraya seldom came to church, and when the letters from America arrived she would scoff, but then she'd read them avidly, and Mariam knew her mother fantasised about going too, of taking her daughter with her and starting a new life somewhere else. It was only a fantasy, and there was no harm in it. Like the way her mother would sometimes cut out pictures from magazines, the full-colour ones, showing amazing kitchen appliances from America, the latest fashions from Paris, and beautiful homes behind white picket fences where happy, prosperous families posed for the photographer's lens.

Their life in the new Zabbaleen City was very different from these images, which may as well have been beamed down from space. The narrow streets were piled high with all the city's junk, the dogs climbing over it to catch the rats, and the pigs were scattered from the endless traffic of bikes and small trucks that came and went at all hours.

In all of this, though, Mariam was happy. She was surrounded by her family, lulled by the re-established routine of work, school and church. Many of the children didn't go to school but Soraya insisted that Mariam did. The nuns who taught her were strict, but one or two were young and kind, and even the older ones would let a sudden ray of sweetness shine through and belie their terrifying appearance. Mariam was good at mathematics. Soon she was helping Grandfather Hani with his books, for the Khouris' trade was flourishing, and Mariam's uncles, with a combination of muscle and diplomacy, were expanding the area under their control.

Inside Zabbaleen City the world was perhaps much as it had been for her people for decades. But outside, the world was changing, and it filtered in and entered their bubble the way everything did, through the trash. The nuns taught variously in English and French, but everyone preferred English now. People watched American movies and wanted to drive American cars. Egypt looked to the West now that Nasser was gone, and the huge Soviet embassy on the Nile in Dokki, which Mariam saw once from a distance, looked these days more like a fossilised elephant, slowly bleaching in the sun.

What Mariam loved was the endless river of print that came into Mokattam on the carts. She would look through the piles, pull out copies of *Al-Kawākib* and follow the glamorous lives of film stars like Zubaida Tharwat, who had the eyes of Nefertiti, Samia Gamal, who danced her way across the screen next to Farid al-Atrash, and Soad Hosny, the Egyptian Cinderella. She pored over *Al-Ahram* every day, to keep up with world and local news, often seeking out tales of spies as though they may offer some hint as to her mysterious father. Once she came across the mention of a German, Lotz, who spied for Israel and was imprisoned in Tora, and she wondered if he had known her father. Soraya would never be drawn on the topic. What mattered was not some man, but family.

'Get your head out of the trash, binti, and start *thinking*,' Soraya said. 'A woman's always alone in this world. You have to be smart.'

How one could be both always alone and yet dependent on family was a mystery to Mariam, but then many things were. How come there was so much trash in Cairo? How did the ancients build the pyramids? How did one become a movie star like Faten Hamamah?

Most of all, she loved it when Soraya took her to the Metro or the Diana or Cinema Miami to watch the movies. There was something about the darkness of the great cavernous spaces, the flickering beam of light from the projector above, the sound and the fury on the screen, that reminded her of church. They watched *Sunset and Sunrise*, *The Killers* and *Adrift on the Nile*, *City Lights* and *Children of Silence*. They watched *Funny Lady* with Barbra Streisand and Omar Sharif. Soraya loved Omar Sharif, who was a Christian like them, though not a Copt. But Mariam loved Barbra more, just as she loved Nadia Lufti in *Wild Flowers* and Shadia in *The Fugitive*. The women on the screen were Egyptian just like her, but they were somehow more than that, for they had been turned to light and lived magnified, like ancient goddesses risen from the ruined temples of Abu Simbel and Luxor, to be worshipped and adored.

She wanted to be like them, and she cut out their photos from the pages of *Al-Kawākib* and stuck them to the wall next to her bed, so that they could watch over her as she slept.

36

THE SCRATCHING OF THE JOURNALIST'S PEN WAS THE only sound in the room. A copy of *Cinema Nuovo* sat on the dresser, a picture of Bernardo Bertolucci on the cover. He had deep-set eyes. Mariam was all but promised the next cover. She just had to give good story.

'I would like some water now,' she said. 'Do you mind?'

'Of course not,' Flavia said. 'Please, Miss Khouri.'

'Mrs Gallo, soon,' Mariam said.

'Of course,' Flavia said. Mariam smiled with pleasure. She extended her hand to the journalist. Flavia admired the new ring, that shiny stone.

'And how does it feel to be getting married to the great Enrique Gallo?' Flavia said.

'We haven't got to that part of the story yet,' Mariam said, laughing. Flavia laughed too.

'So you always knew you wanted to be a movie star?' she said.

'No, not at all,' Mariam said. 'It seemed unimaginable to me.'

'But it wasn't.'

'Miracles happen,' Mariam said.

'You believe in miracles?'

'We must have faith,' Mariam said.

'Of course, of course.' The journalist wrote that one down. Good. They were devout people, the Italians. 'Tits, blood and priests,' Enrique told her. 'That's what the people want to see on screen. It is very hard to make a good movie, my love. It's very hard to make any kind of movie.' They'd just come out of a private screening for Joe D'Amato's *Convent of Sinners*. 'I want to make a *great* movie, Mariam!' Enrique said. 'And I want you to star in it.'

It was the night he proposed, with a ring that had belonged to his grandmother. Enrique was sweet, and he loved her very much. There could be worse matches, even if he never did make a good movie.

'Mariam. Mariam!'

It was Fuad, come running through the mounds of trash that looked like hills set against a setting sun. Dogs yelped and sprinted away from their resting places in his wake, his beaming face turning Mokattam into an enchanted land, because he only had eyes for her. There was a gladness that came alive inside her only when she was with Fuad.

'What is it?' she said, laughing. He rushed to her side and then stopped, looking suddenly sheepish.

'I got this for you,' he said. 'It's from the rich people's trash. In Zamalek.'

Zamalek was the prized jewel of the Khouris, Cairo's wealthiest neighbourhood, a place where the very air smelled rich and perfumed, where people ate rubies and pooped out gold. Their trash was the best in all of the city, and it was the source of the Khouris' wealth. *They* controlled the rubbish collection for the neighbourhood now. It took time, negotiations and bloodshed, but it was theirs at last, it was their right.

Fuad worked for Mariam's grandfather. He was a year older than Mariam. More worldly. He was out there day after day, learning the ropes, seeing the city, sometimes even getting tips from the kindlier residents of Zamalek. He always wore the same things on his rounds, trousers too large for him, with holes in them, sandals that were coming apart, a shirt that wouldn't have been new even back in the time of the Khedive. He smudged his face with soot. He made a sorry sight. It made the tips better.

He grinned at her expectantly. 'Here,' he said.

'What is it?'

'Open it.'

She looked at the heavy package. It was gift wrapped. She said, 'You *wrapped* it, Fuad?'

He beamed.

'Found it like that,' he said. 'It was in the trash. I had a peek inside, though.'

Mariam saw the rip, and how he'd taped it back over.

'Come on, what is it?' she said again.

'Open it!'

She put the package on the ground. She hesitated. No one had given her such a heavy gift before.

'Come on!'

Mariam ripped the wrapping. The paper was so delicate and expensive! There was even a little bow taped to the top. People stared at them, but then people always watched everything you were doing. Mariam tore the wrappings and set them to one side to put into the paper pulp vats later for recycling.

'No,' she said.

'Yes!' Fuad said.

She stared at it in incomprehension.

'But who would throw something like this away?' she said.

'It was for a lady,' Fuad said. 'A very fancy lady on the third floor of an apartment building on El-Malek El-Fadl, near the Supreme Council of Antiquities building. She tips me sometimes. But not recently. Recently she has been very angry.'

'Why is she angry?'

'It is because of a man,' Fuad said. 'Her boyfriend. He is a no-good man. He cheated on her, Mariam. So she threw him out. And he bought her this to say sorry, but she shouted at him on the street, and everyone heard the names she called him. And then she threw this in the trash.'

Mariam looked at the machine in wonder.

'It's a video player,' she said.

'Brand new,' Fuad said proudly.

'Does it work?' Mariam said.

'Work? Of course it works!'

'Is it Betamax?'

'No, VHS,' Fuad said.

'Oh.'

'VHS is better!' he said, even though they both knew it wasn't true.

'You should sell it,' Mariam said. 'It's too expensive.'

'I wanted to give it to you,' he said.

'I can't take it, Fuad!' she said. 'It costs a fortune!'

'You're worth it, Mariam,' he said. 'Besides, I got these in Dr Saleh's trash, he lives on the second floor of that building.' And he brandished two VHS tapes at her which he materialised, magician-like, from under his jacket.

Mariam took them from him. Fuad couldn't read, but you didn't need to be able to read when it came to cassettes. These ones were genuine, not even pirate tapes like they sold in the Khan el-Khalili, but the real thing.

'Lemora, Lady Dracula,' Mariam read aloud. The cover showed the disembodied pale face of a woman grinning maniacally against a dark background. The lettering dripped red. A blue stamp on the back screamed VIDEO ENTERTAINMENT!

'And...' she frowned. 'Eegah?' The cover showed a giant caveman with a club. '"The crazed love of a pre... a prehistoric giant for a ravishing teen-age girl",' she said. She looked on the back. 'Who is Richard Kiel?' she said.

'It doesn't matter!' Fuad said. 'I'll tell you what, Mariam. Let's plug it into your grandfather's TV. At least we can watch them before I sell it. What do you say?'

'Deal,' Mariam said quickly. She put her hand out and Fuad, grinning, shook it. Something like happiness, like a spark, coursed through her as their skins touched.

'I don't like you hanging with that boy, Fuad,' her mother said. 'People who live in trash can still keep their hands clean.'

'Fuad is my friend!' Mariam said.

'A boy is nobody's friend, Mariam. They're selfish and

hungry and if you're not a wife you're a used tissue that ends up in the garbage.' Soraya brooded. 'Even if you are a wife,' she said. 'Anyway, you are not marrying that boy. He is going nowhere.'

'He works in Zamalek!' Mariam said. Working in Zamalek was like, like... words deserted her. It was like you were already rich.

'And this machine doesn't belong to him to give away,' Soraya said. 'It belongs to your grandfather. All the trash from Zamalek belongs to the Khouris.'

'He was just being *nice*,' Mariam said. She felt the anger, never these days far below the surface, threaten to rise. She loved her mother. It was her duty to obey her mother. But every time Mariam spoke to Soraya she wanted to scream at her.

They were in the living room of the new house. No more tin shacks, not after nearly a decade in Mokattam. Hani Khouri and his sons built the house from bricks, connected it to electricity with a high wire running off the main grid, and furnished it with brand-new rugs, a shrink-wrapped sofa from the store, tables and chairs, all with the money they made on the trash. There was nothing used in the new house, all was new, and the sofa squeaked with the plastic every time Mariam sat on it.

Grandma Sandra – Umm Nader to all her acquaintances – was in the kitchen outside, making meat broth on the fire and baking bread. She distrusted modern appliances. Earlier, Uncle Nader and Uncle Farid slaughtered one of the pigs outside and, having done so, carefully separated and packaged the meat to be sold to the upmarket hotels downtown. They were gone now, along with the pig, and the blood baked into the dark dry ground. Mariam's stomach rumbled. She was always hungry these days.

The VCR sat next to the brand-new television, which was bought from an electronics store on Sidi Abd El-Gawad Square in Bulaq only two months before. The day it was brought, carried with all pomp on the back of her uncle's truck through the alleys of Mokattam, people came to gape, and to murmur in envy of the Khouris' prosperity.

'We can just watch the movie, Mama,' Mariam said. 'Then Uncle can sell it.'

'Who puts such a thing in the trash?' Soraya said, transferring the object of her outrage seamlessly onto the nameless scorned woman of Zamalek. 'To throw away such a thing, it's, it's… immoral, Mariam.'

'Maybe she just didn't want it,' Mariam said.

'Then she should have sold it!' her mother snapped. 'The wise person throws nothing away.'

Mariam thought of the endless piles of rubbish outside.

'There must be few wise people in Cairo, then,' she said, and her mother gave a sudden, surprised bark of laughter.

'Let's watch this movie then,' Soraya said. 'Somehow, you always get your way.'

But she no longer sounded angry.

Fade in. Desert. The image revealed only lasted five seconds. The desert was not like the one outside Cairo, or perhaps it was, in that all deserts, Mariam reflected, must in some way be the same. She didn't know. She was no Bedouin. She was a city girl. There were young Americans driving around in large cars. A giant caveman with a club in his hand. People in nice suits dining in something like a club. More desert, a helicopter. A boy played an electric guitar as a girl swam in a pool. The pool looked nice. The sort of pool only rich people ever got to swim in. Girls in bikinis and young men who had never gone hungry. Mariam wished she could lounge by a pool like that, too.

Grandfather Hani tsked disapproval at the girls in bikinis, then grinned. More desert, then the giant caveman was back. The boy with the guitar now had a gun. He fought the giant caveman. Then a pool party and a rock'n'roll band. The giant caveman disrupted the party. The caveman tried to take the girl away. He was shot by the sheriff. He floated face down in the water.

The camera lingered on the giant's club in the pool, a dark spot that might have been the giant's loincloth.

'Poor devil,' the narrator's gravelly voice said.

Soraya cried. She was a sucker for doomed love and tragic heroes. Grandfather Hani said, 'I've seen worse,' and went off to find his wife outside.

Mariam remained in front of the television, though. It wasn't the movie, with its strangely wooden actors, the frequent and inexplicable musical interludes or the male lead, the boyfriend with his expression of constant constipation that arrested her, but that near-final shot, of the club and the black thing floating in the water, the camera drifting across them until it finally pulled away. Somehow there was magic in it, and Mariam rewound the tape and watched the movie again, alone, as her mother wandered off, her grandmother called her in vain to come have supper, as the moon rose outside and the heaps of garbage, ever present, stood serene in the moonlight's glare, the rats awake and sniffing for action as Cairo, asleep under the hot day sun, woke up slowly into night-time.

'Poor devil,' Mariam said. 'Poor devil.'

37

'HOW ARE WE DOING?' ENRIQUE SAID, STICKING HIS head into the dressing room. He saw Flavia, smiled, extended his arm and entered fully into the room.

'Ciao, Flavia! Ciao, ciao!'

A kiss on both cheeks, an affectionate holding of the hands, then he turned to Mariam, his bride to be, taking her hand (the one with the diamond ring) and kissing it, always theatrical, saying, 'My darling. Is she treating you right?'

'It's only an interview, darling,' Mariam said.

'Only an interview!' Enrique said in mock outrage. 'It's *Cinema Nuovo*, darling!'

'Yes, darling,' Mariam said, lowering her eyes and smiling. Flavia took it all in and shrugged at their antics.

'She's in good hands, Enrique,' she said. 'You can rest easy.'

'And the cover, Flavia? She gets the cover, yes?'

'You worry too much, Enrique, I already said it was a done deal.'

'Then I will take up no more of your time,' Enrique said. He blew kisses as he retreated to the door. 'Ciao! Ciao!'

'You are very close?' Flavia said when the door shut.

'Close? Of course,' Mariam said.

'Any thought of children yet, Mariam? Once you're married, of course.'

'Children?' Mariam said. 'Oh, no, no. It's too soon to think about that.'

'It's never too soon to think about children,' Flavia said. A look came into her eyes that was part sadness and part curiosity. Mariam looked away, looked at the lights round the mirror and at her reflection.

Children complicated everything. That was what Soraya always used to say.

'Family,' Flavia said. 'It's important to you, yes?'

'Of course,' Mariam said. 'Very.'

'Your mother was a positive influence?'

'She was a wonderful woman,' Mariam said. 'A wonderful mother.'

'And your father, Mariam?'

'He died,' Mariam said. 'I never knew him.'

'I'm so sorry,' Flavia said.

Mariam smiled bravely. Just as she had hundreds of times before. 'He was a wonderful man,' she said. 'I wish I got to know him.'

'What did he do?'

'He was in trade.'

Flavia made notes in her notebook. Her pen scratched the page, making a sound like a chicken trying to escape at the door of its coop.

Once a month, a man named Gregor came to see Mariam's grandfather. It was not always the same man but he always had the same name. Sometimes one of the Gregors, the one who came most frequently, would stop by the kitchen and make small talk with Soraya, if she was there, and always made some comment on Mariam and how well she was doing. It was important, Gregor said, that she keep going to school and get good grades. The Gregor who came most often had kind eyes and once, just once, when they were alone in the kitchen, he said unexpectedly, 'Your father is always thinking of you.' He hesitated, as though he had said something wrong, then took a small box from his pocket and gave it to her. It had Cyrillic letters on it and when she opened it she discovered a wooden doll, lovingly painted, inside which nestled a smaller doll, inside which nestled yet another. There were six dolls in all, from the largest to the smallest, all similar in shape yet painted in different colours.

After that visit the Gregor didn't come back for a long time, and other Gregors came in his place, but they continued to arrive, punctually, once a month, late in the evening, handing her grandfather an envelope and receiving in return a satchel full of papers from the junk. These visits had gone on for as long as Mariam could remember, beginning in Imbaba and continuing in Mokattam.

There came a time, near her seventeenth birthday, when things grew tense in the capital. There were riots in the streets, and some blamed the Soviet Union for fomenting unrest, and some blamed Al-Gama'a al-Islamiyya, and some blamed the president for all of society's ills. Whoever was truly at fault, in such a climate it was not good to be a Copt. The Zabbaleen went about their business all the same, for trash needed to be collected, and in October a victory parade was organised, to march through Cairo, and

Mirage jets flew overhead. Mariam had wanted to go out to see the parade as it passed but her grandfather forbade it, and for once she did not argue. They stayed in, and watched the parade on the television. Tanks rolled in the streets and soldiers marched. The president stood at the back of a truck, saluting the troops. They came to the main stage and he took his place, a small, thin blade of a man, amidst the other dignitaries. There were men from Ireland and Cuba and America with him, and a Coptic bishop, too. They all stood there and watched the military might of Egypt on display.

When it happened, it was so confusing, and happened so quickly that it was hard to say at first what it was. Some of the soldiers, dismounting from a vehicle, approached the stands and opened fire. The television signal cut and was replaced with music, then recitations from the Quran. Mariam could hear the sudden silence everywhere, the breathless, nervous anticipation of everyone watching: the sense of something terrible that had happened and was still to come.

It was broken just as quickly as it rose, that silence, that anticipation which, years later, she still thought of as the magic moment in a darkened cinema, the instant where the audience, put under a spell, collectively succumbs to something larger than reality and yet flimsier. The cobwebs of magic which is spectacle in its pure form, of actors transitioned into light, dancing upon motes of dust.

Word travelled fast. It was an assassination. The president, shot several times, was airlifted to hospital but died two hours later. The foreign dignitaries were wounded and one died, two generals also died, as did the photographer and the bishop. Cairo was put under a state of emergency and even the Zabbaleen did not go on their rounds the next day. There was an uprising in Asyut, but it was put down.

The president was buried four days later. This time, too, Mariam watched it on the television. It held a strong pull on her, the sadness and the spectacle. Men in uniforms marched with guns, then came the palm bearers. At last came the horse and cart, much like her grandfather's, and in the back of the cart lay the coffin. Finally came the mourners, men in suits, who marched behind the coffin. There were no women to mourn the president, not here, not on the television, and the coffin was carried to its last resting place, at the pyramid-shaped Monument to the Unknown Soldier, which was ordered into being by the president himself some years back when he was still alive.

Soraya cried. She was a sucker for doomed love and tragic heroes. Grandfather Hani said solemnly, 'Now things will be worse for us,' and went off to find his wife outside.

Mariam remained in front of the television. It wasn't the funeral, with its strangely wooden actors, nor the pomp and circumstance of the occasion which arrested her, but that near-final shot, of the coffin carried, as though floating in air, the camera lingering over it until it finally pulled away. Somehow there was magic in it, and she realised sadness and happiness were merely two effects of the same medium, and that the moving pictures on the screen could evoke either one.

Her grandmother called her in vain to dinner. The moon rose and the heaps of garbage, ever present, stood to attention outside like soldiers on parade.

'Poor devil,' Mariam said. 'Poor devil.'

★

The next month, no Gregor came to the house, nor the month after or the one after that. But Mariam kept the dolls, all nestled inside each other, and when she looked at them she imagined her father was still alive, somewhere out there, and that he was thinking of her; he loved her. The new president was much like the old president, insofar as the city still stood and trash still had to be collected every day. The Zabbaleen continued to do so, and to sort it, and to use or sell what was usable or sellable, and the pigs kept eating the food that was thrown away every day, until they grew fat and were slaughtered and sold to the hotels.

Life, in other words, continued. For Mariam, suspended in between adolescence and adulthood, every day seemed like an agony of waiting, the same minuet of daily routines enacted as though life was a film reel forever looping on the projector.

One day Fuad came again from his rounds and they stood and spoke in the shade.

'You know my cousin Fayez, from the village?' Fuad said.

'No?' Mariam said.

'He sent me a letter,' Fuad said. 'I am going to go up there to see him.'

'To the village?' Mariam said.

'The village is my heart,' Fuad said. 'Cairo is just where I live.'

'You've been there, what, twice, in all the time I've known you?' Mariam said.

'Many times,' Fuad said. 'When I marry it will be to a girl from the village. She will come to live in Cairo with me.'

'And there I was thinking you were going to ask for my hand in marriage,' Mariam said, and gave a small curtsey. Fuad didn't laugh. He looked at her very seriously and at last shook his head.

'Your grandfather would never allow it,' he said. 'And besides, you are a handful, Mariam.'

She stared at him, outraged beyond words.

'It's true,' Fuad said. 'You are more than one man could manage, and you don't know what you want. A woman needs to know her own mind.' He sounded like he was quoting someone older.

'Anyway, I found this,' he said, before she had a chance to come up with a reply. He thrust a folder of stained paper at her.

'What is it?' Mariam said.

'I don't know, but it looks important,' Fuad said. 'There's pictures of gold in it. I found it in the trash of the Supreme Council of Antiquities. They never tip, and the guard is often rude to me.'

Mariam studied the folder.

'It's a report on a new dig site near Aswan,' she said. 'Look, they found pottery shards and a bracelet, and they think there might be a tomb there. There's a map.' She stabbed at the page.

'This shouldn't be in the trash,' she said. 'If anyone found it...'

'I found it,' Fuad said. He looked excited. 'Is it near the village, this grave?'

'Not really,' Mariam said.

Fuad studied the map and pursed his lips.

'It's close enough,' he said. 'With a truck.'

'Where will you get a truck?' Mariam said.

'Fayez's uncle has a truck,' Fuad said.

'Grave robbing is a crime,' Mariam said.

'Being poor is a crime,' Fuad said. 'Thanks, Mariam. I'll see you.'

He took his folder back and sauntered away. Mariam stared after him.

What did he *mean* she was a handful! she thought furiously.

38

THE LIGHTS WAITED. OUTSIDE THE THEATRE, PEOPLE would be getting ready for the show. They'd be putting on their evening clothes, going out for an early drink, perhaps queuing up for the last remaining tickets. The lights waited, murmuring softly to Mariam, willing her to come alive for them. No matter how much time might pass, they seemed to say, she will always be there, now, alive and young, for as long as there was film and for as long as it was threaded onto a projector.

Then she will rise, a being of pure light, and act once more upon the gaze of spectators. And if not film then video cassettes, on television screens, or late-night cable like they had in America. The ancient pharaohs sought immortality in building pyramids and tombs filled up with gold. But Mariam had something better.

'Favourite films?' Flavia said. Mariam stared into the mirror.

'There was Shadi Abdel Salam's *The Night of Counting the Years*, of course,' Mariam said. '*Al-Mummia*.'

Flavia looked up with some surprise. 'The one produced by Rossellini?' she said. 'About the grave robbers.'

'Yes. There is a beautiful shot of the funeral, at the beginning of the movie,' Mariam said. 'The coffin is carried slowly through the desert. The tombstones are stark white, like ivory pieces. The women wait, head to toe black, each woman stands alone and yet they all stand together. All you can hear is the wind.'

She'd watched it with Soraya at the Metro back when she was seven years old or so. Soraya always dressed for the cinema. Where she walked, heads turned. To Mariam she was the most glamorous person in the world, equal to or even surpassing Nadia Lufti on the screen.

The journalist wrote something in her notebook, then put down her pen and sighed. 'I could kill for a coffee,' she said.

'I will go get some,' Mariam said. She was happy to leave the dressing room for a while. She went out into the corridor. Her name was on the door. That made her happy. In the old days there were no dressing rooms or trailers, and often she had had to do her own make-up on set. She went into the small staff kitchen and filled the moka pot with water and ground coffee, then placed it carefully on the stove. She often missed coffee cooked the Egyptian way, stirred into the water in the pot and brewed carefully on the fire, but this was Italy, and she'd taken to it well enough.

There was so much *food*, now, pastas and meat stews and seafood and fish, *ice cream*, and when Enrique and crew had dinners they were always so long and had so many dishes. She had to watch her figure, so she ate salad a lot and tried to stay off the bread. She missed ful medames, but no one in Italy had that for breakfast. They mostly had chocolate pastry and coffee.

When the coffee was ready she took it off the stove and placed the moka pot on a tray, with two small cups, a bowl of sugar and some cookies. She carried it all back to the dressing room.

'Here, let me help you with that,' Flavia said. She took the tray from Mariam and put it on a stool. They sat across from each other and Mariam poured.

'Sugar?' she said.

Flavia waved the offer away, but did accept a cookie. The coffee was bitter and strong, and it made Mariam think of home, though it was strange: she did not miss it as much as perhaps she thought she should. It was as if there were two Mariams: one who came before *Black Dirt* and one who came after, and the woman she became simply had no *time* to be homesick, because there was so much that was new and exciting still ahead.

'That was your first time in front of a camera? *Black Dirt?*' Flavia said, as though reading her mind. The coffee was finished and the pen was back in her hand, poised to turn words into print and story into truth. You could never trust what you read in those actor interviews, Mariam thought. Everyone just said what they thought you wanted to hear.

'*La Spia,*' Mariam said. 'Yes. It was not a big role.' She laughed. 'I'm surprised you remember it. I was only supposed to be in the background, to begin with...'

'It is time you found work, Mariam,' Soraya said. 'You can sort through the rubbish or you can come work in the hotel with me. I can get you a job as a maid.'

'I don't want to be a maid,' Mariam said.

'Do you want to pick through trash?' Soraya said.

'There's no shame in picking through trash,' Mariam said.

Soraya shrugged.

'Then work for your grandfather,' she said.

'I will come with you,' Mariam said.

'That's what I thought,' her mother said.

They walked, then took a bus downtown the next day. Mariam had been to the Balmoral hotel before, twice with her mother, once with her grandfather when she was small, when he went on his route to collect the trash. Then, she had been at the back of the hotel, and marvelled at how much trash there was, and in what rich variety. Now she came in through the staff entrance on the side, and was deposited into the hands of Umm Zayed, a formidable presence, who looked Mariam up and down once and said, 'You can work in the laundry room.'

'I was told I would be a maid,' Mariam said.

'You, a maid?' Umm Zayed said. 'Can you even make a bed, girl?'

'I... yes?'

'Aha. Go get changed into uniform. They will be deducted from your pay. Then go report to Umm Jalil in Laundry.'

'Can I—?'

'What?' Umm Zayed said.

Mariam shook her head.

'Yes, Umm Zayed,' she said.

Mariam changed into the uniform they gave her. It had belonged to someone else before, and didn't fit her, but it was starched and ironed and smelled faintly of lavender detergent. Mariam wandered the back of house quarters, passed the kitchens, turned back, turned left and found the laundry, a huge room with electric machines lining one wall, baskets of sheets and bed coverings, and women busy hanging, folding and ironing, which made the room fill with a constant cloud of steam.

Umm Jalil, with a Cleopatra Luxe cigarette dangling from her lips, spoke little and had the arms of a wrestler. She pointed to an unattended ironing table, then waited, the ash growing longer on the end of her cigarette but never falling off, until Mariam picked up the iron. For the next eight hours she worked until her arms threatened to fall off, her hands blistering and her face growing red and hot in the steam. The amount of laundry seemed endless, and as soon as a crate of clean sheets went out a new one came in, and the huge washing machines turned and turned, sloshing water and soap. When Mariam got her break there was no sign of her mother, and she sat with the other women in the adjacent room as they ate the food they'd brought from home.

'Hi,' a girl her age said, approaching Mariam. 'I'm Mona. Are you new? You're so pretty.'

'I'm Mariam,' Mariam said. 'Do you work in the laundry too?'

'I'm a cook,' Mona said. 'I mean, I help the cooks. But I want to be a pastry chef.'

'I don't like the laundry,' Mariam said, and Mona laughed.

'No one likes the laundry,' she said. 'Where are you from?'

'Mokattam,' Mariam said. 'My mother works here as a floor manager.'

She said it with some bitterness. It was not fair that her

mother was in a position of such authority and yet here Mariam was in the most menial job.

'You're Soraya's daughter!' Mona said. 'I should have realised. You look so much like her.'

'Do I?' Mariam said self-consciously. She tucked a strand of damp hair behind her ear. She felt so gawky next to her mother.

'I'm from downtown,' Mona said. 'Right here, born and raised. My mother's a nurse at the Coptic Hospital in al-Zahir.'

'You're a Copt?' Mariam said.

'No, Muslim,' Mona said. 'What music do you like to listen to? Do you like ABBA? I love ABBA. Do you have a record player?'

'No,' Mariam said. 'I like movies. We have a video player at home.'

She felt a rush of pleasure when she saw Mona's eyes open wide at that news.

'What movies do you like?' Mona said. 'Did you see *The Gods Must Be Crazy*? It's so funny.'

'It was!' Mariam said. 'Did you see *Where Do You Hide the Sun*? It's with Nadia Lufti.'

'I like foreign movies more,' Mona said. 'Hey, we should—'

She was interrupted in that by Umm Zayed, who had been chatting in low voices to Umm Jalil.

'Get back to work, girls,' Umm Zayed said. 'The head of the lazy is the home of Satan.'

Umm Jalil grunted assent. Mona turned an apologetic smile on Mariam, shrugged, and said, 'I'll see you later, Mariam.'

'I'll see you, Mona.'

She went back to work. The iron moving, back and forth, back and forth. Her back hurt and her feet hurt and her face grew blotchy and red. At last it was over, and she changed back into her day clothes and sought out her mother, but her mother was nowhere to be found. When she asked for Soraya the other girls turned reticent and didn't answer. At last Mariam ran into Mona on the way out.

'She has a friend who is a guest here,' Mona said uncomfortably. 'Did your mother never mention it?'

'No,' Mariam said.

'You can get home by yourself, can't you?' Mona said. 'Hey, you want to go get a soda?'

'I want to go home and sleep forever,' Mariam said, and Mona laughed.

'It gets easier,' she said. 'And it's not easy to get work, you're lucky that you have your mother.'

Mariam said goodbye. When she re-entered Mokattam it was like visiting it for the first time. She had seen nothing of the hotel itself; but just being there, with that smell of fresh laundry, was to be aware of another, hidden world just above her, where guests in fabulous clothes shimmered as they strolled on marble, drinks in hand, laughing and speaking in foreign tongues. It was like a movie, whereas Mokattam, with its smell of rotting carcasses and exhaust fumes, its tired laundry hanging overhead, its dogs and pigs rooting in the piles of trash, was all too real and suddenly depressing. Her hands were sore from work. Back near the house the fire burned as it always did, her grandfather sat there with his tea, and the women sorted through the endless piles of trash. It was a living, not always a good living but a respectable one all the same, and Mariam felt listless and unexpectedly angry. She didn't know what she wanted, only that it was something else, something different.

Back inside, she closed herself in the room she shared with her mother. She reached for her box of trinkets on the high shelf. She had two things of her father's. The nested dolls, and a small gold pocket watch, old and scratched, that had the barely legible inscription of *Feebes* on its underside. Her mother gave it to her indifferently one day, long ago, when Mariam was small and asking questions.

'Here,' she said. 'This belonged to him. You can have it. I don't need it.'

Mariam kept the watch as though it were a relic – of what faith she wasn't sure. From time to time she'd wind it, set it to the correct time and watch it tick. Sooner or later it always ran out, time slowed and then stopped, stuck in the past.

Now she wrapped her fingers around it as she thought. She felt trapped, by her mother, her circumstances, by the Umm Zayeds and Umm Jalils of this world. Soon they will find her a suitable boy to marry. Then she would stay home, have children, go to market, cook. She realised with an aching clarity, as though for the very first time, that she wanted something else, something impossible, a life only the glamorous women of the screen lived, in the pictures and the society pages.

She was too tired. She went to sleep. The next morning she was up early. Soraya had come back in the night. Once again they went out, dogs barking, cars honking, took the bus downtown, separated at the staff entrance of the Balmoral. Mariam pressed bed sheets and pillowcases, over and over, all day. She felt her life shrinking, the world around her contracting like in an iris shot.

She went home. She wound the old pocket watch. She slept.

In the morning she went back to work.

39

'Henrietta Feebes,' Flavia said.

'Yes,' Mariam said.

'Some would call her your benefactor.'

'She is a dear friend,' Mariam said. She nodded twice to accentuate the point.

'She discovered you?'

'Oh, it wasn't like that,' Mariam said. 'Henrietta was putting up the funding for the picture, that was all. I believe she found the experience enjoyable, which is why she kept her hand in it after. And of course, she funds all kinds of cultural causes.'

'The director, Thomas Greene—'

'Tom, yes. Of course. Gosh,' Mariam said. A word she learned back then that only the English used. 'You take me back, Flavia.'

'Tom Greene,' Flavia said. 'What was he like?'

'He was always so nice,' Mariam said. 'Very professional. But we didn't keep in touch after the shoot, and it was so long ago. I doubt he remembers me at all. I was just the Zabbaleen girl.'

*

About a month after she started at the Balmoral, Mona took Mariam out for a soda after work.

'My friend Fuad's cousin Fayez found some mummies in a burial cave near Aswan,' Mariam said. 'They want me to help sell them.'

'Mummies?' Mona said. 'Eww.'

'And some canopic jars and two gold bracelets and a scarab seal. Also some bones but they think those just came from a dog.'

'There's a Dr Müller who stays in the hotel,' Mona said. 'Two soft boiled eggs, toast, jam and weak milky coffee. The cleaners say his room is always full of old junk like that.'

'What, mummies?'

'Well, not *mummies*,' Mona said. 'But he collects antiques.'

'Is he rich?' Mariam said, and Mona gave her a look.

'They're all rich if they stay at the Balmoral,' she said.

'But how can I talk to him?' Mariam said. 'I never get to go front of house. I hate the laundry room.'

'You need to find some way into maid service,' Mona said. She sipped her Coke noisily through a straw. 'But all front of house staff are male.'

'It's not fair,' Mariam said.

Mona shrugged. 'The cooks are very excited,' she said. 'There's a guest at the hotel with Miss Feebes who says he's going to make a movie here. Head Chef wants to be in it, you know. He thinks he's Omar Sharif.'

'Who is Miss Feebes?' Mariam said.

'Some English lady. She's been coming here for years.'

Mariam thought of her gold watch. Did her father know this lady? He must have, she thought, excited, and then—

'A movie?' she said.

'That's what they say, but I don't believe it,' Mona said. 'Who would want to make a movie here? Maybe you could be in it, Mariam. You could play the—'

'Laundry maid,' Mariam said.

'The lover,' Mona said, and she said it slowly and meaningfully, like *luuuver*, and they both burst out laughing.

'My cousin Fayez is coming up from the village next week,' Fuad said.

'I don't know your cousin Fayez,' Mariam said.

'Look, it doesn't matter if you do or don't,' Fuad said, 'but he's going to bring the stuff.'

'He's going to bring it *here*?' Mariam said.

'Where else do you want him to bring it?' Fuad said. 'Look, are you going to help us out or not? We'll cut you in for ten per cent.'

'Are you crazy, Fuad?' Mariam said. 'That's prison if you get caught.'

'Who is getting caught?' Fuad said. 'No one's getting caught. Just got to do it quiet, got to do it smart. I asked around the dealers at the Khan el-Khalili but they are all thieves and robbers, Mariam. And when I said I'll sell the mummies outside their shops myself they threatened to beat me up. No, we just need to cut them out and find a foreigner with money and then there'd be no problem.'

'My friend Mona says there's a Dr Müller in the hotel

who collects antiques. I just need to find a way to talk to him,' Mariam said.

'See?' Fuad said, beaming. 'I knew I could count on you. We could make enough money for me to lease my own garbage collection route from your grandfather. Maybe even buy my own cart and donkey outright. And you could get yourself a nice dress.'

'Aha,' Mariam said. 'I still don't know how I can get to that Dr Müller.'

'You'll figure it out,' Fuad said. 'You always do.'

The next day, arriving early for work, she was aware of a commotion in front of the hotel. Going over to look, she ran into Mona.

'Photographers,' Mona said. Mariam stared at the men with the cameras as they stood outside in a sort of anticipatory hush.

'What for?' Mariam said.

'There's some famous person staying at the Balmoral,' Mona said.

'Like a famous actor?' Mariam said.

'Nah. Some old lady writer,' Mona said.

Mariam watched. As if on cue, an ancient lady in a kaftan came out of the doors holding an ornate walking stick, the doormen parting in her wake like Cleopatra's attendants.

'Friends!' the woman said, raising her arms and smiling. She wore large black Elizabeth Taylor sunglasses and heavy rings on her fingers. Despite her advanced age, her voice carried and seemed vibrant and alive. 'It is always a pleasure to be back in your beautiful country,' she said. She put her arms down and punctuated the ending with a tap of her stick.

'Mrs St James! Mrs St James!' The man who spoke loudest was rotund and persistent. 'Ali Mubarak, *Al-Ahram*,' he said. 'What can you tell us about your new movie?'

'We're going to be late for work,' Mona said.

'Shhh!' Mariam said.

'I am very blessed,' Mrs St James said, 'to have such a wonderful team who want to make my little book into a movie. I only wish my good friend Agatha could have been here with me. She loved Egypt dearly.'

'She means Agatha Christie!' Mona whispered to Mariam.

'Shhh!'

'I mean Agatha Christie, of course,' Mrs St James said. A few people clapped.

'My book is about a spy,' Mrs St James said. 'But it is also a love story. And it is set right here, in Cairo!' She beamed at the photographers. 'Isn't that wonderful?' she said. 'We were very fortunate to have Mr Ted Lewis adapt my novel for the screen, and as for the director – well, he can speak for himself.' She leaned on her cane, smiled like a theatrical compère, and said, 'Thomas, will you come out now?'

A young, hesitant man stepped out of the hotel doors. Mariam thought he had a kind face and sad eyes. He came to stand by Mrs St James and looked out at the small assembly before him. His eyes found Mariam, hesitated. She found herself looking directly into his eyes. Some sort of recognition, of interest. She looked down. When she looked up again the man was addressing the reporters.

'Hello, everyone,' he said.

'Mr Greene! Mr Greene!' It was the man from *Al-Ahram* again. 'Ali Mubarak, *Al-Ahram*! When will you start filming? What can you tell us of the cast? Will you be using Egyptian actors?'

'We will start soon,' Thomas Greene said. 'The crew will be arriving in a couple of days and we aim for a very tight three week shoot. We will be based out of the hotel, which has gracefully allowed us to film in and around the building, I believe for the first time in its history, and for which we are very grateful.' He paused. He struck Mariam as a shy man, and a man of few words, who did not relish being in front of the cameras. 'I'm glad to say the main role will be played by Mr Eddie Constantine.'

There was scattered applause. Tom Greene smiled. Ali Mubarak of *Al-Ahram* scribbled furiously in a notebook.

'And the girl, Mr Greene?' he said. 'Who plays the girl?'

'A terrific young Italian actress,' Tom Greene said, and he smiled, and Mariam revised her opinion of him: there was a part of the man that enjoyed the game. 'Miss Alessandra Mussolini.'

'Mr Greene!'

'That's all, folks,' Tom Greene said. 'If you'll excuse me, I have a lot of work still to do—'

'What about Egyptian actors, Mr Greene?'

'We will try to cast as many as we can. Thank you. Thank you.' He turned and went back inside.

'We're late!' Mona said. 'Come on!'

She dragged Mariam by the arm. At the staff entrance they were welcomed by Umm Zayed, who looked at them dolefully then just shook her head.

'Go on, then,' she said.

Back inside. Back in uniform, back in the laundry room, back on the ironing board. But today was different. The girls were chattering in low voices, and even Umm Jalil grunted in clear evidence of interest at the conversation from time to time. There were movie folks, the whole hotel was going to become a movie set! No one was sure what that meant. Mr Constantine was already here – he wasn't – he was coming in two days – he arrived last week and was secluding in his room – Miss Mussolini was coming tomorrow – the hotel ballroom has been converted into something called a sound stage – what was a sound stage? – there was a lot of heavy equipment in the storage room – the cooks will be cooking double all month with all the crew expected to arrive – how many? Tens of people, who knew a movie took so many people to make? – add to that the regular guests and the hotel was at full capacity, no rooms available at *all* – Dr Müller has been complaining of the noise – Miss Feebes was back in her regular suite, did you hear? She always tipped generously, unusual for the English – married? No, she never married, though many suitors, she was financing this movie, she had a thing for the director – Mr Greene, *he* didn't tip, but very nice manners – plain omelette, fresh yogurt and coffee, black – Mrs St James, very *spirited* lady, but terrible cough – blood on the pillowcase, yes, but what can you do – that's how it was with my mother, too, poor soul, and so brave – ninety-one, someone told me she was, and she was a personal friend of King Farouk – I wonder if there will be handsome men among the crew – get to work, girls!

The last from Umm Zayed, though not unkindly, and Mariam, bent over the endless laundry to be ironed, thought,

I can't be doing this all my life when there is another life out there that other people get to live. She ironed furiously, thinking.

Her opportunity came not that day or the next, though each morning she hovered by the hotel entrance before going to work, hoping to catch a glimpse of the arrival or presence of the movie people. A couple of bored photographers came and went periodically. Where they stood there gathered a small pile of ash and cigarette butts on the ground.

On the third day of her watch Mariam saw a big truck arrive, and men hauling heavy crates of equipment out of the back and into the hotel. She saw the director, Thomas Greene, supervising them. He saw her again and frowned, then waved.

Mariam stared at him, frozen.

He waved again, more impatiently this time, until she made her legs move, one at a time, and approached him, mortified, her eyes fixed firmly on the ground.

'I keep seeing you standing there like a kid at a candy store with her face pressed to the glass,' Tom Greene said. 'Do you work in the hotel? Do you speak English? I guess you can't even understand me. Do you have candy stores in Cairo? We didn't really have them when I was growing up. I used to save all my money to go to the Electric Cinema on Portobello, it's where I first saw Bergman. That was when I knew I wanted to make movies one day. I'm sorry, you look confused. I don't blame you. I need a—'

'I speak English,' Mariam said.

'You do? I mean, gosh. Of course. Do you work here?'
Greene said.

'I do the laundry.'

'The laundry? Yes, of course.'

'I'm sorry,' Mariam said. 'I am late for work. Excuse me!'

She ran away. Her heart beat wildly. She darted through
the staff entrance and went to her station.

Stupid! Stupid! she thought.

The iron hissed steam. She pressed it down so hard she
almost burned the fabric.

40

'*GLADIATORE 3000*,' FLAVIA SAID.

'Yes,' Mariam said.

'Directed, of course, by the wonderful Enrique Gallo.'

Mariam smiled. 'Yes,' she said.

'How did he propose?' Flavia said, responding with a smile of her own.

'It was at the Cap d'Antibes,' Mariam said. 'We were sailing on Dino De Laurentiis's yacht. Well, I don't know if it was his yacht. But he was hosting a party on it. The sun was setting… Enrique got on one knee.'

'You're positively glowing,' Flavia said.

'It was very romantic,' Mariam said.

'Did you say yes?' Flavia said.

Mariam laughed. So did Flavia.

'It was a big diamond,' Mariam said.

'Can I see it again?'

'Of course.' Mariam extended her hand. Flavia admired the ring.

'You first met how?' she said.

'It was on the set of *Headhunter's Bloodbath*,' Mariam said. 'A Margheriti picture we shot in Almeria in Spain. I

362

die halfway through the movie. Enrique was assistant to the DP.' She shrugged. 'It was just meant to be,' she said.

'You've built an impressive résumé since *Black Dirt*,' Flavia said. 'Genre fare like those two Ferdinando Baldi Westerns you made early on, Margheriti of course, now *Gladiatore 3000* – but you also had roles in art house films, most recently in Derek Jarman's *Caravaggio*, and in Godard's *Je vous salue, Marie*—'

'I go where the work is,' Mariam said. 'To me it is only the role, the chance to play my part.'

Outside on the stage, the lights waited. They murmured soothingly. There were only the lights, and when they were turned on her she came alive, and everything else was just the antechamber. This is what she couldn't say, that she couldn't explain to a reporter: it didn't *matter* if she was a zombie or the girl who drowned or was tied to a stake, the romantic interest or the girl back home or a sad clown (a blink-and-you-miss-it background shot in Verhoeven's *De vierde man*), a woman fighting to save her family (in Yousry Nasrallah's *Summer Thefts*), an alien or a cartoon squirrel (a small but memorable voice role in a Ralph Bakshi short). And she remembered with aching clarity the first time she heard anyone yell 'Action!' and the cameras were turned on, and she walked across the large room from one side to the other, carrying the laundry, trying not to look to where the cameras were…

All that day was ordinary, but she got her break at last as she stood by the laundry room door, about to go to lunch. A man she hadn't seen before, an important man in a service suit with a green name badge on it, with a thin waxed moustache and a sweaty face, stopped her abruptly and barked, 'You!'

'Sir?'

'Where is the usual girl?' the man demanded. 'You lot are like clucking chickens since all this nonsense started. Take this' – he pointed to a basket full of freshly laundered sheets – 'to the second floor immediately.'

'But sir, I have never—'

'Do it!' the man barked. He mopped his brow. His name badge said Mr Ali. 'I don't have time for this,' he said.

'Yes, sir,' Mariam said.

She picked up the laundry basket. She followed the corridor, found the doors, stepped through them.

Suddenly she was in another world.

Marble floors and muted colours, the rich cool shade of high-ceilinged rooms and slow-moving fans. Men and women who looked busy and important wore the sort of clothes one only saw in movies, new and expensive. Ice tinkled in glasses. Front-of-house staff moved with dignified purpose, exuding calm efficiency. No one paid the slightest attention to Mariam.

She walked almost blindly, found the elevators before being grabbed by the arm by a man in a jacket whose name tag said Mr Rahim.

'Use the service elevator, girl!' he said. His thick moustache, white woven into the luxurious blackness of it, quivered as he spoke.

'Where is it?' Mariam said.

'There, girl!'

He took her to one side of the lobby, where a smaller, discreet elevator waited. Mr Rahim pressed the button, waited for the doors to open, pushed Mariam in.

'Where are you going?' he said.

'Second floor. Mr Ali sent me.'

Mr Rahim pressed the button for her, stepped outside the elevator, regarded her with mute disapproval until the doors closed on his visage and she was left alone. She hoped she wouldn't see Soraya. Things had been tense between them for a while now, and Mariam had the distinct impression her mother tried to avoid her at the hotel. Soraya seemed to regret letting her daughter into the place she considered hers, where she had a life of her own, divorced from the realities of Mokattam and their home.

Mariam understood it. Here, her mother could be herself, at least a different version of herself, not the daughter of Zabbaleen, not the mother of a Mariam, but a woman who had her own, separate existence. Mariam didn't begrudge her that. But she felt hurt all the same, and the two emotions, acceptance and resentment, swirled inside her like acid in the pit of her stomach.

The elevator pinged softly. The doors opened. Mariam carried the laundry to the end of the corridor, her feet making no noise on the carpet. Two maids with a trolley were at the far end.

'About time,' one of them said. Neither of them was Soraya. They vanished through the open door of a room with an unmade bed in disarray and piles of clothes on the floor. A tray of food and two empty wine glasses were left outside on the floor. Mariam snuck a look at the room list clipped to a board hanging from the trolley's side. The two women paid her no attention. Dr Müller's room (do not disturb before twelve) was on the third floor.

There was no one else around.

Mariam took the stairs.

'Yes?' Dr Müller said. 'Come in, come in. Don't touch the artefacts.' He was a thin and nervous-looking man with a prominent forehead and weak blond hair. He fiddled with a pipe but never seemed to light it. Mariam stepped in. She looked around her uncertainly.

Mona was right – the room was filled with all kinds of antiquities, old sheesha pipes, hand-carved backgammon boards, rolled-up rugs, loose mosaic tiles and glass fragments and clay pieces. A slowly assembled, beautiful blue glass bottle took pride of place on a low table, its missing pieces lying beside it along with a brush and a pot of glue.

'Stunning, isn't it?' Dr Müller said. 'Byzantine. I'm something of an amateur archaeologist, you might say. You speak German? English? French?' He seemed lonely, eager to talk.

'English,' Mariam said.

Dr Müller made a face. 'Such a barbaric tongue,' he said. 'But there we are, there we are. Well, I won't get in your way, miss. I will go on the veranda.'

'Dr Müller,' Mariam said.

Dr Müller looked startled.

'Yes?' he said.

'I didn't come here to clean.'

'Then why—' An awful suspicion came into his eyes. 'No, no,' he said, waving his hands and retreating, 'I *told* Junker not to send me pr—'

'Dr Müller!' Mariam said. 'I came to talk to you about mummies.'

Dr Müller blinked.

'Mummies?' he said.

'I know where there are some.'

'Mummies, you say? Genuine mummies?'

'Yes.'

Dr Müller finally lit his pipe. He drew smoke and blew it out in a blue cloud.

'Well, that's a relief,' he said. 'I thought Junker sent you. He means well, but I really...' He stared at her in suspicion.

'You are sure you're not a...?'

'Dr Müller!' Mariam said.

'Good, good.' He puffed on his pipe. 'Then I am all ears, young lady! You work here, yes?'

'Yes.'

'No doubt you have some street contacts, yes, yes, perhaps a cousin or a boyfriend? People do offer me finds from time to time. My door is always open!' He looked at her with his watery eyes.

'Dr Müller, what is it that you do?' Mariam said.

'Me?' he said, surprised. 'I'm a chemist. Well, petroleum, mostly. I'm advising your government on some possible drill operations. Fascinating stuff, oil. Do you know, it causes terrible pollution, but we're not to talk about that. Not good for business, eh?' He tapped his nose, almost dropped his pipe, then looked about him in some confusion.

'We are all scientists in my family, do you know,' Dr

Müller said. 'My great-grandfather – or was it my great-great-grandfather? I forget – he knew Darwin. Darwin!' He looked at her in expectation.

'About those mummies,' Mariam said.

Dr Müller nodded. 'Yes,' he said. 'Well, then. I would need to see them, of course. Arrangements will need to be made. It is hard to get such things out of Egypt. A lamentable state of affairs.'

'They will be in Cairo early next week,' Mariam said.

'I go to Alexandria tomorrow for a few days,' Dr Müller said. 'Too much noise here with this film crew around. How can I make contact with you on my return?' He still looked at her with some suspicion. She couldn't blame him. She must seem mad to him, bursting in like this. Only his greed saved her from being reported.

'I will slip a note under your door,' she said.

'Excellent,' Dr Müller said. His pipe had gone out. He fumbled with a match. 'A mummy would be just the thing to round off my collection,' he said. 'I could put it on display in my living room back in Munich.' He lit his pipe; he sank into a reverie; he seemed content. Mariam quietly withdrew from the room.

On her return to the laundry she found everything in disarray, the girls chatting freely, Umm Jalil and Umm Zayed in the middle of an argument, and Mr Ali pacing back and forth and mopping his brow from time to time. No one had noticed Mariam's absence, nor was her sudden return commented upon. The steam continued to rise into the air, the great washing machines kept spinning, and it took Mariam a moment longer, having returned to her station (and attempting to pretend she had been there all along) to realise that there were three strangers in the room.

The first one she already knew. It was Thomas Greene, the director. Beside him was a man who looked quietly competent, and measured things with a small device in his hand, and talked to Thomas Greene animatedly, pointing from time to time and framing little windows with his fingers.

Twice Thomas Greene looked her way, and once he smiled.

The third person with them was a woman in her early to mid fifties, small and trim, impeccably dressed, with no rings on her fingers but a bracelet on her arm, very small and delicate, and two small and delicate diamond earrings, which between them must have cost a small fortune. She looked directly at Mariam once, and said something quietly to the director, who nodded. The woman looked at Mariam again. She motioned her to come over.

Mariam, stupefied, abandoned her iron and approached the foreigners.

'You're Mariam,' the woman said. 'Soraya's daughter?'

'You know my mother?' Mariam said, surprised and a little discomfited.

The woman nodded.

'My name is Henrietta Feebes,' she said. 'I knew your father, long ago.'

'I never met anyone before who knew my father,' Mariam said. She looked at Henrietta Feebes in longing. 'What was he like?'

'He was a man,' Henrietta Feebes said. She said it as if that summed up everything. Then she said the words that were to change Mariam's life.

'How would you like to be in a movie?'

41

'THE FIRST TIME WE SEE YOU IN *BLACK DIRT*,' FLAVIA
said. 'Do you mind if I smoke, by the way?'

'No, not at all,' Mariam said.

Flavia extracted a soft pack of Gauloises from her pocket
and a cheap disposable lighter. She lit up with a sigh of
relief. 'The camera moves in a long tracking shot through
the service corridors,' she said. 'It enters the laundry room.
Steam rises and fogs the camera, and for a moment the
viewer can't see a thing. Then the fog clears as the camera
pushes further into the room, and suddenly an image forms,
of a young woman, looking directly into the camera, her
eyes haunting, her face framed by the steam.'

She was reading from her notebook.

'You're being too kind,' Mariam said.

'It's true,' Flavia said. 'You somehow seem so young and
innocent, yet world-weary. It's a captivating moment in the
picture.'

'It was actually the second scene I was in,' Mariam said.
'The first time Tom yelled "Action!" I had to walk across the
room holding a laundry basket and I was utterly terrified.
I was only in the background. It's the scene where the spy

and the girl first meet in the laundry room, when they have that argument. Eddie Constantine was old for the role but somehow he carried it off, even opposite Alessandra, who was so young and pretty. And of course he dies at the end.'

'There was death on the set too, wasn't there?' Flavia said. She paused with her pen poised and looked sympathetic.

'Off the set, yes,' Mariam said. 'It really was very sad.'

'Mariam! Mariam!' Mona said. They had gone out for soda again after work. 'Guess what?'

'What?' Mariam said.

'I'm going to be in the movie!'

Mona beamed. Mariam had to smile.

'You are?' she said.

'Yes! They want to use the kitchen for one of the scenes. The old detective guy—'

'I think he's a spy,' Mariam said.

'Well, whatever he is, he chases some bad guy across the hotel, and they get into the kitchen and have a big fight. They want us to be there, in the background. And we get paid for it!' Mona beamed. 'Oh, and the chef even gets to say a line!'

'What's his line?' Mariam said.

Mona stood up to her full height, pointed a quivering finger in the air and said, 'Get... out!'

She collapsed back on the chair laughing. 'Poor Mr Mohamed is terrified!' she said. 'He was so eager to do it and now all he does is practise. Do you think it's better if he uses a big spoon instead of pointing? He could shake it at them, like he's threatening them with it.'

'I'm going to be in the movie too,' Mariam said. 'They want to film in the laundry room. But they asked if I could be available for a couple of other scenes. Apparently the director likes the way I look. I don't even know what this movie is about! Is the Italian girl supposed to be Egyptian?'

'I think so,' Mona said. 'They'll all speak English anyway. Hey, that's amazing news, Mariam. Are you excited?'

'I'm scared,' Mariam admitted. 'I don't know what to do.'

'You just stand where they tell you to stand, and say what they tell you to say,' Mona said. 'That's acting.'

'When did you become such an expert?' Mariam said.

'It's not hard!' Mona said. 'Looking after dying patients in a hospital is hard. Cleaning pots and pans all day is hard. Acting is just pretending. Kids do it all the time.'

Mariam reflected that this seemed a cruel way of describing what, as she now realised, she had been so desperate to do and so afraid to admit to herself. To act was not to pretend, it was to *be*, for a little while, someone else, but no less real for that. Movies made people happy. They allowed the nurse to be snatched away from the world of the dying, for the patients to escape momentarily the prison of their failing bodies, for the dishwasher to find solace in a world of light where everything was possible, for just a little while.

Mona was wrong, Mariam thought. But she didn't know how to say it.

They finished their sodas and said their goodbyes. Mariam went home, as she always did, the crowded roads filled with cars and motorbikes, buses and trucks, and pedestrians weaving their way in and out of the traffic. She barely noticed. She felt she was in a dream. At home her grandmother stood by the cooking coals, stirring a pot with a long wooden spoon.

'I'm going to be in a movie, teta,' Mariam said. Her grandmother smiled. She put her hand on Mariam's face. Her hand was rough and warm.

'God gives what the heart desires,' she said, 'but the heart is seldom wise. Is this what you want, Mariam?'

'It is,' Mariam said.

'Taste this,' her grandmother said. She lifted the spoon to Mariam's lips. The stew was rich and smoky, more lentils than meat.

'It's delicious,' Mariam said.

Her grandmother nodded. She reached for the salt and scattered some into the stew with a thoughtful expression, then looked up and smiled.

'Go with God, Mariam,' she said.

Time passed. Mariam did the ironing. She carried laundry across a room in a camera's gaze. She watched the spy and the girl's first kiss on the balcony, illuminated by lamps that burned like the sun. She saw soundmen and doormen share cigarettes as they skulked outside on a rare break. She saw Mona in the kitchen, in a scene, stirring a pot as the spy chased a baddie across the room, throwing utensils and pushing over pots. She saw the chef shout angrily while waving a spoon, saying, 'Get – out!' as Mona tried not to laugh. She saw the old lady, Edna St James, speak intensely with Tom Greene as they went over lines of script. She saw Soraya, talking quietly with Henrietta Feebes.

The order of the world had been irrevocably upset, Mariam thought. She had been offered a glimpse of what lay behind the scenery, and of those who move behind it and repaint the world. She tried to read a worn-out copy of *The Spy* someone had left out one day on a chair in the dining room, but she found the going hard and abandoned it after a while. It was full of guns and pretty girls and that kind of thing.

Dr Müller came back from Alexandria. Umm Zayed still frowned whenever Mariam was late, but she didn't say anything. One day Tom Greene gave Mariam a line to say. It was a scene where the spy walks in the street outside. It was a Cairo of the movies.

Mariam sat with her back to the wall, a begging bowl by her feet. The spy hesitated when he saw her. Something like compassion filled his rugged face, and he dropped a coin in her bowl. She looked up at him (really at a camera lens) and said, 'Thank you, mister.' The spy walked on. Unbeknown to him he was being followed by a sinister man in a black hat.

The director yelled 'Cut!'

'It's arranged,' Mariam said.

Fuad and his cousin Fayez were passing the long-stemmed hose of a sheesha pipe between them. The water in the bowl gurgled as they drew smoke in turns. Fuad grinned at her excitedly.

'We're going to get so rich,' he said.

'I don't want anything more to do with this,' Mariam said.

'What exactly did you do?' Fayez said. He looked at

her with eyes that were a little too bright. He didn't smile. Mariam didn't like him.

'I put a note under Dr Müller's door, like we agreed,' Mariam said. 'The place near the necropolis, two days from now. The rest is up to you.'

'He better pay up,' Fayez said. 'Or else.'

'Or else what?' Mariam said.

'Or else I don't know,' Fayez said, staring at her. Fuad slapped him on the shoulder.

'It's just business, Fayez,' he said.

'You're soft here in the city,' Fayez said. 'Too rich and too fat.'

'Soon we'll all be rich,' Fuad said. He sounded like he was trying to convince himself as much as his cousin.

'Where are the mummies?' Mariam said.

Fayez gestured carelessly behind him.

'Can I see?'

'Do what you like.'

Mariam went around them. She peered into the small storage room. The two shapes inside were smaller than she expected. It was dark, she couldn't make out details, and she withdrew quickly. She thought, these were hardly pharaohs that Fayez was trying to sell. Just some dead people from long ago. It made her feel sad.

'I'll see you, Fuad,' she said, coming back.

'Thanks for arranging it, Mariam,' Fuad said. He elbowed his cousin.

'What?' Fayez said, irritated. He stared at Mariam. 'Why are you still here?' he said.

'I'm not,' Mariam said. She left, not looking back.

★

The hotel was no longer its usual cool, refined space. A madness took hold of the bricks and mortar, of guests and staff alike. Hot tungsten lights burned unnaturally in nooks and crannies, men and women who looked busy and important moved from place to place carrying things or ordering other people to do things. Even Mr Rahim, the elderly doorman, looked different in the new lights; taller, younger, his moustache more black, as though it had been varnished anew with shoe polish. He stood proudly by the elevators as men with a heavy camera on a tripod tested out shots and a boom operator rested standing against one wall. No one paid the slightest attention to Mariam. She peered into the hotel bar. She had never been to a bar before. She saw the reporter from *Al-Ahram*, Ali Mubarak. He sat chatting to Mrs St James.

'Do you see,' Mrs St James said, 'it *has* to happen that way, the death of the spy is in*evitable*, it is the moral im*perative*, and yet as he lies on the rubbish heap, the blood ebbing out of his body, we never know for *sure* if he lives or dies, and so we're offered hope...' She paused, then laughed. 'Of a sequel, anyway!'

Ali Mubarak laughed with her. Mrs St James lifted her drink with a shaking hand. The ice tinkled in the glass. 'Of course, I don't know if they will keep my ending or not. Tom is undecided. A movie is never the book, you know.'

Ali Mubarak said something; Mariam didn't hear what.

'The overall theme of my books?' Mrs St James said. She took a sip of her drink. The glass hovered unsteadily in the air. 'Moral choices, I would say. Well, that and fucking.' She brayed a laugh again, then looked confused. She blinked. The glass slipped from her fingers. It fell to the floor. The glass broke. Mrs St James looked surprised. Then she slowly toppled in her chair.

Ali Mubarak sat there looking stupefied. Mariam was the first to run to the fallen woman. Mrs St James lay on the floor like a broken doll. Mariam lifted her head gently, and Mrs St James's eyes opened, for just a moment. Her lips moved without sound.

'Don't try to speak,' Mariam said. She looked around her. 'Help!' she shouted. 'Somebody help!'

When she looked down at Mrs St James again, the old woman's eyes were closed, and she was no longer breathing. The body slackened and relaxed suddenly. A long, mournful fart emanated unexpectedly from Mrs St James. With it came a horrible smell as the dead woman expelled the contents of her last supper into the world.

A laugh escaped Mariam's lips, startling her, and she began to hiccup. The old woman didn't look peaceful in death. Mariam gently laid down the head, with its eyes that would no longer see, its mouth that would no longer speak, onto the floor. She wiped her eyes from tears she wasn't aware of.

That's how they found her, with Mr Mubarak of the newspaper still gaping stupidly to one side, and Tom Greene took Mariam, helped her up, and held her as she clung to him, crying at something, she didn't know what.

42

THE NEW BRITISH PROTESTANT CEMETERY WAS A WAY
out of town for Mariam, adjacent to a busy road and the
train tracks that went into Misr Station. Beyond its high
wall, the sounds of traffic gave way to a sense of peace. Palm
trees moved gently in the breeze. The grass was manicured
like the lawns of some sprawling British estate from the
days of the Khedive, and the white tombstones stood erect
and orderly in neat rows all evenly spaced.

It was a small party of mourners who gathered there that
day to bury Edna St James. There had been some confusion
as to her eventual destination: whether the body should be
flown back to England for burial, and what the novelist's
wishes on the subject might have been. It was Henrietta
Feebes who made the arrangements in the end, stating that
Edna had loved Cairo, and often expressed a wish for her
bones to be laid there, where she would always be warm.
Work on the film was suspended for half the day. An air-
conditioned bus took the main principals from the hotel
to the cemetery. Mariam and Mona took the public bus to
get there.

But it didn't matter, Mariam thought. They were the background actors to someone else's final act.

Henrietta Feebes wore black mirror-shades. The coffin was carried by the gaffers and grips. An English priest with a face so pale that it seemed powdered with bone dust gave a short eulogy. Henrietta spoke next.

'She was funny, vicious, silly and wise,' she said. 'A keeper of secrets and a teller of tales. She lived, goddamn it. All that remains now are her words.'

The priest blanched at the curse, but he swallowed it without voicing objection. Tom Greene touched Henrietta's shoulder, then turned to the others.

'Let's get to work,' he said. 'She would have wanted it this way.'

'Amen,' someone said. Mariam once again tried to swallow laughter. She didn't know why. Death made her act strange.

The coffin was lowered into the ground. A group of girls from the nearby convent school sang a hymn. Their voices rose, the notes pure and lovely.

Mariam cried. Mona held her hand. The coffin was covered in dirt.

'Thank you for coming,' Henrietta Feebes said near the gates. 'She was very fond of you, you know.'

Mariam looked at her in bemusement. She had never spoken to Mrs St James before the old lady's demise.

'We can give you a lift back to the hotel,' Henrietta said. 'Since you both came all this way.'

'Thank you, miss,' Mona said shyly.

They rode back to the Balmoral. At the hotel there was

a small, sombre reception, with drinks and buckets of ice placed on top of a black tablecloth. Mariam felt the cloth between her fingers. She had ironed it earlier.

'I saw you in the scene you're in,' a voice said. Mariam looked up, startled to find a man she'd never met before standing there. He was in his late forties or early fifties, with a big, broad open face that'd taken a knock or two in its time. 'You were good.'

He put out his hand, smiling disarmingly. 'Sean Doyle,' he said. 'I'm one of the financiers of the movie.'

'Mr Doyle. Thank you,' Mariam said. 'How did you... I mean, how did you see it?'

'Oh,' he said. 'Tom showed me the dailies. I'm an old friend of Henrietta's – of Miss Feebes's, I should say. My business still takes me to Cairo sometimes.'

'What is your business, Mr Doyle?'

'Call me Sean, please.'

'Sean.' She felt awkward saying it.

'And you're Mariam, aren't you,' he said, not as a question.

'How do you—?'

'I take an interest,' he said. 'Putting cash into a movie, you know. It has its benefits whether the damn thing makes money or not. Piqued my interest, when Henrietta mentioned it. She's always looking for investment opportunities for me. Lots of connections.'

'What do you do?' Mariam said again.

He looked at her with an easy smile. 'I might as well level with you,' he said. 'I don't get to, not too often. Not as much as I'd like. I'm trying to free my country, but to fight you need guns and guns cost money. Even when you have money, people like to keep track of where it goes and what it's used for. So you need banks to make it all... clean.'

'Like a laundry,' Mariam said.

'Exactly like that, yes. You put it in dirty and it comes out smelling of...' He rubbed the black tablecloth between his fingers, then smelled them. 'Rosewater?' he said.

'But is that legal?' Mariam said.

'Is it legal, or is it moral?' Sean Doyle said. 'Those are not the same thing. Not that banks care for either. Money only cares for money, and the Feebes family has been making it for a long time now. You wouldn't think it to look at Henrietta, would you? So small and so demure. So classy. But she scares the shit out of me, Mariam. I might not look it, and I might do unsavoury things, but I still have principles. Henrietta wouldn't know what one is. Be careful with her. I think she likes you.'

'I don't understand,' Mariam said.

'And maybe you'll never have to.' He picked up his bourbon and downed it in one. 'You're good,' he said. 'There's something sad in your eyes when the camera catches you. It's very... natural.'

'I don't think I'm sad,' Mariam said.

'No,' Sean Doyle said, and he shook his head quickly, 'but you have it in you to be.' He motioned a waiter with his glass. It was swiftly replaced. Sean took a sip and sighed.

'I'm getting too old to be doing what I do,' he said. 'And the fight's not even close to coming to an end. I don't have a lot of sadness in me either, but when I've had a couple of drinks... Plus, we *should* feel a little sad after a funeral.'

'Of course,' Mariam said. 'I *am* sad about poor Mrs St James. I didn't know her very well, but it is sad.'

Sean smiled and raised his glass. 'To feeling sad for people we didn't know very well,' he said.

Mariam raised her glass of water.

'Sláinte,' she said. Sean Doyle's delighted laughter rolled through the room and people turned and watched them, then went back to their own drinks.

'Now where did you pick that up?' Sean said.

'I saw it in a movie. Did I say it right?'

'You made a credible attempt.'

Mariam smiled, raised her glass again and drank a sip of water.

'I knew her secret, you know,' Sean said.

'She had a secret?' Mariam said.

'It was a sad, old secret,' Sean said. 'The Feebeses found out so the Feebeses owned her. It's what they do, you know. You can make a bargain with them, but they will own you after. Something to bear in mind, perhaps... Henrietta owns Edna's estate, you know. Fifty-plus novels, movie rights, the lot. She never sold as well as Christie, but it's still worth a fair bit of cash.'

'What did she do?' Mariam said.

'She fell pregnant to a man who forced himself on her. She killed him. The old Feebes, he was Admiral of the Fleet, he helped keep it quiet and the child was given up for adoption. Edna kept secretly sending the boy money for years after. He's a barrister in York now, I understand.'

'Now I do feel sad,' Mariam said.

'She was never married, you know,' Sean said. 'She

changed her name to St James and called herself Mrs because it sounded more respectable. She used to tell people her husband died in the Great War.'

'How do you know all this?' Mariam said.

'I've been around a long time,' Sean said. 'And like the Feebeses I also deal in secrets.'

'It's dirty work,' Mariam said. 'What my family does is more clean.'

'What does your family do?' Sean said.

'We're Zabbaleen. We collect the trash.'

'That's the thing about dirt,' Sean Doyle said. 'It doesn't matter how much you sweep it away, there is always going to be more.'

Their glasses touched. He downed his drink. Mariam sipped her water.

She thought of colours in autumn; not of Cairo's but those on film, like in *All That Heaven Allows*. She felt sorry for the old lady but Mariam was young, and had her own life to lead. She knew she would have to decide what she wanted. She couldn't go back and she couldn't stand still. It was not yet her time to face winter. Even her summer had not yet come. She was in her spring.

At that moment she decided she would do what it took. She would go speak to this Henrietta Feebes, and she would ask her, and if she had to she would beg. She could chart a new future, a clean one for herself.

Mona came running through the thin crowds just then, her face anxious.

'Mariam,' she said. 'There's a call for you at the desk.'

'A call? For me?'

She had never received a call. The thought of someone

asking for her here was something she couldn't imagine. She said, 'Excuse me,' to Sean Doyle and followed Mona. As they reached reception she saw Dr Müller checking out. He looked to be in a hurry and when he glanced her way he blanched and looked away.

The man on the reception glared at her and said, 'Staff do not receive calls at the desk.' Nevertheless he handed her the receiver. Mariam pressed it to her ear.

'Mariam! Mariam!' It was Fuad. 'You have to help us, we're in the police station, they were waiting for us when we got to the necropolis—'

Dr Müller finished his business at the desk and turned to leave. His bags were packed by the door. He looked at Mariam. She looked at him.

'So sorry,' the doctor mumbled. It was barely audible. 'There was nothing I could do.'

He rushed to the door. The porter picked up his bags and carried them to the taxi waiting outside.

'Fuad, I can't do anything,' Mariam said, 'I told you I can't be involved—'

'Mariam, please!'

'I will ask my grandfather. He will send someone,' she said helplessly. On the other side of the line, Fuad began to cry. The line went dead.

Mariam handed the receiver back to the taciturn man at reception.

'Thank you,' she said.

'No more calls,' the man said.

Mariam nodded.

No more calls, she thought.

Then she went to look for Henrietta.

*

Flavia wrote. Mariam watched the smoke from Flavia's cigarette as it drifted towards the ceiling.

Mariam's story seemed to her like ancient history suddenly. It was only a few years ago, yet a lifetime away. She put her hand over her belly, thinking of the unborn baby growing inside. They hadn't told anyone yet, not even Enrique's parents. And she had not spoken to Soraya in years. Not since their big argument, after the string of successful local films where Mariam got increasingly bigger roles, and when Henrietta, having helped her initially (a bit part in *The Peacock*, with Salah Zulfikar) came back into their lives. She had offered Mariam the chance to go abroad, and to star in her first big picture, a *Day of the Jackal* knock-off called *Operazione Istanbul*, which despite being set in Turkey was to be filmed on location in Malta and Milan.

Why Henrietta was still financing movies was a bit of a mystery, other than that she seemed to enjoy it. When you were as rich as Henrietta that was enough reason, or so Mariam figured. Henrietta came to the house, driven to Mokattam in a black limousine that had to be parked a few roads away. She came the rest of the way on foot.

What she made of her visit to the house, with the piles of trash rising outside, the rats and the pigs, she showed no outward sign of it. She may as well have been taking tea with the English queen. The Zabbaleen watched as she came. A small dark figure in conservative attire that no doubt cost more than the house.

Mariam watched her from a distance, framed the shot:

Henrietta Feebes, picking her way confidently through the no-man's land of trash.

When she came she smiled. She wore dark glasses. She clasped Soraya's arm in mute acknowledgement. The two women, their shared history one Mariam could not guess at, seemed to communicate without words. Then Soraya nodded, once, and they let go of each other.

Inside the house, Soraya made tea. She brought out the best pastries. Henrietta looked Mariam over. She said, 'Are you happy here?'

'It's home,' Mariam said.

'Home,' Henrietta said thoughtfully. The word sounded foreign in her mouth. 'I grew up in a boarding school in Switzerland,' she said. 'I didn't tell you that, did I?'

They had only had one real conversation before. Mariam made no mention of that. But she hadn't forgotten, and she didn't think Henrietta had either.

'There is an opportunity for an actor like you, Mariam,' Henrietta said. 'I won't pretend that the world will give you all the roles you perhaps deserve. But there are options, outside of Egypt as well as within. I could offer you a contract, right now, for three pictures. Once you make those you will have more choices. You could travel, you could see the world. It is perhaps selfish of me to make this offer. I don't know. But I felt I should make it all the same. The decision is yours to make.'

You can make a bargain with them, Sean Doyle told her. But they will own you after. Something to bear in mind, perhaps.

Mariam understood.

'Can I think about it?' Mariam said. She realised she

was having doubts. When the choice came at last it was overwhelming. She didn't know what to say.

'You can, but we start shooting in two weeks in Malta,' Henrietta said. She stood up.

'You have a lovely home,' she said.

She looked not to Mariam then, but to Soraya. Who said nothing, but her eyes brimmed with unshed tears.

Soraya walked her outside. She was gone a while. When she came back her mouth was set in an angry line. There were no more tears.

'It's all decided,' she said. 'You will leave for Milan tomorrow.'

'But Mama!'

'It's decided,' Soraya said. 'It's for your own good. I will not discuss it further.'

'I am my own woman,' Mariam said. 'I can make my own decisions!'

'There is something in you, Mariam,' Soraya said. 'Confounding, irritating, vain. But you have *something*, a spark, and when the light hits you, you *shine*. I want you out of here.' Her hand gestured, over the house, over the world beyond. 'And I don't ever want you to come back.'

'You're mad,' Mariam said. Her mother's voice was the voice of a stranger.

'I want you to get out! Do you understand me?' Soraya said. 'I want you to leave!'

'Why are you like this? What did she say to you?' Mariam said. 'Did she pay you? Is that it? Did she buy you off?'

'Get out!' Soraya said. Mariam cried. Soraya went to her, to try and hug her. Mariam pushed her away. Her mother stumbled back, almost fell. Mariam suddenly realised her mother had aged. She went to her, to hold her.

Soraya said, 'Go.'

Mariam went out into the night. She looked back only once, saw her mother in the window, saw the ghosts that were no longer there. Her grandfather by his fire, her grandmother by his side. She searched for the ghost of her father but had no idea what he looked like. She walked away.

She never came back.

'You look sad,' Flavia said.

'Do I?' Mariam touched her eyes. She dabbed the corners with a handkerchief. 'I'm so sorry,' she said. 'This will ruin my make-up.'

'I'll call Yvonne back,' Flavia said.

'Yvonne?'

'The make-up lady.'

'Of course,' Mariam said. Flavia stood. She put a comforting hand on Mariam's shoulder.

'Let me get her for you,' she said.

She left. The door shut behind her. Mariam took a deep breath, held up her shoulders. She put her hand on her belly again. Another life. She looked into the mirror and her reflection looked back at her. Mariam smiled, and the reflection returned the smile to her; Mariam practised until the smile was perfect. Fuad and Fayez got five years each in Tora Prison.

Then Yvonne bustled in, tutted and fussed and fixed

Mariam's make-up. Flavia lit another cigarette and reopened her notebook in her lap. Yvonne was at last persuaded to leave. Mariam sipped water from a glass, careful not to smudge her lipstick.

Outside, people would be finishing their drinks, the last of the tickets would have been sold. The lights waited, ready to come on. The ushers moved between the seats, collecting any remaining rubbish, popcorn boxes, drinks, or gum some thoughtless prick left stuck on the underside of a chair. Enrique would be getting ready to welcome the crowds, dazzle them with his smile, shake hands and slap backs. He was good at that.

Mariam wondered what Henrietta was doing. She was in London probably, or New York. Perhaps Hong Kong. The last time Mariam saw her, Henrietta told her that they had an offer from the Hongkong and Shanghai Banking Corporation to buy Feebes Bank. Henrietta was going to accept the deal.

'A clean break,' she said. She didn't say from what.

The lights waited. It was almost time. Mariam took a last sip of water. She put on her best, most genuine smile.

'Any more questions?' she said.

PART SIX

NEW YORK

ISABELLE

2012

43

THE CALL CAME AT THREE IN THE MORNING, JOLTING
Isabelle Feebes from the sleep she'd just managed, at last,
to fall into. Her heart beat too fast as she searched for the
phone by her bedside. The phone kept playing 'Diamonds'
by Rihanna. She picked it up, dropped it with a dull thud,
felt for it on the floor. The phone kept playing the damned
song. At last she grabbed it, the screen lit up, and she
breathed out a sigh of relief.

'Yes?' she said. 'What is it!'

'Oh, I'm sorry, Miss Feebes. Is it late over there?'

'It's three in the morning, you tit.'

'I see. Apologies. It's Dr Steinmeier, Miss Feebes—'

'I know who you are!' Isabelle said. 'What is it, Dr
Steinmeier?'

She reached for the switch, turned on the bedside lamp.
So much for sleeping. There was a box of pills and a bottle
of mineral water on the bedside table. She popped open the
cap, palmed one pill and swallowed as she swigged water.

'It's about your mother. I'm afraid it's not long now, Miss
Feebes. I really am very sorry.'

'This couldn't wait?' Isabelle said. She got up, opened

the blinds, stared out of the dark window. A quiet street in Kensington, a fox regarded her from the bushes, its eyes reflecting the light from the street lamp. Isabelle usually liked the foxes, but she found this one disconcerting. 'Only this is the third time this month,' she said.

Her cigarettes. Where were her cigarettes? She remembered she quit, cursed silently, then remembered she still had a pack (for emergencies only) in the pocket of a vintage Steve McQueen-style leather jacket she'd found second-hand in a charity shop in Primrose Hill (now hanging in the wardrobe).

'It really is not long now, Miss Feebes. Again, I am terribly sorry. You should—'

Ah, there they were. She felt in the pocket, pulled out the cigarettes (Marlboro Lights) and a Bic lighter she picked up who-knew-where. She fumbled with the pack, extracted one crumpled cigarette and lit it. The rush of her first drag almost knocked her off her feet. It felt good. She said, 'Come to New York?'

'Exactly, Miss Feebes,' Dr Steinmeier said.

She stared out at the empty street. The clock by the bedside flashed 03:05.

'I have too much keeping me here,' Isabelle said.

'Miss Feebes...'

Isabelle sighed.

'Fine,' she said, defeated.

'Goodnight, Miss Feebes.'

'Goodnight, Dr Steinmeier.'

Shit, Isabelle thought. Shit, shit!

She went downstairs. Put on all the lights, the house (one of many owned by the House of Feebes) blazing out illumination. That should put off the foxes, she thought. There were bars she knew of still open at this hour. They'd let her in. She had memberships to half the private clubs in London for just such an eventuality. But going out would mean other people. She went to the fridge, got the bottle of vodka from the freezer. A row of frosted shot glasses stared at her from the fridge at eye level. She picked one, filled it up, drank.

Her head cleared. Things came back into focus. She took a drag on the cigarette, couldn't find an ashtray, dumped it into a half-empty mug of cold coffee. It made a satisfying little *hisss* when it hit the water.

New York, she thought. She didn't want to go to New York.

Isabelle Feebes, twenty-five, rich, with the best that private education could provide (a boarding school in Switzerland, another in Italy and a third and final one in England, all terminated by mutual agreement, then a year at King's College, Cambridge, also terminated by mutual agreement, then most of a degree in London at the Royal College of Art), had managed, for most of the past two years, to avoid dealing with the vexing issue of her mother.

The Honourable Henrietta Feebes had long since retired across the pond to her apartments on the Upper West Side in New York, from which she could gaze out upon the world from a suitable height without having to go out into it too often. From time to time she'd venture forth. A private jet to Northolt, then a limousine. She would arrive, unannounced and inevitably at the worst possible moment, whenever Isabelle had *just* managed to relax her shoulders a little; she would fuss over Isabelle, and take her out to dinner at some expensive place only very old, very rich people went to, where the chefs were inevitably French, the views inevitably panoramic, and where Isabelle and her mother would inevitably proceed to have a blazing row.

What they fought *about*, or over, was never of much importance. Over the past few years of relative stability for Isabelle in London, it was the ritual itself, more than anything else, that mattered; that became almost a sort of comfort in the end. Henrietta needed – wanted – love. She demanded it. Isabelle, in her turn, craved a love her mother seemed unable to give or even understand. It was a source of constant incomprehension between them, for though they did love each other, they could yet never seem to express it in a way the other would understand.

Then came the cancer, as inevitable as a shovel shovels shit (a saying of Henrietta's she was fond of repeating after a couple of martinis). Henrietta remained in New York, where she underwent treatment. Isabelle stayed in London, where she ran a small boutique art gallery in rapidly gentrifying Shoreditch. She went over to the States twice in those two years, where her mother drifted from room to room like a Hamlet played by Frances de la Tour at the Half Moon Theatre in Limehouse, suffering the slings and arrows of outrageous fortune. The first time, they went to Katz's and her mother wore a headscarf and they fought over a corned beef sandwich and matzo ball soup. The second time, her mother wore a wig and they dined at a private reception at MoMA, to which Henrietta had just given a donation to establish a new Feebes Wing.

'I am getting sentimental in my old age, darling,' she said. That time there was no fight left in either of them, and when they returned, sitting in the back of the car that Carl, the old chauffeur, was driving, Isabelle saw her mother's hands tremble in her lap, when she thought Isabelle wasn't looking, and the skin was thin and almost translucent, and Isabelle was afraid.

She ran back to London like a coward, making excuses about work and the gallery no one, neither her mother nor herself, remotely believed, but if Henrietta was hurt by this decamping she didn't show it. When they spoke on the phone both were cordial; the treatments were working well; work at the gallery was going well; the weather was fine, and there was talk of some rain; they must see each other soon, just as soon as things ease up; 'Well, goodbye then' – 'Goodbye.'

Somehow, the fox was still out there, still watching Isabelle. She wondered if it was an emissary of the netherworld, sent to watch her, or if it was just lost. She watched the fox. The fox watched Isabelle. Somehow her shot glass was full again and then empty again. A pleasant lightness suffused her now.

'Damn you, Mother,' she said.

Then she started to cry, out of nowhere and startling herself. Big ugly sobs wracked her, her body shaking as she tried to hold down nausea. The fox watched her through the window, and then it scuttled off, and she was all alone.

When Isabelle was seven years old, Henrietta took her little orphan, as she sometimes called Isabelle back then, on a walk to Madison Square Park, across from the Flatiron Building where some subsidiary of a German firm was in the book business. Isabelle wasn't sure what a 'subsidiary' was, and didn't know anything about the book business, but she liked the little park, where mothers pushed babies in prams, men walked little dogs around on a leash, and where she saw a squirrel for the first time. Henrietta bought them both hotdogs.

'What do you want to be when you grow up?' Henrietta asked her. They sat on a bench and people-watched.

'I like to draw,' Isabelle said. She had got some mustard on her nose and tried to lick it off without success.

'Drawing isn't a career,' Henrietta said, not even laughing at the faces Isabelle was pulling.

'It was for Van Gogh,' Isabelle said. Henrietta looked momentarily bemused.

'Where did you learn about Van Gogh?' she said.

'You have that painting of a wheat field on the wall in the library room,' Isabelle said. 'He made that.'

'Van Gogh barely ever sold a painting and he died poor,' Henrietta said.

'But he was happy, wasn't he?' Isabelle said. 'He got to make beautiful paintings.'

'I don't think he was very happy, no,' Henrietta said. 'I don't think art makes many artists happy.'

'So why do they do it?' Isabelle said.

'I don't know,' Henrietta said.

'I like drawing,' Isabelle said. 'It makes me happy.'

Henrietta looked like she wanted to say a couple of things about that – grown-up things, if Isabelle was any judge. But then Henrietta just smiled, and it was a nice smile, and the light hit her eyes in a nice way and made them sparkle, and she said, 'Let's get ice cream.'

It had been a nice day.

Isabelle, in truth, did not spend a lot of time in New York growing up. Henrietta liked the city, but she had old-fashioned ideas, a crumbling pile of a mansion house back in England, half a lifetime spent in Egypt and Hong Kong, and America seemed a little too democratic to her, its rich a little too rich, its art a little too modern, its poor too poor and its tired too tired, its huddled masses a little too wretched, and its multitudes (here Henrietta switching abruptly from Emma Lazarus to Walt Whitman) containing too many multitudes. New York was fine for Henrietta, but Isabelle needed a proper education, proper manners, proper people, and the sort of accent that opened doors without you having to ask. So Europe it was, for most of the time.

The cigarette was out. Isabelle didn't feel like lighting another one. The darkness outside pressed on the house. The silence outside pressed on the house. Isabelle would have welcomed the sound of drunks staggering home, of a bottle rolling on the pavement, of a siren screaming as it went past. But even the birds were asleep, and Henrietta was in New York, and she was finally dying. Dr Steinmeier had called twice before, and each time the prognosis was imminent. But this time Isabelle knew it was true.

She had not spoken to Henrietta in over a month. Henrietta wouldn't take her calls. She did not want Isabelle to come, did not want her 'To see me like this, darling. You have your life to lead. How is the gallery? How is darling Simon, are you still seeing him? No? Well, no great loss.' She coughed. It lasted a long while. 'Don't call again. Dr Steinmeier will be in touch,' she said. That was five weeks ago. Nothing since then.

Selfish! It was selfish. Henrietta was a loner for most of her life. Girls' boarding school, a series of finishing schools, then the family business, but no real family. She had many homes and no permanent one, plenty of acquaintances but no real friends. If she had lovers, affairs, she never did say. She lived in hotels, hung out with barons and bankers and artists and spies. Now she wanted to die alone. As if Isabelle being there was just another inconvenience.

The only thing in Henrietta's life that never made sense, that was the cause of all their fighting, was Isabelle herself.

44

Isabelle could remember parts of her old life. They were hazy and incomplete, broken into fragments. Mama's smell of sweat and Chanel, how warm her skin was when she snuggled into her. Mama was love, comfort, laughter. Papa was strong hands lifting her up in the air, tossing her high and catching her, laughing. Papa's smell was cologne and cigarettes, his unshaved cheek tickling, and he made faces at her and made her laugh. Mama's face she only knew from later, from watching her in the films she had appeared in. But in her memory Mama had no face, she was just there.

Isabelle could remember being happy, which was a strange thing to remember, because happiness was not a feeling that came to her often these days. She was uncomfortable with the idea. Art required misery, or so she told the moneyed clients who came through her gallery, citing Van Gogh with his severed ear, Kahlo with her chronic pain, Dadd's insanity and fratricide, Caravaggio's murderous rage, Nazi architects and Fascist fashion designers. Then she tried to flog them a Gilbert & George. In truth the gallery never made any money, the crowd Isabelle hung out with were promising art students with a taste for cheap wine and expensive dope, and she lived in a house that was too big for her as she tried to figure out what to do with the rest of her life.

The little girl who liked to draw, who she remembered from that time in Madison Square Park almost with affection, was given the best private tuition and art teachers money could buy. The one thing those kind, well-meaning adults taught her was that she wasn't good enough. What was once fun became a chore, then a subject of hatred. Henrietta, in her own way, meant well, but as usual, in her own way, had simply taken away Isabelle's joy in what was once a simple pleasurable activity.

Still, Isabelle liked running the gallery. No point letting all that education go to waste.

Her telephone rang again, Rihanna's 'Diamonds' making her jump. She picked up.

'Yes?'

'Isabelle? It's Melanie. So sorry to hear the news, sweetie.'

'Thanks.'

'I managed to find you a ready plane with crew in Biggin Hill, I'm sending a car over for you now.'

'Thanks, Melanie. You're a dream,' Isabelle said.

'I really am so sorry. She was a lovely lady, your mum.'

'She's still hanging on, Melanie,' Isabelle said.

'Yes, of course. Of course.'

Isabelle had never met Melanie. She knew her only as a voice on the phone, imagined her in some office somewhere, in some woollen skirt and jacket, or maybe tweed, with a view out of the window, but not too good a view, somewhere in Canary Wharf, anyway, with a computer in front of her and that competent voice, and long nails painted burgundy and tapping, always tapping on a keyboard. She was just the sort of person who got things done so you didn't have to do them yourself.

'What about Uncle James?' Isabelle said now.

'The baron is not well enough to travel, sweetie,' Melanie said. 'You know that. He barely knows what day of the week it is.'

Isabelle took a deep breath. 'I meant, has anyone told him yet?'

'In the morning, sweetie.' Melanie's voice softened. 'For now, it's just you.'

It was always just her. Isabelle felt the tears well up again, threaten to come out. She fought them, lit a cigarette instead.

'You really must give that up, you know,' Melanie said. 'It's not good for you.'

'Fuck off, Melanie.'

'Car,' Melanie said, not in the least perturbed. Isabelle wasn't sure Melanie ever slept. And she never got ruffled. 'Plane. Then car again to the apartment. You can manage, right?'

'Yes... Thanks, Melanie.'

'Don't mention it. Condolences again. Call me if you need anything.'

'I will.'

The line went dead with a click. Isabelle stared at the phone. She swiped aimlessly. *Cut The Rope. Fruit Ninja. Angry Birds.* She wondered if she had anyone to call. She scrolled through her contacts list. Pressed *Simon*.

It took eight rings before he answered and he sounded dazed. 'Hello?'

'It's me,' she said.

'Jesus, Isabelle. It's four in the fucking morning!'

'I just wanted to… I don't know. Did I wake you?' she said.

'It's four in the morning!'

'I know what time it is!' Isabelle snapped. 'Are you alone?'

'Does it matter?' Simon said. Then he sighed, said, 'Yes, I'm alone. I guess you are, too.'

'Yes.'

'Is everything all right, Isabelle?'

'I'm… Not really.'

'I'm seeing someone, you know,' he said.

'I didn't know.'

'Well, I am. Look, can this wait until the morning? I have to go to work in three hours.'

'I just… Yeah,' Isabelle said. 'Yeah, it can wait.'

'All right. Call me tomorrow. I mean later today. Hey. Just… Go back to bed.'

'Yeah,' Isabelle said. 'I will.' She thought of saying something else but nothing came out. She heard his breathing on the line. Then he hung up.

Why the *fuck* did she call Simon? She wanted to throw the phone at the wall. They'd met at a book launch, at an Aztec-themed restaurant in Camden. He went to Cambridge, his grandfather was a former ambassador and knighted, his mother was the daughter of a baronet, his uncle was something high up in the BBC. Simon was charming, suave, with beautiful white teeth and blond hair cut carelessly at great expense down to his shoulders. He played acoustic guitar. He worked in investment banking.

He went to Glastonbury every year. He always closed the toothpaste tube properly after he brushed his teeth.

Simon was... *easy*, she thought. Easy to get along with, easy to go out with, easy to stay in with, easy to see friends with. He opened doors for her, he held her hand, he got tickets to see Florence and the Machine, he was...

He was fucking boring, is what he was, but he was so convenient that she stayed. It was like sinking into a warm scented bath of domesticity, luxuriating in that normality of *settling*, until she almost began to imagine this was her life and her future, until she almost began to imagine the kids (a boy and a girl), the dog (a collie), their house (West London, close to the river and all good schools, a weekend home near the New Forest), until she suffocated in it all and had a one-night stand with a punk band roadie she met in Kentish Town, staggered back to Simon's apartment at three o'clock in the morning still reeking of sex, and threw up on his carpet. It felt better than leaving a Dear John letter. After that, Simon was reduced to an entry in her contacts list and someone she still saw occasionally at parties.

'Well, we could still be friends,' he'd said, and the sheer staggering banality of it threw her so much that she agreed.

Why the hell did she call him now? Well, what's done was done. It made her feel better, anyway. At least she woke someone else up, to stare into the night. She went upstairs, ran the shower hot, washed. She picked dark jeans, a blazer, a black tee, a pair of Nikes. A black car drove smoothly to the front of the house and stopped. A driver in a suit stepped out and waited by the car. Isabelle grabbed her travel bag and went outside.

'Morning, miss,' the driver said.

'Just take me to the airport,' she said tiredly.

Before the accident, before Henrietta, before she was ever a Feebes or had a notion of what a Feebes was, Isabelle lived in a stone farmhouse in the Italian countryside, with a vineyard that spread out from the back of the house towards the dirt road that led to the village. There was an old donkey called Bianco in a little enclosure, a couple of chickens that ran free and laid eggs, and an Alfa Romeo parked right up front, which her father loved more than he loved anything in the world, or so he sometimes told her.

When they weren't living in the farmhouse they were in all kinds of other places, that were often busy and confusing, where her mother pretended to be other people and her father yelled at people for not doing things the way he wanted them to.

Since they were very busy people she was most often looked after by a Spanish nanny called Esmeralda, who made funny faces and liked listening to BBC World Service and liked fresh cut flowers from the garden, and sometimes helped Isabelle's father look for things he lost in the bedroom when Isabelle's mother wasn't there.

Isabelle rested her head against the window of the black car. It was the sort of car that was fast and sleek and very, very comfortable, the engine purring, the driver staring ahead, the road quiet at this time of night, dawn not yet near to breaking. Isabelle watched London end and the outer dark begin, the world of woods and hills and giant trucks parked by the wayside where the truckers grabbed a few hours' sleep. No more foxes, not on the main road. There might still be some foxes in the woods, she thought, though more lived in the city now, joining the squirrels and the rats, west London's green parakeets and north London's terrapins, newcomers onto the vibrant urban landscape drawn by the culture, world-class banking facilities and convenient air connections to all points on the globe.

She didn't want to go to New York. She didn't want to think about Henrietta. She waited for her phone to ring, for Dr Steinmeier to cough his dry little cough and say, 'I'm so sorry, but...'

But the phone did not ring, Dr Steinmeier didn't call, and somewhere in New York, high above Central Park, Henrietta Feebes lay small in her opulent bed, her face wan, as she waited for the end.

Fuck, it was depressing. 'Can you put on the radio?' Isabelle said.

'Sure, miss. Any preference?'

'Don't care.'

The driver put on the radio.

'What the hell is that, jazz?' Isabelle said.

'Miss?'

'Can't you change it?'

'Miss.'

The driver pressed the button again. The Lighthouse Family came on with 'Ain't No Sunshine'.

'A bit on the nose,' Isabelle said.

'Miss? You want me to change it?'

'It's fine. Just drive.'

She remembered Bill Withers singing it on the radio in the kitchen in the farmhouse that day, too. She didn't know what the song was or who sang it. She only learned the name of it later. But she remembered the music, and the sudden silence outside, and then the sound of a car that wasn't the Alfa Romeo, of quiet wheels and a German engine, gliding along the dirt track to the house.

Esmeralda had been crying all that day but wouldn't say why. It had rained, and the air smelled of pine needles and wood smoke, and snails came out after the rain and danced their slow dances outside. When the car came it carelessly drove over two of the snails and crushed them. Isabelle was watching out of the kitchen window. She saw the big black car, and the driver in the peaked cap get out and open the passenger door, and she saw the small, determined woman who stepped out, looked at the house, looked up at the window and saw Isabelle in her turn.

The woman wore black, the sort of black only rich people wore. Esmeralda came out to welcome her. She was still crying. The woman in black said something to Esmeralda and Esmeralda nodded miserably and stepped aside, and the woman in black entered the farmhouse as though she owned it, which Isabelle much later found out that she did.

The woman in black came in and Isabelle stayed at the kitchen window. The driver outside lit a cigarette and smoked it leaning against the car. Isabelle could hear the small woman moving through the house. She heard her enter the kitchen, and there she stopped, but Isabelle didn't turn around.

The woman said, 'Isabelle.'

At that Isabelle did finally and reluctantly turn. The sky clouded again outside. It was going to rain.

'What?' she said. Something awful took hold of her. The

whole day had been wrong. The woman's appearance was a wrongness too many, and she stared at her in hate, though hate was a strong word. Perhaps it was fear.

'My name is Henrietta Feebes,' the woman said. She came closer then, and knelt down to be at Isabelle's height, and she took Isabelle's hands in hers as she spoke.

'Something sad happened,' Henrietta said.

'Something sad?' Isabelle said. 'Did you do it?'

'Goodness, no,' Henrietta said. 'It's about your parents, Isabelle. There was an accident.'

'An accident?' Isabelle said. 'Are they all right?'

'I'm afraid they're not,' Henrietta said. Thinking about it later, picturing it over and over in her head, Isabelle was astounded at how badly the conversation went. How uncomfortable Henrietta must have been, how horrified Isabelle herself was. She just knew, without being told. Knew something terrible had happened, that this woman represented it, had brought it down upon Isabelle's life. And every word Isabelle spoke was a brick, being put up one by one to make a wall, to stop the bad that Henrietta Feebes represented from engulfing Isabelle.

'What happened to them?' Isabelle said.

'They were on a boat,' Henrietta said. 'Well, a yacht. They were having a party for a new movie they'd just finished. I knew your mother when she was a young woman, you know. I helped her – well, this is neither here or there. There was a storm.'

'What sort of storm?' Isabelle said.

'A bad one,' Henrietta said. 'Look,' she said. 'I don't know how to do this. Your parents died. I don't know what to say. There is nothing I could say that would fix this. I am so sorry.' She reached out for Isabelle and engulfed her in an awkward hug. Isabelle screamed, the brick wall collapsing, the monster reaching across it to trap her in its tentacles. She pushed Henrietta desperately away.

'Let me go!' Isabelle screamed. 'Let me go!'

She kicked Henrietta in the shin. The woman, startled, pulled away. Isabelle ran, terrified of being chased. She ran down the corridor and out of the door, past the driver who, caught off guard, dropped his cigarette and tried to grab her. She ran as fast as she ever ran, out of the gate, along the dirt track, into the vineyard, trying to lose herself between the hanging vines. She could hear them behind her, calling her name, the driver cursing, Esmeralda crying. Isabelle ran and ran, the blood pounding in her head, until she reached the toolshed and took shelter inside. She hid, in the darkest place she could find, huddling with her arms round her knees and her head down.

None of it seemed real. Mama and Papa were going to come back any minute. The Alfa Romeo's engine would sound and the car itself would glide into the driveway and they would come out, calling her name, both of them smiling, arms open for a hug. It would all be just like it was. It would all be like it should be.

Silence outside. Birds calling. Isabelle cried. Someone tried the door handle outside and she froze. The door creaked open, soft footsteps came in. Henrietta knelt beside her.

'I can't bring your parents back,' she said. 'But I can give you a good life, Isabelle. Please. Get up.'

Isabelle looked up. Henrietta's face, though alien to her, was nevertheless open, sympathetic. It was the only friendly face she'd see. The realisation almost crushed her. Henrietta swept damp hair from Isabelle's eyes. She took out a handkerchief, embroidered in gold thread with the letters HF. She wiped Isabelle's tears.

'Everything will be fine,' she said. 'You'll see. Come along, now.'

She took Isabelle's hand. Isabelle didn't resist. Henrietta pulled her to her feet. She didn't try to hug her again. She held on to Isabelle's hand and Isabelle followed her, out of the door, through the vineyard, back to the house and the waiting car.

45

'Miss?'

'What—?'

She woke up with a start, her face pressed to the window, her eyes gummy with dried tears.

'What?' she said again.

'We're here, miss.'

Lights shone wet in the dark, but over on the horizon she could see a faint dawn trying to break through. Guards on the gate, she flashed her passport, the car eased in, a porter in a top hat came to open the door for her and let her inside into a comfortable waiting lounge.

'Anything I could get you, miss?'

'Coffee.'

'Right away.'

The place looked like the foyer of a Cairo hotel. Her luggage was taken directly from the car and whisked to the hangar. Her coffee arrived and she drank it. She didn't like being inside. She took her coffee outside, escorted discreetly by the porter, lit up a cigarette and smoked it against the cold. She watched a helicopter arrive over the dark skies as though fleeing the dawn.

'Who's that?' she said.

'Feebes,' the porter said.

'I'm Feebes,' Isabelle said.

'Bank,' the porter said.

'Oh, the bank.'

'Bank.'

'Yeah, you said.' She tossed the cigarette into the wind. Went to the helicopter landing pad, heedless of the whirring blades. An old man in a dark suit and coat stepped out of the helicopter and walked over.

'Uncle Daniel?' Isabelle said.

'Isabelle!' Daniel Pikorski hugged her. He felt frail, more than she remembered. But his cheek was as smoothly shaved as ever, his cologne understated and pricey just like always, his white hair beautifully cut. 'I'm so sorry,' he said.

'Yeah. Me too,' Isabelle said. 'Is it still Feebes Bank?'

'Futures and Investment Holdings,' Pikorski said. 'HSBC kept the brand name. We just do what we always did. Move money around.'

'Of course.'

'I'm glad I could be here for you, Isabelle,' Pikorski said. 'The plane should be ready, if you are.'

'I'm ready. I mean...' She took a deep breath. 'As ready as I can be.'

'I understand. I knew her for a long time, you know. Your mother. We were friends... Good friends.'

'It's hard for me to imagine,' Isabelle said. 'Mother having friends.'

'Well, you are her daughter,' Pikorski said. 'It's always hard for a child to perceive their parents as, well, individuals.

As people. You know what I mean. But she wasn't always your mother.'

'You can say that again,' Isabelle said.

'Come on, Isabelle.'

'Do you think she loved me?' Isabelle said.

'I think she does love you. Very much so.'

'Was she ever capable of love?' Isabelle said.

Pikorski didn't reply. They went inside, had a quick show of their passports to the immigration officers, and were escorted through the lounge and onto the plane. Pikorski said hello to the pilots as Isabelle sat down. It was just the two of them and the crew.

'All set?' Pikorski said. He came and sat down and strapped in.

'Good to go,' Isabelle said.

'I'm sorry it has to be like this,' Pikorski said.

'Are you going just for her?' Isabelle said.

'I do have some business in New York, but yes. Dr Steinmeier called me.'

'Thank you for the ride,' Isabelle said. The engine hummed. The plane taxied to the runway.

'Anything for you, Isabelle. How is the gallery going?'

'All right.'

'I should put you in touch with my assistant, Sam. She's looking to put up some new art on the walls. For the office, you know. I don't know why I didn't think of it before.'

'That would be great. Thanks, Uncle Daniel.'

He smiled. 'No one ever calls me that,' he said. 'Only you.'

The plane sped across the runway. It took to the skies. Neither of them commented on it. The lights of cars on the highway below, the dawn rising now, giving the skies a look of wet, grey laundry. The plane rose, rose towards the clouds. Isabelle held her breath.

Then it happened, like she knew it would, like she always dreamed it. The plane cut through the clouds and emerged above. Sunlight flooded the window, touching her face, making her exhale. She put her hand on the window, her fingertips touching the stretched acrylic surface. She smiled.

The seatbelt sign bleeped gently and went off. The flight attendant came in, a coffee for Pikorski, a gin and tonic for Isabelle – 'But hold the tonic.' Uncle Daniel had his laptop already open, ready for work. Mother always called him Pikorski. He was in the CIA back when there were good guys and bad guys. Now what was left of Feebes Bank cleaned Mexican and Colombian cartels' money, a fact that was only recently in the papers, but which did not seem to bother anyone unduly, least of all Uncle Daniel. 'If you're too big to fail, you're too big to jail,' she heard him say more than once.

It wasn't her business. Money was money. There was no such thing as clean money or dirty money, honest or crooked. There was just the thing in itself. What it could do, what people would do to get it. Isabelle accepted her gin. She drank it slowly. Her head hurt and she was tired. She felt herself nodding off.

'Why don't you take the bedroom?' Pikorski said. 'Get some rest. It's going to be a long day. I'll wake you up for breakfast before we land.'

'Yeah,' Isabelle said. 'Yeah, I think I will. Thanks.' She put down the gin. She didn't want it anymore. She went into the bedroom cabin and shut the door. It was going to be a long day, she thought. She took off her shoes, brushed her teeth in the sink. She washed her face, stared in the mirror. A face she didn't know stared back at her. Fuck. She crawled into bed and pulled on the duvet and slept.

She dreamed she was on a ship sailing to the Americas. This was not an uncommon dream for her, and she knew this, just as she knew that she was dreaming. Fish in the ocean jumped into the air and their scales caught the light. Men in old-style hats and coats walked the deck and smoked tobacco. She checked her pocket watch for the time. It was gold and new and shiny, and it said *Feebes* on the base. It was the same watch Henrietta had given her on her eighth birthday, the same watch that had belonged to her birth mother, to her grandfather before her, and so on into the murky past. Here it was as yet new, and she was comforted holding it. The wind picked up and the sails billowed and the ship picked up speed. Three lonely islands appeared in the distance, a dark rain cloud hovering over them, and it was only when she strained to look that she realised it was made up of thousands of birds.

She woke up with the dream fading, a bad taste in her mouth, a hangover of grief. She got up, washed her face, brushed her teeth, feeling like she was doing everything in reverse. She went back into the main cabin where Pikorski was sitting for breakfast.

'Coffee?' he said.

'Please.'

She sat opposite. Pikorski poured her a cup. A selection

of pastries, jams and honey awaited. Isabelle stirred milk and sugar. Pikorski buttered a croissant, put it on her plate.

'Sleep all right?' he said.

'I slept.'

He nodded.

'I spoke to Dr Steinmeier earlier,' he said. 'She's hanging on, still, your mother.'

'Would you?' Isabelle said.

'Would I what?' Pikorski said.

'Hang on.'

He sipped his coffee, considered, put the cup down.

'I don't know,' he said. 'I think so. It's natural to want to, well, still be. Stay you, for as long as you can.'

'But not being, is that so bad?' Isabelle said. 'I wasn't, and then I was. My mother – my birth mother – was and then, just like that, she wasn't.' The raw hurt was still there. 'I don't know what I mean,' she said.

'I do,' Pikorski said. 'I remember as a kid, wondering how it was I came to be. How something can come out of nothing. And then, as I grew up, I saw people cease to be. And how quickly that happens, and how the world... Well, the world goes on just the same without them in it. The world doesn't need people. Only other people do.'

'Well, this is morbid,' Isabelle said.

He looked at her. 'Appropriately,' he said. He looked so serious that she suddenly laughed.

'Appropriately, yes,' she said. He smiled.

'Considering!' Isabelle said. She started to laugh. 'I mean...'

'Given the circumstances,' Pikorski said. Now he was

laughing too. Isabelle laughed. She couldn't stop. She started to cry.

'It will be all right,' Pikorski said. He passed her a napkin. Isabelle cried into the cloth.

'It's a nice napkin,' she said. 'It's a really nice napkin.'

She put it on the table and bit into her croissant. It tasted like butter and tears.

'It's so confusing,' she said. 'You don't know what to feel.'

She took another bite.

'It's a good croissant,' she said.

Pikorski sat there, his silence waiting.

'It's like, I'm angry,' Isabelle said, 'and I think I'm sad, or I think I think I should be sad, but I don't know if I am or not. And I'm tired, and I don't like New York, and the last time I saw Mother was the last time we had a fight, and now... Now there'll be no more fighting.' The croissant was finished. She rubbed the tips of her fingers to get at the crumbs. 'I think about it and then I just feel numb,' she said.

'It's normal,' Pikorski said. 'And it's difficult. I could tell you to be strong but...' He shrugged. 'That's just a thing people say. Hell, I've said it plenty of times before.'

'Does it ever help?'

'It doesn't hurt.'

'Then I'll try to be strong, Uncle Daniel.'

'We're landing soon,' he said. 'Do you need to get ready?'

'I'm as ready as I can be, I think,' Isabelle said. 'What was she like, Uncle Daniel? When you first met her?'

'Henrietta?' He smiled. 'She was exciting,' he said. 'She gave you the impression everything was possible and you never knew what she'd do. She dragged me to climb Khufu's pyramid one night, along with... Well, never mind. I was just a kid, trying to make a name for myself. She grew up in wealth, they were already old money by then, the House of Feebes. I liked her.'

'And then?' Isabelle said.

'And then fifty years go past in the blink of an eye,' Pikorski said. 'And suddenly it's over. And you'll never... share a laugh or just sit there quietly, not saying anything because you don't need to. I'm sorry.' He covered his eyes.

'I'm sorry, too,' Isabelle said.

Manhattan through the window was like the opening title sequence of a wintry film. Isabelle didn't care for it. They landed in Teterboro and Pikorski shook hands with the pilots, thanked the crew. Isabelle was just pleased to get off. She wrapped her coat around her, hurried to the lounge and the warmth. Already everything was bigger, brasher, louder, more Gatsbyed. Pikorski joined her. They showed their passports to Border Protection and were ushered through to Pikorski's limousine. Isabelle pulled out her cigarettes, lit up with shaking hands. She drew in smoke gratefully.

A grey morning, gulls cried in the distance over the Hackensack. Trucks honked on Route 46. She felt an urgency, she felt nervous. She took another drag, coughed and tossed the cigarette. She got into the car next to Pikorski, who was making small talk with the driver.

'Good trip, Mr Pikorski?' the driver said. 'Beautiful morning here.'

'An ugly dawn but a beautiful day,' Pikorski said.

'Sir?'

'Something a friend of mine used to say. I never really understood it.'

'Sure,' the driver said. The engine hummed. The car pulled out. In moments they were out of the airport and driving through New Jersey.

'Take the Lincoln Tunnel,' Pikorski said.

'Sure thing.'

Isabelle said nothing. She stared out of the window. She should phone Claire, tell her she wouldn't be in today for the gallery, to go ahead and open without her. But Claire was used to Isabelle not showing up. She wondered who she could call. She'd never been all that good at making friends. She stared out of the window, wishing the car would go faster.

'Why is this taking so long?' she said.

'Traffic,' the driver said.

'We need to get there,' Isabelle said, 'I need to see her.'

Thinking, why did Henrietta leave it so late, why hadn't Isabelle insisted on going anyway, why did she—

That feeling of waiting for something awful to happen, and knowing there was nothing you could do to stop it.

Pikorski dozed. She looked at him, saw an old, frail man under that tailored suit and expensive haircut. Money and power, whether gained or inherited, gave you a sheen of invincibility, but fall asleep in the back of a car and that illusion vanished. She checked her watch. The phone didn't ring. She had no one to call. The car drove on.

She saw the Hudson River in the distance. They came to the tunnel. Like Gilgamesh she entered the tunnel in the double-hours of darkness. Marker lights flashed, the other cars, like a herd of scorpion men or some other Babylonian monsters, rushed alongside them, there under the river and the press of water, disconnected from the sun, the moon and cell reception. On and on the tunnel went and then it ended and the car emerged into sunlight and Isabelle could have cried.

Manhattan with its traffic-jammed avenues and lofty towers, this kingdom of the shore with all its rich proud cost of outworn buried age – damn it, why was she mangling Shakespeare now?

'Please hurry,' she said.

The driver nodded, said, 'Sure thing,' but didn't alter the speed of his slow progression through honking cars and yellow cabs and too many pedestrians, too many traffic lights and crossings, too many distractions and delays, until at *last*, the building came into view, rising into the sky with the park behind it, and the car slowed and the doorman came hurrying out with an umbrella, since it had began to rain.

Isabelle emerged into grey mid-morning. She hurried inside, hurried to the elevator which waited for her, stood there as Pikorski, slower, somewhat bleary-eyed, followed.

They went up to Henrietta's floor. The door opened. Isabelle rushed in.

Dr Steinmeier looked up from a cup of tea and put his spoon down gently on the saucer.

'I'm sorry,' he said. 'You just missed her.'

46

JOE DASSIN SANG 'LES CHAMPS-ÉLYSÉES' ON THE HI-FI system. Henrietta lay in the bed, as small as a rag doll and as still. The blinds were open, the wan sunlight illuminating Central Park far below. The dark wood bookshelves groaned under the weight of hardcover novels, art and photography books, dictionaries and travel guides and various knick-knacks Henrietta had collected on her travels. A blue stone statuette of Anubis sat near the bed next to the lamp and an untouched glass of water. Van Gogh's *Wheat Field with Cypresses* hung on the opposite wall away to the bed.

'She moved the painting,' Isabelle said.

'She liked to look at it,' Dr Steinmeier said.

Joe Dassin kept singing about the Champs-Élysées. Isabelle couldn't take it. She didn't want to look at the small, still figure on the bed.

'Why this song?' she said. 'Did she like it or something? I never heard her play it.'

'Beats me,' Dr Steinmeier said.

'Can you turn it off?'

'Sure.'

He did something with a remote control. The sudden

silence came as a relief. Isabelle sat on the side of the bed. She took her mother's hand.

'I'm sorry,' she said. 'I'm sorry I wasn't here.'

'Don't be,' Dr Steinmeier said. 'She didn't want you to see her.'

He was blunt, Isabelle forgot that about him. Also, how much she disliked the man.

'Could you...?' she said.

'What? Oh. Of course.' He nodded curtly and left the room.

Alone with Henrietta, Isabelle looked at her mother's face, searching it for... what, exactly? Henrietta was so thin, the animating force that had made her such a strong, *infuriating* presence was gone and there was nothing in its place. Isabelle breathed, inhaled the smell of old books, polished wood, death. The sunlight dappled the treetops as it broke through the clouds over the park, and the air smelled of fresh rain and flowers. There were freshly cut roses in a bowl on the desk by the window. Henrietta's nails were freshly painted. Isabelle wondered which of the maids had done it for her.

The whole apartment felt hushed, but she knew it would soon get busy, that now that the ritual of death had concluded, the elaborate ceremony of its aftermath would begin. She should call Uncle James. She put her mother's hand down gently on the bed sheet. She stood up, paced the room. Ran her finger along the spines of Henrietta's books.

Pacific US Foreign Policy in the Aftermath of the Guano War: 1855–1890. Pioneering Photographers Series: Lady Julia Montmorency, a Monograph. Baedeker's *Egypt.* Edgar

Waverley's *A Quiet Spy: A Memoir. Death in the Morning* by Edna St James.

She frowned at an old copy of Marx's *Capital*, pulled it out, opened it to the flyleaf. *To Henry from Edith.* A little heart drawing. She put it back, kept pacing.

She stopped when she saw the small framed poster half-hidden on the wall next to the bookshelves.

Her mother – her birth mother – looked young and happy and pretty in the picture. Her face dominated the poster, half in profile, looking to the distance.

She looked so lovely, Isabelle thought. She looked so young. Mariam Khouri never got the chance to grow old. Never got the chance to see her daughter grow up. The poster was for one of her early films, a breakout role, with a real director and a real script. *In The Yellow Sun* was a British-French-Egyptian co-production. It was made before Isabelle was born.

Isabelle had watched it once, years later, coming home unexpectedly one afternoon, in between school expulsions. Henrietta was sitting in the dark, the movie cast onto the wall from an old 35mm projector. Mariam rode on a horse through the desert, pursuing a figure far ahead. Though her head was covered, her face was bare. The sunlight made her glow.

Isabelle stood in the doorway, not daring to breathe. Henrietta hadn't noticed her. Henrietta's eyes were on the movie, and she was crying without sound, the tears streaking down her face.

Isabelle had felt like an intruder. Had stood there, for a long moment, not sure what to do, and then she left. She went out again and then to Macy's, where she did some shopping and then got stoned in the toilets. When she got back to the apartment the projector was nowhere, Henrietta had gone out to some charity function, and Isabelle had a takeout pizza and watched cable until she fell asleep.

She'd forgotten that day. She looked at the poster now and wondered. When she looked away it was raining again beyond the window, the sunlight gone and the joggers in the park moving like tiny ants below. Henrietta lay in the bed. She looked at peace.

Could you be at peace? Isabelle wondered. Or was it just something people said? She took one last look and went out and shut the door, quietly.

Dr Steinmeier was in the kitchen with Pikorski. They both looked up when she came in and Pikorski got up and poured Isabelle a cup of coffee. Isabelle sat down and Pikorski put his hand on her shoulder, then let go. He left the room.

'They were old friends,' Isabelle said.

'I know,' the doctor said. He pushed a plate towards her. 'Cookie?'

Isabelle took a cookie. Butter and sugar, so delicate the pastry flaked on her tongue. She sipped coffee.

'My family has been looking after Feebeses for generations, also,' Dr Steinmeier said. 'My great-great-grandfather was in Peru when Edward Feebes expanded the guano mining operations in the Chincha Islands. Family legend is that my grandfather looked after Edward as he recovered from his... Well. A little breakdown brought about by an over-dependence on opium, if family lore is to be believed. He was a great man, my great-great-grandfather. He made a fortune in Lima in construction.

Then his grandson lost it all playing cards against Emiliano Zapata, the revolutionary. Or that's the story, anyway. We made our fortune back in the forties, during the… well, the war. As did the House of Feebes, I must add. We have been together a long time, Steinmeierses and Feebeses. And now here we are, Isabelle. It is like a wheel, I think. It turns and the faces change but all the people remain the same.'

'Yeah, whatever,' Isabelle said. She searched for her cigarettes. Fuck it, she thought. She could smoke. Dr Steinmeier watched her without commenting, but she could read the disapproval.

She never liked Steinmeier, she didn't think Henrietta had liked him either.

She fished out the pack, shook it. She was low on smokes. She pulled out a cigarette, couldn't find her lighter, checked her pocket, felt that she was putting on a show. So much of smoking was a performance, even when you were alone. She finally found the lighter, put the cigarette in her mouth, applied the flame to the tip and watched it glow. She took in her first drag and held it, then released the smoke slowly, watching it waft across the table.

'I have informed the baron,' Dr Steinmeier said. 'Well. Your cousin Alfred. The baron is, how do you say, he has his good moments and his bad ones.'

'What did Alfie say?' Isabelle said.

'He was very sorry. He said he'll call you.'

'That'll be nice.'

'And then there is the funeral to arrange, of course,' Dr Steinmeier said. 'Ah, just in time.' He got up as the elevator arrived. Isabelle followed him out, to see the doors open and busy-looking men in sombre black suits emerge with a stretcher.

'Through there,' Dr Steinmeier said, directing them. Isabelle watched it all with a sense of unreality. The men went to Henrietta's bedroom. Pikorski opened the door for them. They spoke softly. He came out and went to Isabelle.

'Let's go into the library,' he said. 'Let them do their job.'

Isabelle numbly agreed. She had said goodbye. She didn't need to see Henrietta carried away, out of her own home, like so much garbage being removed.

'So what happens now?' she said. They sat down in the reading chairs. Isabelle liked the library. It was full of books no one had opened in years, but it was always a good hiding place to nurse a hangover whenever she was back in New York.

There were no clocks in the library room. Nothing ticked or tocked or indicated the passage of time. Rain fell outside and drummed impatient fingers on the window.

Isabelle waited.

For two weeks Isabelle continued to wait: the sort of heavy-limbed, uncertain period akin to being in limbo, that waiting place between heaven and hell which is nevertheless closer to hell in Catholic theology. The House of Feebes, of course, were good old-fashioned Anglicans, that is to say, they always had an angle. Isabelle stayed in the apartment, sleeping in her own room, which felt too small, where her posters of the Backstreet Boys and Boyzone from when she was eleven still hung on the wall. The apartment felt too large, its silence too oppressive. When she went out into the city proper its crowds felt overwhelming, the noise deafening, the buildings too tall. She was too used to the relative quiet of London.

Henrietta had arranged her own death in advance. For the funeral, she had hired Lillian Oberman of the Oberman Group, her go-to for social planning. Lillian had burst into the apartment on that first day, all white even teeth a horse would be proud of, a mane of blonde hair and contact lens blue eyes, and immediately took charge.

Planning was under way. The funeral date was arranged, a church booked, and 'We must discuss the invitation list, we *must*,' she said.

In the event, Isabelle left her to it. Isabelle was not needed, the invite list decided long before, for what was sure to turn out to be 'The *hottest* invite of the season, Issy, anyone who's *anyone* wants to come pay their respects—'

No one called Isabelle Issy. She longed for a friendly face, but even Pikorski, after the first day, retired to his own place in the city and had since gone to Hong Kong, promising to return for the funeral. The service staff for the apartment were retained, and they moved like efficient ghosts around Isabelle, keeping the place just the way Henrietta had liked it, making Isabelle feel even more of a stranger.

She assumed she would inherit the apartment now, but she didn't know. Arrangements will be made after the funeral, she was told. A few photographers waited for her downstairs the first time she came out. Her photo – looking wan and withdrawn – appeared in the papers, with *Heiress to the Feebes Fortune?* splashed across page six.

She spoke to Claire, twice. Claire was more than capable of running the gallery back in London, what there was of it. In truth it was only kept afloat with Isabelle's allowance. They chit-chatted about the weather. Rainy, cold, dark: the usual. Condolences on the death, then the inevitable question: What happens next?

'I don't know,' Isabelle admitted. 'It's all in a sort of holding pattern until after the funeral.'

'Is your uncle going?'

'I don't think so. He's feeble.'

'He's a feeble Feebes,' Claire said. Isabelle didn't laugh.

'Got offered a couple of George Shaw paintings on commission,' Claire said, to fill in the silence. 'He's pretty hot right now after that Turner nomination last year.'

'That's great,' Isabelle said.

'Well, stay strong,' Claire said. 'And all the other things people are supposed to say, you know.'

'I know,' Isabelle said. 'Thanks.'

She spoke to Simon, once.

'We're not together anymore, you know,' he said.

'I know.'

'You've got to stop calling me.'

'I know.'

'I'm really sorry,' he said, his voice softening. 'About your mum.'

'Thanks.'

'Well, I've got to run.' He hung up abruptly.

So that was that. She went for long walks, to nowhere in particular. Manhattan in the winter. Steam stacks wafted fog into the sky, office workers huddled in corners sharing miserable cigarettes. Tourists took pictures outside St

Patrick's. She walked through Midtown to the East Village to Chinatown, stopped to eat dumplings in a place where the steam fogged the windows. She stepped out into more fog, darkness fast falling, under Manhattan Bridge she watched the lights across the river, lit a cigarette and added yet more obfuscation to the city's air.

Passing the Angelika Film Center in SoHo a couple of days later she saw her mother's face looking down on her from the marquee, which advertised an Italian B-movie retrospective, tonight's screening being of *Black Dirt* – Mariam Khouri, impossibly young, tiny behind the two leads but still recognisable, if not from memory then from the mirror, whenever Isabelle looked.

She went in, purchased a ticket. She sat in the dark cinema. The blue light from the projector reflected off the dust motes above her head. On the screen it turned into moving pictures. She watched the spy meet the girl for the first time, watched their love bloom, but she only had eyes for the young Zabbaleen girl in the background. She waited for each one of her appearances, from the moment she first arrives, a being of pure light, carrying a pile of laundry from one side of a room to another.

Isabelle cried, quietly. There were few people in the audience. No one noticed or, if they had, they left her to it. You were supposed to cry at the movies, anyway.

She felt better when she left the movie theatre. The fog cleared, a little bit.

47

'ONE PAINTING, VAN GOGH, VARIATION ON *WHEAT FIELD With Cypresses*, one Picasso, blue period, two Degas in the drawing room, one *Still Life with Apples* Cézanne in the dining room, I mean honestly, sweetheart, but the *placement*! Excuse me, miss, if you could just get out of the way...'

'Who the hell are you?' Isabelle said. She'd woken up, too late and not hung-over enough, to a phone call from Lillian Oberman informing her the final arrangements for the funeral had been made, and that it was to take place tomorrow. Then these people showed up out of nowhere and began moving through the apartment like locusts.

A grey-haired man in a comfortable suit extended his hand for a shake.

'Martin Greeves,' he said. 'Paintings and Modern Art.' He made a business card materialise. Isabelle examined it suspiciously.

'Boucher's?' she said. 'The auction house?'

The man gestured to his two younger companions, a man in a shirt and tie with his sleeves rolled up, and a woman in a conservative suit and haircut. 'This is Philip, he's Books and Manuscripts, and this is Rebecca, she's—'

'Cataloguer,' the woman said. She shook Isabelle's hand. 'A pleasure to meet you, Miss Feebes.'

'John from Wine and Spirits is in the wine room,' Martin Greeves said. 'The rest of the team should be over momentarily.'

'The rest of the team?' Isabelle said.

'Furniture, Jewellery, Handbags and Accessories, plus our Egypt expert and our East Asia specialist. Now, I have a list of inventory here, but I can't seem to find—'

'Who let you in?' Isabelle demanded.

'Let us in?' Greeves said. 'The foundation hired us to do a full evaluation. For the auction, you see.'

'What foundation?' Isabelle said.

'The Henrietta Feebes Foundation,' Greeves said.

'I never heard of that,' Isabelle said. She felt sick inside.

'Then I am as confused as you must be,' Greeves said. 'But we have a job to do, so, if you'll excuse me. I'm trying to locate an item described as "gold-plated shovel, mid-nineteenth century". The inventory list says it should be hanging above the fireplace in the foyer, but I can't seem to find it.'

'The what?' Isabelle said.

Then, in her confused state, a memory came back.

She was fourteen or so, had just been expelled from that school in Switzerland. She'd hated that school, for no good reason other than she felt that she did not belong; all the other girls, well-brought up and mannered, just as smart, but born into their wealth, knew how to wave and how to dress and how to exit from a helicopter, knew how to execute a perfect pirouette and how to ride a horse and how to shoot—

Henrietta was in London that summer, disapproving of Isabelle's fate. She sent Isabelle to Feebes Manor. Isabelle remembered being driven to the old pile of a house, this huge edifice that must have been amazing a century back but was now, in Henrietta's own words, 'An absolute *drain*, just the upkeep on the place is going to bankrupt us.' Cousin Alfie, a year older, was on the seat beside her, a practised bored look on his face, hair down to his shoulders; in the heart of the overgrown maze they both tried to smoke cigarettes and coughed out their lungs. In the dusty library, later, he tried to feel her up.

Isabelle wandered from room to room, dead people's paintings hanging on the walls. Birds nested in the upper rooms and foxes made a mess of the shrubbery. Nature had reclaimed the grounds.

Mice ran in the dark and nibbled at the rotting curtains, the lights fizzed as wires frayed and the current fluctuated unpredictably. There was something fun about being there, camped out in the library. They went on excursions, finding a hoard of stuffed animals in one upstairs room, owls and deer, an elephant-foot umbrella stand and an armadillo ashtray. In another, the remnants of beds were piled up like kindling for a bonfire.

Once, they tried going down to the cellar, found rows and rows of bottles of wine and got drunk and threw up on the floor. One small door at the back was closed shut with a big heavy lock, leading Isabelle didn't know where. Something about the door scared her.

She was at Feebes Manor as punishment for being expelled. Cousin Alfie for whatever he did – he wouldn't tell her. They were to clean the place up. It seemed like forever, but it was only a long weekend. When Henrietta and Uncle James arrived, each driving in a separate Rolls-Royce up the driveway, it was clear the cousins had done nothing useful, nor were they expected to.

'We're putting the place up for sale,' Henrietta announced. 'It's time.'

'Many fond memories,' Uncle James murmured. 'So many.'

'Aha,' Henrietta said. 'Listen, kids. We're going to do a clear-out before the sales agents arrive. Just bring everything down to the lawn.'

'Must do something about the cellar,' Uncle James murmured.

Henrietta shot him a sharp glance and he flinched.

'Father would not have wanted to...' Uncle James said, and then faded away.

'I will take care of the cellar,' Henrietta said.

'Good, good,' Uncle James said. 'So many fond memories. Sherry, anyone?' He wandered up the stairs and vanished into the house.

Isabelle looked at Alfie, who looked back at her and shrugged.

'Race you,' he said.

They ran inside. They began ransacking the place, hauling old candelabras, paintings pulled from the wall, cracked glassware and moth-eaten tapestries onto the lawn. Soon they were dirty and dusty and hot. In the El Torturador upstairs a bed still stood, as sturdy as it was seventy, a hundred years ago. Isabelle pushed Alfie onto the bed.

'Go on, then,' she said. She pressed herself on him. Her

lips sought his. Alfie lay still under her. When she kissed him his lips were dry.

'I'm not sure I like girls,' Alfie said. He pushed her off. She sat on the bed beside him.

'Fair enough,' Isabelle said. 'Want to get drunk again instead?'

'Think they'll notice?' Alfie said.

'Nah.'

'Sure,' Alfie said.

They snuck back down to the cellars. The dusty bottles lay in rows.

'Do you think we have to lug these all up for them?' Alfie said.

'Maybe,' Isabelle said. She picked a bottle off the shelf at random.

'You got the opener?' she said.

'Yeah.'

The wine was warm. It tasted fruity. After a few sips it made her limbs feel heavy and nice. The locked door at the far end was still locked. It was the old baron's place. She went up to it. She held the lock. It was new, it had no dust on it.

'What are you doing?'

She jumped. It was Henrietta, standing there, looking at her.

'N... nothing.'

'There's nothing in there, Isabelle.' She turned her gaze on Alfie.

'Alfred, put that bottle away.'

'Yes, Aunt Henrietta.'

'Both of you, come with me.'

Isabelle followed her mother up the stairs, seething with a mixture of embarrassment and resentment. Once back above ground, Henrietta sent Alfie to find Uncle James. She led Isabelle back into the library and then just stood there, looking severe.

'What am I going to do with you, Isabelle?' she said.

'I don't know, Mother,' Isabelle said. 'What would you like to do with me?'

'Don't be cheeky.'

Isabelle was going to say something, thought better of it. Henrietta went to the fireplace. No one had lit it in years. She reached for a thing on the wall.

'What's that?' Isabelle said.

'It's a shovel.'

'Why is it hanging on the wall?' Isabelle said, bemused.

'It belonged to old Edward Feebes,' Henrietta said. 'He had it plated in gold.'

'That's a weird thing to do.'

'I used to be fascinated with it when I was a girl,' Henrietta said. She took the shovel off the wall and held it like a weapon, trying it out. 'It killed a man once, right here in this room.'

'Who?' Isabelle said.

'Some employee of my father.'

'Was it murder?' Isabelle said, eyes wide.

'Just an accident, I think. Still. There were always stories.' She whooshed it through the air then smiled unexpectedly. 'I think I'll take it back to New York,' she said. 'As for you, young lady, you need to go back to school. London this time, I think. And I expect you to stick at it for once.'

'Can't I go back home with you?' Isabelle said. She tried not to show she was hurt, but it was there.

'You need structure,' Henrietta said. 'Discipline. I can't give you that in New York.'

'But Mother...'

'Come here,' Henrietta said, softening. Isabelle went to her, submitting to the unexpected hug.

'You know I love you,' Henrietta said.

'Miss Feebes?'

'Huh?'

'The inventory?'

'Oh, right.' She came back to herself, stared stupidly at Martin Greeves (Paintings and Modern Art). 'The shovel.'

'That's right.'

'No, it's not here,' Isabelle said. 'Mother did a big clear-out a few years ago. I think it went in the rubbish. It was just gold paint, you know. On it. I don't think it was worth anything.'

'All right, thank you,' Greeves said. He scribbled a note in his paperwork. 'I had better get back to it, then.'

Isabelle stared after him. She called Dr Steinmeier.

'What's the Henrietta Feebes Foundation?' she said.

'Oh, that,' Dr Steinmeier said. 'You'd have to speak to the lawyers. I understand it's what your mother wanted. The foundation, I mean. A charitable enterprise. Not unusual. I really don't know, Isabelle. I'm sorry.'

He hung up, still mumbling apologies. Isabelle stared at the phone.

'What the hell?' she said.

'Isabelle?'

She turned. A young man with perfectly cut hair and suit stood there watching her with a sardonic smile.

'Alfie!'

She ran to him. Holding him felt good. He pulled back, looked her over, said, 'You look like shit.'

'Thanks.'

'I'm sorry about Aunt Henrietta,' he said.

'When did you get into town?' Isabelle said.

'Just now. Beatrice is staying at the Carlyle. She sends her love. She'll see you tomorrow for the funeral.'

'And Uncle James?'

Alfie shook his head. 'Couldn't make it,' he said.

'Not good, huh?'

'He has his good days,' Alfie said. 'But there's less and less of those. You know how it is.'

'I'm sorry.'

'At least he's sticking around,' Alfie said. 'I'm in no hurry to become the next baron. I wish I could chuck the whole thing and become, I don't know.'

'A commoner?'

'God, no,' he said.

Isabelle laughed. 'Then what?' she said.

'I don't know. I never see you in London anymore. We shouldn't leave it for funerals and weddings.'

'Is anyone getting married?' Isabelle said.

'Beatrice is engaged,' Alfie said. He put his finger to his lips. 'Gareth finally proposed.'

'Good for Beatrice,' Isabelle said. 'Hey, Alfie?'

'Yeah?' he said.

'It's good to see you.'

She hadn't realised how alone she felt. He put his arm around her.

'Let's go shopping,' he said.

439

48

IT RAINED ON THE DAY OF THE FUNERAL. THE CITY DIDN'T stop. It didn't stop for the dead, and it wouldn't stop for anything. Isabelle was driven to the funeral home. She wore her best black suit. Alfie had taken her shopping the day before, then to the hairdresser, the nail salon, more shopping, then back to the apartment where the appraisers were gone. He made her take a shower. He made her wash her hair.

'When is the last time you washed your hair?' he said.

'I dunno.'

'Get it together, Isabelle, for fuck's sake,' he said.

'I don't want to, Alfie. I don't want to get it together. I don't even know what's going on. I don't even know if I want to go back to London. The gallery's shit, Alfie. It's shit. I've never done a single useful thing with my life. All I did was get kicked out of places. At least Mother did stuff. She travelled. She had interesting friends.' She felt so sorry for herself and it felt good.

'Aunt Henrietta was awful, Isabelle,' Alfie said. 'They all are. Were. She tried to make you into something you weren't, some replica of her that wouldn't behave the way she wanted, so she lost interest and only dumped what guilt she could on you. Her friends were crooks and her business was dirty. Hey, I'm not pointing fingers. It's in all of us. We were born to the House of Feebes. But you weren't. You didn't get a choice. She took you, she *collected* you like she collected everything else. You don't owe her anything, and least of all you don't owe her yourself.'

He looked quite emotional, standing there. She stared at him in surprise.

'I didn't know you felt this way,' she said.

'Isabelle,' he said, 'why do you think I always *liked* you? Every time you stood up for yourself, every time you got kicked out of school or ran away or... Do you remember that time they made us go to Feebes Manor? And you bought cigarettes, and we tried to smoke them in the maze, and we coughed our lungs out? That was the first time I tried smoking.'

'You brought the cigarettes!' Isabelle said.

'If I did it was only because you gave me the courage to,' Alfie said. 'You helped me, Isabelle. By showing me how to stand up to them. We got drunk in the cellar, do you remember?'

'That wasn't your first time,' Isabelle said.

'Well, no,' Alfie said. He laughed, but the laugh died down. 'But then we, you know. We tried making out. And I realised I didn't like girls that way. Look, I'm just saying. I'm always going to be a Feebes. There's always going to be a door down in the cellar with a big lock on it and something awful hiding inside. But it doesn't have to be like that for you. You can still be... free.'

'Free,' Isabelle said. The word sounded strange. She

stared around her, at the walls of the apartment, closing in on her, holding her in their opulent embrace.

'I'm not sure I know what that is,' she said.

'Maybe you don't think so,' Alfie said. 'But to me you were always the most free person I ever knew. Get some rest. It's going to be a big day tomorrow.'

He kissed her on the forehead. Isabelle went to her room. She lay in bed for a long while, unable to sleep, not thinking of anything in particular.

Cousin Alfred and Cousin Beatrice were already at the funeral parlour. Pikorski came soon after. Dr Steinmeier hovered. The coffin sat in wait. It was a closed casket, mercifully. Henrietta did not approve of being showy. The men from the funeral home – 'The funeral chaps,' Alfred said, for which Beatrice shot him a dirty look and said, 'Funeral service operatives' – carried it outside and to the waiting hearse.

It rained. The hearse glided slowly through the street, Isabelle and the others following, and those invitees who chose to brave the procession. It was only a short walk to the church, on the Upper East Side, and Isabelle could smell the trees in the rain, mixing with the car exhaust fumes. The vicar came out of the church, nodded to them. The coffin was carried inside. Isabelle followed behind, the dutiful daughter playing her role one last time. As the coffin was placed on a dais near the front it was covered in flowers.

'Showtime,' Alfie said. He squeezed her hand.

The mourners began to filter in. Photographers outside – Isabelle had done her best to ignore them. Black cars came to a halt, discharging dignitaries. Men in black suits and ties, women in black dresses, and Lillian Oberman moving between them like a bird in a gilded cage, ushering and reassuring.

Bankers and art collectors and the sort of people who sat on charity boards; minor royals from across the pond and old friends of Henrietta from Cairo and Hong Kong. Isabelle didn't know any of them. They came in accompanied by camera flashes, removed dark sunglasses, shook hands and murmured meaningless words of condolences before taking their seats. The church was full. The vicar came to the front of the church. Isabelle sat with her cousins and Pikorski.

The vicar said, 'Welcome. Today we celebrate the life of Henrietta Feebes, beloved mother, aunt and patron of the arts. Please turn to Psalm twenty-three.' He cleared his throat. 'The Lord is my shepherd...' he began.

Isabelle's mind wandered through the long service. She stood up dutifully to sing 'Amazing Grace'. Another Bible reading, another hymn. The coffin just sat there, Henrietta's photo sitting atop it in a black frame, and Isabelle wondered where the picture was even taken and when. Henrietta smiled in the frame. She looked full of life. She looked absurd, sitting there on top of her coffin.

The vicar gave the eulogy. Isabelle wanted to escape. The church was stifling, the crowd of people in black was only broken by the gold of watches and jewellery, the sparkle of a diamond earring. It was her turn to go up in front of them. She blinked nervously at all their blank faces.

'My mother,' she said. 'My mother was...'

She didn't feel like crying. She hid her face in her shawl and Alfie mercifully came up and hugged her shoulders, and the crowd murmured sympathetically, and Isabelle resumed her seat with relief. Alfie took her place.

'What can I say of my beloved aunt Henrietta?' he said. He had a nice voice, good for public speaking. 'She was always full of joy and full of life, right up to the last moment. I well remember, as children, we—'

He went on in that vein for a while. Isabelle's mind wandered again. The years peeled back, she was a child again, feeling sleepy but not wanting to sleep. Papa said, 'You can sleep in your bed tonight, sweetheart.'

'But I don't *want* to,' Isabelle said. She was nestled in the big bed between her parents. 'I want to sleep in *this* bed. *My* bed is too cold.'

Papa laughed, and Isabelle snuggled closer into Mama, laying her head on her chest. She yawned.

'I don't *want* to go to sleep,' she said.

'Night-night, sweetheart,' Mama said. She wrapped her arms around Isabelle. Isabelle stretched between them, feeling warm, feeling safe. She put her arm around Papa and nestled into his back. He felt warm and comfortable. Her breathing eased.

She fell asleep, sandwiched there between them, feeling happy.

'And this is your room,' Henrietta said. She opened the door onto a dark box of space. A rectangle of light spilled from the window onto the single bed pushed against the wall. 'I hope you'll be happy here.'

Isabelle stared. She mumbled something inaudible.

'What was that, dear?'

'Thank you.'

'You're welcome. Goodnight now.'

Henrietta pushed her in gently. Isabelle sat on the bed.

Henrietta closed the door softly and Isabelle was left all alone.

'And now for the Lord's Prayer,' the vicar said.

Alfie nudged Isabelle sharply.

'What?' she said.

'Stand up,' he whispered.

She stood.

'Our Father, who art in heaven, hallowed be thy name...'

The coffin was lifted by the funeral people. It was carried out of the church into the waiting hearse. Isabelle and her cousins followed with Pikorski. They stood outside under black umbrellas as the mourners filed out, shaking their hands, murmuring condolences.

Then into a limousine, and they followed the hearse to the cemetery, and there they buried Henrietta.

The rain fell. Cobwebs spun of gossamer threads between the leaves of a chestnut captured the drops and caught the light unexpectedly. Isabelle inhaled the scent of fresh earth and mulch. A smell of renewal. The ground was muddy. Black umbrellas bloomed. The coffin like a crushed, malevolent bug was lowered into the dirt. Isabelle took a handful of earth and threw it on the coffin.

Goodbye, Mother. Goodbye, Henrietta Feebes.

'So sorry for your loss,' the lawyer said. The lawyer was one of the few to come to the funeral, neither close family nor friend. She was a stooped, white-haired woman in a grey suit. 'How are you taking it?'

'It's hard,' Isabelle said.

'Of course, of course. The terms of the will must have come as a shock.'

'The terms of the will?' Isabelle said.

'The foundation,' the lawyer said. 'But it was what she wanted.'

'The Henrietta Feebes Foundation,' Isabelle said hollowly. Remembered Greeves, the man from the auction house, mentioning it as he was inventorying the contents of the apartment. She should have followed it up. But she had let it pass her by.

'Yes,' the lawyer said. 'She was always very fond of cats.'

'Cats?' Isabelle said. They'd never even had a cat. She had wanted one, had dreamed of a kitten to snuggle with in bed, a fluffy thing that would be all hers, to play with and feed. Henrietta wouldn't hear of it.

'So many street cats in Cairo,' the lawyer said.

'Yes.'

'But you still get a stipend for a couple more years,' the lawyer said. 'You have received the paperwork, of course?'

'The paperwork?'

She thought of the unopened mail on the kitchen table back in the apartment.

'Yes,' the lawyer said. 'And there is always a seat on the board for you, conditions permitting. But it's like she said in the will, she wishes you independence. Children must not be encumbered by their parents, after all. Encumbered by wealth, like she said.'

'Did she,' Isabelle said. 'Did she say that.'

She stole a glance at the grave. The fury rose in her, the afterwave of the shock. She tasted bile. She was never a Feebes, she realised. Had known all along, but had let herself

believe that maybe she was, that maybe she *did* belong. The
door in the cellar of the old baron's house. That's where a
Feebes went. She had thought herself one of them. But she
was like the kitten she was never allowed to have. A pet to
keep around, until it wasn't needed anymore.

'Damn you, Mother,' she whispered, and the loss and the
hurt turned into a wild laugh that burst out of her, along
with sudden tears, and the lawyer, taken aback, didn't resist
when Isabelle hugged her. The lawyer awkwardly patted
Isabelle's back.

'But of course,' she said. 'You are hardly poor. And you
can remain in the apartment for a couple more weeks before
it goes on the market.'

'Of course,' Isabelle said, still laughing or crying, she
wasn't sure which. 'One wouldn't like to be poor.'

'Of course not,' the lawyer said. 'I really must go, Isabelle.
Again, I am—'

'Sorry, yes,' Isabelle said. 'Well, goodbye.' She let go of
the lawyer, who hesitated, then nodded, once, and hurried
away through the rain.

'Isabelle, the car's waiting,' Alfie said, appearing. 'We
need to go on to the reception.'

'Did you know, Alfie?'

'Know what?'

'About the will.'

He looked suddenly uncomfortable.

'I thought you knew,' he said. 'I mean...'

Isabelle laughed again. It burst out of her like the cry of
a bird high in the sky, forlorn and free.

'Of course you did,' she said.

'Isabelle, we need to go—'

'You go,' she said. 'I'll walk.'

Cousin Beatrice, overhearing something, came to join them and stood there with that stupid look on her face, part scowl and part curious indifference.

'It's pouring down with rain!' Alfie said.

'It's just water,' Isabelle said.

'Isabelle, come on—'

'Goodbye, Alfie. I'll see you later.'

She turned so they wouldn't see her crying.

Beyond the small cemetery the world continued to turn, joggers jogged and dogs barked and cars crawled along the avenues. Rain rained and snails snailed and squirrels squirrelled squirrelly things; and the dead, resting in their gilded tombs that worms enfold, rested in the dirt that was all there was and is to be.

Isabelle, with a cry of defiance, left Feebeses both living and dead behind her and ran. Out of the gates and past the parked black cars and all along the pavement and across the road, dodging traffic; seeking shelter at last in the maze of roads and buildings that lay between death and water.

49

THE EAST RIVER WAS SOMEWHERE AHEAD. CENTRAL Park at her back, along with cemetery, church, and the hotel where the reception held for Henrietta Feebes's demise was no doubt currently kicking up a notch. Waiters would be circling with trays aloft holding glasses of wine, business would be discussed in murmured tones, and a piano player no doubt played sad tunes that had people nodding their heads in appreciation. For some, life was nothing but a series of black tie events, while others wore only the final tie that was the hangman's noose—

Isabelle couldn't say her thoughts made much sense at that moment, and as she ran, falling into the half-forgotten rhythm of a jog, she had the sense that all around her the world was covered in a greasy smoke. Voices rose in pain from the shadows, the sound of spades hitting dry dirt over and over clanged in a din all about her, somewhere the sound of horses and the roll of heavy wheels in mud, men laughing, women calling from dark alleyways to them, and as Isabelle ran a ghostly monk dogged her footsteps, and there was a discharge of gunshots in the distance, but they sounded olde-worlde and besides, this was the Upper East Side.

She slowed down, her heart rate easing as her eyes adjusted to the real world again, not knowing where she was other than that it was somewhere near the river. She heard the call of gulls and the foghorn cries of barges as they floated past, and she saw that there was a bar across the road with a sign above it that said *Annie's*.

She walked to it under the rain and pushed the heavy wood door open and went inside.

The lighting was dim, the way a bar should be lit. There was a long counter with glass bottles on shelves behind it and a solitary barman watching an old-fashioned television set hanging on the wall. There was a pool table no one was playing on just then, a dartboard similarly abandoned, a few low tables and chairs scattered haphazardly across the space, and two or maybe three solitary drinkers sitting in the corners and doing whatever drinking they did alone and without conversation. It was the sort of place that could have been anywhere, in any century, waiting for a stranger to just walk in from the rain.

Isabelle went to the counter and sat down on a stool. The bartender, without looking over and without saying a word, poured her a measure of whiskey and slid the glass across and went back to watching the television. Isabelle knocked back the drink and a flame shot through her and warmed her through, and without thinking she reached for her cigarettes, flicked her lighter and lit one.

'No smoking,' the bartender said.

'Huh?'

'No smoking.'

'I had a rough day.'

The bartender shrugged, reached under the counter and came back with a heavy old glass ashtray and plonked it on the bar next to Isabelle's elbow.

'Thanks.'

The smoke dribbled blue out of her nostrils. It rose towards the flickering screen of the old television.

'What are you watching?' Isabelle said.

The bartender grunted. Isabelle stared – some sort of documentary. The sound was down low. Talking heads. She tried to make out what they were saying. Old men speaking, grey archival footage. An old man came out of a house with a white picket fence, glared at the camera. *Soviet defector 'Gregor' speaks to PBS*.

Isabelle couldn't hear what he had to say. She lost interest. The bartender grunted, switched off the television abruptly, poured her another drink and slid over a bill.

'End of shift,' he said.

He vanished through a door. Isabelle sat staring. A younger man came out of the same door. He went behind the counter, smiled, said, 'It will stop raining eventually.' He had a light Irish lilt in his voice.

'I don't mind the rain,' Isabelle said.

'Jack Doyle,' the man said, extending his hand. Isabelle took it. Jack's hand was warm and dry.

'Isabelle F...' she said, then stopped. 'Just Isabelle,' she said.

He shook her hand, still smiling. He had a nice smile.

'Isabelle,' he said. 'You look like you've just come back from a funeral.'

'I buried my mother today,' Isabelle said.

'I'm sorry,' Jack said.

'It's my second one.'

She couldn't really remember her birth parents' funeral. She knew she had been there. But the memory was hidden; when she tried to prod for it it flittered away, seeking shelter in some dark corner of her mind. She didn't know who she was anymore. The past and the present seemed all about her at that moment, entwined, and she knew that once the rain eased she would have to step back out of that dark comforting space of the bar that felt as warm as a womb, and face the question of what to do next – of who to be.

She sipped her whiskey and looked at Jack Doyle and wondered who he was and if he ever felt the same as her. But Jack went around the bar, a bottle in his hand, and vanished to serve the other patrons who were still sitting, silent and wreathed in dark, as though they were merely ghosts having come to Annie's to haunt Isabelle.

She listened to the rain outside. It eased by degrees, then stopped. Perhaps, she thought, the past and the future were all just a series of stories that kept being told. To be herself she'd have to write her own chapter in a never-ending chain of human lives, as small and compressed as diamonds. She finished her drink, looked in her handbag for cash and found the gold pocket watch, which she had meant to do something with, she was sure of it, when she took it with her that morning to the funeral.

She examined it now, the faded cheap gold, the mechanism that measured out the time of the lives that had carried it until they ran out. She put her finger across the inscription on the base of the watch but it no longer meant much to her, at least not at that moment.

She placed the watch gently on the counter and went outside into the brightening day.

About the Author

LAVIE TIDHAR's work encompasses literary fiction (*Maror* and *Adama*), cross-genre classics such as Jerwood Prize-winner *A Man Lies Dreaming* (2014) and World Fantasy Award-winner *Osama* (2011), and genre works like the Campbell and Neukom prize-winner *Central Station* (2016). He has also written comics (*Adler*, 2020) and children's books such as *Candy* (2018) and *The Children's Book of the Future* (2024). He is a former columnist for the *Washington Post* and a current honorary Visiting Professor and Writer in Residence at the American International University in London.